The Temple
Of the
Three Whispers

Book Four:

The Denselands

BRIAN HARMON

The Temple of the Three Whispers
Book Four: The Denselands

ISBN: 978-1-945559-28-0

Don't miss these other great books by Brian Harmon!

The Temple of the Blind series:

The Box (Book I)
Gilbert House (Book II)
The Temple of the Blind (Book III)
Road Beneath The Wood (Book IV)
Secret of the Labyrinth (Book V)
The Judgment of the Sentinels (Book VI)

The Temple of the Three Whispers series:

The Lady of Cedric's Cove (Book I)
Circles in Hermes' Footsteps (Book II)
Misplaced in Mysteria (Book III)
The Denselands (Book IV)
The Impassible Wall (Book V)
The City Beyond Memory (Book VI)
The Keeper's Dollhouse (Book VII)
Priestess of Ruin (Book VIII)
The Temple of the Three Whispers (Book IX)
Whispers in the Murk (Book X)

The Rushed series:

Rushed (Book 1)
Rushed: The Unseen (Book 2)
Rushed: Something Wicked (Book 3)
Rushed: Hedge Lake (Book 4)
Rushed: A Matter of Time (Book 5)
Rushed: All Fun and Games (Book 6)
Rushed: Something Wickeder (Book 7)
Rushed: Evancurt (Book 8)
Rushed: Relic (Book 9)

Hands of the Architects trilogy:

Spirit Ears and Prophet Sight (Book 1)
Pretty Faces and Peculiar Places (Book 2)
Broken Clocks and Amber Threads (Book 3)

For Chrisy. Until we meet again.

Chapter 1

"Excuse me," said Erin, trying her best to look warm and friendly. She held out the small, brown box she was carrying. "We have this little tradition in our family for weddings. We give these to the bridesmaids on the special day. It's a sort of good luck charm."

The woman standing before her was stunningly beautiful. She was somewhat chubbier than the other bridesmaids, but that did her no disservice whatsoever. She was perfectly curvy and buxom and positively *gorgeous*. She had the kind of sweet face and friendly smile that could melt the most frozen of hearts. And she looked so happy standing here in the shade with what was so obviously her mother and her sister.

They were *all* so beautiful. Erin found herself wondering if perhaps these women had descended straight from Aphrodite, herself. It wouldn't necessarily surprise her, after all, given even half of what she'd learned to be true of the world these past few years.

The lovely bridesmaid reached out, her hands and nails as perfect and lovely as her smile, and took the box from her, curious.

It wasn't a terribly attractive piece of jewelry. It wasn't particularly pretty or dainty. It was something of a rush job. It couldn't be helped. She didn't have time to plan better.

It wasn't even supposed to be like this. She intended to wait until *after* the reception to approach her. But the plan had changed. There were...*things*...lurking in the crowd here. Shadowy, menacing things that none of these people could see. They prowled and they crept, sniffing and prodding at the feet of everyone who passed by them.

Did they follow her here? Was it her fault these things were poking around this beautiful wedding?

They'd already taken notice of her. The thorn wouldn't be safe. Just hiding it in clay and wearing it as an unassuming necklace wasn't going to be enough to fool them anymore.

It was time to improvise.

"I know it's going to sound kind of silly," she said, hoping she didn't sound as fake as she felt, "but it's based off a little-known old Chickasaw legend. If you put this on before midnight and wear it for three days without taking it off, it's said to bring good fortune in all matters of love and family for the rest of your life."

"Oh," said the beautiful bridesmaid. "Well, that's a nice thought, isn't it?"

"That's a sweet gesture," agreed her mother. "What a lovely tradition."

Her sister nodded. "It's so sweet. I like it."

"I know, right?" said Erin, putting on her best smile. "I'm not going to tell you it works, but my mom swears by it. She says no woman who's ever put one of these around her neck on a wedding day ever divorces or has difficulty bearing children or loses a loved one too young."

"A *very* nice thought," amended the bridesmaid.

"It is," agreed her sister.

"I've never been very superstitious," said her mother, "but I've also never seen any reason to turn down a good luck blessing. I mean, why not?"

"Exactly," said her sister. "If all you have to do is wear it for three days, what could it hurt?"

Erin felt a little guilty. The thorn held no such power, as far as she knew. In fact, if anything, it might bring this poor, lovely woman an entire mountain of grief. Heaven knew that's what it brought *her*.

But she *needed* her to take it. She needed her to put it on, to keep it close, to keep it *safe*.

Three days should be long enough.

At least, she hoped so…

"Enjoy it," she said, flashing her best smile. "And all the happy tomorrows it promises." Then she turned and walked away, her smile fading almost immediately.

Things were going to get worse now. She could feel it. Inescapable fate was bearing down on her. But this was where she was supposed to be right now. This was how things were always going to go. The man with the antlers told her as much, after all.

She picked up her pace and headed for the parking lot. The sooner she put distance between herself and the lovely bridesmaid the better.

She could see them in the corners of her eyes, slipping unnoticed through the crowd, keeping pace with her. *Stalking* her. Wispy, darkling things that glinted and gleamed in strange, gyrating patterns, but only in the very edges of her peripheral vision. They melted away like fleeting dreams whenever she tried to look directly at them.

But this was good. Their attention was entirely fixed on *her*. They didn't seem to realize that she no longer had what they wanted. And they didn't seem to know who the lovely bridesmaid was, either, that she was the rightful owner of the thorn, chosen by the Keeper, himself. She knew that pretty face the moment she caught sight of her, the very same face she'd seen so many times in her dreams the past few months, but the things lurking in the crowd showed no such recognition. Not yet, anyway. And they wouldn't. Not as long as she kept drawing their attention away from her. All she had to do was keep leading them away. The thorn would find its way to where it needed to be and her job would be done.

And yet, a great sorrow was closing around her heart. She didn't know what was going to happen to her in the next few hours, but she knew deep in her soul that she was never going home again.

All she could do was hope that fate had kinder plans for the pretty bridesmaid.

Chapter 2

Olivia was lying with her head on Wayne's chest as he slept, listening to the beating of his heart, the soothing rhythm of his breathing and the occasional soft grumbling of his belly. She loved every sound his body made, every reminder that he was here with her, safe and sound. She never wanted to be apart from him again. But while she lay soaking up the sounds of him, her eyes and her thoughts were fixed on the thorn. She was holding it in front of her face, staring at it. She couldn't stop thinking about Erin Laplede, the woman who gave her life to place this unassuming little thing around her neck. And then she managed to save her from that awful fairy circle…which, quite honestly, seemed like a rather impressive feat, given the specific order of those events.

Was it really her back there, though? Was it really Erin's disembodied spirit watching over her? Or was it only some strange manifestation of Maeve's magic? Or perhaps even the power of the thorn, itself? She was still unclear on the details, after all.

Maeve called it Yggdrasil's thorn. Like the tree from Norse Mythology, Wayne said. But she didn't really understand it. He tried to explain it to her before he fell asleep, but she only became more confused the more she learned of it. It sounded to her like Yggdrasil was less a tree than a concept of heaven, earth and hell. But perhaps she'd missed something, because how did a *concept* have *thorns*?

She supposed the name was likely some kind of metaphor, but even so…

Maeve said it was a key. And like a key, it had opened the way to the train station. But Maeve also told them specifically that they'd have to take it deep into the vast expanse of the Wood, meaning they were going to need it again before this was over. Additionally, using it made it change. It was as if it had melted and then cooled into this new shape, from a pendant-like spade to this sort of fishhook-like design.

It still didn't *look* like a key, no matter how much she stared at it.

It still looked like a fancy pendant. But whatever it was, whatever purpose it was meant to serve, it was important enough for Erin to give up her life protecting. And it was important enough that the creepy scarecrow man wanted to steal it from them. Which only meant that it was likely to continue attracting trouble as long as they were carrying it.

Would they really be all right?

Her gaze drifted past the thorn to the small room. Nadia had shown them to this sleeper car shortly after they left the station. It wasn't huge, but it was plenty big enough for the two of them, with a full-size bed and its own attached bathroom. There were clean clothes in their size waiting for them in the closet. Practical khaki pants, plain tee shirts, socks and comfortable running shoes. Even a change of underwear. (A brand-new pair of panties to replace the ones those horrid little monsters stole, thankfully.) And everything in just the right sizes. There were also fresh toiletries. They enjoyed a hot shower together. She tended to all the scrapes and scratches she and Wayne collected in those awful woods, removing most of the bandages Everett gave her but replacing the one covering the ugly mark above her right eye. And when they stepped out of the bathroom, a much-appreciated hot meal was waiting for them. Fried chicken, mashed potatoes and buttered corn to fill their growling bellies. And apple crumble for dessert. They ate their fill (then ate a little more) and then crawled into bed together. They even found the energy to make love before falling asleep in each other's arms.

Surprisingly, she didn't have any nightmares, even though those awful never-children and that freaky scarecrow man provided enough fuel for a lifetime of night terrors. She wasn't entirely sure why, but she kept wondering if maybe it was Max and Nadia's presence here on this train that kept the bad dreams away.

They were another mystery, after all. Just who were they? *What* were they? They were anything but ordinary sisters. Were they like Maeve? Powerful spirits of some kind? *Angels*, perhaps? It seemed like all sorts of very *scary* stuff was turning out to be real. Why not something good for a change?

She let go of the thorn and squeezed Wayne a little tighter. She still didn't want to be doing this, of course. But after all that had happened, she'd decided it was better to be *anywhere* with him than without him. So if this was where he had to be, then so be it. She'd take whatever came her way.

Right now, she almost felt like she could handle anything the Keeper threw at them.

She closed her eyes and listened to Wayne's heartbeat. In just a few months, that was going to be the sound of her *husband's* heartbeat. It was a silly thought she kept indulging herself in, as if changing the word from "fiancé" to "husband" changed who he was in any way. They'd already been living together for several years. And yet, thinking about it always filled her with such an overwhelming and almost *giddy* sense of joy that she could barely contain herself.

She did the same thing with the words "boyfriend" and "fiancé" those first few months after he proposed to her. There'd been so many times she'd caught herself thinking about it and realized that she probably looked like some kind of freak, giggling, blushing and grinning like an idiot for no apparent reason...

But she didn't care. Wayne had been her big, strong hero from the moment she first met him. Nothing was going to tear her away from him.

And yet, this conviction had barely crossed her mind when there was a knock at the door.

Wayne gave a startled snort and opened his eyes. Instinctively, his arms closed around her, ready to protect her. (Always her hero.)

"Are you guys up?" called Everett. "Because Nadia says breakfast is ready."

"Okay," grunted Wayne.

"Thank you," Olivia called out.

"Sure thing," chirped Everett. Then he was gone again.

The two of them lay there a moment in silence, holding each other, enjoying the peaceful rumble of the train beneath them, their thoughts heavy with the burden of the unknown waiting for them.

"What do you think's going to happen next?" whispered Olivia.

"Breakfast, sounds like."

She giggled. "*After* that, obviously."

"How should I know? *You're* the one who's supposed to be able to see the future."

She looked up and crinkled her nose at him. "You're supposed to tell me everything's going to be okay because you're going to be right there with me."

He gave her a tired smile. "But see? You already knew that."

She pursed her lips at him, which only made him smile bigger back at her. (He was always telling her that he loved those faces she made at him and calling her "adorable," even when she was being serious.) "I mean it, though," she pressed, nuzzling her face against his chest again. "All that stuff we went through in those awful woods...

Do you think…?" She paused. No. It wasn't really a question, was it? She already *knew* the answer. "It's going to get worse, isn't it?"

But Wayne didn't hesitate. "No," he said firmly. "Nothing can be worse than being separated from you. And I don't intend on letting *that* happen again."

She closed her eyes and squeezed him. It was a sweet gesture and she appreciated it, but she knew he couldn't stop something like that from happening again. It wasn't as if they just became distracted and wandered down different paths back there. That forest was a broken place, mangled by a deranged scientist's twisted experiments and poisoned by evil fairy magic. It didn't matter how special Sandy said they were; at the end of the day, they were both only human.

Maeve said that the rest of their journey would be dangerous. She said something was standing in their way. Something worse than the scarecrow man and those awful never-children. Something strong enough to interfere with the Keeper's plans…

"Come on," she sighed. "They're waiting for us." She pushed herself up onto her elbows and watched as Wayne's eyes gravitated toward her bare chest. She'd never once felt embarrassed when she saw him looking at her like that. Not even when they first became lovers. She used to think that was something she'd never get used to, back when she was single and could only *imagine* what being intimately involved with someone would be like. But it turned out she *liked* it when he looked at her. She *wanted* him to look. She never in her life felt prettier than when he couldn't take his eyes off her.

She leaned forward and kissed him.

She didn't *want* to get up. She didn't want to get dressed. She didn't want to go out there and find out where those strange sisters were taking them. She just wanted to stay right here in his arms. As long as possible. Preferably *forever*.

But they didn't have forever. For better or worse, they were on the Keeper's schedule.

Finally, she sat up and pouted, letting the blanket fall away. "If we ever get through all this and make it back home…"

"*When* we make it home," insisted Wayne, his gaze still fixed on her naked chest, admiring the way the lamplight glinted off the golden thorn hanging between her breasts.

She reached up and brushed back her long hair. "Take me somewhere nice?"

"Take you somewhere?" he asked, finally meeting her gaze. "You don't think you'll have gone *far enough* by then?"

She gave him an embarrassed smile. "I want something *better* than this to remember when it's all done. A *real* vacation. Somewhere *not* in the woods," she quickly added. "A nice hotel, maybe? A fancy dinner or two?"

Wayne smiled up at her. "Anything you want," he promised. "You know I can't say no to you when you're naked."

She giggled and leaned over him again. "Take me somewhere nice and I promise I'll be naked *all you want.*"

"Sold! No takebacks!"

"Wouldn't dream of it," she laughed.

She kissed him again, long and slow, savoring him. Then, finally, she sighed and sat up again. "We'd better go. I kind of don't want Max getting mad at us."

Wayne's eyes opened wide at this. "Yeah, that's a good point."

The two of them dressed and stepped out into the hallway. The curtains in their room had remained closed the whole time they were in there. They'd both found the darkness far too unnerving to leave them open. Out here, however, the entire outer wall was uncovered windows, revealing nothing but that ominous darkness outside. In the soft overhead lights of the car, only their own reflections stared back at them.

"What time is it?" Olivia wondered. Everett told them breakfast was waiting, but it wasn't morning yet. But then again morning wasn't coming, was it? Because there were no mornings in the Wood. There was only that bleak, eternal night.

"Time doesn't really work right out here," said Nadia. She was standing at the end of the hallway, smiling back at them. "Right now, it's sometime early Friday morning in your world."

"Friday?" asked Wayne, surprised. They'd lost the entire *week*? It was a good thing he arranged to have his work projects covered for an extended amount of time. He told them he had the flu and might be out for a while, but he never dreamed they'd actually be gone this long. God, he hoped he didn't end up pissing off his boss. Dalton was a pretty easy-going sort of guy and he took good care of his employees, but this felt like he might be pushing his luck...

Olivia found herself more focused on the last part of that sentence, however. *In your world...* She felt an uneasy lump deep in her belly every time she thought about where they were. She'd managed to push the awful fact to the back of her mind while she was safe and sound with Wayne in their bed, but the truth was that it was the Wood out there.

Wayne cupped his hands to the glass and tried to peer into that oppressive darkness.

Curious, she did the same. Everything out there was swallowed in that all-enveloping gloom, but she could see those awful trees flashing past in the glow of the train's lights. They were moving far too fast to make out any real details—it was nothing more than a lot of shadowy blurs passing them by—but she could see enough to recognize those naked, coiling branches. There was no lush July foliage. Not a glimmer of green to be seen. Everything looked as bare as the dead of winter. And up in the sky… No moon. No stars. No clouds. Nothing but endless emptiness.

"The Wood," sighed Wayne.

Olivia groaned. The Wood… The very sight of them sent a sick feeling burrowing deep into her gut. She spent hours lost and alone in those trees, waiting for someone to come rescue her, hurt and terrified, wondering if she'd ever see her family again. She really didn't want to go back into that awful forest.

Wayne could feel it too, she knew. She glanced up at him, knowing how much he must be haunted right now by unwanted, long-buried memories bubbling up like water from a poisoned spring. Memories of a long, terrifying tunnel filled with imagined horrors with the potential to become real at the slightest slip-up. Wandering lost in a forest filled with living corpses yearning to tear him limb from limb.

"*So* cool!" exclaimed Everett. He'd appeared at Nadia's side as if by magic while they were looking out the window, his nose pressed to the glass.

"It is *not!*" snapped Wayne.

Olivia and Nadia both giggled.

Everett wasn't dissuaded in the least. He stared out at those passing trees with childlike wonder. "So this is another world, right? And that station where we got on was, like, the gateway or something?"

"Something like that," confirmed Nadia.

"*Awesome…*" he breathed.

"That place is *not* awesome!" growled Wayne. "It's a death trap! And we're in the *middle of it!*"

But Nadia only beamed at him. "Don't worry. This train is a safe place. These rails are one of three roads hidden by the Faceless Ones when this universe was first created."

Faceless Ones? Did she mean the sentinels? Those creepy statues down in the temple? Those naked, towering men with freakishly elongated bodies and nothing where their faces should have been? Supposed ancestors of the Sentinel Queen? She looked up at Wayne and saw the same understanding mirrored in his expression. The sentinels were the architects responsible for the Temple of the Blind. And they'd already determined that the station and even the tracks they were riding on were made from the same gray stone...

"This road can only be entered through the station where you boarded," Nadia continued, "which was, itself, hidden deep within that fairy circle, basically unreachable to anyone but you three."

"So, we're like...the *first* to see this stuff?" asked Everett. He looked like he was about to explode.

Nadia turned and pressed her small hands to the glass, staring out into that passing darkness with those wondering emerald eyes. "The path this road carves through the forest is a meticulously crafted anomaly woven into the very *existence* of the Wood that makes it possible to travel vast distances in very little time." She was so full of energy. She was standing on her toes, bouncing up and down as she spoke. "The sheer scale of it is almost impossible for the human mind to really comprehend. To put it just a little bit into perspective, using today's technology, you could travel to the far side of the galaxy and back in less time than it would take to get this far without the roads."

"No way!" gasped Everett.

"How is that even possible?" challenged Wayne.

It was a good question. Olivia didn't know much about space travel, but she knew that most of that stuff was measured in millions of light years. They'd only been traveling a single night. Hadn't they?

Nadia giggled. "Anything's possible when the rules defining what's possible stop applying. And out here, distance is as uncertain as time." She was still staring through the glass, seemingly fascinated by the darkness out there. "These tracks take advantage of all that broken stuff, making the unreachable reachable."

Olivia and Wayne both found their gazes drawn there, too. That endless black forest, crawling with dead things that didn't stay dead and nasty man-eating trees and freakish, flying carrion eaters that circled in the empty sky like buzzards.

"The Wood is a graveyard for dead worlds," she explained. "Everything that ever lives and dies ends up there eventually, in some way or another."

"When can we go out there?" wondered Everett.

"*How stupid are you?*" boomed Wayne, surprising him.

Olivia jabbed him in the ribs with her finger. "Don't be mean!"

"Sorry..." said Everett.

"You're fine," Olivia assured him.

But Wayne stalked past him, frustrated, and made his way to the next car, where they first boarded the train. There was a little sitting area in the very front. He plopped down on one of the couches, looking irritated.

Olivia followed him and smooshed herself into the seat beside him, intentionally crowding him. When they first started dating, she remembered being a little intimidated when he got like that. And he got like that a lot. Lots of things annoyed him. Everett's incessant optimism was only the newest in a long list of things that got under his skin. Like his family's constant criticism. Pretty much *everyone* else on the road when he had to drive somewhere. And back in those early days it was frequently his roommate, Charlie, that put him in bad moods. That guy was a piece of work. She didn't like him very much. And then there was Charlie's ever-present, obnoxious, foul-mouthed and blatantly *slutty* girlfriend, Laura, who was always flirting with Wayne whenever Charlie wasn't in the room.

(It probably went without saying that she didn't like Laura very much. But that was another story.)

She kept thinking he'd get irritated with *her*, too. That she'd say the wrong thing and he'd blow up at her. But that never happened. In fact, it didn't take her very long to figure out that for all his grumpiness, Wayne never felt an ounce of anger toward *her*. And once she learned that she was immune to his bearish moods, she found that if she just inserted herself into his personal bubble, he *always* softened up for her. And that was probably one of her favorite things about him. She loved that she, alone, had the power to soothe the savage beast whenever she wanted.

Now, she laid her head on his shoulder and looked up at him, batting her pretty eyes at him, and she could actually see that tenseness in his jaw ease up a little.

"Don't be a grumpy-pants," she said without speaking a word.

The Sentinel Queen told her that she was psychic. Sandy told her that she had the power to see the threads of fate, itself, allowing her to predict the very future, but she was convinced that *this* would always be her favorite superpower.

Nadia came skipping into the sitting area and plopped onto the seat across from them, bouncing on the cushions. Did she *ever* stop moving? It was like she was on a constant sugar high. "You know, the Wood is an absolute death sentence for most of the people who lay eyes on it." Her cheerful tone was a stark contrast to the dark words she was speaking. "Bridges between it and the living worlds, places like

Gilbert House, are almost unheard of. What happened to you two five years ago isn't typical. Not by any means."

"So...*what?*" asked Wayne, bemused. "We've used up all our luck for a lifetime?"

Nadia leaned forward, emerald eyes shining at them. "No. Luck had nothing to do with it. Don't you understand? The two of you were *supposed* to be there."

"Are you talking about the Keeper?" asked Olivia. Maeve said it was all about him. He was the one who gave her the land where she built her circle. And Sandy told them that he was the one who sent Erin to give her the thorn.

"Hey, I remember that name..." said Everett. He was standing in the doorway, as if hesitant to approach. "You guys were talking about that guy before."

"It's still a long story," grumbled Wayne.

Olivia glanced around. "Hey, where'd that other guy go? Austin?" The unfriendly looking man who was on the train with them. He was sitting in one of the seats near the back of the car when they boarded, reading a book and pretty much ignoring them. But he was nowhere to be seen now. She'd almost forgotten about him.

"He's around," replied Nadia. "Don't worry about him. He has a job to do here, just like you do."

She looked toward the door leading back to the sleeping cars. She wondered what his story was.

Nadia smiled that cheerful smile and then hopped to her feet. "I'll go get your breakfast. Eggs, hashbrowns, toast and bacon." Then, her bright eyes fixed on Wayne, she added, "I made *lots* of bacon."

Wayne's eyebrows crept up at this. Olivia could actually hear his stomach grumble in response.

Chapter 3

Nicole stood in a passageway of smooth, gray stone, a flashlight clenched in one trembling hand. She was cold. She was naked and tired. And she was *afraid*. Her heart was racing, her stomach clenched in a steaming knot.

There was a chamber looming in the darkness ahead of her. She could see where the smooth ground gave way to coarse, black earth.

"Stay away from the meadow," the Keeper warned her in his forced and gravelly voice. "There is nothing for you there but pain and death."

She shook her head and took a step backward. Why was she here? She wasn't supposed to be here. This place was five years in her past. It didn't even exist anymore. It was swallowed up with the rest of the temple after Brandy threw open that door. She couldn't come here if she'd wanted to.

And yet, she could feel the cold stone beneath the aching soles of her weary bare feet. She could feel the cool air raising gooseflesh on her exposed skin. Her hair was still damp from crossing those deep, frigid pools. And she could feel the hard rubber handle of the flashlight in her clenched fist.

She backed away, her gaze fixed on that darkness, half-convinced that something horrible was going to come rushing out at her.

Why did it feel so bad in there? What was *wrong* with that room? It was just one of the many mysteries buried forever that frightful night, never to be unearthed again.

Or so she thought…

Finally, she tore her eyes away from it long enough to turn and shine her light down the tunnel behind her, making sure there was nothing back there. Thankfully, she was alone. No monstrous hounds or man-eating trees were about to devour her.

And yet…*why* was she alone in this place? Where did Brandy and Albert go? Weren't they with her almost the whole time?

When she looked forward again, she caught just a glimpse of Albert's naked back as he vanished into that ominous darkness. Her heart leaping with fresh terror, she rushed forward to stop him.

The first time they were here, something about that room got into his head. It *lured* him somehow. It tried to make him enter. If she hadn't stopped him when she did, he would have walked right out into it.

And now it had him again!

But when she reached the end of the tunnel, he was nowhere to be seen.

"Albert?" she whispered. Then, a little louder. "*Albert?*"

There was nowhere else for him to have gone. He had to be in there.

She shined her light across that black soil, where it glinted off the rippling surface of a pool of water. Above it, the dead and naked branches of a shadowy tree jutted toward her like jagged bones. "Where are you?"

An awful dread had settled into her belly. She felt as if she might throw up.

She didn't really see what she thought she saw. Albert didn't go in there. He *couldn't* have gone in there. She only imagined that she saw him. But even as she told herself this, she aimed her flashlight to the left and caught just a glimpse of his pale form vanishing deeper into the darkness.

"Albert!"

What was he doing? Why would he go in there? Did something make him do it? Was he being controlled somehow?

"*Albert!*" She could feel tears welling up in her eyes again. She hated feeling helpless like this. It was awful.

"Nikki…"

She swung the light back to the right, her heart leaping again. That was *Brandy's* voice!

"Nikki…"

"Brandy?"

"Help me…"

She shook her head. No. They weren't in there. They couldn't be. This place didn't even exist anymore. It was long gone.

"Please… They're hurting me…"

She shined her light down at the black soil in front of her feet. It was moving. Something unseen was churning beneath it. Something small and dark skittered just into view and then vanished again before she could aim her light at it.

Something splashed in the water out of sight, sending twinkling ripples racing through the gloom.

"…hurts…so much…"

"Brandy!" Every part of her brain wanted to rush into that darkness. That was her best friend in there. She couldn't just leave her to suffer.

But that wasn't Brandy. It *couldn't* be Brandy. Brandy and Albert weren't here in these awful tunnels with her. They were in Tennessee. They were on their honeymoon.

They were *safe*.

"Just leave us then," said Albert. There was such an awful tone of accusation in his voice that it pierced her heart like a blade. "Just run away."

She shook her head. Those welling tears overflowed and spilled down her cheeks. "No…"

Brandy's sobs drifted through the darkness. "…make it stop…"

"It's not real…" she breathed.

She felt something on her outstretched arm. Looking down, she found that there were drops of blood on her bare skin.

She stepped backward, looking down at herself. There were drops of blood *all over her.*

Brandy's blood?

"…please make it stop…" begged Brandy.

"Just let her die," snarled Albert. "What do you care?"

She clenched her teeth. No. That was *not* Albert. Albert would never say such things to her.

"…please…" sobbed Brandy.

Nicole backed away from the meadow and its hideous lies. None of this was real.

She turned to run, desperate to leave this place, only to find herself staring into the rotten eyes of Albert's long-dead corpse.

She let out a startled gasp and opened her eyes. She wasn't in those awful tunnels. She was in bed, in the small master stateroom of Keith's boat. Andrea and Gina were snuggled up together beside her, both of them sound asleep.

It was only a nightmare…

But it felt so *real*. Even the tears she'd cried were still wet upon her cheeks. She wriggled her arm out from under Gina's pillow and wiped them away, sniffling.

She needed to get ahold of herself. Why was she dreaming of the meadow of all things? And why now? There was no shortage of *new* things to have nightmares about. The barely-there. Tristesse Lane. Cedric's Cove and those horrors that lurked beneath its flooded streets.

And yet...why did it feel like that wasn't the first time she'd visited that awful place in her dreams? Why did it suddenly feel as if she'd been having similar nightmares ever since that frightful night?

Or was that part of the dream, too? It was so hard to recall...

Careful not to disturb her friends, she slipped out of bed and began to dress. Unlike Andrea there, she couldn't sleep in her clothes. She couldn't get comfortable. They tangled up around her every time she rolled over. It always felt like they were strangling her. She was used to sleeping completely naked. But in the interest of not making it weird, she compromised and kept her underwear on.

Gina told her she didn't mind. In fact, she took her skirt off, too. Although she kept her blouse on.

She put on her socks and shoes, made a half-hearted effort to tie back her messy hair, then collected her phone from the charger and slipped quietly out of the cabin.

Chapter 4

Gina opened her eyes and watched as Nicole left the stateroom, then continued to watch her, even after she was out of sight, using that accursed second sight to follow her through the trawler's interior, out the door and onto the walkway outside, where she stopped and gazed out over the water.

She shouldn't be alone right now. Glum or his barely-there could still be following them, for all they knew, lurking somewhere just beyond her senses, waiting for another chance to sink their claws into her vulnerable brain. Or something even worse. The goddess confirmed that Elias Hochog was dead but warned them that the ancient deity he worshipped was quite real and wouldn't let something as minor as the death of his insane servant get in the way of stopping them from reaching their destination.

(What comes back will be different and in many ways more dangerous.)

She'd felt no trace of those presences since before they found the Lady of Cedric's Cove, but she didn't dare let her guard down. Nicole and Andrea had been so nice to her, right from the start, even though they barely knew her. She couldn't bear the thought of letting anything happen to either of them.

It still pained her how adamantly she'd insisted that Andrea forget about her roommate and leave that apartment before something else came looking for the Whisper. If she'd listened…if they'd been gone before Nicole escaped that dangerous pocket world…what would've become of her? Would the barely-there have seized her again? Would she have ended up suffering in Tristesse Lane's miserable depths forever? She knew she shouldn't blame herself. She didn't yet know what they were dealing with. She was only doing as the goddess instructed. But the very thought of that possibility, of a reality where they left without Nicole and Andrea never saw her again and she'd never even meet her… She couldn't stand it.

Shortly after setting off from the dock in Cedric's Cove, Nicole grew agitated with their captain—who also, unbelievably, turned out to be her ex-boyfriend, of all the people in the world—and announced that she was going below deck to shower and get some sleep. Gina tried to stop her, of course, telling her that they shouldn't be alone, that the barely-there might still be watching, and she simply informed her that, if it bothered her, she was welcome to join her.

Andrea was already telling Keith all about their long journey and all the misadventures they'd stumbled into along the way. There was a lot of story left to tell and she didn't seem to have slowed down at all, so she opted to follow Nicole.

She was muttering to herself as she made her way below deck. She sounded irritable. And Gina found herself hesitant to follow too closely, half-expecting her to lash out at her. In her experience, it was never a good idea to be in anyone's space when they were angry. That was when people stopped pretending to be nice. So she didn't dare try speaking to her. She'd stay just close enough to keep them both safe from barely-theres.

Nicole paused as she passed the little kitchen to see what was inside the refrigerator, muttered something about someone at least getting *something* right, and then plucked a bottle off the shelf. She held it out at arm's length for her to see. "Beer?"

"No, thank you," she replied timidly. She'd never developed a taste for alcohol. Once, back when she first turned twenty-one, she bought herself a case of cheap beer and tried getting drunk, thinking that it might dull the awful things her psychic mind showed her. It didn't work. In fact, it had the opposite effect: only dulling her normal senses while seemingly magnifying the scary one. It was one of the worst nights of her life. Definitely not worth the hangover the next morning.

"Suit yourself," Nicole told her. She closed the fridge, then opened the bottle and took a long drink as she made her way toward the back of the trawler, exploring.

The stateroom was fully stocked for them. There were brand new toothbrushes, toothpaste, hairbrushes, deodorant, fresh bandages and disinfectant for their various injuries, soap and shampoo for the shower and even a pair of cell phone chargers already plugged into the wall outlet.

She couldn't help wondering if there were only two because that was how many outlets there were by the bed or because whoever stocked the place knew she'd lost hers.

"Of all fucking people..." Nicole muttered to herself as she looked around.

"Sorry," was all she could think to say.

"Not like it's *your* fault."

No, it wasn't. But still… She was the one who showed up and up-ended their lives. She couldn't help feeling at least a little responsible for everything they were going through.

Nicole took another swig from her beer, then set it aside and plugged in her phone. Then, with no warning, she began stripping off her clothes.

It was kind of weird how casual she was about it. She didn't even bother looking around to make sure no one had followed them below deck. But then again, the only other people on the boat were her roommate and her ex-boyfriend. If she wasn't bashful around someone she'd only known since the night of that wedding, she wasn't going to care if she was seen by literally the two people most likely to have seen her naked on a regular basis.

Embarrassed, she turned around and closed the door behind her. Not that it mattered, she supposed. She really didn't seem to care who saw her. Andrea apologized for her when they first met and referred to her as a nudist. But from what she'd heard about their experience five years ago, it sounded like they all somehow ended up naked together, even though most of them didn't even know each other yet. It wasn't too hard to imagine something like that making a person immune to that sort of bashfulness. At some point, she probably just simply *got over it.*

And with a body like that, she wasn't sure she blamed her…

She caught herself staring and forced herself to look around at the room, instead. This was awkward. She felt like an intruder. "We shouldn't be alone," she said again.

"So you keep reminding me," replied Nicole.

She wilted a little at this. Right. She *did* keep saying that. It wasn't as if they needed reminding. She was only making herself sound foolish. "Sorry."

"You're fine." She tossed aside her panties, then picked up her beer and took another long drink.

Gina's gaze washed over her, her eyes seemingly moving on their own. She was positively gorgeous. Lean and fit, with exquisite muscle tone. And such perfect breasts. She looked the way women in magazines looked after a heavy dose of airbrushing. All the dirt and grime and sweat she'd collected during their travels did nothing to sully her amazing body. Even her smeared and makeup and messy hair looked remarkably good on her. If anything it only added to that surprising sexiness. Even the bandages over those painful claw marks and those strange barely-there marks on her chest and belly couldn't take away from her exquisite beauty.

She felt so uncomfortable, and yet she couldn't seem to tear her eyes away.

Nicole returned the beer to the table with a grimace and picked up the soap and the shampoo bottle. "So I guess that means we're showering together."

She stood there a moment, surprised, a hot flush spreading up her face. "That wasn't really what...I..."

But Nicole was already walking to the bathroom. "That means *you* can't be alone, too," she reasoned.

"I mean, yeah...but..."

"So come on."

Timidly, she followed her into the bathroom. Telling people "no" wasn't exactly her strong suit. She had a bad habit of just going with the flow, for better or worse.

Besides, she wouldn't actually get in the *shower* with her. She'd just sort of hover in the doorway while she washed up. She doubted they'd both even fit. But it was surprisingly roomy in there. And there was, indeed, room for two in the shower. "I can just stand out here," she offered as Nicole untied the stained gauze wrapped around her wrist and examined the injuries the hospital monster left with its ghostly claws. Those scabs looked painful, but she wasn't bleeding anymore, so she wadded it up and then leaned out and tossed it in the trash.

"Suit yourself," she replied as she removed the other bandages and tossed them away as well.

She nodded, relieved. For a moment there she thought she might insist. And she was so bad at refusing people. It was who she was. A fear reaction, in all honesty, a response to all the people who mistreated her over the years, a desperate attempt to please everyone in hopes that they wouldn't get mad at her. And of course a part of her was intimidated by the strong, chiseled beauty standing before her, a form she couldn't compete with in a million years.

Although, she'd be lying if she said there wasn't something alluring about the idea of such a closeness, of a friendship so comfortable, of a relationship so candid. She'd never had a friend she felt that comfortable with before. And she doubted she ever would.

Nicole turned on the water and adjusted it.

Why was her heart beating so fast? This was silly. She pulled the door closed as Nicole stepped under the hot stream and began to soap up. Then she turned around and perched herself on the toilet lid, politely looking away. It felt so strangely surreal sitting here while someone showered right next to her, with only a clear shower door between them. Such a private moment. So *intimate*. So *awkwardly voyeuristic*... Her heart was still beating so hard. It felt like she was doing something wrong. But it was only a shower. They were both adults. They were both girls... That made it okay, right? Athletes showered in front of each other every day.

"Listen," said Nicole as she began lathering her hair. "Don't mind anything I say about Keith, okay? We have a history. Things got sort of messy. I've got some pretty big feelings about the whole thing, I guess. But he's not a bad guy in any way, I promise."

"Okay..." was all she could think to respond with.

"I just don't want you feeling like you can't trust him just because of anything I say or do, you know? You can. He's..." She seemed to struggle for a moment before blurting out, "He's a *nice guy*. That's all."

"Okay," she said again. She wasn't too worried. Andrea had already told her that Keith was a nice guy, that the issues between those two were just that: *between them*. But it was good to hear it from Nicole, too, she supposed. Hopefully it meant that whatever hard feelings might exist between the two of them wouldn't jeopardize their safety in any way.

Nicole sighed, her hands working their way through her hair, suds were sliding down her body, tracing the tantalizing outline of her figure.

Again, Gina tore her gaze away. She looked into the mirror instead, at her own bruised and bandaged face, her plain and unremarkable features. She didn't even remotely compare to the bewitching woman standing bare before her. Not that it mattered, she supposed. What would she do with a body like that? It would probably only bring her more trouble. The last thing she needed was to attract more attention.

"Fuck knows we need to stick together if we're going back to the Wood."

The Wood... Even the way she said it sounded awful. She practically sneered the word, as if she were talking about hell, itself, rather than some otherworldly forest.

"Sorry."

"Not *your* fault."

"Okay."

Nicole turned and rinsed her hair. Gina caught herself watching again as she arched her back and pushed out her impressive chest. She was so distractingly shapely. It didn't seem natural. If she were someone else, she might have suspected that she'd had some cosmetic work done. But that was one of those things she tended to know at just a glance. She obviously worked out, but she also was simply blessed with the sort of natural body other women paid fortunes for.

Finally, she turned off the water, slid open the door and snatched a towel off the rack. "That feels *so* much better!" she sighed as she began wrapping her hair.

"That's good," Gina replied, unsure what else to say. She felt like she might be in the way sitting on the toilet lid like this, so she stood up and backed against the wall. Making herself as small as possible was another old defense mechanism. If she stayed out of everyone's way and didn't stand out, then maybe they wouldn't notice her. And if they didn't notice her, they wouldn't mistreat her.

She finished with her hair and reached for another towel to dry off her body. "Have you been able to feel anything dangerous since we left the dock?"

"Not really. Glimpses of some things I couldn't recognize far out in the water when we first set sail. But nothing that seemed to pay us any attention."

"Things in the water…" she repeated, sounding exhausted. "Just what we fucking need while stuck on a *boat*…"

"Sorry."

"Not your fault," she said again.

"Okay."

She bent forward and began drying her legs, her full, perfect breasts hanging downward and swaying seductively with the motion. "I'm not upset with you or anything. I'm just tired."

"Sorry."

"Hey." Nicole reached out and grabbed her arm, surprising a startled gasp out of her. "I get that you've been through some shit and that's totally okay. But seriously, you should stop saying you're sorry for every little thing like that. You deserve better."

She opened her mouth to reply but realized that she was only about to apologize again, so she snapped it shut.

"There's nothing to be sorry for. You don't *owe* anyone an apology. Least of all me, okay?"

"Okay," she said, her voice failing her a little as it passed over her lips.

Then Nicole hugged her.

She stood there, frozen in place, too surprised to move, Nicole's damp body pressed against her. She was so warm. The mingling smells of shampoo and soap filled her nose.

"You're a really awesome person," she said, "no matter what anyone might have ever told you. And I swear to God, if I ever catch anyone telling you otherwise, I will kick their ass *so* hard."

Again, she wasn't sure how to respond. She felt embarrassed by this sudden attention, for one thing. She wasn't used to it. And she was completely flustered by how *close* they were. She felt lightheaded.

Then, finally, she let go and went back to drying herself off. "Your turn," she said.

Gina was still staring at her, still distracted, still confused. "What?"

"In the shower."

"Oh..." She looked down at her stained blouse and dirty fingernails. "Yeah. Okay."

Now, hours later, as she lay next to Andrea in the trawler's master stateroom, she watched with that unwanted eye as Nicole made her way up to the bridge, where Keith was sitting at the helm. She'd be safe there with him. She could relax again.

What an unusual experience... Was that really something lots of friends did? Just...hang out in the bathroom? Watch each other shower? She couldn't decide which felt more awkward, watching or being watched. It was uncomfortable...but not entirely bad... She didn't exactly mind it. It was just...not something she'd ever even thought about, really.

She remembered the way Nicole looked washing her hair and squeezed her eyes shut, blushing at the mental image.

This wasn't what she thought she was signing up for when the goddess sent her south to that wedding...

Chapter 5

Albert lay in the bed of the strange carriage, reading the shaman's obscene spellbook by the queer, bluish light. Brandy was snuggled up against him, her face pressed against his chest, the rhythm of her warm breath a welcome comfort against the endless darkness looming on the other side of the window above him.

Violet and Corey insisted that they were fine with them taking the bed, that they were used to catching sleep on the go and in shifts. Apparently, it was blatantly obvious that they were exhausted from their ordeal in Lucianna's monstrous hotel. Or, as Violet had so delicately pointed out, they "looked like shit."

He had no idea how long ago they pulled the curtain closed and settled into these silky blankets. It was long enough for both of them to have caught a decent amount of much-appreciated sleep, at least. Between the long rest and the meal Lucianna packed for them—an unexpectedly fancy, piping-hot steak and shrimp dinner for all four of them, complete with garlic mashed potatoes, seasonal vegetables and an entire lemon meringue pie to share for dessert—he hadn't felt this clearheaded since they stumbled into the pervy shaman's copycat sex room. And at least some of that was thanks to the unexpected comfort of this strange carriage. In addition to the fact that the bed was surprisingly cozy, it was a much smoother ride than he'd expected. And quieter, too, considering the speed they seemed to be going. There was a steady drone of wind and runner drag as they plowed forward, but it was little more than soothing white noise in the background.

Lucianna told them that the sentinels built this road. And the stone tunnel *did* look like something right out of the Temple of the Blind. But they never saw anything like this carriage down there. Everything in the temple was stone. This seemed to be made from some kind of metal. And the technology behind it was well beyond his comprehension. He couldn't even quite understand how the *door* on the thing worked, much less how it was able to carry them such a vast distance so quickly. And without any noticeable discomfort? Was it the carriage, or the tunnel, itself, that gave it such power? And most of all, just what the hell was pulling them? There wasn't a single clue about the identity of those mysterious beasts. They made no noise that he could hear. They left no tracks. Were they truly being pulled by something that existed entirely in another dimension from this one?

It was such a uniquely *bizarre* experience that he found it impossible to spend too much time thinking about it. It was utterly *surreal*. Even by their standards!

He turned the page. There were more of those strange, illegible symbols. When the pervert shaman first handed him this book, they covered almost every page. But each time he opened it, there were fewer and fewer passages he couldn't read. He still couldn't understand how it worked. Was it really magic? Was the ink literally rearranging itself on the paper, like something out of *Harry Potter*? Or was it more like some kind of hypnosis trick where it was his mind that was scrambling the letters? He couldn't decide which was harder to believe.

Making love in the dark can be a carnal ritual of electrifying sensations, read the sloppy, cramped handwriting that was legible between a block of indecipherable scribbles and an obscene sketch of a blindfolded woman with her legs spread apart. *When denied the sense it inevitably learns to rely on the most in the visual world we live in, the human brain automatically switches into a state of high alert, dialing up the sensitivity to those remaining senses, creating a unique kind of fear response that can heighten the pleasure of intercourse, especially when performed in an unfamiliar setting. The intensity of exploring another body entirely through skin-against-skin contact, the smell and taste of one's lover and the sounds they make while engaged in the act can intensify every aspect of the art of copulation, often leading to some of the most powerful, trembling orgasms attainable. Utilizing this knowledge in the practice of sexual magic can, under the right conditions, magnify the effectiveness of spells considerably.*

That was an oddly specific tip, he thought. "Not getting enough charge out of your sex spells?" he muttered under his breath, careful not to wake Brandy. "Try doin' it in the dark!" This was absurd. Did the weirdo think they were going to just kill their flashlights and go at it right there in that terrifying forest?

And it only became worse as he scanned the rest of the entry. The pervert next went into excruciating details about the best ways to engage one's partner under the cover of darkness, using far too many descriptive words and more synonyms for "wet" than he'd ever seen in one place before…

Gross.

He turned the page and scanned the next few entries. He'd always thought a spellbook would read something like a cookbook. (A splash of virgin's blood. A pinch of nutmeg. A dash of toad eyeballs.) But this was just thinly veiled smut. Was the old pervert only using this sex magic nonsense as an excuse to insert pornography into every aspect of his sleazy life?

He flipped forward through the pages, weary of wading through obscenities to find anything remotely helpful. So far, the only good magic had done them was to supercharge their latent psychic abilities, which had, admittedly, been helpful. But having to rely on their emotions to make it work was just plain inconvenient. It was too slow. It was only a matter of time before they ran out of luck.

Beside him, Brandy let out a soft groan and reached around him, enveloping him in her arms and nuzzling her face against his chest.

He kissed her forehead, eliciting a muffled, "Mmmmf..." and a firm squeeze.

Slow mornings like this were always the best.

Although...*was* it morning? He had no idea how long he'd slept or even what time it was when they departed Mysteria. Or even when they might've ended up after opening that last lock, now that he was thinking about it. Every time he plunged his hand into one of those statues it also sent them to another point in time in their four-day honeymoon stay. There was no reason to think that the stone under that mutated skeleton would have been any different.

She pressed her face against his chest and kissed him, distracting him from his muddled thoughts. Then she lifted her face, those pretty eyes still closed, and pursed her lips at him, fishing for her morning kiss, which he of course gave her.

He closed his eyes and savored the feel of it. For a moment, he could almost believe that he was home again, in his own bed, safe from all the terrors and perversions of the world.

When he opened his eyes, hers were still closed. But now she was pouting. "It wasn't all just some fucked-up dream, was it?" she whispered.

"No," he replied, although that would've been nice. He would've given anything for them both to have awakened in their own bed in their own home, safe and sound and free to start their life together as husband and wife. "Sorry."

She sighed and pressed her face against his chest again, refusing to open her eyes, as if she might find a way to put off reality long enough to change it.

He gave her a squeeze and kissed her forehead again. It was weird not sleeping naked together. He'd stripped off his shirt in an attempt to be more comfortable, but was still wearing his shorts, and she was still in her shorts and halter top, all of which they stole from their past selves in that freaky hotel. It wasn't what they were used to, and it took them both a bit to settle in, but there was only that one curtain separating them from the other two people riding at the front of the carriage. And no matter what everyone kept saying about their "impressive sexual output," there was simply no way either of them would've been comfortable sleeping naked that close to two complete strangers, no matter how nice they seemed.

He hadn't heard a word spoken between Violet and Corey since he woke up, but two or three times he could hear one of them moving around or rummaging in their bag.

What was the story with those two, anyway? Who were they? How did they fit into all of this? And what strange events brought them to the Lucianna Mysteria just in time to depart on this strange carriage?

"Don't wanna," she muttered, her voice muffled against him, her breath hot on his bare skin.

"Well, we're not there yet," he assured her. The carriage was still plowing forward through that unsettling darkness, after all, showing no sign of slowing down. "For now, we can just focus on breakfast."

At this, she lifted her head and at last opened those pretty blue eyes. "Oh yeah!" she breathed. "Breakfast!" In addition to the amazing meal, Lucianna had packed them all a heavenly spread of bagels, Danishes and muffins to share for breakfast. His stomach rumbled at the mere thought of them all. (Or maybe it was *her* stomach…it was hard to tell sometimes when they were this close.)

She pushed aside the blankets and then rolled over and stretched, the ring in her navel glinting in the curious carriage lights. "Hungry," she yawned, already reaching for her glasses.

"Me, too," he agreed, his gaze lingering on the shiny stud. He'd grab his shirt and fill his belly. And maybe they could get to know their mysterious companions a little better while they ate.

Chapter 6

Violet and Corey sat across the table from each other, their eyes locked. They'd been friends a long time. As long as either of them could remember. They were closer than most siblings. Often, they didn't have to speak. They were of the same mind. And this was certainly no exception.

Violet's phone was lying on the table in front of her. Gina had just disconnected the call and gone silent. She wanted to know about Cedric's Cove.

They'd been searching for the traveling city for over five years with little success, and now here it was, out of the blue. And straight from the mouth of Gina Sarelli, of all people.

Gina was a friend. Or perhaps "friend of a friend" would have been a better phrasing. Not that they didn't consider her a friend. They both thought Gina was a wonderful person, sweet and kind and thoughtful. But she wasn't a very *outgoing* person. In fact, she was practically a shut-in. She never said much. She certainly never went out of her way to have a conversation with anyone. They never would have met her if not for the fact that she lived with two of their other friends. But what made Gina and her roommates particularly special was that they shared something *extraordinary* between them. Like Violet and Corey, they were all three intimately aware of the strange and extraordinary *hidden* side of the world. Gina, in particular, possessed a sixth sense of sorts. She was unnaturally aware of her surroundings. She could see things others couldn't see. She *knew* things.

Violet and Corey had no such abilities between them. They were both as ordinary as any human being was expected to be in this day and age, give or take. But eight years ago, the two of them witnessed a bizarre, unexplainable phenomenon right in their own hometown in Northern Missouri. Local papers called it the "Tunipet Boom," a concussive explosion powerful enough to blow the windows out of a three-story office building and set off car alarms up and down the surrounding streets. It wasn't a bomb. There was no fire or smoke. No discernable epicenter to the blast. And somehow no one was badly injured. No one could explain how or why it happened. Even after all this time, there were no answers. It had become one of those things that were whispered about on those unexplained phenomena websites and creepy story podcasts that Corey was so fond of.

Only three people in the world knew the truth about what actually happened that day. Two of them were sitting at this table. And the third, a dear friend named Jeremy, was gone now. His story was a secret they kept tightly locked away between them. Almost no one would believe it, anyway. And even when they finally began meeting people who might actually believe them—people like Gina, for example—they still chose to keep their story to themselves. It felt private, after all. Almost *sacred*. It was *their* story and theirs alone. And somehow, it worked better for them like this. It was an inspiration to their cause, a *fuel source* for their endless quest to seek out the universe's *other* secrets. They'd promised each other they wouldn't share it with anyone until they finally understood what was really out there. Because during the hours that followed the mysterious Tunipet Boom, they learned that there was far more to the world than their senses revealed to them. There were *monsters* out there, for one thing. Indescribable things that the human mind couldn't even properly comprehend, things that slipped effortlessly in and out of what most people perceived as reality. Things that could disguise themselves as human if they so wanted. But more importantly, there were entire other *worlds* waiting to be discovered. Finding these worlds and mapping them had become their mission. They'd researched hundreds of local legends, seeking out the weird and bizarre, trying to connect them to the existence of portals to other worlds.

And they'd found them.

Most of them weren't very impressive, to be honest. It was difficult to even tell you were inside most of them. They were tiny, rarely much bigger than a few city blocks. And they had a tendency for some reason to mirror their real-world surroundings, making it difficult to tell them apart. In fact, there were alternate dimensions out there that people wandered in and out of all the time, without ever even realizing it.

But those little pocket dimensions were by no means the only ones. There were other worlds, too. Bigger worlds. Darker worlds. *Scarier* worlds.

There was a doorway in a hidden room in the basement of an abandoned church in Arkansas that spewed searing heat and acrid, choking smoke when they tried to open it, forcing them to close it up again. There was an ancient-looking set of hand-carved stone steps hidden away deep in a dense, Kentucky forest that they never made it to the bottom of because the trees there were crawling with strange, blood-red snakes and littered with ominous animal bones. And there was a creepy gravel road in rural Iowa that led to a boarded-up tunnel where someone had hung a sign reading, "WARNING: DEVILS IN-SIDE," and where they both glimpsed a corpse-pale, child-size hand disappearing through a gap between the rotting lumber.

It was dangerous work. *Especially* when they found what they were searching for. But they were smart enough to know when to turn back. They resealed the door in Arkansas. They retreated from the blood snakes in Kentucky. And they sure as hell didn't mess with whatever was behind those boards in Iowa. Knowing where these places were and how to get to them was enough. Maybe someday they'd find a way to go back and explore some of them, but it wasn't worth their lives. Venturing into something unaware was a good way to find themselves trapped. Or stumble into an environment where the atmosphere was toxic or suffocating. Or one filled with hostile life. Because *that* was a real danger, too.

Violet kept a journal of creatures that were sometimes sighted in the vicinity of gateways, fauna native to those other worlds that had ventured into ours, which she'd dubbed "crossers." Most of them weren't really dangerous, but some were. And they were wise enough to know that it only took one.

Corey kept a map detailing all the portals they'd located, as well as anywhere his research led him to believe might contain one or more gateways. Places rich in paranormal history, with lots of unusual activity or mysterious disappearances. Places like Hedge Lake in Northern Michigan, Penaskee and Avelby in Illinois and Crump in Ohio, just to name a few. But Cedric's Cove was one of the most mysterious and elusive. He sometimes referred to it as his white whale. He was convinced it was real and had even uncovered landmarks he believed were part of the path leading there, but in the five years since the stories first caught his attention, they'd never been able to find the gateway.

And now Gina had called them up out of the blue, specifically asking about it.

This might finally be their chance to find it.

They told her everything they knew about the traveling city, which wasn't a whole lot. Mostly, they told her about All Trail's Crossing. That, Corey believed, was where the path leading to Cedric's Cove was hidden, if they could only figure it out.

She thanked them and then hung up.

They didn't discuss the matter with each other. They didn't need to. They were of the same mind, after all. They simply stood up and started gathering their equipment. She said she was in Briar Hills, of all places—another location of interest on Corey's map, interestingly enough—so if they hurried, they should be able to beat her there.

Violet felt a little bad as she tied her shoes, though. Gina said specifically for them *not* to do what they were doing right now. She didn't want them getting involved.

"Gina sometimes receives messages from some kind of *goddess*, telling her to do things," Violet explained. "I know it sounds totally crazy, but who are *we* to judge? I mean we track down *dimensional portals*. She can have a goddess. And according to her, this goddess specifically told her not to involve anyone else, for their own safety. Which apparently meant us."

"Not gonna happen," interjected Corey.

"Right," agreed Violet. "We weren't going to miss a chance to finally find Cedric's Cove."

"So you guys just…ignored your friend and set off to intercept her?" asked Albert.

Violet shrugged. "We're not the best at taking orders."

The carriage was still speeding down the same black tunnel, those mysterious chains stretched taut into the endless darkness before them. And although both Violet and Corey still had their cell phones, it remained impossible to know for sure exactly *how many* hours it had been. Corey had told them that time was inconsistent when it came to crossing world borders, and sure enough, their phones were showing two entirely different times, nearly six hours apart, even though they'd barely left each other's side for the past week.

Albert took another bite of his bagel and chewed pensively. It was strange to think that these people actually did this sort of thing for *fun*. It was almost too bizarre for him to grasp. That was an actual *option*? You could just…*do that*?

Brandy reached out and plucked another muffin from the box. "You weren't worried about her getting mad?"

"Can't really imagine Gina mad," said Corey.

"Yeah, she's not really the type to lose her temper," agreed Violet.

"Still…" said Brandy.

"Honestly," she went on, "we just wanted to check in on her. Make sure she was safe." She was stretched out behind Corey, facing them. At some point while they were resting, she'd changed her clothes and was wearing a plain black, sleeveless tee shirt and a pair of denim shorts that were considerably shorter than the ones she was wearing when they first met her. Corey was wearing a different tee shirt, this one gray and yellow, but was either still wearing the same faded jeans or had changed into a pair that looked exactly the same as what he had on before they went to lie down. "We kind of figured she'd change her mind and let us tag along if we were persistent, you know? It's a weird, scary world out there, once you scratch just a little below the surface. We were worried about her all on her own. But it turns out she *wasn't* traveling alone. There were these two other women with her. They seemed pretty capable. We could tell they were looking out for her."

Two other women? Albert recalled what the crazy cat lady said about there being twelve of them in total. Were those three women the same as them? Together, were they the first seven?

"We tried to go anyway," she went on, "but Gina was super-insistent that we stay out of it. She said it wasn't safe. And besides that, we had another kind of pressing issue to deal with."

"What was that?" inquired Brandy around a bite of muffin.

"Mystery Texter," said Corey.

"Mystery Texter," Violet agreed. "See, we arrived at All Trails Crossing ahead of her, like we wanted, and we just sort of camped out and waited. But Gina never showed up that first day. Or the next. We were worried sick that something happened to her. Then, out of the blue, we get a text from her, saying she wanted us to meet her there after all. No explanation for where she'd been all that time. We tried asking her what was going on, but she didn't answer any of our questions."

"Weird," said Corey.

"Kind of," she agreed. "And it was almost like she knew we were already there, because she didn't give us enough time to drive there if we'd still been home."

"Prob'ly knows us too well," reasoned Corey.

"Probably. So we were ready for her when she got there. I mean, mostly. We weren't ready when they just sort of dropped out of the sky."

Albert scrunched up his eyebrows, confused. "They what?"

"I know, right?" laughed Violet. "They'd fallen into some kind of pocket dimension. A kind we've never seen before. A trap of sorts, I guess?" She shook her head. "I'm not even going to try to get into all the weird shit they told us. But the weirdest part was finding out that Gina never sent those texts. She didn't even have her phone. She'd lost it somewhere. It was someone else entirely."

"Who?" wondered Brandy.

"We still don't really know. But as we were watching them leave for Cedric's Cove, we received *another* text from her phone."

Corey twisted his bulk around in the seat and thrust his phone at them so they could see the screen, but it was too far away for them to read it.

"Directions," explained Violet.

"Which you followed," deduced Albert.

"'Course we did," chuckled Corey.

Violet nodded. "We did. And that's when things started getting *really* weird."

Chapter 7

Erin didn't have to worry about leaving anyone behind, at least. She didn't have a family. She never knew her parents. She didn't even know what happened to them. She grew up in a series of foster homes stretching back as far as she could remember. Always moving around. Never having the chance to grow close to anyone.

That wasn't to say she was miserable, of course. She didn't have any *bad* experiences. No one ever abused her. She was always safe and well cared for. But she never felt like she belonged anywhere. She never felt like she was her own person. In fact, she never felt like she was *anybody at all*. She was always just another kid passing through. So as soon as she was old enough, she set off on her own, determined to find out once and for all who she really was.

When she was ten years old, she spent some time with an older girl named Paxton who taught her, among other things, how to play a guitar. Now she traveled around the country, singing in bars and clubs, scraping out a modest but meaningful life, if she did say so herself.

She came across the job in Ohio a little more than three years ago. A simple gig she found on a flyer tacked to a bulletin board in the back of a bar just outside Columbus. She was already planning on heading south, so it was practically on the way.

But there was something a little off about the town of Crump, Ohio. She felt it as soon as she passed the city limit sign. She'd been to a lot of places. She was plenty familiar with the bad vibes some areas exuded. Places that just didn't feel very friendly. Places that felt strangely tense and unwelcoming. Often it was just a matter of small-town mentality, where everybody knew everybody else and so strangers were always outsiders and outsiders brought trouble. But Crump was an entirely different kind of odd. Somehow, it wasn't the people she found unwelcoming. It was something about the city, itself. Something about the looming brick buildings. Something about the quiet streets. Something about the empty and overgrown parking lots. Something about the *cemeteries* she passed. Those, in particular, kept drawing her gaze.

Why were there so many? There were three of them on Main Street alone.

And then there were the crows. She'd never seen so many of them in one place. They were perched in every tree, on every power line and streetlamp. It looked like a scene from a horror movie. Bad omens everywhere she looked, if she were superstitious. But she wasn't. Not then. Not *yet*. She was still several days shy of her twenty-sixth birthday that day, young enough to still be bold, old enough to have learned that she couldn't afford to run away every time she let herself get a little spooked. It was only *birds*, after all.

So she pushed on.

The club was called the Elysium Fog. She didn't think she would've found it without the directions on the flyer. It didn't turn up when she searched for it on her phone for some reason. And there weren't any signs pointing the way. She turned off Main Street, then down a side-road, past *another* cemetery, then turned again, this time onto a narrow, one-way street that was little more than an alleyway. Wedged between the back of a squat, four-story apartment complex and a nameless off-site warehouse was a small parking lot and some neon signs arranged around a heavy steel door in an unassuming brick wall.

This was either one of those rare hidden gems the locals all talked about or the start of a horror movie. But she was nothing if not tenacious back then. She parked her aging Corolla, collected her guitar from the trunk and tried not to look intimidated as she walked through the door.

Sometimes she wondered how different her life might have turned out if she *had* run away that night. But every time she thought about it, she felt somehow that she was *always* meant to walk through the door of the Elysium Fog. One way or another.

It was dark and gloomy inside, strong with the smell of stale cigarette smoke and spilled beer. There was what appeared to be a ticket window facing the entrance, but the lights were out and the room beyond was dark. There was a closed, unmarked door on the left and a set of dimly lit stairs on the right leading down to a landing, then farther down to the left so that she couldn't see what waited at the bottom.

She could hear music playing somewhere down there but didn't recognize the tune. And she could hear no voices at all.

Had she arrived too early? Was the Elysium Fog not open yet? But then why were the lights on outside? Why would the door be unlocked?

Then a deep, growly sort of voice from the shadows behind the window startled her: "You're good."

She turned and stared at the old man sitting in the gloom behind the window. It was no wonder she didn't see him at first. He wasn't right behind the window, as she would've expected, but rather slumped in an old chair against the back wall, mostly hidden in the gloom, smoking a cigarette. His face was deeply lined and drawn downward with a profound sort of sadness about it, as if he'd spent his entire life carrying the weight of the world and had grown weary beyond words. His hair was long and thin and limp and he had dark bags under his eyes.

Why was he just sitting there in the dark like that? It was a little late in the day to be nursing a hangover, wasn't it? And that was the only reason she could think of.

"I'm…um…here for—"

"The job," the old man finished for her in a shadowy breath of smoke.

It wasn't a question. He seemed to know exactly who she was and why she was here. She felt the hair on the back of her neck stand up. Then, embarrassingly, she realized she was carrying a guitar on her shoulder and clutching the flyer she took from the bulletin board at her last gig. "Right…" she said, feeling stupid. Then, with a bit more confidence, she straightened up and said, "Yes."

"Go on," sighed the old man.

She looked down the dreary staircase again, uncertain.

"Horatio'll call when he's ready."

Horatio? "Is he the manager?"

"He's the Gatherer in the Haze."

She stared at the old man for a moment, bewildered. "Okay…" That seemed like an odd way to describe someone. Gatherer? So…the guy in charge of the talent? The place was called the Elysium Fog, so was "the haze" some kind of nickname the employees here had for it?

She looked down at the lower landing again. Then she looked back at the door she entered through. This place was weird. But she'd been doing this for a while. *Lots* of places out there were weird. She probably would've starved to death a long time ago if she'd run away from every creepy venue she found herself in.

Besides, at the end of the day these places were all *businesses*. They were about money. And getting an attractive woman like her on stage was always good for business. That was one advantage she had. It might not keep the creeps from hitting on her, but it didn't pay to scare away the talent.

This Horatio guy was probably going to want to hear her sing. Make sure she was good enough. That was all.

She descended the stairs, following that strange music, and stepped onto the shiny, black marble floor of what looked like a great, sparkling *cavern*. The walls looked like rough, carved stone, curving outward from the foot of the stairs and opening onto a large space illuminated in a gloomy sort of red and purple glow. There were convincingly realistic stalactites hanging from the ceiling, some of them dripping water into rocky fountains positioned beneath them. Little tables were arranged sparingly around columns of the same rough stone as the walls. Larger booths were set back into shadowy recesses along the walls.

It didn't smell like a cave. There was a dank sort of scent of water from the fountains, but no earthy, underground sort of odor about it. Nor had that cigarettes-and-beer smell from upstairs followed her down here. In fact, it didn't smell quite like most of the bars she'd been in. There was a strange sweetness in the air. A subtle something that made her think of flowers, even though there weren't any flowers to be seen.

The room was roughly T-shaped. To the right, a small stage stood tucked away in the corner, surrounded by more of those little tables. There was a woman sitting on the stage, playing the music she'd heard from all the way up the stairs. To the left, a larger space was occupied by a sizeable bar, tended by a bearded, heavyset man with a great, sagging belly and an uninviting sort of scowl on his bushy face.

There was hardly anyone here. A disheveled man in a wrinkled work shirt was perched on a stool at the bar, looking lost and dejected. A thin and weary looking old man in dirty coveralls was slumped over one of the tables by the stage, staring blankly down at his drink. A man in an expensive suit and pointless sunglasses was sitting in one of the booths, drumming his fingers on his cocktail glass as if bored or irritated. And at a table off to one side, half hidden behind one of the stone columns, a woman was sitting by herself, her eyes red and swollen and mascara streaks painted down her cheeks from crying.

Not the liveliest of crowds, certainly. But it was still early. And if there was one thing she'd learned about people it was that the happy ones didn't often visit bars this early in the afternoon.

Erin placed her guitar next to one of the little tables near the stage and took a seat.

This place felt strange. And not in the same way that all these kinds of businesses felt strange in those early hours of the day before the crowds gathered and woke the place up. She couldn't quite think of a way to describe how it felt. It wasn't like anywhere else she'd ever been. There was something heavy about it, something...*haunting*...

She turned her attention to the woman on the stage. She was older, with streaks of silver running through her long, brown hair, but she was surprisingly beautiful. She was sitting on a chair, playing what appeared to be some kind of bow and string instrument. It looked about the size of a violin, but it was oddly shaped, made of a strange, dark wood with shiny and oddly metallic-looking sparks mixed in with the beautiful wood grain. She seemed to be completely lost in her art, her eyes closed, her hands moving elegantly.

Erin watched the woman play. It was soothing, but also just a little unsettling, as if it reminded her of something warm and familiar, but also of things she didn't want to remember. It was an odd sort of feeling, one she couldn't quite identify. But before she knew it, she was lost in the eerie melody. She found herself staring at the woman's fingers as they danced across the strings. What a curious instrument. Was it some kind of custom build? She couldn't remember ever hearing anything quite like it before.

Like a haunting lullaby, it seemed to carry her away. She drifted...almost *floated*...on the sound...her mind drifting off...

For some reason, she pictured a pale train speeding through a vast, black forest...

Chapter 8

"That's so *awesome!*" exclaimed Everett, his eyes shining with childlike wonder, as if someone had just described a magical wonderland to him instead of a literal portal to hell inside an abandoned men's dormitory.

"It was *not* awesome," growled Wayne. "People *died.* Do you seriously not have the mental capacity to understand what we're trying to tell you?"

"Don't get mad," urged Olivia.

"I'm *trying.* But *come on.*"

They were sitting together at the front of the car as the train plowed on through the endless darkness of the Wood. The empty dishes from breakfast were still laid out on the table between them.

Nadia didn't join them. Instead, she said something about checking on her sister and promptly left. That was a while ago now.

In the meantime, Olivia had decided that they should occupy their extra time by filling Everett in on how the two of them ended up here, starting with those letters that lured them both to Gilbert House.

Which meant, of course, that *Wayne* would tell him the story, because she didn't really want to recount those awful hours she spent trapped in that dormitory from hell.

Wayne's point of view was better, she'd decided. And she wasn't wrong. He didn't witness any of the horrors she did. His story didn't involve all those endless hours cowering in a dark restroom stall, desperately suppressing the sound of her sobbing, terrified beyond words, waiting for help that she had no way of knowing would ever come. He didn't see the blood splattered on the wall. He didn't hear the screaming in the dark. By the time he arrived, those people were already dead. There was only Olivia, who quite clearly made it out of the story in one piece. His story began at the best part. Just before he rescued the damsel in distress, who was destined to fall hopelessly in love with him and someday become his bride.

But Everett just kept testing his patience. He only seemed to be listening to half the story. He was fascinated by the idea of a building half in one world and half in another. He wanted to hear all about the monstrous troll-like thing that was stalking them inside. But he didn't seem to even acknowledge the fact that it *brutally murdered three people in that place.* The whole point of telling him about Gilbert House was to let him know how dangerous a game he was playing. But he was missing the point entirely!

"I'm sorry…" said Everett, wilting into his chair.

"You're fine," Olivia assured him. "It's just kind of hard for us. *We* never went looking for this stuff like you did. We didn't *want* to know about these things. It just happened."

Wayne leaned back in his seat and closed his eyes. Olivia always had so much more patience with people than he did. Sometimes he couldn't understand why she put up with him. Anyone else would've tired of his lousy attitude by now.

"No, I get it," replied Everett. "That totally sucks that that happened. I'm not trying to take anything away from that. Really. I just…" He sighed and leaned forward, his hands resting on his knees. For the first time since they'd met him, a shadow of sadness crossed his face. "I spent so much of my life being afraid of everything that I almost *missed* everything worth experiencing. And the reason I was always so afraid was my mom. She was…*sick.*" He sat up, looking uncomfortable. "She was paranoid. Delusional. She sheltered me. Tried to shield me from *everything.* Never let me leave the house. Convinced me that the world outside was a terrible place filled with evil people. That I'd *die* if I ever tried to leave. That only *she* could protect me. But it wasn't me she was protecting. I was just some kind of *symbol.* Some deluded purpose in her unraveling mind."

Wayne glanced at Olivia, surprised. "That's…pretty messed up…"

He nodded. Then he sort of chuckled. "No kidding. You want to know the absolute *worst* of it? She told me there was no such thing as heaven. She said everyone who dies ends up in hell, just to make sure I was too scared to disobey her."

"That's awful!" gasped Olivia.

"Like I said, she was sick. It was just the two of us. I never knew my dad. She said he left when I was born, but I'm not sure she ever told me the truth about anything, so I can't really say for sure what happened to him. But it never really mattered. He wasn't there. And some people can't handle life on their own, much less trying to raise a kid by themselves, I guess."

"I'm sorry," said Wayne.

He gave them another smile, but it wasn't like the goofy ones he'd been showing them up until now. It was a surprisingly sad smile. "I told you guys I nearly died a few years ago. What I didn't tell you is that it happened because she was trying to kill herself. And take me with her."

Olivia pressed her hands to her mouth, shocked.

"So much for *protecting* you!" exclaimed Wayne.

He nodded. "Yeah. She dragged me out of bed in the middle of the night and made me get in the car. Then she took us out to the middle of nowhere and drove into a lake. All I remember was screaming in the back seat while the car filled up with cold water around me. And her just sitting there in the front, telling me I'd better not take off my seatbelt..."

"Jesus..." Wayne couldn't imagine it. What kind of monster was this woman?

But then Everett smiled his real smile again. "It was scary, for sure. But it ended okay. Some fishermen saw us go in the lake and dragged me out. I don't remember it happening. I remember choking on the water and blacking out. I woke up coughing on the shore. Someone gave me CPR. I found out later that I was actually dead for a few minutes there."

Wayne and Olivia exchanged a surprised look at this, but Everett didn't seem to notice. He was staring down at the floor between his feet, distracted.

"That's when I saw the angel. In those few minutes I was gone. I remember feeling like I was being carried off to somewhere far away. It's difficult to explain. But then she was there. I can't remember exactly what she looked like. And I remember that she spoke to me, but I can't remember what she said. But I do remember that she *sparkled*. Then I woke up. I was coughing and gagging and everything hurt and it was loud and..." He shook his head. "Everything was different after that. I wasn't afraid anymore. And I knew my mom was lying to me about everything. The world wasn't full of evil people. It was those very strangers who jumped into that chilly lake and pulled me out and saved my life." He looked up, still smiling. "And how can there not be a heaven if there're angels?"

"That's a good point," agreed Wayne. It seemed pretty hard to argue with.

Olivia nudged him with her elbow. "He's just like you!"

Everett looked back and forth between them, confused. "What?"

Wayne frowned. "That's..." But he wasn't sure where that sentence was even going. That was *what*? That was impossible? Too much of a coincidence? They were riding a train through the Wood that they found inside a fairy circle... Was *anything* impossible anymore?

"Wayne died in a car wreck when he was little," explained Olivia. "And the doctors brought him back. Just like you described."

Everett's eyes lit up again. "Really?"

"And again a few years ago! The night we were just telling you about." She reached over and tugged at Wayne's shirt. "Show him the scar."

"He doesn't need to see the scar," grumbled Wayne.

But she yanked his shirt up, revealing the pale circle where something strange and shadowy pierced his belly that night. "It went all the way through him."

Wayne pulled his shirt back down. "He doesn't even know what you're talking about. We haven't gotten to that part of the story yet."

"Then keep talking," she told him, as if it were that simple, as if he *enjoyed* reliving that awful night...

Everett nodded. "Yeah! What happened next?"

"Nadia said to trust each other," she reminded him.

"I guess so..." relented Wayne. Then he fixed his gaze on Everett again. "By the way... Your mom..." He didn't want to dredge up any more bad memories for the poor kid, but he wanted to know. "Did she...?"

But Everett didn't seem bothered at all. "Oh. Right. She's in a hospital now. She's getting help. Hopefully she'll get better."

"Oh. Well, that's good." He was relieved. He'd thought for a moment that she died in that lake on top of everything else.

"But I don't visit her," he added.

"Oh..."

He smiled that goofy smile again. "Maybe someday. When she's had time to get better. But for now, I just don't think we were ever good for each other."

"That's probably good," agreed Olivia.

Wayne nodded. Good for him. He was smart enough to stay removed from that toxic relationship, but not so bitter that he'd written her out of his life permanently. It was a very mature course of action, in his opinion. Now it sort of made sense why he was out here on his own at his age.

"So what happened next?" pressed Everett.

Wayne sighed and tried to recall where he left off, but then Nadia appeared in the doorway and announced, "We're approaching a station."

"Already?" gasped Olivia. Wayne felt her nails dig nervously into his arm.

He didn't blame her. His own heart leapt at the idea of whatever came next.

"Don't worry," she laughed. "We're not getting off at this station. There's just something we want to show you."

"What kind of something?" asked Wayne.

"You'll see," giggled Nadia.

Olivia glanced over at him, uncertain.

"I can't wait!" exclaimed Everett.

Chapter 9

Nicole stepped out onto the walkway and looked out over the railing at the endless darkness. The boat's lights only reached so far. All she could see—all she'd been able to see since they pulled away from Cedric's Cove, in fact—was water. It was rather unnerving, if she were being honest. She didn't care for it.

The air here wasn't precisely cold. In fact, it was a nice change of pace from the sweltering heat and humidity they'd left behind. But there was a constant breeze blowing past that was cool enough to send gooseflesh prickling up and down her bare arms.

She rubbed at her shoulders and then made her way to the steps leading up to the bridge.

Keith was sitting at the helm, staring straight ahead into the immense blackness that had been looming before them for so many hours.

"Thought you'd sleep longer than that," he said without looking back at her.

"Nightmare," she replied. She turned away and looked out at the churning water in the boat's wake.

He grunted. "Dreams... Don't get me started..."

When they first met back at the dock, he said something about seeing her in his dreams, but she wasn't interested in the story of how he ended up in Cedric's Cove. She'd just been through several kinds of hell, after all. She was tired and grumpy and she wasn't in a mood for conversation. Especially with her ex, of all people.

Seriously, why'd it have to be *him*?

It wasn't really that she hated him. He was nothing at all like those other jerks she'd dated back when she was going through that nasty, self-destructive phase of her life. In fact, he was probably the nicest guy she'd ever been with. She wasn't sure *anyone* could hate Keith.

When they broke up, everyone she told said the same thing to her. They were all *surprised*. They really thought he was the one. No one came out and said it, but she was fairly sure everyone was disappointed in her, that they all thought she'd screwed up the one decent relationship she'd found. And maybe they were right… But seriously, he drove her crazy babying her all the time!

She stared out over the water. It was eerie how silent it was out here. Except for the soft hum of the boat engine and the occasional sloshing of the churning water behind them, there was *nothing*. Not a bug. Not a frog. Not a bird.

She looked up into the empty black sky looming over them. There didn't appear to be any clouds up there to block out the starlight. There simply *weren't any stars*. There was no moon. No sun. There was nothing at all in the heavens out here.

They really were back in the Wood…

The very thought made her shudder.

And this was going to be an awfully long trip if she couldn't figure out a way to be civil with her ex-boyfriend. Especially for Andrea and Gina. This frigid awkwardness between her and him couldn't be very pleasant for those two to have to endure. She needed to relax. Put the past behind her. Make some small talk.

"How's your mom, by the way?" she tried.

He didn't seem particularly eager to have a conversation with her, either, because he didn't answer for a moment. She thought perhaps he was formulating some snarky way of telling her to stop talking to him. But then he surprised her by replying, "She passed."

"What?" She turned to face him, surprised. "No! That's… Oh shit, I didn't…" She struggled to find the right words, but there didn't seem to be any, so she simply wilted and settled for, "I'm so sorry."

"Cancer came back," he explained. "About four months ago. She went fast after that."

Nicole stood there, unsure what to say. What *was* there to say? What wouldn't sound fake or inadequate? Four months ago? That would've been only about three months after they broke up. She never heard anything about it. But then again, why would she? It wasn't as if she'd bothered to ask anyone how they were doing.

She didn't know Ellen Dorray very long. Meeting the family wasn't a relationship step she typically ever arrived at, after all. It was something serious couples did. And had she ever really been serious about a guy in her life? She didn't even know she was serious about *Josh* until after it was too late. She simply never thought her high school sweetheart could really be the one for her. She'd barely seen anything of the world, after all. But the world was full of disappointments. And of course, by the time she figured it out, he belonged to someone else. And so began a series of brief and meaningless relationships that never amounted to much more than shallow company and casual sex. Meeting the parents wasn't even on the distant horizon for her.

But Keith brought her home after just a few months, far before she ever would have dreamed of bringing *anyone* home to meet her own parents. She remembered being *terrified*. But his mother had turned out to be utterly delightful. She was a wonderfully kind and caring woman, although sickly and frail, having already been battling cancer on and off for many years. It was after that first visit that he explained her sad situation to him. His father died in an accident when he was still a boy, so it was only the two of them. No other living relatives. He had to look after her and he didn't want the first time his mother and girlfriend met to be in some cold, sterile hospital somewhere.

She looked out over that black, silent water again, her jaw set. Dammit... Why did he always have to be so annoyingly *perfect?* The responsible, caring son... The attentive, chivalrous boyfriend... No matter what she did, she was always the *bad guy!*

But...wasn't that her fault? *Wasn't* she the bad guy here? She could've stayed in touch. She could've been friendly. She could've *been there* while he was going through all that. She could've done *something.*

What was wrong with her?

This was working out about as well as she'd expected. There was too much bitterness between them. Maybe she should just stop trying and go back below deck. Maybe she could find somewhere to hide until Andrea woke up. *She'd* make everything better. She was always so cheerful and perky. Everyone liked Andrea. Once she was up and about and chatting away, Keith might just forget his bitchy ex-girlfriend was even here.

"Andrea..." she breathed. She remembered waking up last night when Andrea came downstairs and crawled into bed with them. She said that Keith didn't need anyone to stay with him, that he didn't have to worry about the barely-there.

She didn't understand it at the time, but she was so tired. She simply took her word for it and fell back to sleep. But now that she was awake, she realized that it wasn't any clearer. She turned and faced Keith again. "I thought Andrea was supposed to stay with you last night...or..." She frowned. "...whenever that was, I guess?"

She recalled that Andrea was blabbering away, like she always did, talking about all the crap they'd been through. But she didn't want to sit around chatting up her ex. She was exhausted. All she wanted was to go

below deck, take a long-overdue shower and get some rest. Gina insisted that she not go off alone, though. The barely-there had already gotten its nasty claws in her once. It could easily happen again. So they
split into pairs. Andrea stayed up here with Keith, talking his ear off,
and she went below deck with Gina and showered.

But Andrea didn't stay up here the whole time…meaning Keith
was up here all alone? They were lucky he didn't get snatched away,
leaving the three of them drifting alone and lost in this black hell.

"I sent her down to get some rest," said Keith. "Told her I'd be
fine."

"Gina said none of us should be alone. Because that's when the
barely-there targets people."

"Not worried about the whatever-you-call-it," he replied.

"Gina's not just making shit up. That thing was *real*. If you were
just being all macho—"

"I *know* she isn't making things up," he informed her. He still
didn't look back at her. He kept his eyes forward, staring into that endless darkness. "I saw it myself, remember? I was *there*? I had to slap
some sense into you to get you to stop letting it feel you up?"

She had to bite back the urge to tell him off. So he actually remembered what happened? God, how mortifying.

But…at least it seemed like he'd seen it for what it was and not
what *she'd* seen it as. If he knew that she'd been under some sort of
delusion about sleeping with her best friend's groom on her wedding
night… Well, the thought was positively unbearable.

"Sorry about that, by the way," he grumbled. "I've never once
wanted to hit you. I swear. Never crossed my mind until after I did it.
It's just the way dreams are. Sometimes you're you and you're in control. Sometimes…you're not. And you're not. I felt *sick* about that afterward, for the record. Dream or not."

She stared at the back of his head, her teeth grinding together. Seriously? One thing she could hold against the angelic bastard and she
couldn't even have *that*? "Obviously, I needed a shock to jolt me out of
that sick delusion," she relented. "You saved me. I made it back in time
for my friends to get me away from that thing. *Besides*," she added with
a sharp defiance, "I keep telling you, I'm not fragile. I can take a lot
more than a slap in the face."

"The places that thing took you…" he said, mercifully changing
the subject, "…all those dreary apartments…all that weird, creepy
stuff…"

"Tristesse Lane," she murmured, shivering at the unpleasant

memory. "So you really saw all that..."

"I did. But it's all a little muddled. I've been having strange dreams for weeks now. *Really* weird stuff. Naked women in some kind of dark labyrinth. A river flowing through an endless night. A towering, uncrossable wall. People with no faces."

Nicole frowned. People without faces? Was he talking about the sentinels? The Sentinel Queen? Ada did say that this all started with the Temple of the Blind...

"I was starting to think I was losing it," he went on. "It wasn't just at night, either. I started falling asleep in the middle of the day. But the ones with you in them were especially vivid. And I woke up with these weird thoughts in my head."

"Weird how?"

"Weird like driving all the way to some little lakefront town in Michigan where I found this boat waiting for me."

"Oh." She *had* wondered where he obtained the boat. As far as she knew, he didn't own one when she was dating him. She felt like that would've come up. What kind of guy wouldn't try to impress a date by inviting her out on his own private boat?

"I didn't even know I knew how to *drive* a boat. But it's like I've been doing it my whole life."

"Huh."

"I didn't think it was really you. I thought maybe my brain was just inserting your face because it was familiar. Dreams can be like that sometimes. And why in the hell would *you* be getting into situations like that? If it was real, then I just *knew* it had to be someone else I was seeing."

"Sorry to disappoint you," she grumbled.

Keith chose not to respond to that. He stared into the darkness ahead for a moment, silent. Then, finally, he said, "So yeah. I saw those places you girls went. I don't really understand what they were, but they were functionally very similar to my dreams. I think that's what allowed me to travel between the two when you needed my...*particular set of skills.*"

She glared at him. He intentionally avoided saying the word "help." That was the word around which all the fights started. She'd snap at him for being too pushy and he'd reply that he was, "only trying to help!" But she didn't *need* help. Why couldn't he get that through his dense head?

And yet, that was precisely what happened, wasn't it? She needed his help. She needed him to come to her rescue. She needed him to save her poor damsel-in-destress ass from some big scary monster.

"I don't really understand all of it," he plowed on. "Everything I know about any of this *came from* the dreams. But those dreams took me to you, over and over again. And then they brought me to this boat. And then to that creepy, deserted town back there. So it *can't* just be me going crazy. And one of the things the dreams told me was that that place...that *Tristesse Lane* or whatever...can't get ahold of me like it can you three because it's too much like my dreams, where I can move around freely. It can try to take me but I can just walk right back out. So I sent Andrea below deck to get some rest. She wasn't showing it as much as you and Gina, but I could tell she was exhausted, too."

Nicole rolled her eyes. He was such a fucking *gentleman*. Why did that piss her off so much?

"Besides," he added. "Somehow, I feel like both of them are much safer as long as they stay close to *you*. There's something about you. Maybe it's just your natural strength, but every time I saw you in those dreams, it felt like they were much safer as long as they were by your side."

Nicole turned away and stared out over the water again. Safer with *her*? Why would they be safer with her? She wasn't even supposed to be a part of this. She was just the tagalong. Way back when all this nonsense started, Gina all but confirmed that there was literally nothing special about her.

So why was Keith dreaming about *her*? Why not Andrea? Wasn't this about *her*? She was the one the spear was sent to. She was the one Hotdog Creep set his murderous sights on. She was the one Ada sent Gina to protect.

It didn't make sense. Was this just the universe *punishing* her for sticking her nose in where it didn't belong?

But then, didn't Ada tell her that she had a purpose in all this?

(*The Keeper doesn't make mistakes.*)

This was all so confusing.

She was still staring out into that oppressive darkness when something broke the surface of the water, startling her. She gasped and backed away from the railing. "I just saw something out there!"

"I've been seeing that, too," he replied, not sounding the slightest bit alarmed. "Something under the water."

"And you're not *concerned* about that?"

"It hasn't given me any reason to be. Not yet. It's been a few hours and hasn't gotten any closer."

"A few *hours*?" He was aware of it for that long and didn't bother waking them? "Do you have any idea what kinds of things live in this place?"

"I do," he replied calmly. "I've seen *that* in my dreams, too. Dead but not dead things in the forest. Alien creatures flying in the sky. Even monster trees that look an awful lot like that tattoo on your back."

She bit her lip. There was an edge of accusation there. She had that tattoo already when they met. He'd seen it many times. (And from many different angles.) He probably had it memorized. If he'd seen the night trees in his dreams, then he knew she was aware of this place before they dated.

He knew she'd kept secrets from him.

She felt a pang of guilt at this realization, but she forced it right back down. What was she supposed to do? Just blurt out all that stuff about the temple? He'd have thought she was nuts for sure.

"I don't pretend like I understand any of this," he informed her, "but I'm not completely helpless, either."

She glared at him again. That was *her* line. "I'm not completely helpless," was what she shouted at him when they had their first big fight, back when everything started to unravel. The beginning of the end. And now he'd just thrown it right back in her face.

She stood silently for a moment, staring at the back of his head.

He'd changed. He was never this cold before. In fact, he used to be kind of silly. He was always cracking jokes. Making everyone laugh. It was what first attracted her to him.

Was it just her? Was it only that he hated her now? That was probably it. He wasn't rude to Andrea or Gina, she recalled. He was perfectly nice to them both. And she couldn't honestly blame him if he felt that way about her. But also, he'd been through a lot since they last parted company. He'd lost his mother. Pain like that could take its toll on a person.

Pain like that could *change* a person. Forever.

And regardless of her feelings about him, she couldn't help feeling like that would be a terrible tragedy.

"Just go relax for a while," he said. Never once had he looked at her. He kept those familiar blue eyes aimed forward into that endless darkness. "Maybe try to get some more sleep. It'll be a while yet before we get there."

That sounded fine to her. She started to turn away, but hesitated. "Can you at least tell me where it is we're going?"

"Nope. Don't really know where. Only how to get there."

She lingered a moment, staring at the back of his head, countless conflicting memories circling through her head. Then she turned and walked away.

Chapter 10

Keith sat staring through the trawler's windshield, watching the endless lake unravel itself from the eerie darkness of this bizarre world, his knuckles white from gripping the wheel. He was pissed off. He didn't want to be. He'd never liked being angry. He hated the very feeling, but he couldn't help it. Why did it have to be *her* of all people?

Nicole was just as mean and condescending as she was when they parted ways seven months ago.

"Gina's not just making shit up," she'd snapped at him. "That thing was *real*. If you were just being all macho—" As if that were something he'd do. When had he ever tried to act "macho" around her? Did she bother spending one minute of the time they spent together getting to know him in the least?

She was such an infuriating woman! Seriously, of all the people in the world... Like he hadn't been through enough these past months with all those crazy dreams.

Not that the dreams were exactly anything new. He'd *always* had unusual dreams, as far back as he could remember, full of overwhelming emotions, incomprehensible imagery and strange meaning. He used to wake up crying over haunting visions he couldn't describe to his mother when she came to comfort him. He didn't understand any of it enough to even try to explain it. It was such absurd stuff, after all. An abandoned family station wagon, alone and rotting away in an empty field somewhere. A broken swing, dangling from its one remaining rope. A lost and discarded children's book, its pages fading slowly to white. Silent wind chimes. Empty rocking chairs. Stopped clocks. Dusty toys.

As he grew older, he began to make connections between his dreams and the waking world around him. He once dreamed that all the plants in the yard across the street had died and withered, every tree, every flower, every bush, every blade of grass, as if some deadly poison were oozing from the foundation and creeping through the soil, except that all the death and decay stopped at the fence, leaving the surrounding lawns untouched. A week later, the family there moved away. He remembered sitting on the front steps, watching the moving truck drive away, and realizing that, in a way, life really *had* left that house.

He began to understand that his dreams and his waking life were connected somehow. Through nonsense and metaphors, they were telling him things about the world around him.

When he was in first grade, he had a dream that his grandmother was packing all her things and leaving on a very important trip to the far side of the world. He couldn't remember why she was leaving. Or exactly where she was going. But he remembered her telling him that she wouldn't be back for *twenty years*. It was a few days later that his parents broke the news to him that she was very sick and that she probably wouldn't be getting better. She wasn't going on a trip, exactly…but she really was preparing to go away.

His dreams weren't like other people's dreams. They told him things. He began to think that he might be something special. If he could only learn to decode the baffling riddles they showed him, could he foresee the *future*?

But just a few days after his twelfth birthday, his father died in an automobile accident with no warning whatsoever. It was devastating. It broke his heart. And he was never able to understand why his dreams gave him no warning, why he wasn't allowed a chance to try to save him. Or even to say goodbye.

It wasn't fair.

What was the point in having dreams that told him the future if they didn't let him stop bad things from happening?

After that, he tried his best to forget his dreams. He taught himself to redirect his thoughts as soon as he awoke. He'd turn on the television or start playing a video game. To this day, he still reached for his phone even before his eyes were open, checking the weather, skimming through his emails. His favorite was the various social media apps. Funny stuff worked the best, he'd found. Silly memes. Goofy pet videos. People doing stupid things and hurting themselves just enough to be humorous. Anything to start his day with a chuckle or two and push those unconscious visions far into the very back of his waking mind.

Laughter was the best remedy. It always had been. And not just for himself. It was how he kept his mother's spirits up when she was sick.

But laughter had been hard to find these past few months…

He'd thought that was why the dreams were getting worse. Because humor just wasn't strong enough to push back the gloom anymore. Hard and trying times. A promising relationship turning bitter. His beloved mother leaving him alone in the world. He didn't even know if he had a job anymore. He took a leave of absence to take care of her and then bury her and grieve for her and he'd simply never gone back. Was it any wonder that he couldn't find the humor in anything. He thought it was all just a mopey state of mind, but this vast, black world full of black water, black trees and black sky was proof that there was much more to it all than he'd ever imagined. And maybe, then, the dreams were more than he'd imagined as well…

But the new dreams were so weird. *Much* weirder than any of the dreams he'd ever had before. He'd seen so many strange things these past few months, and like now, it all began with a boat.

It wasn't a boat like this one, though. It was long and narrow, low in the water, wooden. Sort of like the way Viking ships were depicted, he supposed, but not ornate in the least. It was very simple. Very dull, with no motor or sails.

He saw this boat so many times in his dreams during those lonesome weeks following his mother's passing that he could see every detail of it when he closed his eyes. It was tattooed onto his memory. Every time he fell asleep, it seemed, he found himself dreaming of the boat and of the women it carried.

There were fourteen of them in all, each of them stark naked and pregnant. He remembered that not all of them *appeared* pregnant. Some of them weren't very far along. And he couldn't see all of them very clearly, anyway. The only light was a single, burning lamp mounted to the front of the boat. But he simply knew somehow that they were *all* with child. It was the same way he knew that these women were particularly significant in some way.

It was a recurring dream…but not the *same* recurring dream. Sometimes they were guiding the boat up the river, traveling upstream, pushing it along against the current with long poles. Sometimes they were cruising through an immense darkness, as if they were adrift on a vast ocean. Sometimes they were crowded by great, towering walls of stone. And sometimes they were approaching a great, gray mountain at the end of their long journey.

As time went on, he began to see things that came after. Sometimes they were on foot, making their way through a seemingly endless labyrinth of stone, their path illuminated by nothing more than the one lamp that they brought with them from the boat. Sometimes they were walking through a vast, empty city full of towering, cylindrical structures. And sometimes they were emerging from a strange, stone doorway into a blindingly sunny, pristine wilderness. It was always the same group of women. It was always the same dark path. It was always the same *story*, but broken up and out of order, like some kind of enormous word scramble.

One night they'd be disembarking from the boat, onto a stone pathway at the base of the remote mountain. The next night, they'd be getting their first glimpse of sunlight waiting at the end of their journey. The next they'd be back at the beginning of it all, just setting out. But wherever they appeared in his dreams, one thing remained constant. A strange and almost inconceivable sadness hung over them, weighing them down.

In some of the dreams, there was a man accompanying the women. He was much older than they were and sat at the back of the boat, steering the rudder with a simple handle. Like them, he was naked. And he had only one arm.

He wasn't the father of any of the unborn children. Those men were all gone. His job was only to escort the women to their destination. And once they arrived there, they'd part company forever. But he wouldn't return home, either. He *couldn't* return home. Home wasn't there anymore, after all. It was gone. *Everything* was gone.

He didn't understand what that meant. How *everything* could be gone. But that was the thought that filled his head each morning when he awoke. That was the source of that intense sadness that followed those people.

Everything was gone and there was no way back.

Even the man was soon gone. He stayed behind, on the other side of a door that would never open again, a strange, golden object hanging by a chain around his thin neck. He sometimes saw him all alone, climbing in the pitch-black darkness, up a stone ladder of sorts and into a small, dark space, like a boy climbing up into a treehouse. And there he stayed for an impossible amount of time, it seemed, his spirit lingering, waiting, watching, as unfathomable ages passed in a world he never lived to see.

Until someone one day finally came to claim the treasure around his skeletal neck.

He thought for a while that these bizarre dreams were going to go on forever, until they drove him mad. But about a week ago, those dreams finally stopped.

Instead, he began having even more vivid dreams. He began seeing things he didn't understand. Like a forest full of twisting, coiling black trees with bark like glistening flesh. An old building bathed in darkness, surrounded by creepy, shuffling things he couldn't see. Corridors of gray stone stretching forever through black depths. And things he couldn't see that made terrible, machine-like noises he couldn't explain.

And then there were the dreams about *Nicole*, of all people.

Nicole caught in the arms of some strange and monstrous thing with a wormlike snout and teeth like a giant leech. Nicole lost and wandering in some foul, oozing labyrinth that vaguely resembled some kind of apartment building but was clearly something alive and horrible. Nicole alone and in terrible danger in some kind of endless, abandoned hospital corridor.

But the worst part was that the dreams no longer tormented him only at night. At all times of the day, he felt himself suddenly overcome by a feeling of intense weariness, like he could barely keep his eyes open. And the moment he sat down somewhere, he was out again, and back in another of those weird Nicole dreams.

Of course, he now knew that those weren't just dreams. Those things really happened. And Nicole actually saw him in those places where he dreamed he approached her, though he couldn't possibly understand how that was possible.

And if those dreams were real...were the fourteen women and the one-armed man real, too?

Just what *was* reality anymore? Was *everything* real? Was *anything*?

He stared through the windshield for a moment, his thoughts churning.

"Just being macho..." he muttered to himself, gripping the wheel again.

He was still pissed off.

Chapter 11

The directions sent from Gina's missing phone had instructed Violet to drive to the nearest town and find Washington Street. That was easy enough. It was one of the main downtown roads. But from Washington street, they were supposed to turn onto January Street. And that's where things stopped making sense.

"Should be here," insisted Corey. He squinted out at the passing buildings, as if perhaps they were only overlooking it. "Somewhere."

"We've been this way at least a dozen times now," Violet reminded him. Once again, she stopped at the light and turned right, circling back once more. "Obviously we're in the wrong place."

There was no January Street. There wasn't even anywhere a January Street would fit. All the signs they passed had tree names. Maple... Pine... Oak... Why would there just randomly be a January between Walnut and Spruce?

She'd attempted to look it up on her phone but could find no evidence of a January Street existing anywhere in this city.

"We followed the directions."

"I'm starting to think Mystery Texter is full of shit."

He shrugged his broad shoulders. "Maybe. Don't know." He never looked up at her. He was staring down at his phone, scanning the internet for clues.

She circled the block and headed back again. Washington Street wasn't terribly long. Eight city blocks of squat little brick buildings crowded close together. They'd triple-checked to see if they were in the wrong town, but this was where the text told them to go. And no other nearby towns had a January Street, either.

She'd even tried using her looking glass shard, but her mysterious magic trinket revealed nothing that wasn't there without it.

Had they misunderstood the message? Were they in the wrong *state* or something?

"What if it's all bullshit?" she wondered aloud as she drove past the same shuttered hardware store that wasn't getting any less depressing the more she saw of it. "I mean, what if it's just Gina sending us on a wild goose chase because she doesn't want us following her?"

"She wouldn't do that," said Corey. He didn't waste a second thinking about it.

"I guess not..." But maybe the mystery texter was someone who *would* do something like that. Maybe this was just a way to keep them from trying to follow Gina and her friends into those woods.

That would seriously piss her off.

A black and white cat darted across the street in front of them. "Oh no, kitty!" gasped Violet, her foot pressing down on the brake even though she wasn't remotely close to hitting it. She'd always had a soft spot for cats and dogs. She hated the thought of seeing one get hurt. "Go home! That's not safe!"

But as she watched the cat, making sure it didn't try to dart back in front of her again at the last second, it disappeared down a narrow alley between two buildings. There was a wooden sign on one of the walls, jutting out from the brick. In what looked like bright red spray paint, someone had scrawled JANUARY STREET.

"Wait... *That's* January Street?"

Corey looked up from his phone, surprised. "Didn't see that before."

She hadn't noticed it, either. And she'd had her eyes open the whole time, searching for it. Had she always just looked past it because it was a narrow alley instead of a proper street? It wasn't hidden in a way that she needed her looking glass to see it. It was simply as if it had appeared out of thin air.

She turned slowly into the narrow space. The cat had already vanished from sight, which was good because there wasn't a lot of room to navigate. There appeared to be a small lot at the end, though, behind the buildings she was driving between.

There were three little shops crammed together back here in what she thought was the lousiest business location she'd ever seen. Two of them didn't even have proper signs. The third only had a broken neon light identifying it as what she was quite sure was the *sketchiest* tattoo parlor she'd ever seen. One had only a single piece of paper taped to the door with a phone number and hours scribbled out in sloppy handwriting with what appeared to be Sharpie marker. And the third business had only an OPEN sign and looked like some kind of pawn shop, with a random assortment of dingy looking junk sitting in the dust-covered windows. There were no other cars in the little lot. It looked deserted.

"Is this right?" she wondered, uncertain. Even in broad daylight, this place was nothing short of creepy. It had an odd feeling to it.

"Weird," agreed Corey. "Don't match the surroundings. Completely different style from the rest of the neighborhood."

She glanced around and realized he was right. The rest of Washington Street was comprised of buildings made up of attractive cream-colored bricks. *These* buildings, however, were constructed from larger, dark-colored blocks and aging gray wood flecked with remnants of long-peeled paint.

"Like it don't belong here," he observed.

"You think it's another pocket dimension?"

"Possible." He looked down at his phone. "Says it's on the right."

They both eyed the pawn shop. Or perhaps it was supposed to pass as an antique store? It was difficult to tell.

It reminded Violet of the junk dealer they encountered in St. Louis years ago, the one who sold her the looking glass shard. He didn't have a store. Instead, he had a run-down old truck with a bed full of old luggage. Most of his wares had looked like the stuff in this window. Nothing but garbage. She remembered taking one look at the guy and then pretending she never saw him. He looked sort of scuzzy, after all.

She remembered feeling relieved to be past him, only for him to say something they couldn't ignore: "There's a reason no one can find Obadiah Hinx's grave."

Obadiah Hinx was the reason they were in St. Louis that week. In his research, Corey had dug up letters from a man by that name. In these letters, he claimed to have found a gateway to another world. It was considered to be the insane rantings of a lunatic, describing a world of strange beauty filled with a mysterious race of almost-but-not-quite-human people. But there were compelling details hidden in those same letters that perfectly described the portals they'd theorized. The problem was that Hinx refused to tell anyone where the doorway to this wonderful world was hidden while he still lived and boasted that he'd leave the secret to finding it encoded on his headstone.

Except, there was no record of where he was buried.

Only the mysterious merchant's looking glass shard revealed the answer. But that was another story. One for another day.

This place had the same feeling as that mysterious merchant's collection of garbage trunks, though. It wasn't the sort of place she'd look twice at, and yet the strange, otherworldly side of the universe called out to them from somewhere inside, beckoning them.

"So we just sort of steeled ourselves and walked inside," said Violet.

"So what was inside?" wondered Brandy. She was listening raptly, squeezing Albert's hand.

"Lotsa junk," replied Corey.

Violet nodded. "It looked less like a store than someone's basement. There was all sorts of stuff, none of it matching in any way. There were, like, rusty tools and broken bikes and lawn ornaments all mixed in with old dishes and kitchen utensils. Random light bulbs and plumbing fittings. Just...*junk*, you know?"

"Old toys," recalled Corey. "Real creepy."

"No shelves. No organization. Just a bunch of folding tables arranged in rows. Like a flea market stall or something. And lots of old cardboard boxes full of random stuff."

"Everything covered in dust."

"Right! Like it'd all been sitting there for *years*. It was *so* creepy."

"Not as creepy as the twins, though," added Corey.

"Twins?" asked Albert.

Violet chuckled. "Yeah. *Them...*"

They were still looking around the strange little shop, trying to understand why they needed to be there, when a man standing behind the counter called out, "Good afternoon."

He was a very thin man, tall, rather sloppy looking in a baggy brown tee shirt with long, greasy blond hair and oversized glasses.

Then, from behind them, a second man who looked exactly like the first said, "Welcome. We've been expecting you."

Corey turned his formidable bulk and looked back and forth, surprised. At the same time he reached out with one big hand, ready to shield Violet if necessary.

It was less a protective gesture than a display of intent. She didn't need him to protect her and he damned well knew it. But if things went sour, he'd do whatever was necessary to protect his best friend. When it came to dealing with strangers, often times his formidable size and that subtle, protective gesture was enough to make any would-be aggressors hesitant. And anyone who still intended them harm would be focused entirely on the big guy and completely unprepared for the smaller but far more dangerous of the two. But they preferred to avoid any actual confrontations, if possible. And in their line of work, it was more often the location than the locals that presented dangers. More than once, he'd been known to simply scoop her up like a doll and haul ass out of whatever mess they'd gotten themselves into. And given the difference in their size, she didn't have much say in the matter when that happened. At that point, she was just along for the ride. But the fact was that she trusted his judgment. If Corey decided he needed to get her out of something fast, he was usually right. In the end, they trusted each other.

"You're the guys texting us?" she asked, looking back and forth. Why were they on opposite sides of the room? Were they trying to keep their attention divided? She didn't know who to look at. "You have Gina's phone?"

"We didn't send any texts," said the twin behind the counter.

"We don't have her phone," said the other one.

They looked *and* sounded identical. They were dressed the same. Their *hair* was even the exact same kind of messy. It was eerie, like they were entirely *too* identical.

"We're just one of many cogs," said the second twin.

"The Keeper's machine has many," added the first.

"Keeper," huffed Corey. They'd heard that name before.

"Who are you?" Violet demanded.

"Friends," replied the first twin.

"Allies of the cycle," added the second.

"The cycle?" she asked, glancing up at Corey. He raised a bushy eyebrow at her in return. That was another familiar word. The cycle was something both Gina and her roommates had talked about. Apparently, the universe existed in an endless loop of decay and rebirth. Periodically, as one died, humankind migrated via some kind of mass exodus to a brand new one crafted by godlike beings called Architects. (Yet *another* long story…)

They hadn't found any proof of the existence of any such cycle in their own research, but they also didn't receive orders directly from a *goddess*, either.

"I'm Cray," said the first twin.

"I'm Cob," said the second.

"You know you guys are kind of creepy, right?" Violet dared.

"Yes," said Cray, not seeming the least bit insulted.

"We get that a lot," agreed Cob.

Neither of them moved. They both stood motionless, only their mouths moving. They looked weirdly unnatural, almost *staged*, as if they were trying too hard to pass for normal shop owners.

Violet for some reason found herself bothered by the fact that she couldn't see their feet. Cray remained behind the counter. Cob stared back at them from behind an old magazine rack. In her spooked state of mind, she found it surprisingly easy to imagine that Cray and Cob weren't people at all, but mere puppets, controlled by something disturbing lurking unseen beneath them.

"Okay…" she said, uncertain. "So, who *did* send us those texts?"

"Someone else," replied Cob.

"Another friend," Cray assured them.

"An ally of the cycle," added Cob.

She supposed that was a better answer than "*not* a friend," but it didn't exactly answer her question, did it? "So then…*why* did this *friend* send us here?"

"We have something you're going to need," replied Cob.

"Very important," said Cray.

"Critical," agreed Cob.

Finally, the creepy twins moved. In unsettlingly perfect unison, they both turned and walked toward the same corner of the room. Violet watched them, noting that they did, in fact, have feet. They were wearing identical worn-out sneakers with no socks and baggy cargo shorts. Their legs were scrawny and hairy. Not the most attractive of sights, but at least there was no unspeakable eldritch horror crawling around down there with its monstrous hands shoved up their asses.

"Three roads converge in the black depths of the Wood," said Cray as they drew closer together in the far corner of the room.

Again, Violet glanced up at Corey. The Wood. Didn't one of Gina's friends use that word? Everything seemed to fit together somehow, if she only understood what any of it meant.

"One by water," said Cob.

"One by land," said Cray.

"And one by shadow," said Cob.

There was a metal pole leaning against the wall in the corner, about six feet long. The twins picked it up together, as if it were too heavy for just one of them to manage. It looked at first like tarnished silver, but as they turned and carried it closer, she saw that it wasn't tarnished. It was a marbled pattern of shiny silver and a much darker metal.

"They are roads, but they are more than roads," said Cob.

"Engineering marvels of a long-lost civilization," explained Cray.

"They are shortcuts carved across impossible distances," added Cob.

"And a safe haven against the countless horrors of the Wood," finished Cray.

"'Kay," replied Corey, nodding.

Violet glanced up at him, her lip curled in a bewildered sort of sneer. After hearing all that weirdness spew from these two creepy mouths, that was what he had to say? Just…'Kay? As if he were following along just fine? Really? She'd known him all her life, but sometimes she seriously couldn't understand how his mind worked.

"But finding the roads is only half the challenge," said Cob.

"To traverse the infinite acres beyond," said Cray, "they'll need a means of travel."

"We've provided almost everything," explained Cob, "to ride the shadows."

"But you'll need this," said Cray.

The twins walked up to Corey and lifted it up for him to take. He looked the curious object over, glanced uncertainly at Violet, and then reached out and took it from them.

It wasn't as heavy as they made it appear.

They took a step backward, their hands dropping to their sides again.

Violet leaned closer and examined it. It was just a metal cylinder, about two inches in diameter. "So…what're we supposed to do with the magic curtain rod?"

The twins both smiled at this. It should have made them look less creepy, but it didn't. There was something weirdly unnatural about those identical smiles.

"You'll know," said Cray.

"It'll be clear," assured Cob.

"If you say so…" She looked up at Corey again, who only shrugged.

Then Corey's cell phone chimed in his pocket. He stood the rod on its end like a staff and pulled it from his pocket.

"That will be your next instructions, I'd wager," said Cob.

Corey stared at the screen for a moment, then turned it and showed it to her.

"The Lucianna Mysteria," she read. "What's that?"

But he didn't know. He'd have to look it up.

"Good luck," said Cray.

"But beware the Ruin," added Cob.

"The what?" she asked.

But the twins had apparently run out of creepy things to say because they merely turned and walked through an open doorway, leaving the two of them alone in the shop.

Brandy frowned. "That was all? Take this *stick* and go? Seems like a lot of extra work for the two of you."

"I know, right?" agreed Violet. "Like, here's this crazy mystery texter with our friend's phone giving us these weird directions, and when we get there it's just like, 'Great, can you deliver this package? Thanks.' I mean what the hell?"

"That stuff about three roads, though…" pondered Albert. *Three roads converge in the black depths of the Wood…*

"That was interesting," said Corey.

It was, indeed. That creepy cat lady said there were twelve of them. Was that where the other eight were? On the other two roads?

And then there was that stuff about the roads being the product of ancient engineering that made them both shortcuts and safe paths through the Wood? How did something like *that* work?

"So you guys took the rod from them and made your way to Wevenwert," guessed Brandy. "Where we first met you."

Violet nodded. "Yeah, I didn't stick around to see if they'd come back. That place was *spooky*."

Corey followed her out of the building. The July heat was sweltering, but it was far better than being inside. Violet climbed into the driver's seat of the Liberty while he slid the mystery rod into the back seat. But he paused in the open passenger door and looked back at the strange little junk shop. "That was weird," he seemed to decide.

"No shit it was weird! Come on, let's get out of here. Those guys seriously gave me the creeps."

But he didn't move. "Not like that," he said, still staring back at the storefront. "Before. When I was on my phone. January Street. January was named for the Roman god, Janus." Now he turned and met her gaze. "Janus was known for having two faces."

Violet stared at him for a moment, letting that little piece of information process. Then her gaze drifted to the door again, thoughtful. Two faces…? And those creepy twins with the *same* face? "I mean…that's probably not—"

"There's more. He was the god of changes. Transitions. Time. Beginnings and Endings." He raised those bushy eyebrows again. "Sort of like a *cycle*."

"Oh…"

"He was also the god of *doors*," he added.

This caught her attention. Doors? As in the doorways to other worlds that they'd spent the past eight years searching for?

"Just saying."

They stared at each other for a moment, letting it all sink in. Then she shook her head and started the engine. "Shut up and get in. You spend *way* too much time on the internet. We've got to get you a girlfriend or something."

Chapter 12

Erin blinked, distracted. Her mind had wandered a bit there, carried away by the woman's beautiful and strangely haunting music.

How long had she been playing? It seemed to go on forever...and yet, hadn't she only been sitting here a moment? Why did it feel like lots of people were coming and going?

When she finally managed to turn her eyes away, the weary looking man was gone and there was a woman in a stained work shirt sitting at another table who wasn't there before, sucking on a bottle of beer. She watched her for a moment, distracted, then became aware of a strangely dark area beyond where the new woman was sitting. The room seemed to extend in that direction, but there were no lights on in that space.

How did she not notice that before?

But as she stared into that darkness, she slowly realized that there was a figure standing there, tall and imposing. It wasn't quite man-shaped...but what else could it be but a man? The sight filled her with a strange sort of dread that she didn't quite understand. Then the figure turned and retreated into the mysterious depths of the shadows, vanishing like a phantom.

That was odd... Did she only imagine it? This was such a strange place. Perhaps it was making her imagination run wild.

She was still trying to figure out just what she saw when a strangely pale woman in a long, gray dress appeared next to her. "Horatio is ready for you," she said in an odd, hoarse whisper.

Erin blinked up at her, confused. "What?"

The woman pointed a bony finger at the dark part of the room where she imagined the creepy figure standing. "His office," she informed her. "Through there." Then she turned and drifted off toward the bar.

She watched the woman. She didn't walk so much as *glide* away. She practically *floated* across the floor.

Maybe it was some kind of gimmick?

She stood up, collected her guitar and set off toward that creepy dark section.

When she first started doing this work, she was frightened of a lot of the places it took her. She had to learn quickly to convince herself not to run away. Her years in foster care helped. She was already used to being in new and unfamiliar places, standing in front of strangers, looking out of unfamiliar windows. She never had a choice back then. She couldn't have run away if she wanted to. She learned to stand her ground. This wasn't so unlike that, really.

If she'd believed in the sorts of things they showed in horror movies, maybe she would have left while there was still time. But strange and unsettling were just words for an unfamiliar atmosphere. And weird and creepy people—to put it simply—almost always turned out to be strung out on some drug or another.

But there was something more to *this* strangeness. Deep down, she could feel it. Something about that haunting music… Something about that unfamiliar smell… Something about the people here…

She walked into that intimidating darkness, determined not to be afraid of a little gloom. The spooky pale lady said his office was right through here. There should be a door, one she'd see as soon as her eyes properly adjusted. But as the darkness closed around her, she quickly became lost.

The space was far bigger than it appeared. In fact, it was a lot bigger than it had any business being. *Impossibly* big. She turned around, scanning her shadowy surroundings, but somehow she couldn't even see her way back to the illuminated part of the club. She could still hear that strange, haunting music, but she could no longer tell which direction it was coming from. It seemed to be everywhere at once, all around her. Or maybe…inside her head?

That was an odd thought… Why would she think something like that?

And when did it get so smoky? That strange, sweet smell she noticed when she first descended into the club was stronger here, and she still couldn't identify it.

Then she turned around and found herself standing before a dark, towering figure. Eyes like golden flames burned down onto her through the haze, flickering like faraway lanterns in the depths of a strange darkness where a face should have been. And above those eyes loomed a great tangle of monstrous antlers.

She remembered being afraid. *Terrified*, even. But not by the figure, itself. It was the words Horatio spoke to her in that strange, vast darkness that chilled her to her very bones.

And yet…she couldn't remember what those words were…

The next thing she knew, she was sitting behind the wheel of her Corolla again, staring through the windshield at a sprawling cemetery she had no recollection of driving to.

Something strange had happened to her. Something about her had *changed*. There were three thoughts in her head that she didn't understand but knew to be absolute truths.

First, she understood that she had a very important job to do. Second, she knew exactly where to find the thorn and what she must do with it once she possessed it. And third, she was not going to live through this.

In the months that followed, she learned a great many things about the world lurking just beneath the surface. She learned that monsters were real. As were spirits. And gods. And *other* things. Horrible, *unspeakable* things. Things there were no words for. Not in this language. Not in any language spoken since days long, long forgotten.

She ventured into places that appeared on no maps. She glimpsed hidden worlds that no one had ever written about in any book. She witnessed miraculous events that she couldn't begin to explain. And she discovered the existence of ancient evils that schemed to end mankind forever.

Most of all, she learned to see the things that lurked in the shadows. Things unseen by the vast majority of blissfully ignorant human beings. Things like the ones swarming that beautiful wedding reception.

Now, three years and some weeks after that bizarre and fateful visit to the strange and eerie city of Crump, a few frightful hours after passing the thorn to its rightful owner, the lovely bridesmaid, deep in the witching hour of her final and briefest day, she stood alone beneath the starry sky, her back to the lake that would become her grave, facing the monster that she always knew was going to come for her.

"Where is it?" snarled one of the thing's mouths, though she wasn't sure which one.

The crows were gathering again, as they had so many times since that day she ventured into the city limits of Crump. They were everywhere. In every tree and bush. Watching. Waiting. But they weren't really crows. She was finally starting to understand that they were never crows. They'd always been something else entirely.

"Gone," she replied, managing to sound as if she weren't terrified out of her own mind, as if she hadn't, in fact, just wet herself a little.

She managed to look positively defiant, standing there in her ripped and mud-caked dress, her black hair plastered to her dirty face. "Somewhere you'll never reach it."

The ancient and horrid thing standing before her shifted itself, changing shape again. It was gooey and oozing, almost gelatinous, but at the same time it was stubbornly solid. Somewhere inside, she could hear what sounded like bones cracking and popping as it rearranged itself.

She took a step backward and felt her foot sink into the warm lake water. It was oddly familiar, as if she'd felt that wet, squelching sensation countless times in her nightmares since the fateful day she stepped through the doors of the Elysium Fog.

This was the end Horatio warned her about. This was as far as she was going.

She took one last breath of humid night air. Then something cold and wet and reeking of decay closed around her throat and dragged her beneath the surface.

It was every bit as painful as she knew it would be. And it seemed to take forever. She remained conscious long enough to feel several of her bones break, her flesh rend and something vile and torturous wriggle deep inside her guts.

But then, at long last, it was over.

Chapter 13

A shudder passed through the car and the train began to slow.

Nadia opened the door to the platform, letting in the full roar of the previously muffled engine. "We're here," she announced. "Come check it out."

Wayne and Olivia exchanged an uncertain glance, but Everett was on his feet and out the door in an instant. He, for one, couldn't wait to see what was out there!

"Come on," Nadia urged, waving them over.

They gathered onto the platform. On either side of them was an endless sea of silent night trees with their gnarled and coiling branches and their shiny black bark that gleamed like slick, naked flesh in the train's lights.

Everett leaned over the railing, trying to get as close as possible. There was so *much* of it! Had anyone ever set foot in those black acres before? Would they be the very first?

This was exactly what he'd been looking for all this time. A whole new world, right in front of his nose. The answer to his ultimate question, the truth of the universe. It was almost more than he could stand!

"It feels *awful* out here," observed Olivia, shouting to be heard over the roar of the engine.

And she wasn't wrong. Everett could feel it, too. The air was strangely thick. His body felt heavy, as if the very atmosphere were sapping away his strength. It was wide-open, and yet he found himself grasped in the oppressive grip of claustrophobia, as if he were locked in a box somewhere.

It was *indescribably cool!*

Nadia pointed forward, her small finger aimed at the darkness into which the train was still slowly chugging.

The night trees parted, revealing a large, stone platform like the one back in Maeve's circle. Except there was one on either side. And beyond these platforms stood several great, square pillars that jutted high up into the sky, their tops lost from view.

Then a giant appeared from the gloom!

Olivia screamed.

Everett didn't blame her in the least. The face appeared so suddenly from the darkness that it startled him, too. It looked to be carved from the same stone as the platform and its accompanying pillars. Its mouth stretched open in a permanent scream as wide as the doors of an airport hangar, dwarfing the train as they drew closer. They were driving right into its yawning maw, as if they were about to be devoured. "*Awesome!*" he exclaimed.

"It's like the statues in the temple..." Olivia realized.

Wayne nodded. He noticed that, too.

Everett glanced over at them, curious. Temple? Statues? They hadn't told him about those things yet. Had they seen something like this before? The train's lights didn't quite reach all the way to the giant's eyes, making it difficult to tell exactly what the expression was, but the details were *incredible*. He could see creases in its lips, gaps in its teeth, even blemishes on its cheeks. It really did look as if it could come alive.

"This isn't the same Wood you guys remember," said Nadia as she stood grinning up at that massive face. "This is the entrance to the Denselands. Everything's going to be a little bit different here."

"Different as in *worse?*" guessed Wayne.

"Just different," she replied.

"So definitely not better," he surmised.

They stood watching as the train carried them deep into the black gullet of the giant's mouth.

Glancing over again, he saw that Olivia was clinging to Wayne's arm. She looked frightened. But what was so scary about a giant statue? He felt like he was missing something.

"I mentioned earlier that the Wood is essentially a graveyard for dead worlds," explained Nadia as the train began picking up speed again. "It's littered with countless remnants of long-lost civilizations."

"So cool!" squealed Everett. He was hanging on her every word.

Nadia giggled. "But these remnants are scattered so far apart that the odds of simply stumbling across them are practically astronomical. It would be like dumping a bucket of sand out the door of an airplane over a vast forest and then trying to find any of the grains." She turned her cheerful smile on Wayne and Olivia. "The vast majority is empty forest, just like what you saw outside Gilbert House five years ago. The Denselands, however, is different. It's a very specific area deep within the Wood where an anomalous number of remnants have accumulated over the eons for unknown reasons. I guess you could say that if the Wood is a graveyard for dead worlds, the Denselands is a *mass grave of horrific proportions.*"

"That sounds so cool…" sighed Everett.

"It sounds like a *nightmare!*" growled Wayne, making him flinch a little.

Olivia didn't bother telling him to be nice this time, he noticed. She was too busy clinging to Wayne's shirt, looking practically sick with worry.

He stared at her, at the way her beautiful eyes shimmered with unshed tears. The sight hurt his heart. Suddenly, he felt guilty. Maybe he *was* taking his enthusiasm a little too far. This wasn't just about him. He knew it wasn't. But he wasn't acting like it. He found himself remembering the pathetic state she was in when he found her wandering that strange, old-growth forest. The gash above her right eye was still bandaged. There was still a faint scratch on her left cheek. No wonder Wayne didn't seem to like him very much…

They passed out of the tunnel again and back under that black sky. Those gnarly trees stretched out on either side of them, as far as the lights would reach.

"The Denselands are filled with mysteries," Nadia went on. "It's littered with the relics of countless histories. No one knows what might still exist out there. Treasures untold, no doubt. But also horrors beyond measure."

Everett actually heard Olivia whimper at this over the roar of the engine. She was *really* afraid of this forest…

"But the path doesn't end where these rails stop," she added. "The road continues on, through the Denselands, all the way to your final destination. It possesses the same curious properties as these rails, creating a shortcut of sorts, allowing you to traverse the immense distance stretched out before you in an amazingly short amount of time."

Everett felt another pressing urge to express just how awesome that sounded, but this time managed to keep it to himself.

"But even more importantly," said Nadia, "it has certain safety features built into it. As long as you stay on the path, you won't draw attention to yourselves."

"Wait…" said Wayne. "So those zombies won't be attracted to our lights and stuff?"

"That's right. And neither will any of the other things out there."

"What other things?" worried Olivia.

"All sorts, really," she replied. "Shadow beings. Scavengers. Feral spirits. Psychic parasites. Fester vermin. Lingering remnants of past worlds that can never die."

"Okay," interrupted Wayne. "I think we get it."

"Nothing ever dies in the Wood," she warned them. "Not really. And in all the worlds that have withered and ended up here, there can always be found things that were never alive *or* dead. Those are the most dangerous of all."

Everett knew these things should frighten him. And perhaps somewhere deep inside, he *was* a little frightened. There was probably at least a small lingering piece of the terrified boy he used to be hiding somewhere inside. But mostly, he was exhilarated. He wanted to know *more*. He wanted to *see* it with his own eyes!

"But the Faceless Ones' stone road will keep you safe from most of that."

"Most?" pressed Wayne.

"Sometimes things wander across the stone road, and there's nothing to protect you once something *does* happen to notice you. You'll have to stay on your toes. Watch each other's backs. Definitely don't get separated." Then she beamed at them again. "But it'll still be a little while before we reach our final station."

She slipped past them and began gathering up the dishes from breakfast.

Wayne and Olivia followed after her, eager to get back inside and out from under the oppressive darkness.

But Everett lingered there on the platform for a moment, looking up into that empty sky, emotions boiling deep in his chest like rolling storm clouds.

He couldn't wait to see what came next!

Chapter 14

Andrea couldn't remember how long she'd been lost in these cold, dark depths. Had it only been hours? Or had entire days passed since she lost her way? It seemed to her that there was something wrong with the passage of time here. Sometimes it sped out of control, on and on, for days and weeks, months, even *years*. But other times it didn't seem to move at all.

Sometimes she wondered where everyone had gone, why they'd left her here all alone to fend for herself in these frightful passageways. Other times, however, she found herself quite sure that there'd never been anyone else in this endless darkness. She'd *always* been alone here.

And sometimes she was overcome with this strange and persistent feeling like none of this should even be here, as if she could almost remember it all falling down around her...

She could see nothing. She walked blind and naked through this unending darkness, alone and vulnerable, cold and frightened. For longer than she could recall, it seemed, she'd been following the same empty tunnel, one hand pressed against the smooth, gray stone of the wall.

But now, suddenly, the wall ended, her fingers plunging into a blind, black void.

Another tunnel intersecting this one?

No... Somehow she sensed that the space around her had grown to enormous proportions. She'd stepped out into an open chamber of some sort, one much bigger than any room she'd seen in what felt like ages. Yet, strangely, she felt a sudden and wild urge to turn and flee back into the familiar confines of the tunnel she'd been walking through for so very long. There was something dreadful about feeling so small in such a vast emptiness.

But backward wouldn't get her out of here. She needed to be brave. She needed to be strong.

Before she could steel her nerves and push deeper into the gloom, however, the endless silence was broken by a strange grinding sound, like something incredibly heavy being pushed across the stone floor somewhere in front of her.

The sound froze her in place. An awful, freezing terror washed over her like an icy tide, chilling her all the way to her bones as she realized that she wasn't alone at all. Something was here with her. Something *big*.

She was staring into the same endless darkness that had loomed before her for as long as she could remember, but now there was something there. A great, towering shape that seemed to stir in that darkness.

"You really think you can do this?" whispered a voice in her ear. It was Stella's voice. She could feel her standing back there, leaning over her shoulder. "*You*?" she pressed.

Andrea wanted to tell her to shut up. The thing might hear her. But of course Stella wasn't really here. She'd never been here. It was only her imagination. It was only the voice of her own fear speaking the words she felt deep inside.

Stella leaned closer. She could almost feel her there. Long, curly hair brushed her bare shoulder. Warm breath tickled her ear. "What do you think will happen to your soul when you die in a place like this?"

Before she could react to such a terrifying question, the thing in the darkness lashed out at her. Huge, gaping jaws with fangs like gleaming swords descended on her with tremendous speed.

She jolted awake, breathless, a scream caught in her tight throat, her heart slamming against her ribs.

"Are you okay?" asked Gina. She was sitting up in the bed, her gentle brown eyes peering down at her.

Andrea blinked up at her for a few seconds, confused. "Yeah. Sorry. Bad dream."

"Those're going around," said Nicole. She was stretched out on the little sofa, frowning at her phone, her bare feet stuck out in front of the door.

Gina nodded and rubbed at her eyes. "This world is significantly different from ours. I'm guessing we can all probably feel that in some capacity or another." She yawned, then added, "Stuff like that has a way of bleeding through when we sleep."

Andrea stared at her for a moment, her thoughts still haunted by the image of that great, toothy maw descending on her in the oppressive darkness. "Did *you* have a bad dream, too?"

"My dreams are always bad," she replied, as if it were the most normal response in the world.

"Oh..." She glanced over at Nicole. Their eyes met, a note of concern passing between them.

Gina sat there a moment, blinking tiredly at the wall. She'd removed the bandages from her face when she showered. Somehow, the scabbed skin underneath didn't look as bad without them. "Felt like we slept a good amount, though," she added. "That's good."

"Yeah," agreed Nicole, looking down at her phone. "No idea *how* long. No reception, of course. It still thinks it's Wednesday..." But according to Keith, it was Thursday night when they met up at the dock, so that couldn't be right...

It felt like a full night's sleep, in spite of the weird dreams, and that was all that really mattered, Andrea supposed.

What do you think will happen to your soul when you die in a place like this? she recalled Stella whispering into her ear. The memory made her shiver. What was it Albert said about the Wood? Something about there being nowhere for souls to go when they died? That was why Wayne was able to come back. Because his soul wasn't dragged off to the afterlife the moment he left. The Keeper was able to repair his body and keep it functioning during those long hours so that he could return to it.

Or that was the way she understood it, anyway. It was all so crazy and confusing...

Of course *Stella* would be the one to show up in her dreams to say stuff like that. She was the only person she knew who'd actually blurt out something so blatantly unhelpful. Everyone else she knew was nice enough to keep their crazy to themselves.

But was it all only a dream? Or was it some kind of message?

Her gaze drifted across the room, to the oppressive darkness on the other side of the window and she wondered, not for the first time, if she should really be here. Ada said she was special, that she had some kind of weird connection to the world of the dead or something, but...was she really the right person for this? Surely there must have been someone else who could do this. Someone stronger. Someone braver. Someone who knew what the heck they were doing, maybe?

She reached over and checked her own phone. The chargers had come with the boat. It was fully stocked with food and drinks and toiletries, everything they needed to freshen up and get comfortable.

"Mine thinks it's Monday," she reported when it came back to life. She frowned. "But it was already Tuesday when we landed in All Trails Crossing. Did it go *backward?*"

"Time distortions and electronics don't really go together very well," explained Gina. "It's almost impossible to know the real time out here. There's no such thing as an accurate clock when you're crossing boundaries."

Andrea dropped her phone into her lap and laid back down. "I don't wanna keep doing this," she yawned. "My legs hurt."

"I hear ya," grumbled Nicole.

"That's not really how the goddess' jobs work," said Gina. "But I agree. I didn't expect to do so much walking…"

"Goddess…" sighed Andrea, sitting up again. "That still sounds so weird. Even *after* I met her." She picked her phone up again and examined herself in the selfie camera, wrinkling her nose at what she saw. There were toothbrushes, toothpaste, hairbrushes, soap and shampoo stocked in the stateroom bathroom for them, and even a fully stocked medicine cabinet and first aid supplies, but no makeup, which was fine. What did it matter? She didn't wear a lot of makeup anyway. But she had some pretty dreadful bedhead.

"Yeah. It takes some getting used to."

"But she said she wasn't a goddess," recalled Nicole. "She was born a normal girl, just like us. Her name was Ada."

"But she didn't *stay* normal," said Andrea. "I mean, *isn't* she basically a goddess?" She hopped up from the bed and walked to the bathroom. "She's been alive a ridiculously long time." She frowned as she took the ties out of her ponytail and began brushing her hair. "I mean what're the qualifications for being a goddess? I feel like *immortality* is probably pretty high on the list. And, like, *omnipotence*."

"She's the Great Beholder," said Gina in that same, sleepy tone. "She knows everything about everybody. She's a goddess to me, anyway."

Andrea glanced out at her. She remembered the goddess saying something about a promise. Something about finally finding what she was searching for.

It's kind of private, she remembered Ada telling her when she asked about it. *She'll talk about it when she's ready.*

She gathered up one side of her hair and tied it into a simple low pigtail as she wondered about her soft-spoken companion. What was her story, anyway? What had the poor girl been through? And what was it she wanted from life badly enough to dedicate herself to a goddess who was willing to put her in this much danger?

The trawler's engines had been humming along at a steady pace throughout the entire trip, a soft, almost soothing hum as they slept, but now it suddenly dropped. The boat began to slow down.

Nicole sat up, eyes wide open. "What's going on?"

"Do you think we're there?" wondered Andrea. The very idea made her stomach clench with fresh dread. She quickly tied back the other pigtail and then hurried out and grabbed her shoes.

Gina didn't seem to get in any hurry. She sat up, rubbing at her eye again. Her long hair spilled down around her and pooled over her bare legs. "We've got a ways to go," she said through another yawn. "But we're not out in open lake anymore."

Nicole jumped up and hurried out of the cabin.

Andrea finished tying her shoes, then collected her phone and the spear lying next to it. (Except it was really a leaf?) She'd tried leaving it in her shorts while she slept, keeping it as close as possible, but with that new pricklier shape it had taken, it kept poking her whenever she moved, so she settled for keeping it close by instead.

While Gina pulled on her skirt, Andrea stepped out of the cabin. Nicole was up ahead, looking out the windshield into that eternal night. "Are we on a river?"

"More like passing between islands, I think," said Gina as she stepped from the stateroom, carrying her sandals.

Nicole set off out the door and Andrea and Gina followed.

"Shorelines are closing in," Keith called down to them from his seat at the helm.

Andrea thought that was a bit of an understatement. Looking around, she saw that there were thirty-foot-high walls of black stone looming on either side of them. Jagged rocks jutted outward, threatening to shred the trawler's hull if it drifted too close.

"You better know how to handle this thing," worried Nicole.

"I know what I'm doing," Keith snapped at her.

Andrea's gaze drifted up to the tops of those black cliffs. In the harsh glare of the trawler's flood lights, she could make out the skeletal shapes of large, black trees looming there. "Night trees..." she sighed. Seeing them again sent an icy shiver down her spine. She couldn't help recalling their last encounter with one of those, when Nicole was very nearly dragged up into its strangling branches and devoured.

Nicole recalled it, too. She could tell. She was staring up at those ominous branches, her hand rubbing absently at her throat, where the tiny scars from that encounter were still visible if you looked closely enough.

That was almost the end for her. If not for that ghostly voice telling Andrea to use the fire, she wouldn't be with them today. And Albert and Brandy would have been devoured right alongside her, as neither of them had any intention of abandoning her to such an awful fate. All three of them were hopelessly entangled in those nasty, toothy tendrils when she shoved the flaming backpack up into its writhing branches.

But she didn't want to think about that right now. In the months that followed that frightful night, she had enough nightmares about those awful trees to last a lifetime. And those weren't even the only nightmare-inducing things she saw that night. There were real-life zombies, hounds and the Caggo. And then there were those foul carrion eaters, grotesque flying abominations with backward-looking wings and no heads that pooped all over everything and pushed careless girls off cliffs without warning.

Nicole made her way around and up to the bridge and Andrea followed her.

"We're not lost are we?" shouted Nicole.

"We're still on course," insisted Keith.

"We're on a path," said Gina. "I've been able to feel it. It's like a stone road. Laid out underneath us. At the bottom of the lake."

Keith glanced back at her. "Well, you're officially more helpful than any of this equipment." He gestured at the displays built into the helm in front of him, none of which were working.

"Electronics," recalled Andrea. "Glitchy."

Gina nodded. "You don't need them. Or me. I can tell. It's like you've memorized the way."

"Yeah..." He stared into the dark canyon stretching into the darkness ahead of them. "That's what it feels like, all right. It's like somebody planted a map in my head or something. I know where I'm going, even though I don't know *where* I'm going..." He curled his lip, frustrated. "...if that makes any sense."

"It does," she assured him. "I get it."

Those towering stone walls drew even closer. There was less than twenty feet on each side of the boat, which was, of course, plenty of space to navigate, but nevertheless made Andrea nervous. What would they do if they hit something and sank? There was nothing in sight but those vertical walls. Would they be able to climb out of the water? And even if they could, *then* what? That was the Wood up there.

"I don't understand any of it," said Keith. "But somehow I know exactly what I'm doing."

She turned and watched him as he steered the boat between those ominous cliffs. She remembered sitting here with him for a while last night after Nicole and Gina went below deck, chattering away like she always ended up doing. She told him their story, starting at the wedding and leading all the way up to their audience with Gina's goddess. He didn't say much. An occasional, "Huh," or, "Wow," without much emotion behind it. After a while, she became convinced he wasn't really listening to her, but she just babbled on, unsure what else to do, until she reached the end of her story and ended with a lame-sounding, "And that's when we found *you*."

But he *had* been listening. When she was done, he told her that it all sort of added up. He told her about the strange dreams he'd been having for some time, and how suddenly Nicole started turning up in them, of all people. It seemed that he was dreaming about her every time she got into trouble. When the barely-there had her. When they were trapped on Tristesse Lane. When she was nearly left behind in that awful hospital. And even when Hotdog sent her *back* to the hospital. He saw it all. And even more surprising, it turned out that he might've been the reason they escaped all those times.

In his dreams, he seemed to have some sort of connection to Nicole. Which was kind of weird, since they weren't exactly on the friendliest of terms...

She didn't really understand it, of course. He told her he didn't understand it, himself. And even if he *had* been able to explain it to her, by then she'd started to get really sleepy. That was when he told her to go down and get some rest, that the barely-there wouldn't be able to do anything to him. Apparently, she wasn't fooling him in the least when she told him she was fine to stay up longer.

He was such a sweetheart. She couldn't understand why Nicole ever broke up with him. But she had no intention of saying anything to her about it. It was kind of a sore subject.

Nicole wasn't interested in anything her ex-boyfriend had to say, though. She'd had her back turned to him this whole time, staring out over that black water behind them. "I saw something out there when I was up here before," she recalled. She glanced back at Gina. "Can you feel whatever *that* is?"

"There are things in the water," she confirmed. "I don't know what they are. They're not really fish. Or any other kind of animal. They're something else. Something that can only exist in a place like this. But they're big. And they've been circling the boat since shortly after we left Cedric's Cove."

"Okay, that's a little concerning," groaned Andrea.

"No shit," grumbled Nicole.

Andrea remembered Gina saying that the fish people under

Cedric's Cove came from the lake but wouldn't go back to it. Were these the things they were afraid of? She didn't care for the thought of monsters so scary that *other* terrifying monsters wouldn't dare go near…

"Don't worry about them," said Gina. "It doesn't feel like we're in any danger." She looked out the window, at the gleaming sparkle of the boat's lights reflecting in the wake. "Although I don't think it would be a good thing if we fell in the water."

Andrea let out a squeak of a groan at the thought.

"Sorry," said Gina.

"I told you they weren't anything to be worried about," said Keith.

"I know what you told me!" snapped Nicole.

"Do you know how far we have left to go?" asked Andrea, quickly changing the subject.

"I don't," replied Keith. "I know which way we're supposed to go, and that I'll know when we arrive, but I can't really articulate distances. It's…*weird*."

"The things we can do are so different that it can be difficult to fit them into any frame of logic we as human beings are used to thinking in," explained Gina. "You can't really explain it. It just sort of happens."

Keith nodded. "Right. It's like that." He glanced over his shoulder at her, curious. "You just know things, too, don't you? Do you get them from your dreams, too?"

"No. The goddess appears in my dreams when she gives me jobs, but otherwise, they have nothing to do with it. As far as I know, anyway."

"Oh."

Andrea told him last night (or whenever that was) about Gina being able to sense things about her surroundings, but she didn't think she did a very good job of explaining it. She told him a little about her own abilities, too, how she was able to sense ghostly things. She also told him that Nicole, unlike the rest of them, seemed to have no special abilities whatsoever…and now she found herself glancing back at her and biting her lip. Was that too much information? Was she going to get mad at her if Keith told her he knew about that?

People had been telling her all her life that she had a big mouth…

Gina walked to the front of the bridge and stood beside Keith, her gaze fixed on the narrow path before them. "There's something up there," she reported.

"Something good?" asked Andrea, unsure if she really wanted the answer. "Or something bad?"

But Gina shook her head. "Just…something."

Keith nodded. "Yeah… I kind of feel it, too. Like a…" He struggled for a moment, trying to find the right word. "A *landmark*, maybe? A waypoint?"

She leaned closer to the glass, squinting, trying to peer through the ever-present gloom. "A gateway."

"What?" He leaned forward, trying to see better. "Can you see something?"

Andrea stepped forward, too, curious. Something was there. Something *big*. Something that gave her an ominous sort of sinking feeling deep in her gut.

It appeared like something out of a movie, a great and monstrous form emerging from the endless darkness like a leviathan rising from the deep. It was such an eerie and ominous sight that she couldn't fully stifle the startled cry that forced its way up her throat.

A giant stone face loomed before them, so enormous that the trawler's lights barely reached its flared nostrils. A massive mouth, stretched into a great, silent scream, framed the narrow passage before them. Huge, stone teeth stretched overhead like the trusses beneath a bridge and an ominous darkness loomed beyond.

"That's a big mouth…" muttered Keith.

"It looks like…" said Andrea, distracted.

"Back in the temple," said Nicole as she stepped up beside her for a better look. "The entrances to the emotion rooms."

"Faces," she agreed, nodding. "Mouths as doors…" She stared at the great, yawning lips as they approached. It even looked like the same gray stone from which the temple had been built. But those faces had acted as warnings. Did that mean *this* face was intended as a warning?

But that didn't seem right. They couldn't see above the nose. If it portrayed an emotion of some sort, like those doorways in the temple, it was impossible to tell what it was. And what use was a warning if they couldn't properly see it?

Nicole glanced over at Gina. "You called it a gateway…"

She nodded.

"Gateway to *what*?" asked Andrea.

She glanced over at them, a frightened look overtaking her sleepy features, and replied, "It's the Denselands. We've arrived."

Chapter 15

"Okay," conceded Violet. She was sitting across from Albert and Brandy, her legs curled casually under her. "You win. Your weirdo pervert shaman *does* sound creepier than our twins…"

"Told you," said Brandy. She was lying down on the seat, her head on Albert's thigh, her bare feet propped up on the window of the carriage. "That guy made my *skin crawl.*"

"Seriously, though… *Sex magic?* Really?"

"Yeah, that was pretty much our reaction, too."

"Magic might be one of the only things I wasn't ready to believe after some of the stuff we'd seen," said Albert. "But he wasn't wrong. There's something to it. I've felt it. I've *used* it."

"It's emotional," said Brandy. "Not physical." She glanced up at him, blushing a little. "I feel like that's an important point. We didn't have to be like *him* to make it work. Like, we're *nothing* like that creep."

He nodded. "It was about the *feelings* behind it, not the physical action, itself. *Emotional energy.* A kind of…*building up* of it, I guess. And then redirecting it."

"I can sort of get that," said Violet. "I mean, I think. So Sex Offender Gandalf just…sent you to that hotel and told you to use his obscene brand of magic to unlock the door where we met you guys?"

"Pretty much," said Brandy. "I mean, there was more to it than that, but…" She recalled all the things they'd done in their blind effort to utilize their untapped psychic abilities and felt sick at the thought of sharing such humiliating details with these strangers, even if they did seem like nice people. Hell, she wasn't sure she could tell some of those things to *Nicole*, and she told Nicole practically *everything.* "Long story short," she said instead, "we found the two locks hidden in the hotel. Then we found the last door and met you guys." She glanced at Albert. "Right?"

"Sums it up nicely," he replied. "There's a lot more to it, of course…but some of it goes back pretty far. I mean, we first stumbled onto this stuff *six years* ago. It's…*complicated.*"

"*Really* complicated," she agreed. She didn't want to talk about *that*, either. The sex room. Wandering lost and afraid through that darkness in their birthday suits. Why couldn't she have stumbled into a PG-rated adventure?

"So you guys have seen some shit, too," said Violet. "It's weird out there, right?"

"*Very* weird," he agreed. He glanced out at the endless tunnel of stone passing behind the glass. "And now it looks like we're heading deeper into it than ever before. You said those twins talked about three roads converging in the Wood."

"We keep hearing that word," said Violet. "What *is* the Wood, exactly?"

"You've never been to the Wood?" asked Albert, surprised. "But you've explored all kinds of other worlds."

"Well there's a *lot* of worlds out there," she said. "I mean, I *know* we haven't seen them all."

Brandy glanced over at him. "Yeah, but…I thought the Wood was what surrounded our world and separated us from the others." Wayne told them that. It was how Lucas Kneede explained it to him the first time they met, long before any of them knew he had a name, even before the Sentinel Queen accused him of being the literal devil. It was supposedly a sort of buffer between worlds, preventing crossovers. "I thought you'd have to go through the Wood to get to any others."

Albert nodded. "Yeah. I thought so, too."

But Violet shook her head. "The worlds we find are just…*right there.* Like, hiding right below the surface. It's just a matter of finding the way in."

He shook his head, thoughtful. "We don't know much about it, but the Wood's not like the little worlds you described. It's huge. *Way* bigger than our world. It's a giant *forest*, full of all sorts of scary stuff."

"Zombies," recalled Brandy. "Those're real, it turns out."

"We know," said Violet.

"Oh. Okay."

"I've fought those before," bragged Corey.

"Cool," said Albert, bemused.

"But in a swamp. Not woods."

"It was a marsh, actually," said Violet.

"Same difference."

"It's not, really."

"And these freaky, man-eating trees," Brandy went on.

"Night trees," recalled Albert. That was what Wayne called them, anyway. Another morsel of information given by Kneede when they met in that terrifying-sounding tunnel the Sentinel Queen sent him into all by himself.

"We've heard of those, too," said Violet. She untucked her legs and stretched out on the bench. "Our friends ran into some of them."

"Stole their shirts," recalled Corey.

"Just one of their shirts," she corrected him. "She lost her sweater getting away." Then she frowned. "Why is *that* the detail you remember?"

"Just remember 'em talkin' 'bout it."

She shook her head. "Most of what we see are small, empty worlds, but we've seen bigger worlds, too. Some with their own ecosystems. But we've never had to go through a monster-infested forest to reach any of them."

"Big world surrounding ours..." pondered Corey. "Wood outside. Pockets inside." He glanced at Violet. "Could change the model for how I map the worlds we find."

"It could," she agreed.

Albert chuckled. "Is it weird that I'm kind of relieved to meet someone who looks at all this weird stuff with a *scientific* eye?"

Brandy nodded. "It kind of makes me feel a little less crazy."

"A lot better than all that *magic* nonsense, that's for sure."

"Right?"

"We want to understand it all," explained Violet, "not just experience it. But then you have shit going on like *Warner Harr*, and it feels like science just flies right out the window."

"Yeah, that guy creeps me out, too," groaned Brandy. "I did *not* appreciate getting possessed like that."

"We'd already heard of him, too," said Violet. "Our friends had some experiences with him, so we sort of knew what we were dealing with. Even so, it was freaky having some woman with all-black eyes just walk up as soon as we entered the front door and start giving us orders. He seriously needs to work on his social skills, but he really is one of the good guys in all this."

"That's good to know," said Brandy. "But if he could stay the fuck out of my body from now on, that'd be great."

"Yeah, put me down for that, too," agreed Violet.

"But seriously, how do you already know about Warner Harr, zombies and night trees, but not the Wood?"

Violet shrugged.

"Three roads..." said Albert. He kept circling back to that in his head. "By land, water and shadow."

"This is shadow," said Corey. The creepy twins had pretty much told them so.

Kneed had called it that, too, Albert recalled. "And your friend with her two friends, on their way to somewhere called Cedric's Cove."

"Water road," Corey deduced.

"Yeah. Most likely."

"Does that mean we're going to meet back up with them when we get where we're going?" wondered Brandy.

But of course he didn't know. According to Violet, those freaky twins said, "three roads converge in the black depths of the Wood," so it reasoned they were all going to the same place. But that didn't necessarily mean they'd meet. As they'd already established, the Wood was a *big* place.

And it wasn't as if the Keeper had let anyone in on his grand plan. They still knew almost nothing about what to expect when they finally arrived at the end of this tunnel.

"And where's the land road, then?" wondered Brandy. "Who's on *that* one?"

"That crazy cat lady said there were twelve of us," he recalled.

"There's a crazy cat lady now?" asked Violet, bewildered.

"Yeah, don't get us started on *her*," he grumbled.

"She also said two of us wouldn't come home," Brandy reminded him.

"Well *that* sounds like a shit deal!" gasped Violet.

"Not cool," agreed Corey.

"We don't know anything," Albert assured them. "Not really."

"She said Lucianna wasn't what she claimed to be and she was right about that."

That was a difficult point to argue with. If not for the cat lady, they might not have realized something was wrong before it was too late. "Still... I have no intention of just accepting that any of us won't make it home."

Brandy stared at the darkness beyond the window. "I really hope you're right."

For the first time since they set off on this strange journey through the darkness, the carriage gave a jarring lurch.

"What the fuck was *that*?" gasped Brandy. She sat up and grabbed for Albert's arm. There weren't any seatbelts in this thing. She thought for a second there that she was going to end up on the floor.

"Don't know," replied Corey. He was still facing forward, watching the chains that stretched into the distance. "Maybe we're there?"

Violet turned around and joined him at the front of the carriage. "Are we slowing down?"

"Tunnel's gettin' bigger," he said.

"What?"

"He's right," observed Albert. He leaned forward. Those gray stone walls made for a tight fit before, but they were gradually withdrawing in the glare of the carriage's lights. It was already about thirty percent bigger, he estimated. And still opening wider. "Feels like we're approaching something."

Brandy watched those mysterious chains. It was such an ominous feeling, not knowing what awaited them in that ever-present darkness ahead, with no control of the carriage whatsoever. She grasped Albert's arm and hugged it. Whatever was there, she wasn't ready for it.

Lucianna assured them that her impostor was dead, that it wouldn't be causing them any more trouble. As was the bogey that got inside his head and pretended to be the Sentinel Queen, among other things. But those weren't the only ones of their kind. There was a whole world out there that was *crawling* with things like that.

The Ruin. That awful, twisted place looming outside the nightmarish "Mysteria" half of Lucianna's honeymoon resort. The one that looked like some kind of post-apocalyptic movie setting.

Around them, the tunnel walls had been receding gradually, but now they suddenly opened up into a vast, cavernous void.

"We there?" wondered Corey.

"We're still not stopping," observed Violet. Although the carriage had slowed almost to a crawl, they were still moving forward. Those mysterious chains remained taught. "You guys think there's a toll or something?"

"Better not be," grumbled Brandy. "They can bill it to the fucking Keeper."

Violet laughed. "No shit, right?" But then her laugh was cut short by a startled gasp as an enormous face materialized from the gloom in front of them.

Brandy vaguely realized that her fingernails were again digging into her husband's arm, but she couldn't help it. It was such a startling sight. A great, yawning mouth barreling toward them, lips stretched wide, upper teeth bared, ready to swallow them whole.

And they weren't stopping! They were heading straight down the giant's gullet, with no control whatsoever.

But then they passed beneath its lips and teeth and were gulped down into more darkness.

"That was freaky," was what Corey had to say on the matter as the walls of the giant's throat closed in around them and the mysterious beasts picked up their pace again. "We almost went full *Attack on Titan* back there."

"Attack of *what?*" asked Brandy.

But he only shook his head. "Nothin'. Forget it."

"Okay…"

"That was a temple statue…" Albert realized.

Brandy looked over at him, confused. "Temple…?" But even as the word passed her lips, she realized that he was right. That face was made of the same stone as the surrounding tunnel walls, the same stone that was ever-present down in those twisting depths. The carriage's lights didn't reach far enough to reveal more than a shadow of its enormous nostrils, so that it was little more than a gaping mouth, but the details she *could* see were unmistakably Temple of the Blind. She remembered seeing tiny wrinkles and creases in the skin. She even thought she glimpsed a mole on one cheek. "What does that mean?" she wondered. "Are we in trouble?"

"I don't think so, but…." He shook his head. "I'm sure it means *something*."

"Means we're inside that big dude now," decided Corey. "Like, in his guts."

"Ew," said Violet.

Brandy wrinkled her nose at the passing walls. "I sure hope not."

"That's not how statues really work," said Violet.

"Things might be different here."

"Well, whatever it was," said Brandy, "it was fucking *terrifying*. Who the fuck came up with something like that?"

"I'm more worried 'bout there being an exit to match the entrance," said Corey.

Violet made a face at him. "Okay, *yuck*. You can be done now."

"Just sayin'."

"The Denselands," recalled Albert. "That's where Lucianna said we were going."

"You think that was, like, the equivalent of a city limit sign?" asked Brandy. "'Welcome to the Denselands. We hope you enjoy your stay,' or something?"

"Maybe." He looked back. There was a window there, but nothing to see. It was as black as every other direction. Lucianna's haunting words came floating back to him from somewhere in the depths of his mind. (*...the weight of all those fallen worlds breaks any semblance of natural law that the Wood allows. Reality, itself, is broken there...*) "Or maybe more of a 'last chance to turn back' kind of deal?"

She grimaced. "Let's not go with that one."

"We're not stopping, though," observed Corey. And he was right. In fact, the carriage was still picking up speed. Whatever mysterious beasts were in charge of this ride had apparently only slowed down to pass through the creepy giant mouth.

Albert shrugged. "I guess just because you find the city limit sign, doesn't mean you're at your destination. We have no idea how big the Denselands are."

Violet turned around in her seat and looked at Albert. "What was that you called it before? A 'temple statue,' was it? What does that mean? Have you seen stuff like that before?"

He glanced at Brandy. "We've seen statues made from that same kind of stone before. And with the same level of detail. There used to be an entire temple carved from the stuff somewhere under Briar Hills. It was filled with all sorts of statues."

"Used to be?" pressed Violet.

"Yeah. It's gone now."

"We broke it," said Brandy.

"How d'ya break a whole temple?" wondered Corey.

"I guess the entire structure was some sort of doorway," Albert recalled. "We opened it. It was an all-or-nothing kind of thing, apparently..."

Brandy nodded. "Yeah, it wasn't the kind of door you close behind you."

"You guys really *have* seen some shit," said Violet.

"I wanna hear more 'bout this temple," decided Corey.

Violet turned and slipped into the rear-facing seat again, tucking her legs under her, making herself comfortable. "Yeah, me too."

Albert glanced at Brandy. "That's really going back, isn't it?"

It was, indeed. Six years ago. She was a college sophomore. He was a freshman. Lab partners who'd shared a handful of polite conversations...

Then that box showed up.

That stupid and wonderful wooden box...

Chapter 16

Erin sat in one of the booths, looking out at the quiet floor of the Elysium Fog. It was a little livelier than it was the last time she was here, although not much. There were three people sitting at the bar this time and another half-dozen seated at different tables while the beautiful musician played her haunting music.

But how did she get here? The last thing she remembered was... She frowned as she tried to recall what came before this moment. The last thing she remembered clearly was...well...the *end*. That monster at the lake. The fear and the pain. Dirty water flooding her lungs. Her body breaking and tearing. Then, mercifully, the numbing darkness. Cold death, like weary sleep, swept away the pain. And then, finally, it was all over.

Or...she *thought* it was over. And yet, here she was, whole again somehow. She looked down at her hands, half-expecting to find that she could see through them or something.

There were fragmented memories floating around in her head now that didn't feel like her own, of places she'd never been, of people she'd never met, of things she'd never done. A strange sensation, like being lost and adrift in a vast, churning ocean. Voices blowing over her like dizzying winds. Flashes of strange awareness like lightning on the horizon, memories that she never made while she was alive.

She remembered a strange awakening sort of sensation, like opening her eyes for the very first time and finally seeing the world for what it really was, as if she'd been locked inside a suffocating box all her life and was only now discovering what it meant to be free. And she remembered the lovely young woman from the wedding reception...

Except time seemed to have passed. She was no longer in her pretty bridesmaid dress. Instead, she was wearing a lovely sundress and sandals, as if ready for a relaxing summer picnic. But she was dirty and disheveled. Frightened and alone. In terrible danger.

But she was okay now. Somehow, she was able to help the poor girl escape those frightful woods. Although she couldn't remember exactly *how* she was able to do such a thing. She couldn't seem to recall any details about what happened. It was all lost in a strange haze...

And she had no recollection whatsoever of how she came to be back in *this* place.

She looked down at herself. Despite having a clear memory of her watery demise, she was neither wet nor bloody. She had no bruises or scratches. She had no scars. She seemed completely unharmed. But...when did she change? She was wearing her yellow tank top and distressed jeans. She had on her favorite sneakers.

In fact, wasn't this what she was wearing last time she was in this bar?

"It's normal to feel confused."

She looked up again and was surprised to find that the antlered man was sitting in the booth with her.

Horatio. The mysterious proprietor of the Elysium Fog. The monstrous, shadowy figure that first confronted her three years ago and set her down her destined path to that agonizing end in the lake.

(The Gatherer in the Haze.)

This booth was far brighter than that strange darkness in which she first confronted him. But the light didn't help much. He was draped in layers of black, threadbare fabric like some kind of mummy. It hung from those strange antlers, doing nothing at all to hide them, but only giving them a strange, shadowy, cobwebbed sort of appearance. The horns, themselves, looked strangely ancient, worn and chipped and spotted with greenish-gray moss, making her wonder what sort of face he kept shrouded behind that unnatural and unsettling darkness that seemed to gather beneath that deep hood, with only those golden, burning eyes visible.

There was something deeply unsettling about those eyes. Something about the shapes of those deep and flickering flames. Was it only her imagination or did they sort of look like people dancing...? Or perhaps...writhing in agony...?

Unable to meet those burning eyes any longer, she looked down at his hands. They were the only parts of him that weren't completely covered. His fingers protruded from the black cloth and lay upon the table before him, long and grayish and wrinkled, with an odd pattern of fine black lines crisscrossing the exposed surface of his skin. His nails were a dark and sickly green, long and jagged, with odd little bumps and spurs jutting out from their surfaces. Strangest of all, however, was that there were *seven* fingers on each hand.

She had no idea what this thing was, but it was certainly no man. And yet, not one person here seemed the least bit bothered by the fact that there was a monstrous, fourteen-fingered, antlered, glowing-eyed man sitting in plain sight with her at this booth.

She looked around at the other patrons simply going about their business as if nothing were amiss.

And yet…she found herself feeling as if all was not as it appeared.

Some of those people didn't look quite right. There was something off about the two women drinking and talking at a nearby table. Something about the way their heads were moving as they laughed, perhaps? Or maybe something in the way they held their cigarettes? The more she looked at them, the more wrong they looked, and yet she couldn't quite pinpoint *where* they were wrong…

"This club exists at a point in space and time where the natural and supernatural worlds overlap," explained Horatio, his voice clear and deep, but strangely distant, as if he were speaking not from just beneath that shadowy hood, but from somewhere far away, "accessible to both the living and the dead, as long as they know how to find it."

She watched a man walk past the booth. He was perfectly normal, unassuming, perhaps in his late thirties, his hair receding at his temples, with glasses and a shadow of a beard, dressed in a polo shirt and faded jeans. But at the same time, there was something wrong about him. Nothing about his appearance seemed…well…*real.* It was as if he were wearing a blatantly obvious fake mustache or something. The more she watched him, the more obvious it became that he was something other than he appeared to be. And yet, she couldn't seem to see through the disguise, no matter how hard she tried.

Looking around the room, she found that he wasn't alone. There was a woman sitting at a nearby table with a face she could clearly see but couldn't quite *comprehend.* As if it were weirdly impossible for her brain to transfer the data that was being sent from her eyes.

And one of the people sitting at the bar looked strangely cartoonish, like some kind of theme park animatronic setup or something.

"We are sitting in an anomalous wrinkle in the fabric of reality where it becomes possible for the physical and the spiritual to trade places."

"Trade places?" asked Erin, confused.

"Inside the parameters of this club, it's possible for your spirit to take on a form identical to the one you had when you were still alive."

She pressed her hand to her chest as she let those words sink in. She *felt* perfectly alive. "I'm really…dead?"

"That depends entirely on your definition of the word. Define 'death' simply as everything that comes after the moment you leave your mortal body behind, and the answer will very much be yes. You are dead. Erin Laplede's human remains were cremated and are no more."

Hearing that sentence, spoken so casually at her, no less, made her feel nauseous. Her stomach soured. Her *remains*...?

"By that definition," Horatio went on, "death is what begins at the moment life ends and you most certainly are dead. If, however, you think of 'death' as the purely *spiritual* state of being, outside the biological confines of the human body, and in contrast define 'life' as specifically that *physical* state of being..." He turned his head slightly, that intimidating tangle of antlers shifting and swaying above him. "...and if certain conditions makes it possible to shift back and forth between those two states...then death is *not* a permanent state and one can, in fact, find themselves very much alive again." He lifted one of those strange, seven-fingered hands and gestured at her. "As you are right now."

She looked down at herself, confused. "So...is this my body or isn't it?" She still had her sunflower tattoo. She reached up and felt all of her familiar earrings. They were still pierced. She looked at her hand and found that the scar was still there from when she cut her finger peeling potatoes when she was eleven. If she'd somehow *regrown* her body, those things hadn't reset.

"As I've already explained, your original body no longer exists. This is a *physical construct*, woven into existence from the very essence of your spiritual form. You've *remade* yourself into a familiar vessel. It's very rare for a spirit to possess the strength necessary to do such a thing, but by no means unheard of. There are many spirits like you walking around out there, indistinguishable from the living. You probably encountered dozens of them during your lifetime."

She was prodding at the fingers of her left hand. This was a brand-new body? It felt no different than it ever had.

"In this form, a spirit can do almost anything it could do when it was alive. Eat. Speak. Touch. In your case, perhaps...*play music*."

She looked up at him, surprised. That sort of sounded as if she weren't dead at all, as if she still had her life...as if the terrifying ordeal at the lake never happened.

As if reading her mind, Horatio said, "For many who find themselves in this situation, it would, indeed, be a second chance to pick up where they left off. And many have. But *you* still have work to do."

She stared at him, confused. "Work?"

She remembered the first time she met Horatio, deep in that ominous, unlit area that she suddenly realized wasn't actually there. When she looked in that direction, there was no open space, dark or otherwise. There was only the club's stone wall. And yet that dark place was undeniably real. She remembered walking into it. And he did, indeed, tell her that she had a job to do.

But hadn't she done her job? She found the thorn. She protected it. And she delivered it to the lovely bridesmaid. At the cost of her life, no less. At least...*mostly* at that cost...she supposed...

And yet, a new memory now floated to the surface of her murky mind. A black, endless forest stretching forever into an eternal, moonless night. Towering walls of gray stone in a city ancient beyond imagining.

She squeezed her eyes closed, frustrated. Why was it so hard to remember things?

Again, as if reading the question directly from her bemused mind, Horatio explained, "The human body and mind is limited in how it can interact with the physical world around it. Reality is only what your brain perceives it to be through the various limited senses it has access to. It's an entirely different perspective from the spiritual form, which has no such limitations. When you're in *this* state, you're simply unable to comprehend the vastness of the things you experience when you're in pure spirit. That's why you can't fully recall what you've been doing for the past five days."

Five days? Had it really been so long since she...?

"And it's why you can't fully recall the entirety of our first conversation three years ago. Just as you became physical from the spiritual today, I made you spiritual from the physical that day. Only when you're fully separated from any physical form does it all become clear."

"So...I just...can't remember when I'm alive what happens when I'm dead?" (What bizarre words to hear coming out of her own mouth!)

"An oversimplification," replied Horatio, "but accurate."

This was all so frustrating. Looking around again, she found herself feeling strangely as if everything were all out of order. How was she here right now? Not just the infuriatingly confusing concept of being both alive and dead, but *here in this place*. Wasn't this club all the way back in Ohio? She should be far, *far* away from here right now. She felt like she'd traveled a vast distance, following the pretty bridesmaid into that endless, black forest, farther and farther from home... Toward those towering walls in the distance...

But it was so hard to grasp those memories. They were like dreams slipping away in the waking morning. She couldn't hold onto them.

And there was something dark about those memories, too. Something unpleasant. Something she didn't quite *want* to remember.

It was so much easier to just let go.

"Then why am I here like this now?" she asked instead. "Why bring me back to..." She clapped her hands together. Solid flesh striking solid flesh. A living, breathing, human body.

"Because it will be necessary for you to transition between your physical and spiritual forms like this in order to complete the task you've accepted."

"And what task is that?" she asked, not sure if she really wanted to know the answer.

There was something oddly familiar about this conversation. She could almost remember talking about this stuff in those hazy, half-there memories that she couldn't quite grasp. And something about those memories made her feel unpleasant, as if it were something she really didn't want to do.

And indeed, Horatio's next words made her blood turn cold: "To kill one of the Keeper's chosen ones."

"What...?" Again, she thought about that lovely bridesmaid, her brilliant, beautiful smile, standing there with her equally lovely mother and sister. "I can't *kill* anyone!"

"You have the details already." He pointed at her forehead with one of those many long, bony fingers. "They're locked away with the rest of your knowledge of the other side."

She shook her head. "No... That doesn't sound right."

"That is normal," he assured her. "Don't worry yourself over it. For now..." He reached across the table with one of those strange hands and placed something in front of her. "What you came here for."

She stared at the object for a moment, her mind swirling with thoughts that were both strangely familiar and utterly alien.

"Remember. You have to do it before they reach the walls of the City Beyond Memory. If not, all will be lost."

Chapter 17

"So hold on..." said Keith, trying to wrap his head around this absurd concept. "These rooms just, *made you feel whatever emotion the statues depicted?*"

Andrea nodded. "Exactly. Our friends stumbled into the first one without knowing what was going on and went totally crazy with lust. They barely knew each other and they just tore each other's clothes off. They completely *lost it.*"

"Holy shit..." That was, without a doubt, the most *fake-sounding* nonsense he'd ever heard. It was like a feeble plot device for a lazy porn flick.

Shortly after they passed through the mouth of that creepy stone giant, the walls closing in on them began to recede back into the gloom again, spreading wider and wider until only the black water of the lake remained. He had no idea how far they'd come or how far they had left to go, but by some strange power, he *knew* they were still on course and that they were right where they were meant to be.

"And they were just...*statues?*" he pressed.

"Just statues," said Andrea.

He remembered Andrea from when he and Nicole were dating. She was her roommate, so he talked with her quite a few times during those months. And he'd always liked her. She was an absolute sweetheart. Although he'd always found all her piercings to be kind of distracting. He kept finding his gaze drawn to one decoration or another when he talked to her. Even now, he found himself staring at the stud in her eyebrow instead of looking her in the eye. It felt like he was being rude, and he wasn't trying to. But she never really seemed to notice, so maybe it was okay.

Maybe she was used to it?

"I mean, super-realistic ones," she added, still talking about the temple statues. "Kind of reminded me of that famous David statue with all the crazy details? You know the one? With the naked...?" She pointed at her lap.

"I know it," he assured her. And he knew what she meant. He'd always been astonished by all the amazing details on David, right down to the creases, wrinkles and veins on his hands and feet.

"But even *more* detailed," she said. "Like, they could've been *real people* turned to stone. Fingerprints. Individual *hairs*. *Super* freaky."

"And all of them *getting* freaky," added Nicole. She was stretched out on the bench behind them, relaxing.

Andrea nodded. "Yeah. Lots of sex." Her pretty blue eyes widened dramatically as she added, "Like, *lots* of it."

"Did anyone *else* see them?"

She hesitated.

He glanced over and saw that her cheeks had flushed slightly. "Did *you?*"

"Yep," said Nicole without looking up. "She *totally* peeked."

"I was *curious*," she whined. "I mean, can you blame me? And I only saw a *little*. Like…*one* statue. That was all." (Actually it was two of them, but it was embarrassing enough to tell people she saw *one*.)

"And?"

She blushed a little brighter and nodded. "Yeah. It…um…" Somewhere inside her head, she heard Stella's voice cry out, *Like a super-soaker!* and she felt her ears growing hot with embarrassment. "It affected me," she said instead. "Yes."

She remembered stepping out of that room feeling all out of sorts. Her body was hot. She was super distracted. She was positively *mortified*. (And that was *before* Wayne took off his clothes in front of her…)

"What happened?" asked Keith, curious.

"I didn't lose control like they did or anything!" she insisted. "It just…kinda got in my head, I guess. It was just *weird*."

"Huh…"

"The fear room was worse," she pushed on, changing the subject before he could ask any more embarrassing questions. "The first time Brandy and Albert went down there, they got so scared they couldn't go on. It got in your head in a different way. It didn't just fill you with fear until you couldn't control yourself. It *gave* you things to fear."

Keith considered this for a bit. "So…what? Like, it preyed on your phobias or something? Like if you're afraid of spiders?"

"No. Not like that. They were *all new fears*."

"*New* fears?" he asked, intrigued. Somehow that sounded even scarier than facing your *worst* fear.

"It's a little hard to explain. Because I didn't actually see any of those statues. I was *way* too scared." (Especially after what she felt from that one little look back in the sex room.) "Albert and Wayne were the ones leading the way through all that stuff. So all I know is what they told us afterward. And they both described catching glimpses of statues—like, not even the whole thing, just bits and pieces, blurry shapes—stuff like that—and then getting these freaky images in their heads, almost like they were picking up memories of whatever the statues were depicting. Almost like they were *there!*"

"That's...wow. Crazy."

"Yeah. Like, pure nightmare fuel. Those statues weren't just people *being* scared, like the other one was people being all horny. It was the stuff *doing* the scaring. And it was *really* scary stuff. Monsters. People being killed in horrible ways. *Bad stuff.*"

"Freaky," said Keith.

She nodded. "Like I said, I was way too scared to even dare sneak a peek."

"It's not unheard of for places or objects to hold onto powerful emotions," said Gina. She was sitting by herself across from Nicole, looking small and timid. "Or even for them to impart those emotions onto anyone they come into contact with. But I've never heard of it being used in such a specific way. It's kind of disturbing. Almost like someone figured out how to weaponize raw emotion."

Nicole glanced over at her, one eyebrow raised. "Well *that's* a horrible thought."

"Sorry."

"Albert and Wayne always referred to the emotion rooms as traps," recalled Andrea. "So yeah, I mean, *kinda.*"

Keith gave a decisive nod. "Yeah, I think I'd rather face my own fears. Facing brand new ones sounds a million times worse."

Andrea considered this for a little bit. "I wonder what we would've seen if it had worked like that, though? I mean I'm totally scared of snakes, so maybe them?" She shuddered at the thought of finding herself surrounded by snakes in that already unnerving darkness. That wasn't something she wanted to dwell on. But then again, that wouldn't be very different from what Tristesse Lane did to her. It made her live her fear of being left all alone. But she didn't want to think about that right now. She shoved it out of her mind and looked back at Nicole. "What do you think *you'd* have seen?"

"I don't know," she grumbled.

"Commitment," muttered Keith.

"Oh, fuck you!"

He chuckled.

Andrea had to stifle a laugh of her own. That was actually pretty funny. And it sounded like he might've even struck a nerve. But the last thing she wanted was to be on Nicole's bad side. "What about you?" she asked Gina.

"I don't know," she replied. "I've seen a lot of things that scared me really bad…"

"Oh… Sorry."

"It's fine."

She turned her attention to Keith. "What about you?"

"Canned biscuits," he replied without hesitation.

She burst out laughing at this. "*What?*"

"It's like handling an antique grenade! You never know when they might go off! Hands-down, scariest thing I've ever encountered."

Andrea couldn't stop laughing. Even Gina smiled a little at this, Nicole noticed. *That* was a little taste of the Keith she used to know, the Keith who could charm a smile out of any girl in the room. He *was* still in there somewhere. She supposed that coldness she felt from him earlier really was reserved just for her.

That was good. It would've been sad if he'd lost all the joy he used to carry around inside him. And yet there was a part of her that felt surprisingly bitter about it. What was wrong with her? What did she care? Why did everything have to be so confusing?

She stood up, annoyed and frustrated, and walked off the bridge, toward the back of the boat. She didn't feel very good. The humidity was back. It weighed heavy on her chest, making it harder to breathe. And she was tired. Her whole body felt heavy.

Keith watched her walk away. It was weird being around her again. He thought that chapter of his life had closed for good.

Dating Nicole was quite the adventure. Stunningly beautiful, quick-witted and brilliant, passionately protective of her friends and family. (And an absolute dream in the bedroom, though he was too much of a gentleman to go bragging about such things.) And then there was the fact that she was practically a nudist. Whenever they were alone, she was almost *always* naked! Or at least in *some* state of partial undress or another. She'd seemed too good to be true. Which, of course, she very much was.

It was all great in the beginning. The first few months were heavenly. They had a lot of fun together. They talked a lot about all sorts of things. (And again, the sex was *unbelievable!*) But at some point something just changed. She started turning cold and he couldn't understand it. He *still* didn't understand it. All he did was try to treat her like any lady deserved to be treated. At what point did offering to carry a bag make him an asshole? She started using words like "controlling" and "suffocating," as if he were trying to tell her how to live her life instead of offering to open a jar for her.

He was trying to be *nice*. How the hell did that make him the bad guy?

And she hadn't changed one bit. She made that clear right from the start. Her first words to him the moment she recognized him were, "What the fuck are *you* doing here?" then she accused him of *stalking* her.

And now he was stuck on this boat with her, all those old, buried emotions bubbling up from deep inside, confusing him.

Because she still looked incredible...

He realized he was still staring at her and forced his eyes forward again.

No. He was *not* interested in dredging up *that* trainwreck of a relationship. Nicole was probably the hottest girlfriend he'd ever had, but she was also the craziest. There was something seriously off about her.

Although...

Staring into the darkness of this endless lake, it didn't escape him that *he* seemed to have gone a little crazy, too. Strange dreams. Irresistible compulsions to drive to Michigan. Spontaneously acquired *boating skills*. What the hell was happening to him? How did he go from a nobody with a dead-end factory job to sailing the black waves of a mystery lake in a nightmare world with no sky with his crazy ex-girlfriend?

Was *he* the crazy one all along?

He glanced back at Nicole again. She was standing at the rear of the boat, bending over the railing, looking down at the water. He could see the tattoo on her lower back peeking out beneath her shirt.

The tree...

Back when they were dating, she called it a Tree of Life. A sort of good luck symbol. A metaphor for prosperity. But that was no Tree of Life. He'd seen trees like those in his dreams. They grew along the river those women were traveling in their boat. They were real. And they were *mean*. He glanced out at the darkness surrounding them. They were *right out there*. He couldn't see them, but he knew they were there. All around them.

She lied to him back then. She'd seen those trees with her own eyes. Up close and personal. Somehow, she'd been to this dark world before. Five years ago, to be exact. Andrea had already told him about their frightening trip inside something called Gilbert House, then a frightful-sounding journey deep underground, where they found some kind of temple filled with *emotion-imbuing statues* of all things.

Perhaps it only made sense that she was a little off if she'd already been to this world when he met her. Maybe this place just did that to people. Maybe before they were done here, he'd finally understand her.

Or maybe they'd only learn to hate the very sight of each other...

"The worst part of it all was having to be naked the whole time," said Andrea.

In an instant, every thought in Keith's brain scattered like a school of fish from the path of a hungry shark. "Wait... *What?*"

Chapter 18

Albert talked about the box and its strange clues and mysterious maps. He talked about the vast network of tunnels they found under the streets of Briar Hills. He talked about the corridors of strangely immaculate stone, the enormous labyrinth that was the Temple of the Blind with its countless silent statues. He even described the sex room and how those strange statues played with their minds. In *brief* detail, of course. It was an abridged version. He didn't care to talk about how they lost all control in the sex room and ended up stranded in those scary passageways butt naked. That was just a little too embarrassing to share with a pair of strangers. But he talked about the hate room and how they found a way to navigate it safely by using Brandy's poor eyesight. And about the fear room, and how, even with that helpful trick, they were still too afraid to reach the end.

He described the phone calls that summoned them back a year later. He didn't bother talking about Gilbert House. He wasn't sure it was relevant in the end. It was only a distraction. A means of separating them. Part of Kneede's convoluted scheme to stop them from opening the door. Or was it part of the Sentinel Queen's convoluted scheme to stop Kneede from trying to stop them from opening the door? (That part was all still a little confusing…neither's claim really seemed to make sense…) But more than anything, he didn't want to talk about Gilbert House because of the bodies they'd left there. The three unfortunate souls who entered that awful place with Olivia and never left. They had the answers to a five-year-old unsolved disappearance, after all. And he still didn't know how much trouble might rain down on them if anyone ever connected them to it.

They never really had a choice, though. The authorities would never believe their story. Not without seeing the truth for themselves. And that would only lead to *more* lost lives. A police force would charge through that whole building. And while that monstrous troll thing might not be there anymore, having escaped into the wilderness, there was still something terrible up on the fourth floor. Something the Sentinel Queen warned them they never wanted to see.

He didn't even care to mention the others who went there with them. Nicole. Wayne and Olivia. Andrea. He didn't attempt to tell their stories at all. Instead, he focused on the details of the temple, itself. The City of the Blind deep within and its enigmatic Sentinel Queen. Those vicious hounds with their slashing, razored flesh. The vast, winding labyrinth with its murderous guardian, the Caggo. The Keeper and Lucas Kneede. The haunted path spiraling up the burning mountain. And of course the doorway that brought the whole thing tumbling down.

"It was all about that doorway. The Sentinel Queen told us to open it. Kneede told us to leave it closed. And the Keeper told us it was our choice to make."

Violet and Corey raised an eyebrow at each other. (Doorways... And the Roman god, Janus...)

"Wasn't much of a choice," grumbled Brandy. "Open the door or stay locked up in that room and be baked alive."

He nodded. She wasn't wrong. If that was supposed to be a test, it felt pretty heavily biased. He couldn't help but wonder if anyone would've chosen differently, given the circumstances.

Something about that whole thing had never fully added up, in his opinion.

"I'm confused about why this Kneede guy wanted to stop you so bad last time but helped you this time," said Violet.

"Yeah, us too," said Brandy.

"There's definitely no love between him and Warner," recalled Albert. "He kept insisting that the Keeper tell us the truth."

"What truth?" wondered Violet.

"Good question," grumbled Brandy.

"Yeah, he still hasn't let us in on it."

"Kind of unsettling to think the Keeper could be lying about something," pondered Violet.

"Fucking Muppet barely tells us anything anyway," growled Brandy.

"'Muppet?'" asked Violet, confused.

"You've never actually *seen* the Keeper?" asked Albert.

"Not us. Our friends have. Scruffy sort of homeless-looking guy, they said."

Albert and Brandy exchanged a confused look. "Um...no..." said Brandy.

"*Our* Keeper looked like something off the set of *The Dark Crys-*

tal."

She frowned. "That's...?"

But before they could discuss it more, the carriage gave another lurch.

"Slowing down," reported Corey.

Violet turned around and slipped into the seat next to him. "Are we there? Or are we going through another mouth?"

"Butthole maybe," he replied.

"There's no butthole. Stop that."

The carriage continued to slow down.

Albert leaned forward and squinted into the darkness ahead of them. The only other time the carriage slowed down was when they approached the giant stone face. What was it going to be this time?

But instead of a face, the tunnel opened into another room much like the one they started this strange journey in. There was an open space on the left and a wall on the right. The carriage slowed to a crawl and crept toward two stone posts protruding from the ichor-coated floor of the track, preventing them from going any farther.

They inched forward, at the mercy of the mysterious beasts pulling them, until the carriage bumped into the posts. Then, with a loud clank, the yoke disengaged and the four of them watched all fourteen of those unearthly chains vanish into the darkness without them.

"Guess that's it," said Corey.

"End of the line," agreed Violet.

As if to confirm, the carriage door slid open.

"Second floor," muttered Albert as he peered out at the empty space beyond. "Gray stone, dark tunnels and unspeakable horrors."

Brandy elbowed him.

"Sorry." He stepped out of the carriage and stretched. The air felt oddly thick here. Humid, sort of, but not really warm or damp. It was difficult to explain.

A wasteland, he thought, recalling what Lucianna told them about this place, *where the very air is heavy with the weight of the inescapable atrophy that awaits all life.*

Brandy exited behind him and took hold of his arm. "I already hate it here," she decided.

He nodded.

"Looks like there's only one way to go," observed Violet, nodding at the single passageway leading out of the room.

Corey lumbered out of the carriage, the heavy duffel bag slung effortlessly over one shoulder. His size was rather intimidating, but he seemed perfectly nice. It was kind of hard not to like him. And the same was true of Violet. She had an endearing sort of smile and such a friendly, outgoing nature. A big sister sort of aura.

"So what's in the bag?" asked Brandy.

"Supplies," replied Violet. "Usually we're loaded down with recording devices to document our finds and equipment we use to help zero in on dimensional anomalies. A lot of it's still theoretical, of course. There are no reliable studies on detecting portals to other worlds, after all. But we've tried a lot of stuff. Corey gets his hands on all kinds of high-tech gadgets. Even I don't know where he finds it all. We've tested for electromagnetic fields, radiation, high-frequency sounds, ultraviolet light…you name it. And we almost always find *something* when using that stuff. But it's not consistent. Every doorway's different. It turns out it's the simpler things that tend to be more reliable. Radio interference. Temperature anomalies. Even cell phone signals are generally a better indication that we're onto something."

"Not this time, though," said Corey, pouting a little at the one measly bag hanging at his hip.

"Warner told us we had to travel light," she explained.

"*That's* traveling light?" asked Albert.

"Just a couple small cameras and multifunction devices, but mostly it's just lights, batteries and camping gear."

"Necessities," grumbled Corey.

"I know," she told him. Then she glanced at Brandy and said, "He had some new toys he was excited to try out."

"Bummer."

Corey nodded. He did, in fact, look quite disappointed.

Violet unzipped one of the pockets of the pouch. She didn't even have to bend over to do it. It was at the perfect height for her right where it hung. She withdrew two pocket-sized flashlights and handed them to Albert.

"It's hard to wrap my head around the fact that you guys just…*do* this sort of thing," he said as he passed one to Brandy. "I mean, where do you even get the money for something like that? It can't be cheap driving all over the country, buying all that equipment. It doesn't exactly sound like you have jobs."

Violet cocked a thumb at her chest. "Spoiled rich daddy's girl with big credit card privilege."

"Oh," said Brandy. "That would explain it, I guess."

Albert nodded. "And Dad's okay with it? I mean, it kind of seems like a dangerous line of work."

"I tell him everything we do. I don't think he believes a word of it, but I *do* tell him. It's not my fault if he'd rather believe I'm just bar hopping my life away."

It was hard to imagine having that kind of freedom. If the Keeper hadn't hijacked the tail end of their honeymoon, when they'd both taken the whole week off, he wasn't sure what he would've done. And then there was Brandy, who obtained her master's degree this past spring in psychology and was taking a well-deserved summer off to focus on the wedding before beginning work on her doctorate in the coming fall. The idea of simply wandering around all the time, looking for portals to other worlds, sounded like pure fantasy.

But then again, they just rode a magic carriage pulled by invisible beasts from some other dimension across the vast expanse of an impossible forest with no sky, so he supposed he couldn't really talk...

A set of steps appeared in the passage ahead of them, leading up. Something about the sight of them made his heart sink a little. Was this the end of their peaceful journey? Were they about to get their first glimpse of the Denselands? And just what would they find waiting for them in this strange new world?

Reality, itself, is broken there, he thought, recalling Lucianna's haunting warnings, *making it the perfect place to hide something invaluable.*

But it wasn't like they had any choice. The Keeper's otherworldly beasts had broken loose from the carriage and vanished into the darkness, stranding them here.

There was no way to go but forward into the unknown.

Chapter 19

It had been a while since they entered the yawning gateway and Max's mysterious train returned to its normal speed. After taking away their breakfast dishes, Nadia disappeared again. None of them saw where she went. Perhaps she was still tidying up the kitchen.

Olivia felt guilty for not asking her if she needed help, but she disappeared before she could quite get ahold of her emotions after hearing about all the terrors waiting for them in these awful Denselands. For a while, she felt like she might hyperventilate. It was a good thing she had Wayne with her or she didn't think she'd be able to handle any of this.

At Everett's urging, Wayne continued their story. He told him about how Olivia was snatched away by the monstrous thing in the Wood and feared dead. He talked about their companions setting off for the mysterious underground temple they discovered the year before. He described the steam tunnels and their long journey deep underground. He described the sprawling labyrinth crafted from that smooth, clean, gray stone. He described the sentinel statues. And of course he described those other statues as best as he could, and how they had the power to instill intense emotions into them at a mere glance.

She kept expecting Everett to blurt out how exciting it all was, how cool, how amazing, how *awesome*…but for some reason he seemed to have somehow taken control of himself. He sat there, looking plenty enthused, practically bouncing in his seat, but he kept his mouth shut. Maybe Wayne had finally managed to be grumpy enough to even intimidate someone like him. She hoped not, though. Wayne could be a grouch, but he wasn't really a mean person. He was just being protective.

He didn't talk much about the others who were there that night. He referred to them only as friends. She understood perfectly. Those parts of the story simply didn't feel like theirs to tell. It didn't seem right to involve them when they weren't even here.

He talked about the City of the Blind, deep inside that labyrinth, omitting how they'd all ended up naked, for which she was thankful. (That was so embarrassing!) He talked about the mysterious, half-human Sentinel Queen and her revelation that Olivia was still alive out there somewhere. He talked about that frightful tunnel. (But she noticed that he left out that awkward part about the "farewell gift" she gave him before abandoning him to that nightmarish darkness.) He talked in depth about the Wood, trying his best to illustrate just how terrifying it was, how the two of them barely escaped with their lives. But she was pretty sure none of it really got through to him. Everett never lost that childlike wonder in his eyes. Not once.

He talked about returning to the temple, this time with Olivia in tow, retracing their steps, confronting the Sentinel Queen. He talked about the labyrinth. Reuniting with their friends. The murderous Caggo. And he talked about how he died in those black depths, run through by something he could scarcely comprehend, much less properly describe.

The rest of the story was Olivia's to tell. He wasn't there, after all. But he had no intention of letting her relive all of that, too. So he jumped to the end.

"Next thing I knew, I woke up and everyone was hovering over me. Everything hurt, but I wasn't dead anymore. The temple was gone. Collapsed into itself. The door the Sentinel Queen wanted us to open was open. It was all over."

"Until now," said Everett. It was the first words he'd spoken since Wayne started talking.

"Until now," he agreed.

"Or at least until last Sunday," amended Olivia.

"Oh yeah…"

"But I was there for most of that, wasn't I?" asked Everett, grinning.

"You were," laughed Olivia. "So you already know that story."

Everett sat there a moment, letting it all process. Then he said, "So I guess whatever door you guys opened must have paved the way for what's happening now, then. I mean, the two things are obviously connected."

"Probably," agreed Wayne. That *was* what Sandy told them, after all. They were here to pick up where they left off with the first doorway.

The very thought of it scared the hell out of Olivia. She couldn't help wondering if she was really strong enough to do this all again.

"And I'm a part of that, too," he said, as if only just now realizing it. "That's…"

She expected him to say, "…awesome!" but he surprised her.

"…kind of heavy, isn't it?"

Even Wayne raised an eyebrow at this.

"I mean, it seems like a really big deal, doesn't it? Like…all of these different things are coming together…things that have been planned out since the world was *created*…and we've just been handed the reigns to the whole thing. I mean, doesn't that sort of make it sound like we're…kind of *important*?"

Olivia glanced over at Wayne, thoughtful. Albert had talked about that before, she recalled, about how if the Sentinel Queen's story was true, if the Temple of the Blind's true function was a doorway that would open the way for all mankind to continue his endless march through the cycle of life and death of universes…then didn't it mean that the future rested entirely in the hands of the six of them and their actions that night? "I don't…know if I want to think too much about that stuff," she decided.

Wayne nodded. "Yeah. Seems like an awful lot of pressure, doesn't it? The three of us, being responsible for whether or not our species has a future?"

"I'd kind of rather just take it one step at a time," agreed Olivia. "I just want to get this over with, go home and have the wedding we've been planning."

Wayne smiled and squeezed her hand. "Yeah. That's all I want, too."

She leaned over and rested her head on his shoulder. Yesterday's events were still tumbling around in her head. But that wasn't even yesterday, was it? According to Nadia, it was Friday. They left normal behind on *Sunday*. It had been almost a week since she saw her apartment.

Looking back on it all, none of it felt real.

And here she was saying things like, "I just want to get this over with," like it was just some mundane chore she had to finish, when in reality she was scared out of her mind of what might be waiting for her in the hours ahead.

She just kept returning to that awful, pitch-black restroom stall and those terrifying hours she spent in there, knowing that at any second she could die a violent, bloody and agonizing death.

Like everyone else who went inside Gilbert House that night.

She pretended like she wasn't still haunted by those experiences, but the truth was that she still felt like she was waiting for that bad end, even after all this time, like she never really escaped, but only delayed the inevitable.

Nadia bounded into the room and plopped down in one of the chairs. "We're approaching our final stop," she announced cheerfully, as if they were all about to arrive at Disneyland instead of literally the most terrifying place Olivia could imagine.

"Here we go…" grumbled Wayne.

Everett, on the other hand, sat up in his chair, his eyes wide with eager anticipation.

Olivia couldn't help but wonder if he'd still have that refreshing adventurous spirit when this was all over or if he'd learn to fear the unknown the way she and Wayne had. Or if he'd even survive in that harsh, black wilderness that long.

She clenched her jaw at the thought. No. That was an awful thing to think. Simply unacceptable. He was such a sweet guy. She couldn't bear the thought.

She was letting her fear get to her.

"I've already told you that the path ahead is dangerous," warned Nadia. She was sitting on the edge of her seat, her feet kicking back and forth, drumming against the front of it. She didn't look or sound like she was talking about unimaginable horrors in a black hell-forest. That cheerful smile never left her face. "Remember to stay on the path as much as possible. The night trees shouldn't be a problem if you don't stay in one place very long. But I'd still caution against touching them. It's rare, but sometimes even in hibernation they can reflexively snatch at things that pass under them."

Olivia had to stifle a groan. She still remembered being caught by the one on that burning mountain. Nicole saved her, but in the process she was entangled herself. And then Brandy and Albert as well when they tried to help her. She was never going to forget sitting on the ground, staring up at the three of them as they were lifted higher and higher into those branches, terrified out of her mind of what was about to happen.

Thank goodness Andrea was there…

"But the night trees aren't the only dangerous plants in the Wood. Beware of anything you find growing out there. Especially if you see thorny black vines with blood-red creepers. A single prick from one of those will instantly tear your soul from your body. You'd be dead before you hit the floor."

Olivia groaned at the very thought.

Wayne uttered a weary curse.

Everett, of course, looked like he'd just been told that it was Christmas morning. But somehow, he managed to stifle whatever exclamation was about to bubble out of that ever-enthusiastic mouth.

"There will be a lot less undead this far out in the Wood," Nadia went on. "But more fester vermin."

"Do we want to know what fester vermin are?" dared Wayne.

"Scavengers, mostly. There are a lot of different kinds. Most of them are skittish. But sometimes they get bold. Especially in larger numbers."

Somehow, Olivia couldn't help envisioning hordes of zombie rats swarming the landscape, and the thought made her feel like she might throw up...

"Far more dangerous are the remnants of all the dead universes that were trapped when the Wood swallowed them. Some of them are old gods who went down with their worlds. Some of them are demon-like entities that couldn't be killed. Some of them are unimaginable things that have no equal in your world or even in your folklore."

Olivia whimpered audibly this time.

"If this is supposed to be a pep talk," grumbled Wayne, "you might want to brush up on your skills."

Nadia giggled at this. "I know how it all must sound. And I'm sorry if I'm freaking you out. But you should be prepared before you go out into that place. Not everyone who gets involved in the Keeper's plans gets to be."

"Like when your sister just dumps people in the middle of a forest like unwanted dogs?" he challenged.

"Just like that, yeah." She flashed him another of those big, happy smiles. "My sister's job is to get people where they need to be. She's just the driver. It's *my* job to help people. I'm the helper."

The train shuddered and began to slow down.

Olivia felt her stomach turn over at the sensation.

"We're here," announced Nadia.

Chapter 20

"I know we weren't sitting this low in the water when we boarded," said Nicole. She was leaning over the railing, looking down at the water passing along the port side of the boat, her night tree tattoo peeking out again.

"We're not taking on water," Keith insisted.

"It's this place," said Gina. She stepped up beside Nicole and peered down at the surface of the lake. "It's the same thing that makes the air feel so thick. It's like a weight. It's pushing down on us, making everything heavier."

Nicole looked over at her, surprised. "You can tell that?"

She nodded. But it wasn't just that she felt it. It was difficult to explain exactly. She just *knew* it to be true, as if she'd known about this place all along, somewhere deep down. In fact, it was almost familiar to her...as if she'd been here before... But of course that was impossible.

"I think I remember something about that from one of my weird dreams," recalled Keith. "Something about dead worlds piled on top of each other... Whatever kind of sense *that* makes..."

"Dead worlds..." considered Gina. That sounded right. Did the goddess tell her something like that at one point? Or was it just something else she knew without being told? It was difficult to remember when most of your conversations with someone took place while you slept.

She glanced back at him, curious. Did those dreams he kept talking about come from the goddess, too? Was he like her?

But of course, no one was like her. Not really.

Andrea stepped up to the railing beside her and looked out over the black lake. "Are the things in the water still following us?"

"They are," she confirmed, relieved to have anything to think about besides how alone she was in the universe and the haunting idea of a dead world graveyard. She leaned over the railing and peered into those black waves again. She'd been feeling those things this whole time. At least six or eight of them at any given moment. They were attracted to the motion of the boat. Mostly they'd remained underneath them, in the black depths below, only occasionally approaching the surface. But that was when the water was deeper. For the past hour or so, however, the lake had been getting shallower. And those mysterious creatures had spread out more. Most of them were trailing behind them now, keeping pace in their wake. She still didn't feel as if they were in any immediate danger as long as they remained on the boat, but if this weird gravity were to push it too far down into the water...

She didn't dare say such a thing aloud. That wouldn't be helpful. It would only serve to frighten everyone else. Besides, it wouldn't make sense for their journey to end like that. According to the goddess, the Keeper arranged all this. Surely he would know enough to send them a mode of transportation capable of actually reaching their destination.

At least, she hoped so. It wasn't just the things in the water that worried her. She wasn't a very good swimmer.

"We're still on course, right?" worried Nicole.

"Yes," replied both Keith and Gina at the same time.

"I told you, I know where we're going," grumbled Keith.

"I can still feel the road under us," added Gina. "He hasn't veered off it once."

"What's that out there?" asked Andrea, pointing out into the darkness.

Gina squinted in the direction she was pointing. There was a shadow atop the water out there, difficult to see at the far edge of the trawler's lights. But that strange eye inside her head had no problem seeing it for what it was. "Shoreline," she replied.

"Land ho, or whatever," announced Keith.

The three of them looked forward as a night tree appeared from the gloom.

Gina turned and looked across the starboard side and saw that there were more night trees over there.

"I really don't like those things," grumbled Nicole.

"Why do they look like that, though?" asked Andrea.

"Weight of the worlds," replied Gina. She'd never seen a night tree with her own eyes before, yet she knew in an instant that there was something wrong with these. They looked sick. Their coiling, tendril-like branches dangled limp, many of them all the way down to the water below, and their mighty boughs sagged miserably, truly as if the weight of countless worlds were dragging them toward the earth.

"Shit..." sighed Nicole. "Even the murder trees are affected by it?"

"Seems like it."

As soon as they were past the depressed-looking trees, the shoreline receded again. But after a few minutes, more of them emerged from the gloom.

"Are those islands?" asked Andrea.

"Little ones," said Gina. "There are lots of them. A little like swampland. We're in shallows now. Lots of mud and silt. But the road's still down there, under it all."

"A road at the bottom of a huge ass lake..." wondered Nicole. "How the fuck do you even build something like that?"

"Maybe the road came first," suggested Gina.

Nicole frowned at this. "You mean that shit about someone out there *building* new universes? Seriously?"

She shrugged. "I can't say for certain. It's not like I've seen it with my own eyes. But I've heard it from more than just the goddess. And it's not just the physical world that starts over. Things change between old universes and new ones. What was and wasn't possible isn't always constant."

"Wow..." sighed Andrea.

"It sounds ridiculous, if you ask me," grumbled Nicole.

Andrea stared down into the water, contemplating it. "Is it really true then? Just...an endless cycle of dying worlds?"

"It's a fairy tale," said Nicole. "That's not how science works."

"There are plenty of things that science has nothing to do with," Gina explained. "Science is only a set of rules that dictates how the natural side of the universe works. And when a universe is created, those rules can be rewritten."

"It's nonsense..." she grumbled.

"It's almost depressing, isn't it?" pondered Andrea. "I mean, when you really stop and think about that. It means our world isn't ours at all. We're like...*aliens* or something. An invasive species, even, when you consider how much we're trashing it."

"You're not wrong there," agreed Nicole.

"And where did we start, then? What world? Where did it go? What was it like?"

"It's a good question," said Gina. She certainly didn't have the answer. Was it even possible to imagine an entire *universe* that hadn't existed in countless eons?

"What were those worlds like?" she went on. "I mean, were they all different? Were they, like, fantasy worlds with completely different kinds of life? Were there ever dragons? Or *unicorns?*"

Gina caught herself smiling a little at this. "Maybe."

"Maybe you can ask Ada about it next time we see her," suggested Nicole. "She said she's seen a few of them."

"She did say that, didn't she?" said Andrea, excited about the idea.

"I've heard magic was real once," said Gina.

Andrea's eyes lit up. "Really?"

"That's what I heard. I can't really say if it's true. Not for sure."

"Still, that's so cool!"

"Yeah…" And it *was* cool, when she stopped to think about it. But it was also kind of scary. A concept like magic was a two-way street, after all. Anything with a potential for such wonder almost always had an equal potential for darkness. For every amazing spell there could be seven terrifying curses. If she'd learned one thing in her unfortunate life, it was that light rarely came without shadow.

But she decided to keep her pessimism to herself this time. She rather enjoyed how happy Andrea looked at the idea of a world where real magic and unicorns were possible.

"What is that?" breathed Nicole.

Gina looked over to see her staring at something above and behind her. When she and Andrea turned to follow her gaze, they found an enormous shape emerging from the darkness in the trawler's flood lights.

"Some kind of structure," observed Keith, cutting back on the throttle.

"Fucking Christ…" sighed Nicole, relieved. "I thought that was some kind of monster for a second there."

"Ruins," said Gina, though like with so many things, she had no idea how she knew this. "Remnants of a world long dead. They've been here a long time. Longer than any of us can imagine."

Andrea walked to the railing on that side and peered up at it as they drifted past. It looked like a dome of some sort. It was mostly metal framework and broken glass. "That's really something from another world?"

"It's hard to explain, but there's something fundamentally different about it. Not just the age. It's the materials it's made from… The energy attached to it…" She shook her head. "It's…" She remembered the word Andrea used a moment ago: "...*alien*."

"You can just tell all that?" asked Nicole, impressed. "I mean, I know you said you know stuff, but...I mean, shit."

She shrugged. "I don't pretend to understand it, but I'm never wrong."

"What else can you tell about it?" wondered Andrea, curious.

"Not a lot." It was still kind of weird. Growing up, no one ever believed her when she tried to tell them about the things she knew. It was only in the past few years that she finally started meeting people who didn't treat her like a freak when they found out what she could do. After all those years, it was difficult opening up to anyone. But these people really did seem genuine. It was refreshing. But it was also a little scary. She couldn't help expecting something bad to happen every time she opened her mouth. "Most of it is underwater," she explained. "But it wasn't always. Only when it came here."

"When it came here?" asked Nicole. "What does that mean?"

"When that world died. That's what happens. When worlds die, the Wood swallows them. Forever."

"Heads up!" Keith called back from the bridge. "It's getting crowded out here!"

The three of them turned and looked forward. The boat was throttling down even more now and veering to the right, around a tall column of grayish, translucent material.

Gina stared up at it as they trudged past. She'd never seen such a thing in her life, but somehow she found herself convinced that it had something to do with energy. A battery, perhaps? Or maybe a trans-former? Or maybe it was some kind of completely unknown technology using completely foreign materials to utilize completely unheard-of energy types. These were entirely different *universes*, after all.

But then why did that queer sixth sense of hers insist she knew that this strange, crystal tower thing had something to do with energy? It was almost as if she'd seen it somewhere before, in some long-buried memory...

But then, her brain was like that sometimes. The way she simply knew things. There wasn't anything logical about it. She was just weird. Just a freak, like everyone always said she was...

Ada said she could sense the things in her environment, but also that she could sense things having to do with that weird, unnatural world. Things like Janon Tane.

Nicole and Andrea turned to watch as a smooth, black tower slid past them in the dark. It was a featureless cylinder, without windows or doors that they could see, stretching well up past the reach of the trawler's lights.

"Did this used to be some kind of city?" wondered Nicole.

"Part of one, I think," replied Gina. "I get an industrial sort of feeling from this stuff. People used to work here. Back when *here* was still somewhere else."

"So weird..." sighed Andrea.

Nicole nodded.

Gina turned and looked around, feeling the space around them. There was a lot of stuff under the water here. Much of it was debris and rubble from weaker structures that had collapsed. But there was a lot of garbage down there as well. Broken glass. Rotten lumber. Broken bricks and concrete. Posts and beams. Cables and pipes. And lots of strands of some kind of purplish papery substance that didn't dissolve or rot in the water, but just sort of collected on things in long, weed-like streamers. Something that sloughed out of the walls of the buildings in the lake's gentle currents over time. A type of insulation, perhaps? Or some kind of weatherproofing? Whatever it was, it didn't seem very eco-friendly.

But more importantly...

She turned and hurried up the steps, onto the bridge and to Keith's side, her usually sleepy eyes wide and alert as she peered into the darkness ahead of them. "There's some debris in the water up ahead," she warned, pointing. "You can't see it, but it's there."

"If you say so," he replied, already steering to port. "Tell me when I'm clear of it."

She glanced over at him. Here was yet another person who didn't look at her like she was crazy, who just accepted whatever senseless-sounding thing she said without wasting time. It still felt kind of unreal, if she were being honest. Like they were only toying with her.

Andrea and Nicole stepped up on the other side of Keith, looking out into that endless darkness ahead of them.

"You can straighten up again," said Gina.

"Aye-aye, ma'am," he replied without question, easing the wheel back to starboard.

The structures had disappeared back into the gloom behind them, but a number of those sickly night trees had appeared on the left again, growing right up out of the water.

There was something else beneath them now. She could feel it. A winding line of boxy objects. Vehicles of some sort? Strewn along a submerged street?

It was difficult to tell what every object she felt down there might have once been. There were too many of them. And they were too *unfamiliar.*

"There's something sticking up on the left," she said, pointing.

Keith leaned forward, eyes peeled. "I see it," he replied, veering starboard again. "Glad we have *you* aboard or we'd be literally sunk by now."

"Isn't she the absolute best?" asked Andrea.

Gina looked over at her, surprised. That awful, wounded part of her brain still insisted they must be making fun of her, but she knew better by now. Still, she wasn't sure how to even respond to something like that.

Not that these were the first people who were ever nice to her. Her roommates were also very kind to her. It was why she was so determined to keep them safe when Violet and Corey asked about them. Seph and Piper were like the family she never had growing up. And all their friends. Wanda and Amethyst. Kaitlyn, Alton and Phoenix. And then there was Seph's mom and Piper's parents. She'd half-convinced herself that they were only kind to her for their sake, but deep down somewhere she knew better than that.

The goddess promised her she'd eventually find what she was looking for if she followed her instructions…

"Keep right for a little bit."

Keith nodded and did as instructed.

She watched for a moment, keeping that strange, third eye fixed on the jagged shapes jutting up onto the left side of the mysterious path lying deep in the lakebed below them. Then she turned and looked behind them, out into the darkness at their backs.

There was something else under the water, too, something she didn't quite dare to mention. Something much bigger and more concerning than the things that had been keeping pace with them throughout the journey.

It wasn't moving. It was only lying there, amidst all the debris, invisible in the murky darkness to all but her with her strange senses. But for a moment, she felt its eyes staring back at her from those mysterious depths.

It saw them.

More than that, it saw *her.*

But it was slipping away with the rest of the unfathomable remnants of that dead world. Uninterested, perhaps. Or else merely biding its time…

"Should be clear now," she informed Keith, trying her best to sound like she wasn't frightened out of her mind.

"Thanks," he replied. "That was incredible. You're really something else."

"Isn't she?" gushed Andrea.

Gina crossed her arms and stared out through the windshield, embarrassed.

"Well, now that that's over, ladies," announced Keith. "I think we might finally be getting close. You might want to start preparing to disembark."

"Goody," grumbled Nicole as she turned and stalked away. "Time to get off the only thing keeping us safe. Can't fucking wait."

Keith looked like he wanted to say something snarky, but he set his jaw and focused on the path before them. "Galley's stocked," he said instead. "Make yourselves a nice meal. Can't say when you might get to eat again."

"I can make us something," volunteered Andrea as she followed Nicole off the bridge.

But Gina lingered a moment longer, her gaze fixed on the path before them. He was right. The lake path was coming to an end. She could almost see the dock in her mind's eye. And it left an unpleasant knot burning deep in the pit of her stomach to think about. This was uncharted territory, after all. Even her mysterious psychic senses couldn't predict what might be waiting for them on the road ahead.

Chapter 21

The stairs leading up from the carriage felt endless. Violet had lost track of the time, but it felt like they'd been climbing for at least an hour straight. Her legs were burning. And that strange heaviness in the air had only grown worse, leaving her gasping for breath in spite of the fact that she kept herself in pretty good shape.

Fortunately, she wasn't the only one. Albert and Brandy were both breathing hard as well. And poor Corey was practically panting.

They might have to stop and rest soon.

They didn't seem to be anywhere near the top yet. Corey's high-powered flashlight revealed nothing but more steps, so he'd pocketed it for the time being to save its battery and continued using the LED lantern to light their path.

Her thoughts kept circling back to the story Albert told them, about an ancient temple buried deep beneath the streets of Briar Hills. It sounded impossible, of course, but then again so did a great many of the things they'd found in their search for the unknown these past eight years.

And then there was the fact that Briar Hills was one of the cities on Corey's map of questionable and suspicious places. It was a veritable hotspot of local urban legends. Including *lots* of intriguing tales of subterranean tunnels of undocumented origin hidden just beneath its streets. Why *couldn't* such a place be hiding the entrance to an ancient underground structure?

Was that what *this* was? Were they inside another temple like the one Albert described? According to him, it was made entirely out of this same gray stone. Countless empty corridors and chambers that sounded just like the carriage house. And much more.

"I never thought I'd say this again..." huffed Brandy, "...but I'm starting to miss that hotel."

Albert gave a breathless nod and said, "Elevators."

"Margarita bar."

Violet chuckled. She liked these two. They were cute together.

She glanced back at them. "So you never really elaborated on that sex magic stuff. Are you guys, like wizards now or something?"

"*Sexy* wizards," Corey reminded her.

"We're *not* wizards," groaned Brandy.

Violet chuckled.

"We told you, we're not like that pervert."

"The whole point was to bring out some kind of latent psychic abilities, I guess," explained Albert. "He told us we could sense things. I know things about my environment. I can kind of tell when there's something that other people can't see. And she can sense things about the people around her."

"Cool," said Corey.

"*Very* cool," agreed Violet. "So *together*, you're like the perfect team."

"I...guess so...?" said Brandy, glancing over at Albert.

"Sort of like Gina," observed Corey.

"That's right," said Violet. "She knows things, too. *Lots* of things. Maybe she could help you guys learn to control it better or something."

"Maybe," agreed Albert. "At the very least, I think I'd be interested in having a conversation with her. Hear what it's like for her."

Brandy nodded.

"You guys'll love her," Violet decided. "She's a total sweetheart. Super shy, though."

"Quiet," agreed Corey.

I hope she's okay out there, she thought, but didn't dare say aloud. She kept thinking about Gina. Where was she? What challenges was she facing? She couldn't help feeling frightened for her. But in her experience, it never paid to give a voice to worries about things she couldn't control. It was far better to stay positive. Things usually worked themselves out.

Besides, Gina might appear small and meek, but she possessed some seriously kick-ass psychic powers. It was virtually impossible to catch her by surprise. She could see everyone coming from almost literally a mile away.

She pushed the pointless thoughts from her mind and focused on the stairs rising endlessly in front of them. They couldn't possibly go on forever.

Probably.

"It was so weird," agreed Violet. "It was just there and then it was gone. We never could find it again. I still can't explain it."

"Pocket dimension," grunted Corey.

"Pocket dimensions," repeated Albert, shaking his head. "That sounds like something out of *Star Trek*."

"It does," agreed Brandy, looking back at the straight path laid out behind them.

"It might have been a pocket," agreed Violet as she probed the surrounding forest with her light. "But it was just that one room, so if it was, it was the smallest one we ever found."

"Never found anyone who could decipher the writing in the pictures you took, either," he recalled.

"Never," she agreed.

"That *does* sound trippy," said Albert.

"Sounds *creepy*," decided Brandy.

The four of them stopped walking, confused.

"Wait…" said Brandy, her face scrunched up in a bewildered grimace. "What were we just talking about?"

"Were we…doing something else?" asked Violet. She turned and shined her light back down the steps. It felt like they were somewhere different for a moment. But…that wasn't true… They'd been climbing these stairs for…well, she wasn't sure how long it had been, but it was a while. The proof was burning away at her calves.

"Don't remember," said Corey, scratching at the back of his head.

"Me neither," said Albert. "But I feel like we missed something."

"Gone now," agreed Brandy.

"That was weird," said Violet. She felt like something had just happened…but she couldn't seem to recall it. She was thinking about Gina…how she was worried about her out there on her goddess-given mission to who-knew-where…and then…?

Nothing…

Then it was just now.

"Look up there," said Corey, lifting the lantern up over his head, letting the light reach out a little farther. Above them, the stone walls receded, opening into a vast and strangely ominous darkness.

"Is that the top?" asked Brandy. "Did we make it?"

"I really hope that wasn't just the first flight," gasped Violet.

They climbed onward, dismissing the strangeness from a moment before, eager to reach the top of this torturous stairway.

Chapter 22

Wayne stood on the platform, looking out into the endless darkness of the black forest that had haunted his nightmares for the past five years. Once again, he was struck by that strange *heaviness*. Was that something in his head, he wondered, or was gravity stronger here than it was back in his own world? Was this what it would feel like to travel to a larger planet?

Olivia had the right idea, he decided. She'd dragged her feet as much as possible, delaying the inevitable task ahead of them any way she could think of. Like deciding that everyone should use the bathroom one last time before setting off, as if she were the self-appointed mom of the group. And double—and triple—checking that they hadn't forgotten anything. She even took a few minutes to tidy up their room, saying it was only polite.

He didn't rush her. She'd come along soon enough. When she was ready. And he could hardly blame her. All he wanted in the entire world was for Max to turn around and take them back home. But that wasn't going to happen.

Everett, of course, was already off the train and roaming the stone platform, staring up at that empty black sky with that annoying look of childish wonder spread across his goofy face. (This kid was going to make this trip feel like an eternity. He was sure of it.)

Nadia had at least provided them each with a flashlight and spare batteries. That was far better than hoping his cell phone charge would hold out until they arrived at their destination.

"Windier than I remember," he observed. It wasn't exactly gusting, but there was a steady flow of air that was a little stronger than what he'd describe as a breeze.

"The compacted nature of the Denselands causes that," Nadia explained. "It pulls at the surrounding atmosphere from its center, which is where you're going, meaning you could even use it like a compass if you were to get lost. But I wouldn't recommend leaving the stone road unless you have absolutely no other choice."

"Gotcha," he grumbled, his gaze cast out over those nightmare trees with their twisted and coiling limbs that refused to even sway in the constant wind. They all looked strangely droopy, but they remained defiantly and unnaturally stiff, refusing to be budged.

"I really don't want to do this," whimpered Olivia as she appeared at his side, finally joining him on the platform.

"I know," he replied. "I don't either."

"Everything will turn out fine," Nadia assured them. "As long as you don't give up, you have everything you need to do this."

Wayne scowled. That seemed easy for her to say. She was staying on the fucking train.

"Hey!" Everett shouted back at them. He was pointing his light at an odd shape mostly hidden in the dark to the left of the platform. "What's that?" The sound of his voice made Wayne cringe. Should he be yelling like that out here? He was going to attract every monster within a five-mile radius!

But Nadia didn't seem concerned. She leaned out over the railing and shouted right back at him: "Debris from long-dead universes. Buildings, mostly. And other garbage. Most of it is wreckage, broken and scattered when the world they came from ended. But a lot of it is still intact. You'll find tons of stuff like that out here."

"That's so cool!"

Nadia giggled. "See? He's got the right attitude."

"What he's got," grumbled Wayne, "is some kind of *brain trauma*, I'm pretty sure."

Olivia jabbed him with her elbow. "Be nice!"

"Sorry."

Again, Nadia giggled.

Wayne lingered a moment, watching the mysterious shape Everett was shining his light at. It looked strange. He couldn't quite wrap his head around it. It looked like walls, but they were tapered and tiered in strange, overlapping patterns. But it was the colors that really stood out, he realized. It was shiny, despite its age, but it wasn't metal. It had an odd, muddy color, and yet it reflected Everett's light as if it were something much brighter.

"Things change when universes are built," said Nadia, as if reading his mind. "There are plenty of things that once existed that don't anymore. And there are things that exist now that once didn't. You won't be able to understand things that are gone. Don't get hung up on it. Leave the past where it landed."

He and Olivia exchanged a worried glance. What, exactly, did that mean? What kinds of things might they see out there?

"Stay on the path," warned Nadia. "Stay together. And use the gifts you've been given. They'll help you on your way."

The gifts they were given? Did she mean Olivia's psychic danger alarm? Or the thorn hanging around her neck?

Both, he quickly assumed. Anything that might give them an advantage. The real question, he supposed, was what did *he* have to offer? The fact that he'd come back from the dead twice? What good was that going to do them? If anything, wasn't he just running dangerously low on luck? And speaking of ill luck... "Back in Gutler's Weep..." he recalled, "Maeve said something was interfering with the cycle. Something a lot worse than that scarecrow man." He looked down at Nadia, into those emerald eyes. "What do you know about that?"

Her cheerful smile was strangely absent as she said, "I know there are few things that could possibly follow you here. But they *are* out there. I've been sensing something since these events began. Something that eludes me every time I try to focus on it. Something troubling... Something *chaotic*..."

He glanced at Olivia. She recognized it, too. That was the word Maeve used. Chaotic.

(*I sense a chaotic energy hovering over you, interfering.*)

Nadia lifted her face and looked up into the sky above. "Even now, eyes are following your every move."

He followed her gaze upward, half-expecting to see something monstrous peering down at him from that endless, empty sky, but he could see nothing.

"You'll have to be careful," she warned. Then she turned those emerald eyes on Olivia. "Trust your instincts. The threads will show you the way."

"Okay..." she said, looking not even remotely confident.

"You should go now," urged Nadia. "It'll only get more dangerous if you put it off."

"Yeah," sighed Wayne. "We're going."

"Wait," said Olivia, looking back at the car behind them. "What about that Austin guy? Isn't he coming?"

"He's already left," replied Nadia.

"He went on alone?" asked Wayne, surprised.

"Yeah, he seemed pretty impatient. He stepped off the rear platform before Maxie even came to a full stop."

He looked out into that darkness ahead of them, but he could see no sign of a light. While Olivia dragged her feet working up the courage she needed to set foot off this train, he must've acquired quite the lead. Would they be able to catch up to him?

Nadia crinkled her nose. "You guys aren't missing much. He wasn't very fun to talk to. He spent the whole trip with his nose in his book. He seemed kind of weird to me."

Wayne thought she was one to talk but decided against telling her so.

"Anyway, he's got his own job to do. Don't worry about him." She lifted her hand and waved. "Bye now. Good luck out there."

He and Olivia exchanged another uncertain glance, but then they stepped off the platform and onto the gray stone.

Nadia called it a station, but like the last one, it was little more than a stone slab raised to a level where they could easily step on and off the train. Which, he supposed was all a station really was... But there were no buildings, only a handful of those odd, square blocks rising up into that empty black sky with no discernable purpose. There wasn't even a sentinel statue to greet them.

A set of steps waited ahead of them, leading down to the path that continued on at ground-level, following the grade of the forest floor, like a wide sidewalk.

Nadia called it the stone road. Not the most creative of names, but certainly accurate, he supposed. There was nothing else to it. Just a smooth stone path leading off into the endless darkness.

He looked back as he approached the steps. She was still standing on the platform, waving cheerfully at them, as if they were off on a fun vacation instead of into some distant hell. He supposed it was better than watching the train speed away, abandoning them the way Max did back in that forest clearing.

Everett caught sight of them and set off down the steps ahead of them, taking the lead.

"Don't get too far ahead," called Olivia, as if she were talking to a child.

Or do, thought Wayne, but didn't dare say. Instead, he shined his light down at the ground in front of him. It really was the same stone he remembered from the temple. He could practically imagine that he was making his way down one of those dark, empty tunnels instead of along an open path with night trees looming on either side of him.

The Temple of the Blind... He couldn't believe they were back to this nonsense again. He hated everything about it.

And what was the deal with that Austin guy? What was he doing?

And how was it that he was fine to just march out into this wilderness alone and apparently utterly unafraid? It didn't make sense.

He's got his own job to do, he thought, remembering what Nadia told them. Did that mean he wasn't here for the same reason they were?

God, this was all so frustrating.

Olivia hugged his arm, pressing herself close to him as they walked. "We're going to get through this, right?"

He looked down at her, surprised. "Of course we are," he told her, as if he knew anything about what the next few hours might have in store for them.

"Promise?"

"Of course I promise. We have a date, remember? Someplace nice. Fancy dinner. No woods."

She giggled softly. "No woods," she agreed.

"Camping trips are *totally* off the table."

"*Please*," she laughed. But it was a short laugh. He watched her as those dark, beautiful eyes swept across the forest around them, at all those deadly night trees.

He couldn't imagine the memories that must be bubbling up from that awful well of nightmares deep inside her. The very thought made his heart ache.

He loved her so very much. All he wanted was to keep her safe. But they had to trek through this monster-infested forest while being stalked by some kind of ancient godlike evil? It was a miracle he even had her in his life right now. He screwed up his first chance at a happy ending. *Royally*. In a disgusting act of utter betrayal, no less.

Her name was Gail. His high school sweetheart. And back then, he truly believed that he loved her deeply and purely. But one crumby day he lost his mind. That was the only way he knew how to describe it. Because it never once even occurred to him that he'd ever even want to have sex with anyone else, much less his friend's girlfriend, Claire. And yet that was exactly what he did. It happened so suddenly. One moment everything was normal and the next moment everything was changed forever.

He never forgave himself for what happened that dark summer. And he was fully prepared to spend his life alone and unhappy because of it. Right up until the second Olivia fell into his arms.

He lived in absolute terror of losing her like he did Gail. He didn't want anyone else but Olivia, but he never wanted Claire, either. It wasn't a secret. He'd told her what happened back then, how afraid he was that there was something wrong inside him. There had to be. But she wouldn't listen to any of it. She insisted he'd never do something like that. Whatever happened back then, she told him, couldn't ever happen again. She said she could just tell.

And somehow, he almost believed her.

But that wasn't the only way to lose someone he loved. This place could take her away from him, too. What if he wasn't strong enough to do it all again? What if he screwed up even worse this time? What if this time he lost it all to the icy embrace of death, itself?

He didn't know what to do. He didn't understand any of this. If the Keeper wanted these doors opened so badly, why didn't he just go and do it himself? That was the part he was never able to understand about five years ago.

She nuzzled against his arm as they stepped between those unhealthy trees and he looked down at her. The feelings inside him were enough to make him feel a slight wave of dizziness.

No. He couldn't fail her. He *wouldn't*.

He'd protect her.

If it *killed* him, he'd protect her.

Chapter 23

Austin walked alone beneath the empty, heavy skies of the Denselands, unmoved by the added weight of the oppressive atmosphere.

He didn't bother watching where he was going. He didn't need to. He knew the way. He'd *always* known the way.

He kept his flashlight aimed at the book he was holding open in his left hand and, without looking up, casually veered around the twisted, drooping branches of a night tree hanging in his path. Although he knew there were plenty of dangerous things out here in this endless darkness, he didn't concern himself with them. Not in the slightest. He didn't care about them. He only cared about the words on the pages.

It was so much nicer out here on this quiet path than back on that train where that annoying, chatty little girl kept interrupting him.

He turned the page and kept reading, uninterested in the broken ruins of some long-dead world that he passed in the darkness. Uninterested in the pitiful, shuffling thing moving in the gloom. Uninterested in the small, dark shape that darted across his path a few yards ahead of him. He didn't care about a great many things, really. He had a job to do and that was all there was to it. He didn't even care about that small, black shape circling high above, the same small, black shape that managed somehow to stow away aboard the train that brought him here.

That was not his job.

That was not his problem.

His light and his gaze focused on the page in front of him, he kept reading and kept walking.

Chapter 24

The dock waiting at the far side of the lake was much like the one that appeared in Cedric's Cove, consisting of a large, rectangular slab of gray temple stone protruding from the shoreline. It looked just like a piece of the Temple of the Blind jutting out at them, and Nicole couldn't help feeling uneasy as she stepped off the boat onto it, like she was once again setting foot inside that same accursed labyrinth from that night five years ago.

But the temple was deep underground, hidden at the end of a convoluted system of manmade tunnels stretching deep beneath the streets of an unassuming Missouri city. This wasn't even underground.

And yet, it might as well have been. Although there were no claustrophobic walls closing in around her, there was little *else*. Beyond the reach of the trawler's lights was nothing but oppressive darkness.

And then there was that odd, *heavy* feeling, as if some great and invisible force were pushing down on everything. The air felt thicker, like those days that were so humid that it took your breath away to step outside, except there was no humidity. It wasn't hot. In fact, it was fairly cool in the constant wind that sent the loose strands of her ponytail fluttering past her face. And like that dense fog back on All Trails Crossing, it wasn't damp. It was just *heavy*.

"This stone path…" said Gina, shining her flashlight around. "It's the same road I felt at the bottom of the lake. It looks like we're supposed to keep following it."

"Do I want to know what you sense about this place?" braved Nicole.

She lifted her gaze and stared out into the surrounding darkness ahead of them. "Time," she replied. "Lots and lots of time. Like layers of rock laid on top of each other deep in the earth, mapping out unimaginable ages. There are things here from a past so distant it might not even be comprehendible to us."

"That's…*lovely*," she sighed. "Poetic. And unsettling as fuck.

Thanks."

"Sorry."

"Any idea how far we have to go now?" asked Andrea. She was still standing on the steps of the trawler, staring out at the dark path laid out before them, looking as anxious as Nicole felt.

"This was as far as the dream map in my brain went," said Keith as he slung his supply bag over his shoulder. "I have no idea what's waiting for us beyond this point."

"Us?" said Nicole, glancing up at him. "*You're* coming, too?"

"You were expecting me to *swim* back? There's not enough fuel for a return trip. This was one-way from the start."

"I vote for keeping him!" exclaimed Andrea. Then, when Nicole shot her a dirty look: "*What?* Safety in numbers? We already had to leave behind one big strong guy."

She rolled her eyes and started forward. "Fine, but he's *your* responsibility. Don't expect me to take him for walkies when he starts whining."

"Remind me how many times I had to save your ass just getting this far," Keith called after her.

"Eat shit."

"Well, this'll be delightful, won't it?" muttered Andrea as she stepped down onto the dock. "Just a happy little walk in the park…"

"Can't wait," agreed Keith.

"You guys really don't get along, huh?" said Gina, stepping up her pace to keep up.

Nicole glanced over at her. "It's complicated. Lots of feelings, I guess. Sorry."

"It's fine."

She glanced back one last time at the trawler with its engine killed and its comforting halo of flood lights extinguished. It felt like they were leaving behind the one safe place in this entire insane forest. But it wasn't as if they could take it with them. The path from this point forward was on land. And if it was really nearly out of gas, it wouldn't be of use to them much longer anyway. But still, she was going to miss that feeling of security, however fragile it might have really been.

They were each armed with a flashlight and Keith was carrying enough batteries to last days under normal conditions, but there was nothing normal about any of this. The weird physics out here had rendered the electronics on the trawler unusable. What if it drained all their batteries in just a few hours? For that matter, just how long were they going to be here? It felt like they'd traveled halfway around the world

Brian Harmon

just to get this far. And she had no idea what might be waiting for them from here forward. If it was half as terrifying as what they'd been through just to get this far, she wasn't sure she was brave enough to get through it. But there was no going back. And now she was being forced to keep traveling with her fucking *ex* of all people?

"Not enough fuel for a round trip," she muttered under her breath as she focused her attention forward again. "Fucking perfect…" Just how were they expected to get back home? And why didn't he bring extra gas cans? He said he picked up the boat in some normal lakefront town. Was he too dense to even check the gas before setting sail? "Dumbass…"

"What?" asked Gina.

"Nothing." She shined her flashlight out over a mound of scattered bricks and stone. "Can you feel if there's anything out here with us that we should be worried about? Living *or* dead?" Last time they were under this black sky, they found themselves under siege from both those flying carrion eater things *and* the shambling undead.

"Not anywhere nearby." Then she added, "Not since we left the water."

Nicole wondered what that meant. She'd already told them about the things keeping pace with the trawler as they traveled. Was there anything else she'd felt in those mysterious depths? But she quickly decided not to press for further information. She'd rather not know.

Gina shined her own light up at a series of dull gray, tightly packed disks sticking up out of the dirt like some kind of giant screw. It was impossible to tell if it was part of a building or some kind of machine. "It's hard to grasp just how old this place is. I've never felt anything like it. I don't even know how I know it. But it's almost overwhelming."

Nicole nodded. "I'm guessing I probably can't even imagine it."

"Probably not."

That was the worst part about all of this, she decided. Why was she so useless? Gina had these amazing powers to sense her surroundings and see things no one else could. Andrea could hear ghosts and see places like that creepy cemetery. Even Keith seemed to have some kind of weird-ass dream powers…

That was exactly what she needed. To feel even *more* useless. It was bad enough to be stuck out here with her ex-boyfriend, did he really have to be better than her at everything, too?

Ada told her there must be a reason she was here, that the Keeper didn't make mistakes. But what if she was wrong? What if she was the exception to the rule? What if she was the one fuckup that the Keeper couldn't plan around? That sounded exactly like the sort of superpower she'd probably end up with…

The four of them trudged along the stone pathway laid before them, their lights darting left and right and back and forth, their eyes peeled for danger. It didn't take long to realize that this was considerably worse than those cramped tunnels deep within the temple labyrinth. At least down there the scary shit could only come from one of two directions most of the time.

"What is this place?" asked Andrea. "I mean, Ada called it the Denselands, but what *is* it? Like, are we on the *other side* of the Wood?"

"This is just one part of that enormous forest," replied Keith. "I saw that much in my dreams. Like how Briar Hills is just one small part of the planet, the Denselands is just a single dot on the greater map. But even that little dot is a *huge* expanse of space. Like, maybe *bigger than our whole world* big."

"Yeah, not intimidating at all," grumbled Nicole. "Piece of cake."

"And we're a *long* way from home," he added. "A lot farther than we should've been able to go in that time on an ordinary boat like that. I don't know how I know it, but I do. And I definitely don't understand it."

"Something about this path we're on," said Gina. "It has built-in shortcuts. I could feel it while we were on the boat. Speed and distance were distorted in ways I can't describe." She looked back over her shoulder, a thoughtful look on her face. "We're way off the map."

"You guys aren't making me feel any better about this," whimpered Andrea.

"Sorry," said Gina.

"Night trees," warned Nicole, her flashlight illuminating those ominous, coiled branches looming uncomfortably close to the path ahead of them. "Don't get too close. They sleep in the dark and start waking up when there's light. Even little flashlights like these. Too much light for too long and they go full-on *Little Shop of Horrors*."

"We remember," said Andrea. She'd wanted to leave the trawler idling, letting the gas run out on its own, since it was only going to sit there abandoned anyway. Those bright lights would have made a nice beacon at their backs for at least a little while. But Nicole and Gina both vetoed it, saying it would only serve to wake up any nearby slumbering trees and perhaps draw the attention of worse things.

"They don't look like much," observed Keith. They still looked rather sickly and wilted, with their drooping branches.

"They looked a lot healthier last time," admitted Andrea. Although they still looked plenty scary, if you asked her.

"Everything about this place is broken," explained Gina. "The ground and the air. Gravity and pressure. Space and time. It's all crinkled up here. It's constantly fighting against anything living. Those trees are struggling just to exist. And the same thing will happen to us if we're here long enough."

Andrea let out a frightened groan. "Don't tell me stuff like that!"

Those droopy limbs weren't the only thing off about these trees, Nicole realized as they crept past. That strange, flesh-like bark looked sickly, too. It was marred and discolored in places. One of them appeared to have a sizeable gash torn out of it and had oozed a black puddle of gory sap onto the lifeless soil around it. Another one appeared to be covered in strange, pale blisters.

And then there was the fact that they weren't moving *at all*, not even in the wind that was blowing through them. Were they even still alive?

"She's not wrong, though," said Gina. "About how dangerous they are. I can feel them. They're not really trees. But they're not animals, either. They're something entirely different from anything in our world. And even sick, they're still incredibly dangerous. When I look at them, all I can picture in my head is blood raining down from their branches."

"No loitering under the trees," concluded Keith. "Got it."

Nicole didn't want to agree with anything Keith said, but she nodded anyway. Those things definitely weren't dead if they were still dangerous. *Could* something like that even die?

They picked up their pace, eager to put distance between themselves and the slumbering night trees. Each of them remained careful to keep their lights aimed at the ground until they were well out of reach of those grasping limbs.

Safety first.

There weren't nearly as many night trees along this path, however, as there were in the areas surrounding Gilbert House and the temple. That was one positive detail Nicole was able to find. The rest of the landscape appeared to be cluttered with rubble and debris.

Gina said the things here were ancient beyond imagining. What did that mean, exactly? How old was she talking? Because this wasn't the remains of some stone-age world. There was *metal* sticking out of the ground over there, part of some kind of machinery, from what she could tell. Were these the remains of *another* world? One of those that mankind migrated from, like the Sentinel Queen claimed?

But those worlds had ended…hadn't they?

Gina stopped walking and looked back the way they came, her sleepy gaze cast out across the dark wasteland.

"What's wrong?" asked Nicole. "You sense something?" If she'd learned anything during this insane nightmare journey, it was to trust Gina's intuition. It had already saved them several times.

"It's hard to tell from here…" she replied, squinting into that eerie darkness. "Everything gets fuzzy at a certain distance. Something about the broken properties of this world."

Nicole glanced around, concerned. She didn't care for the idea of Gina's fantastic psychic senses being limited here of all places.

"But I feel like maybe we should pick up the pace a little," she added, still staring off into the distance at something the rest of them couldn't see or hear, a look of uncertain concern painted across her soft features. "Just in case."

"Yeah…" squeaked Andrea. "Let's do that."

Nicole didn't need to be told twice. She was already moving. "Yeah, you just keep watching whatever it is you think you're feeling and let us know if we should start running."

Chapter 25

As the glow of their flashlights withdrew into the black forest, the trawler creaked and groaned against its mooring, as if complaining to the empty sky that it would never again leave this spot.

But it wasn't alone just yet.

One last passenger remained.

A foul odor sullied the air, undetected by human noses. Soggy boots sloshed water across the deck, unheard. And foul, black gore dripped, unseen, from festering wounds.

One glazed eye stared blind into the oppressive gloom, seeing without seeing, watching the fading flashlights with an inhuman and sadistic hunger.

"Anun amum ut mu…" spoke a choked and gargled voice full of foul and bloody lake water. Swollen, fleshy lips pulled back in an awful mockery of a smile. "Anun Goar Nangup."

Chapter 26

"Okay," wheezed Brandy. "We reached the top. Can we go home yet?"

The stairs leading up from the sentinels' carriage house opened directly onto a stone landing in the middle of a vast and eerily quiet darkness. The only sound was the wind, Albert immediately noticed. Not particularly strong, but constant. It came in from behind them, pushing at their backs as if urging them forward.

Corey pulled out his flashlight and switched it on. Its impressive beam pierced the darkness well beyond the reach of the lantern, revealing a startling landscape of broken walls and strewn debris.

"It looks like a disaster happened here," said Brandy.

"It did," realized Albert. "The worst kind of disaster."

She glanced over at him, surprised.

"Lucianna told us this was a gathering place for dead worlds, remember?"

"Oh fuck..." she sighed, her pretty eyes washing over the crumbling remains of what she realized was once some kind of building.

Corey was already moving forward ahead of them, his powerful light probing the mysterious darkness. All around them, the remains of a building of dingy white stone jutted up from the earth like jagged teeth. An angular chunk of rusty metal and splintered, gray boards were thrust out at them from one side, the possible remains of a roof. Several large posts of dull, orange-tinted metal protruded from the rubble. A simple black box, about the size of a van, was half buried in the remains of a collapsed section of wall. And there were hundreds of bright silver cables strewn through the littered debris that shimmered and glittered when the light passed over it.

"I don't even recognize most of this stuff," observed Brandy as she stepped gingerly through the broken brick and stone.

"Me neither," agreed Violet. "Like, what kind of metal is that?"

Albert didn't need to ask what she meant. He'd already noticed it.

It looked like all this had been lying here for ages. It was covered in thick layers of settled dust, but those cables looked brand-new. They hadn't oxidized or tarnished at all in the time they'd been lying there. "It's literally the remains of another universe. It could be a kind of metal that we never discovered in ours. Or one that doesn't even *exist* anymore."

"Holy shit…" Violet shined her flashlight around, looking at everything. In their work, they'd seen countless abandoned buildings, but she'd never seen anything like this. What were those orange posts? Some kind of structural beams? It all looked so *alien*. But that was exactly what Albert was saying, wasn't it? This stuff all came from *another world*.

"I don't really know any more than you do about it," he went on, "but from what everyone's saying, the universe exists in some sort of cycle. It's born…and then time passes. Maybe millions or billions of years—I don't even know—and then it dies. This stuff could be from the last universe or it could be from a universe that existed a hundred cycles ago. We have no way of knowing."

"Why would anything *that* old still exist, though?" wondered Brandy.

"Broken time," said Corey.

"Time gets wonky across borders," Violet elaborated. "Doing what we do, we almost always experience a loss of time at some point. It's possible that in a place like this, it might slow to a crawl. Or maybe time passes but doesn't affect things the same way. Who knows?"

Albert cast his flashlight beam out over the ruins as they walked through them, taking it all in. It was difficult to imagine that mankind could survive long enough to finish *one* world, much less hop their way through a veritable multiverse of earths. The history books were filled with examples of how humanity seemed to be perpetually on the brink of wiping itself out.

And if advanced civilizations had migrated into the current universe, why was there so little recorded history? Was there some mechanism by which human societies were periodically reset and wiped away?

"You know," said Violet, "according to our friends, the universes weren't just born. They were *crafted*. Constructed by some kind of god-like entities they called *Architects*, with these crazy, all-powerful, cosmic tools."

"Things like the Grim Reaper's scythe," added Corey. "And Rumpelstiltskin's spinning wheel."

"Well *that* sounds made up," grumbled Brandy.

"We're ones to talk," Albert reminded her.

She shrugged. "Still…"

Albert's light fell on a strange and ominously familiar shape jutting up from the debris. It was a gnarled mass of coiled, fleshy branches. "Night tree…" he warned. Proof enough, he supposed, that they really were back in the Wood.

"*That's* a night tree?" Violet stared at it. "I've heard of them, but I've never seen one."

"Doesn't look dangerous," observed Corey, adding his light to hers. "Looks dead."

"Don't shine your lights on it!" exclaimed Brandy. "That's what wakes them up!"

Their flashlight beams dropped to the ground as if they'd suddenly grown heavy.

"Sorry…" said Brandy, grimacing a little at herself. She didn't mean to freak out. "One of those things nearly killed us five years ago."

Violet nodded. "Understood. Safety first."

"Wind don't blow their branches," observed Corey.

She looked up, surprised. "You're right…"

Albert had noticed that, too. He didn't see that five years ago. The trees he saw up close that night were in various stages of waking up. But he remembered Wayne telling them once or twice that he remembered the trees out in that dark forest not being stirred by the breeze, not even the littlest dangling branches. He'd often wondered what kind of wood those things were made of. Were they even wood? Or if he cut through that fleshy bark would he see flesh and bone?

He didn't care to think too much about it.

"So how do we know which way we're supposed to go?" wondered Corey, apparently already over the man-eating trees.

Albert shined his own light down at the ground. "The stone."

The others all looked down. There was, indeed, more of that same gray stone peeking out from under all the debris.

"It's the path the sentinels laid out for us. I noticed it kept going after we reached the top of those steps. So it's not just part of the carriage house structure. It's a *road*."

"Follow the road," said Violet, recalling what the twins said to them back in that creepy junk shop. (*One by water. One by land. And one by shadow.*)

Corey was recalling the same thing. "Shadow road," he agreed, nodding.

She thought they were only talking about the carriage, but the road continued on. *We've provided almost everything,* she recalled Cob telling them, *to ride the shadows.* But the road didn't end where the carriage stopped.

"I'm betting it's important to stay on the path," reasoned Albert.

"Shortcuts," Corey remembered, nodding. "Safe passage."

"Right." Although he had no idea how those things were supposed to work. It was just a stone pathway laid out before them. There was absolutely nothing to protect them out here.

"Sounds like a plan to me," said Violet. "And any plan's better than no plan."

But as they pushed forward, they found that staying on the path wasn't as simple as that. Within minutes, an enormous wall of black metal appeared before them, blocking the way.

"Road ends here," announced Corey, as if they needed his excellent observational skills to tell them that. He pointed his light left, then right, revealing no end in either direction.

"Is this some sort of building?" wondered Violet.

It was a good question. Albert shined his light up at it. It didn't look like it was built here. It was crumpled and creased in places. It looked like something that had fallen across the path. A tower of some sort? A skyscraper?

But then, there weren't any windows he could see...

Corey shined his light up toward the top of the wall. It wasn't vertical. It curved back as it went up. "No way over. Gotta go 'round."

Albert looked back and forth, uncertain. He didn't care for the idea of leaving the road. This was the Wood, after all. And the Wood was dangerous. But Corey wasn't wrong. If there was no way over the obstruction, they had no choice but to circle around it.

Corey examined the debris on either side, then decided that right looked like the better option and simply started in that direction without any discussion.

Violet set off after him without question.

Albert and Brandy hesitated a moment longer, but then they, too, followed the big guy into the black unknown.

Chapter 27

This.

Was.

Awesome!

It was all Everett could do to contain the giddy excitement building up like a geyser inside him as he shined his light out into the forest of strange, black trees all around him. The branches were knotted and twisted, at the same time coiled and bristled. Their bark was shiny and smooth, almost *slimy*, with a strange, latticework sort of pattern. They looked like something from a Tim Burton movie, he thought. Especially the strange, melty way that they drooped toward the ground like that. Wayne said they were dangerous. *Man-eaters*, he said, though he couldn't quite figure out how they could eat anything. He saw no mouth. Did they, like, split open down the middle or something? That would be so cool to see!

They told him there were also zombies in these woods. Not just animal zombies like what attacked them back in the fairy circle, but *real* ones. Reanimated *people*. He hoped he'd get a chance to glimpse at least one of those. They also described some kind of flying scavenger. And then there was all that stuff Nadia mentioned, too.

He had so many questions. Not the least of which was how did a place like this even work? How was there no sun in the sky without everything freezing over? Where were they that they couldn't see a single star? And how did this simple stone path protect them from all the things that were supposed to be prowling out there?

It didn't even feel like the same planet. Gravity felt stronger. The air felt thicker. It felt like the very atmosphere was pressing down on him, as if he were deep underwater instead of walking on dry land.

He could barely contain himself, and yet he didn't dare voice any of these questions. He didn't need to be psychic like Olivia to see that Wayne was done putting up with his childishness. But even more than that, there was something about that frightened look in poor Olivia's eyes that made him keep it all to himself.

He found that he really didn't like seeing her upset.

"How're you doing?" he heard Wayne ask her.

"I'm scared," she replied quickly. "But Nadia was right. It's safer on the path. As long as I focus on going forward, I don't feel too bad, but when I even think about stepping off it and going any other direction…" she shuddered hard at a fresh wave of dread at the very mention of it. "It's *bad*," she finished, those pretty eyes wide with fear.

Everett looked down at the stone path beneath his feet. It ran in a straight line, following that strange, constant breeze, but hugged the contours of the ground perfectly where the terrain rose and fell along the low, rolling hills of the surrounding landscape. Was it really an ancient feature built by a faceless race of monsters? And did it really have the power to protect them from all the dangers out here?

He thought back to the fairy circle, to those mysterious mushrooms he saw growing that pointed the way to the clues leading him to the remains of that old school. Maeve said those were a manifestation of his own special ability, a sign he could follow to her, to finally set her free.

It didn't feel like some kind of supernatural power. They just looked like mushrooms. He didn't remember ever consciously thinking that he should follow them. He sort of did it automatically, almost at random. Would he be able to do something like that again someday? Or was that something only Maeve could make him do?

Or might any of what he was looking at right now be like that? Was there anything here, like those mushrooms, that only he could see?

So many questions…

He shined his light off to the right of the path and onto something lying there. "Is that a car?" he asked, stopping.

Wayne and Olivia turned their lights onto it as they approached. "Looks like it," agreed Wayne. "Sort of?"

It did, indeed, look like a car, but not like any kind of car he'd ever seen before. It was oddly shaped. Rounded in places but squared off in others. It had four wheels, doors, windows, a windshield and headlights. But all of those things were oddly shaped. The wheels were small. The windows were narrow. The headlights seemed to run the full length of the front of the car in a little arc that sort of jutted outward over the bulky bumper. And it was surprisingly small, without much space in either the front or the back. It didn't look like an ordinary engine would fit in it.

It was kind of ugly, he thought. It was an odd shade of orangish gray. There didn't seem to be any rust on it. Instead, whatever it was made of seemed to be shriveling up like the skin of an old plum. The glass was intact, but foggy. And the tires seemed to be crumbling into little brittle pieces. He tried to picture what it might've looked like when it was brand new, but even then he couldn't imagine it looking even remotely attractive. Still, it was intriguing. Was this what people drove around in a past universe? Like, was this what their version of Ford made instead of Mustangs? He shined his light around, but there weren't any more to compare it to. Maybe vehicles were a novelty in whatever world it came from?

"Looks like a deathtrap to me," decided Wayne.

"You think *all* cars are deathtraps," Olivia reminded him.

"They are. How many times do I have to die in one to make my point?"

"Already once too many," she replied, squeezing his arm.

Everett still couldn't believe that both he and Wayne had died and come back. In a vehicle no less! Although they were, admittedly, two very different scenarios.

Wayne kept moving, uninterested in examining the alien Chevy further.

He lingered a moment longer, still curious, but then he followed after them.

A few minutes later they came across a broken concrete cylinder lying across the path, about seven feet in diameter. It looked like a large storm culvert, but there was strange, rusted machinery running through it. Without knowing exactly what it was, he couldn't even guess whether it was always horizontal or if it once stood vertical and fell here at some point.

But it didn't slow them down. Broken as it was, it was easy enough to step over it and continue on their way.

His companions didn't bother trying to make sense out of it, he noticed. They just carried on as if ancient machinery from another world was something they stumbled across every day. He couldn't quite understand it himself. Weren't they the least bit curious? If what they were being told was true, then they were all essentially aliens from another *planet*. This was an astronomically rare chance to get a glimpse of what some of those old worlds were like. He understood better than anyone about being scared, but who wouldn't want to know something like that?

Was he really the weird one here?

But as he glanced back one last time at the puzzling piece of ancient human history, he was distracted by something small and dark darting out from under the broken concrete and vanishing into the woods beyond the reach of his light.

His breath caught in his throat. That was too small to be one of those zombies they warned him about. It looked like some kind of animal, but it disappeared too quickly for him to get a proper look at what kind. It could have been almost anything.

It didn't seem worth it to point it out. They probably didn't want to know anyway. Nadia said this stone path would keep them safe, but he'd keep an eye out and let them know if he saw any more.

When he looked forward again, he saw that one of those unusual trees was drooping over the path. Wayne and Olivia were veering around it, but they didn't quite dare to step all the way off the safety of the path, so they ducked down low and slipped under the branches instead, doing their best not to touch any of them.

It seemed sort of silly. What could little branches like that do? But he followed their lead and did the same.

Alien… The word kept circling in his head. Was that really what they were? Except instead of descending from the stars, they all crossed over through some underground stone temple from an entirely different universe?

The Denselands are a place filled with mysteries, he remembered Nadia telling them. *It's littered with the relics of countless histories. No one knows what might still exist out there.* Those words still thrilled him to his very core. And what she said next: *Treasures untold, no doubt.* His imagination was practically set ablaze with the possibilities. But of course, he'd be foolish not to also recall the warning that came with it: *But also horrors beyond measure.*

He pushed on through the darkness, shining his light out into that endless black forest, wondering what kinds of amazing things he was going to see before it was all over.

He could barely stand it!

This.

Was.

Awesome!

Chapter 28

So this was the Denselands... Or, at least, that was what the goddess called it.

Gina, for one, could understand why it would have such a name. To that mysterious, troublesome part of her weirdo brain that told her all the impossible things, it felt sort of like how water pressure increased against your ears as you dived deeper below the surface. It was like the very atmosphere was weighed down, condensed beneath the unfathomable gravity of all the dead worlds collected here. The air was thick. Her body felt heavy. And the very landscape was strangely compressed.

"Crinkled" was the word she used when they first arrived. And it was still the best way she could think to describe it. It was as if someone had wadded up the world like a map, folding it over on itself, allowing unrelated points to touch so that the distance between any two places became maddeningly inconsistent. They could travel a thousand miles in two steps or walk for hours and go only a few inches.

It was only the curious stone road beneath their feet that kept them on course. It seemed to be immune to the unreliable physics of this broken place, running straight and true even when the landscape, itself, was warped and twisted. But at the same time, it seemed to be able to *use* the crinkles in the map to carve a shortcut, allowing them to cover even greater distances than when they were on the boat.

"Feel anything dangerous?" asked Nicole.

The honest answer was very much yes. She could sense things all around them. Most were small, but some were roughly man-sized. One some distance to their left was about the size of a full-grown dairy cow. Most of them weren't moving very much, if at all, but plenty of them were crawling about the forest floor like scuttling bugs. There was one area, however, ahead of them and to the right some distance, where she could sense several dozen small and unpleasant things swarming about like sewer rats within the remains of some kind of collapsed structure.

But it didn't seem like a good idea to alarm everyone, especially when none of these things appeared to be taking any notice of them. Lying about it didn't feel right, either, though, so she opted for a more neutral response: "Nothing's noticed us."

Nicole nodded, satisfied with that answer.

"Olivia and Wayne said the Wood was filled with zombies when they were stranded out in it," said Andrea. "They said it was, like, full-on *Walking Dead* out there."

"Well *that* sounds like a fun time," muttered Keith.

"There's nothing out here like that," said Gina. These things were different from anything she ever felt in their own world. They were like the trees, neither really plants nor animals but something altogether different. There didn't seem to be any distinction between living and dead here. Although there *were* organic things scattered around this landscape, bits and pieces of dead creatures that she couldn't quite iden-tify, remains of things that had been here a very, very long time, proba-bly having arrived with the ruins and debris of all the worlds collected here. Practically fossils…and yet that strange psychic sense insisted that death wasn't black and white here, that few things were ever really gone.

"I wonder why?" said Andrea, staring out into those trees. "Not that I'm complaining," she quickly added.

Gina didn't know. Zombies weren't something she'd encountered before. But she didn't doubt for a second that they could be real. Why not? It wouldn't be any less believable than half the things she *had* felt roaming the world. Maybe it had something to do with how deep in the Wood they were. There were no people out here to turn into zombies. Except for the four them, she supposed, which wasn't a thought she wanted to dwell on.

"Just let us know if anything gets anywhere near us," insisted Ni-cole.

"I think we're safe on the path," she assured her. She didn't really understand it, but it felt to her like there was some kind of otherworldly protective quality about it. As far as she could tell, nothing had taken any notice of them whatsoever. It was as if it masked their presence somehow, allowing them to slip by undetected.

It was the very same road she felt running along the bottom of the lake beneath the trawler that whole time. Did it have the same pro-tection back there, too? She remembered those mysterious things that were swimming along with the boat. Those had definitely detected them. But they never attacked. Nor did that monstrous thing she sensed lurking deep in the lakebed toward the end of their journey. Was that thanks to the road's curious protective attributes as well?

Before she could ponder it further, she was distracted by a strange collection of broken structures off to the left. It wasn't something they were merely nearing as they traveled. A moment ago, none of it was there. The entire space around them had abruptly changed.

They'd skipped ahead through the crinkled space.

At the same time, she realized that other nearby ruins, like the one with the nest of swarming rat-like things, had vanished. It made her think of a travel montage in the movies, like when the Fellowship of the Ring was shown passing through all the different regions of Middle Earth in *The Lord of the Rings*. It was a little disorienting.

But she didn't dwell on it. She was too distracted by those structures. There were about five of them in all, packed closely together, as if an entire chunk of a city street had dropped out of the sky. Most of them had collapsed into rubble, but one was still partially intact. There was a space still standing in one corner of it, sealed off from the vast and dangerous outside world.

And there was something *in* that space.

At first, she thought it was a person. But that couldn't be a human. Her psychic mind told her that it had been there a very long time, even longer than the goddess had been around.

Far longer than anybody had any right to exist.

There was a terrible aura about that space. A darkness even blacker than the depths of that empty and ever-looming sky above. It felt dreadful, as if something about it were pulling at her, attempting to draw her into it. It filled her mind with unpleasant and twisted emotions. Fear. Loneliness. *Hopelessness*. But also anger. Bitterness. *Hatred*. She suddenly wanted to *hurt* someone.

But of course that wasn't real. That wasn't *her*.

The things in this place couldn't make her like them. She wouldn't allow it.

Whatever was in there was neither alive nor dead. It was now broken and tarnished in terrible ways, filled with overwhelming misery...endless suffering...and *madness*... *So much* madness... She could feel it there, like a living, *pulsating* thing, rhythmic, like the beating of a withered heart. And *time*... So very much time... She could almost *taste* the passage of it, bitter and sour and rancid, capable of slowly eating away one's very humanity, leaving nothing but monstrosities behind.

Then, just as quickly as they appeared, those structures were gone again.

They'd passed through another crinkle in the map. They were somewhere else now. Another structure had appeared up ahead, this one also partially intact, but mercifully empty this time.

It was a relief to be away from that other place, but as she pushed onward, it lingered in her mind, her psychic brain still processing the strange input of data it received from there.

Was that what Andrea meant by zombies? Had somebody been transported here when their world fell apart, only to spend eons trapped inside that space, never truly dying, never truly decaying, only *lingering...*

On and on...

Forever...

She repressed a shudder and forced herself to keep walking. She didn't want to frighten anyone. She needed to focus on keeping every-one safe. That was what was important. That was the job the goddess gave to her.

But as she pushed forward, a brand-new awareness blossomed in her mind, this one so intense that her whole body shuddered and she dropped to her knees, the wind sucked out of her.

"What's wrong?" worried Nicole, crowding over her. She was shining her light around, looking for whatever perilous thing must have caused her to sink to the ground like that. But she wasn't going to be able to see it. She couldn't. By the time it was that close, it would al-ready be too late.

"We have to hide," she gasped.

"What?" asked Andrea, frightened.

"From what?" asked Keith.

Gina stood up, steeling her nerves against the dreadful feeling, then grabbed Nicole by the hand and hurried forward, practically drag-ging her.

The new structure that appeared a moment ago, the one that was still partially intact. That was their best bet.

"What do you see?" asked Nicole. "Where is it?"

But she couldn't answer her if she wanted to. There weren't any words to describe it. It was like nothing she'd ever sensed before. And it wasn't coming from any *direction* at all. It was...moving *sideways?* Or maybe *diagonally?* She wasn't sure how to best describe it. All she knew was that it was coming. It would be here soon. And they couldn't let it see them. "Everybody inside!" she hissed.

"Inside *where?*" asked Andrea, confused.

But then their lights found it. An old, square structure, like the remains of something out of a renaissance fair or something, made from stone and wood, with a broken door and a collapsed roof.

"Everyone be quiet!" she said as she ushered them through the doorway and into the cramped space inside.

"Is it safe?" worried Nicole.

It was a good question, but one they didn't have the luxury of worrying about. She crowded in behind them and urged them deeper inside.

"Nobody make a sound," she whispered. "Or we'll all die."

Chapter 29

The obstruction blocking the shadow road didn't stretch far into the surrounding Wood. It came to an end within a few hundred feet. And yet it still felt entirely too far off the path for Brandy's liking. The longer they spent going around things like this, the longer it was going to take to get this awful ordeal over with so she could finally go home.

Corey didn't seem to share in her hurry, though. He was taking his time, looking around, examining everything. As they circled around the end of the obstruction, he stopped and shined his light up onto it, examining it. "Boat."

The three of them all turned their lights up onto the towering wall to see that the front of the object tapered into a telltale point. It did, indeed, look like the bow of a boat. Although the better word for it was probably *ship*. It was enormous. And it didn't look like any kind of ship Brandy had ever seen. The hull looked like it could have belonged to one of those massive cruise liners, but much larger. Above that, barely visible even in Corey's powerful light, was a tightly packed mass of crowded structures and machinery that looked more like a ruined industrial complex than the deck of any ship she'd ever seen. The entire thing was tipped hard to its port side and partially crushed under its own weight, scattering debris well beyond the reach of the light. To Brandy, it looked like the aftermath of a tornado.

"Why's there a boat?" wondered Violet. She shined her light out into the forest around them, confused. She couldn't see very far, but she certainly hadn't seen any water. This was a forest, not a bay.

"Tsunami?" offered Corey.

"That doesn't sound right," said Albert. "Everything else here would be flattened if a tidal wave that big washed through here."

Corey shrugged. It was the only explanation he had. He showed no interest in coming up with any more.

Getting around the misplaced vessel was going to be harder than any of them anticipated. The debris from the crumpled ship made it impossible to hug the hull of the ship on the way back like they did on their way out. They'd either have to climb over the dangerous wreckage or circle all the way around it. Neither option was particularly ideal, as far as Brandy was concerned.

She never saw a lot of the Wood five years ago. She glimpsed those awful trees from Gilbert House's second- and third-floor windows. But unlike Wayne and Olivia, the only time she spent outside was on the burning mountain, where the night trees were scarce and the only zombies were the broken ones Kneede's corpse monster dumped in their path. But that was more than enough to convince her that she never wanted to see any more of it.

Yet here she was.

She eyed a nearby night tree. It looked strange. Droopy. Sickly. With odd little white blisters on one side of its fleshy trunk like drops of splashed paint. But it was definitely the same monstrous shape that nearly killed her that night. She, Nicole and Albert were all caught in those strangling, biting branches. If not for Andrea's quick thinking, they wouldn't be here today.

Or was it *Wayne's* quick thinking? Andrea always insisted it wasn't her idea to set Albert's backpack ablaze and send it up into those snatching branches. She said a ghost whispered it in her ear. Because apparently a forest of black, fleshy, man-eating trees filled with insatiable zombies in an eternal night under a sky with no moon or stars wasn't terrifying enough. It needed to be haunted on top of it all.

But why did they all look like that? She swept her light back and forth, not letting it linger on any one tree for more than a second or two. Their branches were a lot limper than the ones she remembered on the burning mountain. Had all the wreckage piled up around them stunted their growth or something?

She reached for Albert's hand, but he wasn't standing beside her where she last saw him. He'd stopped and was shining his light out into the darkness.

"What's wrong?" she whispered, her gaze washing across those trees. "Did you see something?"

"No," he replied. He didn't feel the need to whisper, which was a good sign, but he kept his voice down. "And I can't stop wondering *why*."

She frowned at this, confused. "What?"

"Where are all the zombies? I thought Wayne said they were *swarming* out here."

"Sweetie, isn't that a *good thing*?"

He chuckled a little at this. "Yes. It is. But I can't help wondering why. Like, *where are they?*"

She considered the question for a moment, her flashlight drifting from night tree to night tree. "Olivia was out there that whole time waiting for Wayne to rescue her and nothing attacked her," she reasoned. "Well, I mean except for the thing that dragged her out there in the first place, obviously. It sort of sounds like those were only swarmed around Gilbert House."

"That's true," he admitted.

They'd heard the story many times, about how Wayne had wandered through that awful forest, armed only with his flashlight and an old man's cloak that was somehow supposed to smell like something even more terrifying than zombies so that it scared them away.

It didn't make much sense to her. *Could* zombies smell? It seemed to her that a functioning nose was the *last* thing a rotting corpse should have. Albert deduced that it was probably less about scent and more about *presence*, that it was probably something psychic. But that didn't make it any easier to understand. If anything, that made even *less* sense to her.

But it worked. Wayne said that the things he saw scurried from his path as he crept through this nightmare forest in search of Olivia. For a while, anyway. Eventually it began to wear off. And by the time he found her, the dead had already lost their fear of whatever the old cloak imitated. Their escape had been the stuff of suspense stories. A mad dash through a horde of grabbing, biting zombies. Scurrying up a waking night tree to escape a giant, living mass of broken corpses and fleeing for their lives through the blood-soaked hallways of Gilbert House...

"Don't fall behind," Violet called back at them.

Corey was already well ahead of them, searching the wreckage for a clear path.

Brandy grabbed Albert's hand and pulled him along. "Come on."

"Sorry," he sighed, still shining his light out into those droopy night trees. "I know a zombie is the last thing we need to deal with right now, but I also can't stop wondering where they all are."

"I know." She understood why he was concerned. After all, wasn't the whole reason Wayne's cloak worked because there were things out here that even the undead were afraid of? Wasn't that what Kneede told him? Wasn't that precisely the sort of thing he was pretending to be when he used his crazy psychokinetic powers to build the corpse monster and scare them all out of their minds? "Let's just focus on one thing at a time, though. Starting with getting back to the road before we end up hopelessly lost."

"Yeah. You're right."

"Of course I am."

Albert chuckled and gave her hand a loving squeeze. "Of course you are," he agreed.

Ahead of them, Corey climbed over a broken slab of strange, cream-colored material that didn't quite resemble metal. It looked more like a great chunk of plastic. But that didn't seem right. Was it some kind of concrete? Or something closer to fiberglass, perhaps?

He stepped from the slab up onto a barrel-shaped piece of broken machinery and surveyed the area ahead of them. "Looks like there're ways through," he reported. "If you're okay with a little climbing."

Brandy glanced around at the strewn wreckage. Was that a wise choice? They still didn't know very much about this strange new world. What were the dangers out here? What new and deadly monsters might be lurking in such a place?

But Corey was already making his way forward. And Violet was right behind him.

Albert stepped up onto the plastic-looking slab, then helped her up. Always the gentleman. He was always so sweet like that. She loved how thoughtful he was. It gave her that familiar little fluttery feeling in her belly that made her want to stop and stick her tongue in his mouth. (Although, admittedly, a lot of things made her want to do that...) It didn't last very long, though. This wasn't the most romantic of locations, under *any* circumstances.

Ahead of them, Corey paused to examine a great, boxy shape that lay broken on the ground, dumping its strange contents across his path. There were thick, shiny cables and fat, glossy tubes and a weird, unraveled mass of dull, metallic mesh. To Brandy, it looked almost *anatomical.* Those inner workings had spilled out like the guts of some unfortunate beast ripped open by a vicious predator.

"I can't make sense of what any of this stuff used to be," observed Violet as she shined her light onto a cluster of grimy pipes bristling up from the top of a crumpled, rusted-covered tank.

"Dif'rent technology," observed Corey.

"Probably," agreed Albert. "If this really is stuff from a dead world, then it could be the kind of stuff we haven't even dreamed up yet in ours."

"Or never can," countered Corey. "'Cause of different physics."

"That could also be true. We have no way of knowing."

Brandy didn't think she cared much for this topic. She didn't want to think about dead worlds and how similar or different they might have been. It was only a reminder that their own world was dying, too. Would it one day end up just like this? Just a bunch of broken and scattered garbage strewn about this horrible forest?

She turned and looked back the way they came, paranoid that something awful must be stalking them, only to find that there was nothing back there but a black sea of night trees.

Where'd the wreckage go?

She turned back to Albert, but he was gone, too. Everyone was gone. She was standing alone in that awful black forest.

Her heart stuttered in her chest. What happened? How did she get out here? Where was everybody?

She turned around again, panic rapidly welling up inside her.

"You okay?" asked Albert.

She blinked at him, confused. He was standing right in front of her, still holding her hand. Violet and Corey were just ahead of them. They were still surrounded by the alien wreckage of that massive ship.

"Babe?" pressed Albert.

"Yeah... I'm okay... Sorry."

"What's up?"

But she wasn't entirely sure how to even explain it. What was that? Was it only some weird hallucination? Some kind of premonition?

"Building," said Corey.

She looked over to see that he was shining his powerful light over a half-collapsed structure of bluish-hued bricks with odd-looking triangular windows. What little glass remained unbroken was tinted a bright shade of yellow. She stared at it, her muddled thoughts whirling around, processing that the building looked like nothing she'd ever seen before, but only in a distracted, half-aware sort of way. The rest of her mind was still in that other forest with no ruined buildings or beached ships, where there was only her and those awful night trees.

Albert leaned closer, looking her over. He was concerned.

"I'm fine," she insisted. "Just jumpy. Really."

He didn't look convinced, and she didn't exactly blame him. She wouldn't have accepted that answer if *he* were acting like she was right now.

"Come on," she said, pulling at his hand. "We don't want to get too far behind." Whatever it was, it was over now. And she didn't want to linger in this awful forest any longer than absolutely necessary.

They pushed on toward the ruined building. Corey was making

his way around it, shining his light through the broken windows, trying to get a peek at what was inside.

Violet was behind him, tiptoeing through the bricks, her light focused on her feet, watching every step.

Albert clung to Brandy's hand as they made their way toward her.

"Corey says there's a way through," Violet reported when they caught up with her, then turned and slipped inside.

Brandy thought the only thing scarier than wandering around in these woods was wandering around inside some old building that might collapse on them at any moment, but she followed along, not wanting to risk getting separated like in that bizarre hallucination.

The building was bigger than it looked. It stretched far back into a creepy darkness filled with dangling streamers of what appeared to be some time of unraveling wiring. Corey crossed the grimy floor and shined his light through the first doorway he came to, then quickly moved on to the next when he saw that part of the ceiling had caved in.

There was a large metal pipe lying across the next room, having been knocked from the ceiling when the wall to the far left fell in long ago.

Corey peered over it to check what was on the other side, then turned and, without bothering to ask, grabbed Violet by her waist.

Brandy watched, surprised, as he hoisted her up off the ground like she were a mere doll and then placed her down on the other side of it.

Then he turned and looked at her, those bushy eyebrows raised inquisitively. "You too?" the look said.

She didn't think she wanted to be manhandled across the pipe. But she also didn't want to waste time getting back to the path. Instead, she held out the hand she was holding her flashlight in.

He took the hint and grasped her elbow. With him on one side and Albert on the other, they lifted her up and over the pipe, where Violet was waiting to help her down.

Then Albert climbed up on top and slid himself over, followed by Corey, whose formidable bulk made it look easier.

Then they were moving again.

The next room was in far worse shape. A huge chunk of metal and shredded cables had crashed through the wall, making it impossible to cross. Instead, there was a door on the right they'd have to take if they didn't want to backtrack.

Was it really safe to be in here? It looked to her like the whole place was on the verge of falling apart around them. But Corey kept pushing onward, already heading for that doorway, seemingly unconcerned.

Except he stopped short of the exit, his big head tipped to one side as if listening for something.

Brandy started to ask what was going on, but an odd noise caught her attention.

...tok...

...tok...

"Everybody quiet!" hissed Violet, her green eyes wide open and a startled expression overtaking her usually calm features.

...tok...tok...tokka...

The two of them exchanged a worried look.

Brandy wanted to ask what was making that noise, but Violet told them to be quiet and she didn't quite dare disobey her. They were supposed to be the experts on otherworldly things, after all. And this was definitely an "other world."

But then Violet turned toward them and whispered, "We have to go."

"What is it?" Albert whispered back.

But Violet and Corey were already on the move, making their way through the door and into the dark space beyond.

Those strange noises continued, seemingly from the very walls around them.

...tok...tok...

...tokka...tok...

"Seriously!" insisted Brandy, her voice hushed but demanding. "What *is* that?" She didn't like being able to hear something she couldn't see. It was too much like the temple. It was too much like those awful hounds.

"Tokkatoks," whispered Violet.

"What's that?" she pressed.

"Very dangerous. Keep quiet. They're attracted to sound."

"Blind, though," whispered Corey. "Can't see the lights." He found a way out at last and hurried back out beneath that empty sky, only to stop again, his strong arm thrust back, shielding Violet from something.

...tokkatokka...

...tokka...

...tokkatok...

...tok...

...tokkatokkatokka...

Brandy held her breath and tried to hear the noise over the sound of her own racing pulse. What *was* it?

As she watched, Corey swung his flashlight to the left and cast its beam onto a small, strange shape scuttling through the strewn debris.

"What...the *fuck*...is *that*?" breathed Brandy.

It had a somewhat monkey-like shape, with an upright torso and small head, but without any recognizable facial features. Instead, there was a sort of bristly, bony ridge running down the front of its head that flexed and relaxed in a quick and oddly unsettling rhythmic motion. As it skittered forward, more of its strange body came into view. Its lower half was elongated, with six twisted, scrawny legs in addition to its arms, which reached all the way to the floor, allowing them to be used as arms *or* legs. It was difficult to wrap her head around exactly what she was seeing. It had patches of hair on its body like some kind of mammal, especially on its underside, hanging between all those legs, but it also appeared to be partially covered in a bug-like exoskeleton. It was hideous and creepy and didn't look remotely natural. But the worst part was the freakishly long claws at the ends of all those legs. It was these that were making that noise, she realized. It was walking on the tips of them as it skittered through the wreckage and across the hard-packed earth.

Violet pressed her finger to her lips and then leaned close between them and whispered very quietly, "Where there's one there's more. They move in swarms. And they're usually bigger than that."

"How much bigger?" Brandy whispered back.

Then an enormous leg plunged down from the darkness, spearing the smaller creature. It let out a horrible squeal. Then, in an instant, it was snatched away into the darkness.

"Lots," replied Corey.

"Time to move!" hissed Violet. "Go!"

Brandy didn't need to be told twice. She grabbed Albert's hand again and the four of them fled the area.

Chapter 30

Olivia reached up and touched the thorn through the tee shirt Nadia gave her. There was something comforting about the feel of it, although that might've been wishful thinking and the lingering memory of Erin Laplede telling her that it would bring her good fortune, even if that part *had* turned out to be a lie.

Yggdrasil's thorn… It sounded even crazier than the idea of a Temple of the Blind. Like she was carrying something straight out of Norse mythology. Although Wayne said he'd never heard of Yggdrasil having thorns until now. Of course, he was by no means the foremost expert on the subject, so he could have simply missed that detail somewhere. He told her that he doubted the thorn actually had anything to do with any real-life Norse gods, and she supposed he was probably right. Maeve even told them that the name Yggdrasil had been around forever, probably far longer than the concepts of Odin and Midgard and the Bifrost. But still, just hearing her call it by that name made it feel as if she were wielding some mystical weapon around her neck. Something with a name like that *must* have *some* protective power…right?

But then again, it did nothing to protect poor Erin, she supposed…

Wayne caught sight of movement and turned his flashlight out into the forest to their right. Something was crawling on the bare ground among the slumbering night trees, a dark, stiff, *broken* kind of shape, dragging itself along, clawing at the hard, dead ground. It didn't seem to have legs or a head, although it was difficult to tell for certain. It was all twisted and knotted up.

Olivia had to bite back a scream at the mere sight of the thing. A million terrible memories came bubbling up from that well of nightmares she kept buried deep in the back of her mind.

But it wasn't moving toward them. It was heading back the way they came, seemingly oblivious of their existence.

Ahead of them, Everett hadn't noticed it. He was scanning the other side of the path, examining the branches of one of the nearby night trees. Neither of them pointed it out to him. The last thing they wanted was for him to decide he needed a closer look.

She turned and looked up at a night tree whose branches were dangling uncomfortably close to the path. Again, she recalled the way they twisted and writhed and grabbed and strangled, dragging poor Nicole up into its killer boughs. The memory never failed to send a shiver down her spine.

But that tree was fully awakened by the light of the raging inferno belching up from every crack and crevice on that burning mountain. These trees hadn't seen any kind of light in eons. They were like the ones she landed among when the corpse monster dropped her after snatching her from Gilbert House's third-floor windows, deep in their eternal sleep, still waiting for a sunrise that would never come.

She spent hours curled up among several fallen night trees, feeling their clammy, flesh-like bark against her skin as she tried desperately to hide from the thing that dropped her there.

Was that all the proof she needed that darkness was her friend out here? As long as they didn't linger with their lights, those awful trees weren't likely to bother them?

But Nadia also said that sometimes they grabbed out of sheer reflex. That was a scary thought. And here in the Denselands, those coiling branches drooped low, making it far easier to brush against them while stumbling through the dark.

"You still doing okay?" worried Wayne.

She nodded. "Nadia said the path was safe. That's a lot more than we had last time, right?"

"That's right."

"The path is safe," she said again. And she could feel the truth in those words. That strange, psychic part of her brain was telling her that this was the right course.

He looked back the way they came. "*Perfectly* safe," he agreed.

He wasn't a very good liar, but she appreciated the effort.

"How far do you think we'll have to walk?" That oppressive heaviness made it feel like she'd been slogging uphill this entire time. It was draining her energy a lot faster than walking around that cursed fairy forest.

"I don't know. But it can't be that far if we're expected to get there on foot. In this forest of all places." Then his mouth turned downward into a thoughtful frown. "Although maybe 'far' is the wrong word. Nadia said something about space and time not working right out here."

She remembered. According to her, they'd already traveled an immense distance from home. And that thought alone was enough to leave her feeling sick with anxious dread. It was impossible not to wonder if it was even possible to go home again from such a place.

Wayne shook his head. "I wonder what Albert would think about all this." Albert thought a little differently than him, after all. Wayne was very creative-minded. He saw the beauty and the history and the emotions in the world. Albert was logical. Numbers and patterns and connections was his thing. That was why Wayne was an artist and Albert was a computer guy. And Wayne had always appreciated the way the two of them could discuss things. It was enlightening to compare observations.

But Olivia wasn't thinking about any of that. At the mention of Albert's name she remembered that they weren't the only ones caught up in all this. Sandy said he and Brandy were entangled in it too, somehow. And wherever they were, Nicole and Andrea were in terrible danger. And she never heard back from them. Her purse and phone were still in the Explorer when Max towed it away. She was right when she said she wouldn't need them. She probably would only have lost them if she'd been carrying them when those awful never-children attacked her. Wayne still had his because it was in his pocket when she dropped them in that clearing, and he hadn't had service since, so it was pretty much useless.

Where were they all right now? What was happening to them? Were they enduring even scarier trials? Were they even still alive?

No. She couldn't think like that. She *wouldn't*. Her friends were the absolute strongest people she knew. Wherever they were, whatever they were going through, they'd be fine. She was sure of it. She had to believe in them.

It was the only thing she *could* do for them...

"Check this out!" exclaimed Everett. He was rushing ahead, his light shining onto something to their left. A building of some sort?

The walls were a strange, transparent green material that didn't quite look like glass. It was dull and roughly textured. And it didn't reflect Everett's flashlight. Instead, it seemed to take the light *into* it, making the area around wherever he was pointing it glow an eerie shade of sickly green.

"That's so cool!"

"Stay on the path!" snapped Wayne. "Jesus, it's like we're babysitting somebody's sugar-addled ADHD kid…"

She nudged him with her hip, urging him to be nice, but she couldn't quite stifle a giggle.

The structure was about twenty feet tall, roughly round, with a roof made of a coarse, spongy-looking black material that somehow looked both hard and soft at the same time.

Everett continued toward it, barely staying on the path. There was a round opening farther along that looked like a window but appeared to be sealed with a disk of smooth and shiny gold-colored material. Was it some sort of privacy feature? Like a two-way mirror, reflective on one side but transparent on the other? Or was it to protect against weather or intruders, like a heavy-duty shutter?

She was probably the last person who should be hazarding guesses. She didn't know much of anything about architecture in her *own* universe… But she certainly didn't blame Everett for being curious. Looking at the strange, green building, she couldn't help realizing that they were all looking at a piece of some strange, alien civilization that no one alive had ever seen before.

It was strangely exciting to think of it that way.

Even so, she still decided she'd rather be at home right now, snuggling with Wayne in front of one of their favorite shows.

Something moved in the darkness on the other side of the path and all three of them pointed their lights in that direction.

There was someone over there. A pale gray shape was staggering along in the dark on the other side of one of the nearby night trees.

"Zombie!" exclaimed Everett, excited.

"Shut up!" hissed Wayne.

The thing stopped and stood there. Olivia felt her heart stutter in her chest. Had it heard them? Did it know they were here?

But it didn't turn and rush at them. Did it still not know where they were? Was it trying to zero in on them? Or was it only a coincidence that it stopped walking when it did?

She held her breath and squeezed Wayne's arm, praying the thing would just go away.

It wasn't human, she saw. It stood on two legs. It had two arms. It had a head and a torso and all the right things to be a human. And it was even the right size. But something was just a little off about it. Looking closer, she saw that there were thick tufts of mangy looking hair clinging to its lower legs. And its head was just a little misshapen, its skull protruding a little from the back.

For what felt like a very long time, the thing didn't move. It just stood there, seemingly listening, like a silent predator waiting for a chance to strike. And the three of them stood where they were, not daring to move, not daring to make a sound, willing it to just keep walking.

Or...at least, that was what Olivia and Wayne were doing. She couldn't speak for Everett. He was standing on the path ahead of them, shining his light on the thing, looking like a spring wound to its limit, ready to burst at any second. She could almost feel the excited tension radiating from him.

Not for the first time, she found herself feeling afraid for him. Wayne was right. He was going to get himself killed if he couldn't reel in that enthusiasm. This wasn't a game, after all. There were no extra lives. There was no retrying the level. There was no reset button. There was only life and death. And of those, only one was ever guaranteed.

Finally, the gray corpse began to move again, shuffling off in the other direction.

Olivia saw as it moved away that it had a short stub of a tail and a strange, extra toe protruding from its heel.

Definitely not human.

She didn't dare relax until it was out of sight. Even then, she didn't let her guard down. It could suddenly decide to turn around and rush right back at them.

Everett turned his excited eyes back on them. He looked like a kid who thought he'd just spied Santa's sleigh in the sky. "That used to be someone from one of these worlds, didn't it?" he asked, surprising her.

Wayne stared back at him, confused. "What?"

"I mean, that's the only place zombies could come from, right? One of the worlds that got dumped here when they died? You have to have been alive once to be dead, don't you? Was that what we looked like in one of those worlds?"

Wayne looked back out into the forest where the thing disappeared, contemplating it all.

Olvia, too, pondered this for a moment. She remembered seeing things that weren't human during their desperate escape through the undead horde swarming Gilbert House that night. She even remembered Wayne talking about it with Albert, how it meant there must have been other humanoid species in some of those other worlds. It was a fascinating thought, that people might have once shared their world with races who had horns or fur or wings or extra arms or some other fantastic feature. But she remembered thinking that it was also just as possible, knowing what they knew about their own world, that the people in those worlds were at constant war with each other precisely *because of* those differences.

But one thing she'd never considered was whether the human beings they were today had evolved directly from one of those other races. She knew there were such things as vestigial tails, people born with exactly such an extremity as she just witnessed on the thing in the forest just now... What if that thing they just saw was a *direct ancestor*? Her own grandfather-far-too-great-to-count?

She looked up at Wayne as she pondered this. She could almost see him contemplating the possibilities.

Everett, however, had already grown impatient and moved on. He was walking on ahead of them, excitedly swinging his light back and forth, ready for the next amazing thing to appear from the darkness.

Wayne scowled after him for a few seconds, then started walking.

Olivia, still clinging to his arm, went along with him. But her mind still churned with new and fascinating thoughts.

She stared at the strange, green structure as they passed it, wondering if perhaps that was a part of some long-ago city where people of all different shapes and sizes once went about their business together, like some fantastic science-fiction movie scene.

She found that she kind of liked the idea.

But she couldn't help wondering... If past universes were really like that...then where were all the other people now? Why weren't they here anymore?

What happened in the distant past that led to us being the only ones who remained?

Chapter 31

Andrea clenched her teeth and forced down the terrified cries swelling in her chest.

Not a sound, Gina had insisted. Not a whimper. Not a gasp. *Not a single movement.*

They'd taken shelter inside the remains of some kind of building, huddled together in the dark, surrounded by broken concrete, rusted steel and strange, oddly shaped pieces of crushed and crumpled things that she couldn't identify. She didn't have time to take a good look before Gina warned them to kill their flashlights, plunging everything into blackness, but she could feel the sagging ceiling pushing down on them from above and there was something jagged and cold pressing against her left hip. Most of the structure had collapsed in on itself, making it impossible to move away from the gaping doorways and open windows. Even the floor beneath their feet was sunken and canted, as though the building were slowly being swallowed up by the earth. She couldn't help wondering how easily the rest of the structure could come crashing down on top of them.

But the darkness was the worst part. It was utterly black in this place without their flashlights, leaving her at the mercy of her torturous imagination. But she didn't dare disobey Gina and turn her light back on, not even for a second.

Because something was outside.

Something *big.*

Something *terrible.*

But what? Gina didn't say. There was no time. It was already almost upon them.

Fortunately, her psychic eye was able to see this broken building they could hide in, but it offered little shelter. There was barely room for them to squeeze through the door and out of sight. And once inside, the window loomed just above them, its glass shattered long ago, leaving it nothing more than a large, gaping void that anything could reach right into if it only thought to do so. There was nothing to stop it. If it even suspected that it heard a frightened shuffle in the dirt or a faint hiccup of a terrified breath—or if it just felt like being thorough and checking every crack and crevice of these ancient ruins—their strange journey would be over and she'd never see her home or family again.

What do you think will happen to your soul when you die in a place like this?

She clenched her teeth hard against those intrusive words.

Stupid Stella… Even when she wasn't real she managed to find a way to make every situation as uncomfortable as possible.

Her heart hammering in her chest, her lip quivering with fear, struggling to keep her trembling body still and her breath silent, she clung to Gina's small form while Nicole knelt over them, her arms encircling them both.

She was aware of their body heat, their shaky breath on her skin, the subtle smells of their bodies. Sweat. A hint of those granola bars they'd split for breakfast. The shampoo they used on the boat. A hint of Keith's lingering cologne. Someone's deodorant.

She hadn't even thought of that. What if the thing could *smell* them?

You know it can, chuckled Stella somewhere in her cruel imagination.

Shut up! she thought hard at it.

Stupid imaginary Stella!

She took a slow breath, willing herself to calm down, and realized that there was another smell here, too, one that seemed to be coming from the debris around them. A strangely sour sort of smell, unpleasant and sharp, almost overwhelming, that wasn't quite like anything she could identify. Something rancid? Something that subtly tickled and prickled at her throat, making her suddenly want to cough…which would surely be a death sentence…

You're so fucked, laughed that fake Stella.

Nicole must have felt her shudder a little because she closed her fist around the fabric of her shirt and pulled her closer.

That's right. She wasn't alone out here. She was with her friends. They were going to take care of her. Nicole and Gina had been looking out for her this whole time. They were a team.

"It's right outside the window…" whispered Stella's voice in her ear. It didn't sound like a voice inside her head. It sounded like her real voice, as if she were right there with them. She could even feel her hot breath tickling her skin. It gave her such a fright that she jumped, barely suppressing a startled yelp.

Nicole and Gina both squeezed her tighter in response. She probably startled them as much as that imagined voice startled her. She was lucky she didn't make one of them gasp.

Her stupid, cowardly imagination was going to get them all killed!

This was torture. She could feel tears welling up in her eyes. That pressure in her chest was growing. She caught herself holding her breath and realized if she let it out now it would likely explode from her in a great, blubbering sob.

It was quiet. She couldn't hear anything over the thunder of her own pulse pounding in her eardrums. But somehow she knew it was out there. If she gave in to the fear for even a second and let out so much as a groan—if *any* of them made so much as a peep—it would hear them. And then it would come for them.

She squeezed her eyes closed and felt those tears streak down her cheeks in the dark. She had to calm herself. She had to fight this terrible fear.

Why did Ada ever think she could do this?

"It doesn't see you."

Her eyes flashed open in the dark. That wasn't Stella's voice.

"It's moving away now. Just a few seconds longer."

Was that the voice she heard in Cedric's Cove? Ghost Girl? She hadn't heard her say a word since Hotdog plummeted to his death. She thought she left her back there.

It wasn't like how she sounded during her final confrontation with that maniac. No one else seemed to have heard it. She felt no reaction from Nicole or Gina whatsoever when she spoke. But it didn't seem to just be in her head, like it was back in that cemetery, when she could barely tell it apart from her own frightened thoughts. It was more like the way it was back in that hospital. As real as any of them but only audible to her own weird ears.

She closed her eyes again and tried to calm her mind. If Ghost Girl was with her again, then all would be well. She was sure of it. She'd saved her from Hotdog, after all.

Somewhere in her head, she heard Stella let out one of her annoyed sighs. The ones she blew through her teeth that sounded like a hiss. She always did that when she thought things were going to start getting fun but didn't. Like when an argument she'd been following with those eager brown eyes didn't escalate into a proper fight.

She could almost see her stalking away, bored now.

"It's leaving," whispered Gina, confirming what Ghost Girl said.

"Will it be back?" asked Nicole, her voice barely audible, even as close as they were huddled.

Gina let go of Andrea and stood up straight. She was turned toward the window, as if she could see whatever was out there in spite of the inky darkness, which of course she probably could, given her crazy psychic powers.

She was tuned to an entirely different world than Andrea was, after all. What was it Ada said to them? Something about there being *three* worlds? The world of the living, the world of the dead and another that was neither of those? It didn't make any sense to her. How were there only three worlds? Hadn't they explored more than that in just the past few days? And what *was* something if it was neither living nor dead? Like, wasn't that just…rocks? Or something? And yet Gina was supposably attuned to that third world. To something called the Great Enemy and his twelve fangs or something?

"It's gone," said Gina, no longer bothering to whisper.

"Gone *where*?" asked Nicole. She wasn't quite bold enough to raise her voice yet. "It's been, like, *five seconds*. How far could it have gone?"

Gina switched on her flashlight, blinding after the blackness.

Nicole snatched at the light, covering the lens, trying to darken it before the monster could see them.

"It's gone," she repeated. "It doesn't move like we do. It's somewhere far away already. It can't see or hear us anymore."

Andrea switched on her light and looked around. It was even more claustrophobic than she realized. She looked up at the drooping ceiling above them and felt her heart sink at the thought of it all choosing this moment to come crashing down on them. But she also wasn't terribly eager to step back out into the open. "Are there more of those things out there?"

"Probably."

"Oh," she squeaked.

"But it's more dangerous staying in one place too long than it is to keep moving. We're the anomalies here. Eventually we'll attract unwanted attention."

Nicole cursed under her breath and turned on her flashlight. "What *was* that thing, anyway?"

"I don't know if I can describe it," said Gina. "I guess…maybe if you could imagine what the sound of being driven mad might look like if it took physical form?"

Nicole stared at her for a moment, horrified. "Um... Yeah, I don't think I'm going try to imagine that."

"Agreed," said Andrea.

"Fair enough."

Andrea turned all the way around, confused. "Wait... Where's Keith?"

Chapter 32

It was about five years ago, not long after the new year. At that time, they still hadn't found concrete evidence of existing portals. It would be more than a year before the mystery of Obadiah Hinx lured them to St. Louis. They'd uncovered plenty of fantastic stories and wild conspiracy theories, but what they were seeking still remained frustratingly theoretical.

Until they arrived at that deserted estate somewhere deep in the forests of Northern Minnesota.

It was cold as hell, Violet recalled, but Corey's unending research had turned up a lead that he had "a gut feeling about," so they packed up her Jeep and headed north in spite of the plunging temperatures.

Corey had two types of "gut feelings." The first type happened when a potential portal of any particular reputability was located in close proximity to a completely unrelated location he also had an interest in, like the time he had that "gut feeling" about a haunted museum in Texas that "happened" to be located next door to an all-you-can-eat barbecue restaurant he saw featured on the Food Network. Or that time when he had a "gut feeling" about local legends revolving around an abandoned prison just a few short miles from where a major tech convention he'd been wanting to attend just so happened to be taking place. It would surprise no one to know that *these* gut feelings rarely yielded any helpful data for their research. But humoring him never failed to put him in a good mood for a few days.

But Corey also sometimes had *actual* gut feelings about stories he found. He could scroll past hundreds of news stories, articles and social media posts without raising an eyebrow and then some seemingly forgettable little comment would catch his attention. He'd dig deeper and deeper, throwing himself down a random rabbit hole, unearthing little bits and pieces of some deeply buried legend. And before she knew it, they were on the road again, headed for a lonely stretch of road in South Dakota where people had been going missing for decades or a misty lake in rural Ohio where a coven of witches was said to once practice their dark arts or an extravagant mansion in Georgia where an eccentric psychologist was said to have amassed a collection of bizarre books written by disturbed mental asylum patients. Or a lost grave in St. Louis that was said to reveal the location of the entrance to an unbelievable world of fantasy and beauty.

It was *these* gut feelings that had most often brought them face to face with the true depth of the universe and proved to them beyond a doubt that this was not a single world in three dimensions but rather a multitude of separate but intertwined realities that existed simultaneously within the same physical space.

In this instance, the story that caught Corey's eye was about an abandoned estate in the middle of the Minnesota wilderness that was rumored to be incredibly haunted.

Ghost stories didn't usually interest them. That wasn't what they were searching for. There were plenty of people out there doing that already, after all. But sometimes ghost stories turned out to be misidentified sightings of portals. In the case of this place, it wasn't the ghosts that Corey found interesting, but the fact that no one seemed to know who built the estate or what it was used for. No records could be found. No news articles mentioned it. The few people who lived nearby knew nothing about its history.

She had no idea how he kept finding stories like that. He seemed to have an odd natural talent for it. It was like he was born to do these things. She'd tried asking him about it, but he only ever shrugged and replied that it was, "Just a hunch."

They spent three days in that frigid wilderness, exploring the various buildings on the property. Theirs wasn't particularly thrilling work. They spent a lot of time wandering around, doing little worth mentioning. Corey had an arsenal of gauges and meters that he employed at every sight, studying everything from electromagnetic fields to radiation levels, none of which had ever produced any concrete results.

It was on the morning of the third day, as they were walking around the property one final time before giving up and leaving, that Corey caught sight of a small outbuilding that wasn't mentioned in any of his research. It was just a little shed backed into a thicket of trees, almost entirely swallowed by the overgrown brush. If it hadn't been the dead of winter, she was fairly sure they never would've seen it.

Corey beat back the thorns and pried open the door. He was already convinced that this was what they'd been searching for.

She was convinced they'd once again find nothing at all.

This time, she was wrong.

Hidden inside the shed was an old ladder descending down into a vertical shaft in the ground, as if they'd found a long-lost entrance to some forgotten gold mine. Except that on the back wall of the shed, just behind the hole, someone had painted a dire warning across the wood in big, capital letters: BEWARE OF TOKKATOKS!

And below that: STAY QUIET!

They had no idea what a tokkatok was. And at that time, they didn't have the experience they had today. But just like the Tunipet Boom revealed that there were strange new worlds waiting to be found right here on earth, it also taught them that there were also strange and dangerous things lurking in some of those worlds. That knowledge, paired with that curious warning on the wall, was probably what saved their lives that day. It certainly wasn't an overabundance of caution, because they immediately descended that ladder like a couple of fools and began exploring the dark tunnel waiting for them below.

A few yards from the bottom of the ladder they found a strange, rectangular stone, about three feet high, in the middle of the floor of the tunnel. She remembered thinking there was something creepy about it, probably because it reminded her a little of a gravestone. And because it simply didn't seem to belong there. It served no purpose. There was nothing carved on it. It wasn't holding anything. It was just a smooth slab of gray stone. The only distinguishing detail was a strange indention in the back, roughly round, about the size of a cantaloup. But like the stone itself, it seemed to serve no particular purpose.

It was strange.

"Looks familiar..." Corey observed.

"You've seen something like it before?"

He was frowning at it, confused. "Not sure. Feel like I did once, maybe. Can't remember, though."

She stared at the stone for a moment, wondering. *Did* it look familiar? Now that she was really looking at it, she could almost remember seeing something like it somewhere before, too... But that was probably only because he put the idea in her head. It was just a rectangular stone. It probably looked like *lots* of things they'd seen before.

"Maybe not," he seemed to decide. But he stood there a moment longer anyway, staring at it, the corners of his mouth drawn down in that deep, thoughtful frown.

"Let's keep moving," she urged him.

He spent some time snapping pictures of it with his phone and taking readings around it that never told them anything but seemed to make him happy. Then he grew bored with it and turned his attention on the empty passage continuing past it.

It was an odd series of finds, but did it mean anything? Violet found herself contemplating any number of reasons for such a place to exist, not the least of which being that the original owner was a few bushels short of an orchard and simply enjoyed digging tunnels and erecting strange stones.

But things only became stranger as they descended the sloping tunnel deeper into the earth.

First, there was the temperature. It was common knowledge that it leveled out in caves and cellars and other underground places, providing a constant shelter from both the heat of summer and the freezing cold of winter, but within a space of just a few minutes the passage increased from chilly to positively hot. It was as if they'd walked into a sauna. One of Corey's many multifunction devices told them it was almost ninety degrees and still getting warmer. And yet they weren't able to see any steam or feel any heat rising from the hole in the shed above, in spite of the fact that it was freezing cold on the surface. The tunnel was leading downward, so how was the heat not rising?

It was bizarre. She didn't know how to explain such a thing. Embarrassingly, her thoughts raced with fantastic ideas of hidden, underground industrial complexes, top-secret nuclear reactors, military research bunkers and even cloaked alien bases. But that was the sort of nonsense Corey was always blurting out. She didn't think like that. She looked for logical explanations. Such as hot springs. She tried to remember if there was any history of volcanic activity in Minnesota.

But before she could contemplate it, she heard the sound. A low sort of "tok-tok-tokka" noise coming from somewhere in front of them.

Corey did the thing where he stepped forward and sort of crowded in front of her, threatening to protect her, and as he did this, his light pushed back more of the darkness and revealed the first of the holes.

They were everywhere, bored into the earth in every direction, ranging from a few inches to almost two feet in diameter. She remembered stopping, an unsettling feeling rushing through her at the sight of them all. They didn't look manmade. It looked like some kind of animal burrow. Or a *hive*.

She recalled the warning painted on the wall above—BEWARE OF TOKKATOKS!—and felt a shiver race through her in spite of the sweltering temperature in the tunnel.

This was nowhere they should be…

Before she could retreat, however, it appeared. Their first crosser. It came scuttling out of one of the holes, freezing them in their tracks as it reached out with those long, claw-tipped arms and prodded at the earth around it.

The head and chest were oddly monkey-like, but with a face like nothing she'd ever seen before. No eyes or snout, just that strange, bristly ridge running down the front of its head that sort of undulated rhythmically up and down.

It crept a little farther out, revealing thick, shaggy hair on its underside and far too many legs. The rest of its body was mostly bald, with only mangy clumps here and there. It was a corpse-pale shade of gray and partially covered in bony, almost insect-like skeletal protrusions.

They didn't get a picture of it. They were both so surprised to see such a thing that neither of them even thought about it.

And then more showed up. Only a few at first, but then *dozens* of them, skittering along the tunnel floor on those sharp little claws, crawling in and out of those holes, making that eerie "tokka-tokka-tokka" sound as they moved.

Not the most creative of names, she remembered thinking, but it *was* a rather eerie sound. Very fitting, all things considered.

She didn't scream. Her thoughts immediately went to the other half of that message: STAY QUIET!

They both remained frozen, careful not to make a sound.

And it worked. The monsters didn't come straight for them. They skittered this way and that like busy ants, in and out of those holes, just like some giant insect nest. They didn't seem able to see their lights. They didn't seem to smell them. And it was no wonder, given that they had no visible eyes or noses. But when Corey took a cautious step backward, several of them froze and lifted those dagger-like arms into the air, as if listening.

Stay quiet, indeed.

Her heart racing, her stomach boiling with fear, her eyes never leaving those strange little monsters, she very slowly crept backward through the tunnel.

But they weren't quiet enough.

Several of the little monsters were following the soft sounds of their footsteps, stalking them. And she very much doubted they were going to be able to ascend the old ladder silently.

It was Corey who gave them their chance. He very carefully withdrew some change from his pocket and tossed it as far into the tunnel as he could.

The tokkatoks swarmed the noise. Not just the ones following them. They came pouring out of those creepy holes. *Hundreds* of them, all fighting and scrambling over each other, making terrible screeching sounds. And in the chaos, the two of them fled back the way they came, up the ladder and out into the freezing Minnesota winter.

The creatures didn't follow them out of the hole. Corey was immediately convinced that they didn't like the cold, that it was the unusual heat in that tunnel that kept them inside. She wasn't sure, but she thought it was probably a fairly sound theory. All that mattered to her was that by the time they reached the Jeep, there was no sign of the tokkatoks.

But the oddness didn't end there. The *time* was wrong. Although it was still morning when they found the shed, it was almost sunset now. They'd lost half the day somehow, even though they were only in that hole for a few minutes.

It was all the proof they needed. They'd discovered their first portal. And they weren't too stubborn to admit that it was almost their last. They went on to sit down and lay out some general safety guidelines for moving forward. It was why they had their "safety first" motto.

Not that it had ever really kept them from getting into these kinds of messes. Like now, for example, as she ran for her life through the wreckage of the giant beached ship, surrounded by those tok-tok-tokking sounds once again and wondering if she'd finally pushed her luck too far.

She ducked under a great hunk of that strange, plastic-looking material, then looked back over her shoulder as she ran on. That big tokkatok didn't seem to have heard them over the screeching of the smaller one. That was good. She didn't even know they could get *that* big. The biggest ones they saw that cold winter night were only about the size of German shepherds, which was plenty terrifying enough for her.

But she wasn't sure how much longer luck would hold out for them. She could still hear those "tok-tok-tok" noises under the debris on either side of them. And here and there she caught just a glimpse of something darting away from the flashlight's reach.

These tokkatoks seemed more skittish than the ones they encountered that night. Maybe because of the giant ones. It looked like they might be cannibalistic, like spiders, so it was only natural that they'd be cautious. But even so, she doubted they could keep away from these monsters forever. And the big ones certainly wouldn't have any reason to be cautious.

Worse still, it wasn't as if they could simply run back through a portal and escape into the safety of a frigid Minnesota winter like last time. They were kind of stuck here. That carriage ride was a one-way trip. Any chance they had of getting home lay in the unknown ahead of them.

But the landscape was becoming more claustrophobic with each passing minute. There was stone and metal and concrete everywhere. They were ducking under beams and climbing over piles of bricks and veering around strange, broken machinery that she had no way of comprehending.

The mangled bulk of the beached ship was piling higher and higher over them. When Corey shined his powerful light upward, it revealed a labyrinthine cobwebbing of twisted metal, broken pipes and tangled cables, all of it crawling with swiftly scurrying shapes on dagger-like claws.

Would they even be able to find the stone path again in all this wreckage?

Somewhere in the chaotic mess of the ruined ship, something heavy crashed to the ground, nearly wrenching a startled scream from her clenched throat before she could stifle it.

Why were there tokkatoks here? That was the question that kept circling in her head. It didn't make sense. Did the portal in that old shed connect to *this* world? What were the odds of that? According to what they'd learned these past few days, the Wood was different from most of the worlds they'd researched. It was much bigger. It surrounded their own world and all the others as well. So maybe it wasn't all *that* impossible. And yet something about all this felt weirdly implausible.

What would've happened, she couldn't help wondering, if they hadn't been familiar with that sound the tokkatoks made? Were they only alive now because they knew enough to keep quiet and get out of that area before they were heard?

What were even the odds of that?

But of course now wasn't the time for contemplating odds. There was a much more pressing matter requiring her attention at the moment. And it was all around them.

Corey shined his light to the left, revealing just a glimpse of towering legs scurrying past them in the dark.

Before Violet's heart was quite finished leaping into her throat at the sight, another startling crash reverberated from somewhere behind them.

Then something about the size of a horse flashed across their path, freezing them all in place for a moment.

This wasn't going to end well. They were surrounded. And the very landscape was turning into an unsolvable maze around them.

Corey caught her eye, then gestured at another great hunk of that strange, plastic-like material. It was sticking up at an angle, creating a small space underneath big enough for them to all fit in.

She took the hint and slid into the space, pulling Brandy and Albert along with her.

Corey crept a little farther out into the open and pulled something out of one of the pockets of his bag.

"What's he doing?" whispered Brandy.

But Violet only pressed her finger to her mouth again. Corey had a plan. That was all she needed to know.

As they watched, he ignited a road flare. The unexpected glare was blinding. But far worse was the sound of it. The fiery hiss seemed almost deafening in the eerie silence.

Almost immediately, things were on the move, zeroing in on him.

Violet watched, terrified, as several small shapes scurried straight at him.

One even scurried over the top of the slab they were hiding under and dropped to the ground right in front of them.

But Corey didn't panic. He pulled back his arm and then hurled the flare into the distance.

The tokkatoks rushing at him immediately turned, one of them practically at his feet already, and followed the noise.

As the three of them watched the burning torch descend into the wreckage, they caught glimpses of many bug-like shadows converging and descending on it. An even greater commotion arose as the monsters scuffled over the perceived prey.

Corey didn't watch what happened next. He was already on the move. He turned and headed in the opposite direction.

Violet didn't need to be told to follow him. "Come on!" she whispered, already slipping out of their hiding place.

Together, the four of them scurried around and over the wreckage, moving as far from the flare as they could get.

Chapter 33

Austin stopped walking and looked up from his book. For a moment he was blind to the dark world around him, his eyes adjusted to the glare of his flashlight on the clean white pages in front of his nose. But even before he could make out anything, he knew this was the place.

The road stretched straight out ahead of him, vanishing into the constant gloom. But that wasn't his path.

He turned left and set off into the open forest.

He wasn't concerned about the things that prowled these endless trees. They wouldn't bother him. He wasn't like the others, after all. The trials of the Denselands didn't apply to him.

As his light faded behind him, leaving the sentinel's road sinking back into the darkness it had always known, he turned his attention back to the pages of his book and continued reading.

Chapter 34

Wayne's life changed that night five years ago. Before that, he was an unhappy shut-in, dragging himself through college, distancing himself from his old life.

Things had happened, after all. Bad things. Things that were his fault. Things no one should forgive. It was so much easier to just cut himself loose and go his own way, alone, where he wouldn't be able to hurt anyone ever again.

Then that envelope arrived. Gilbert House happened. The Temple of the Blind happened. And when it was over, he had precious new friends.

Even better, he had Olivia.

He looked down at her now, his beautiful fiancée, the love of his life, his best friend in the whole world... It frightened him sometimes just how much he loved her. If anything happened to her, he was sure it would destroy him.

And yet here they were, back in this black nightmare, tempting cruel fate again.

Why did it have to be them? Hadn't he endured enough the first time? He *literally died that night!* But that wasn't enough? They needed to come back? That nightmare inducing experience needed a fucking *sequel?*

There were no words to describe just how much he wanted to punch the Keeper in his freaky, upside-down face. (Although he was the only one from that night who never saw the ugly little creep... He only had everyone else's description of what he actually looked like. It was a little hard to imagine.)

Something small and shadowy darted through the woods on their right and scurried up one of those fleshy trunks, out of sight. It was the third or fourth one of those he'd seen since they lost sight of that alien zombie, which felt like at least an hour ago. None of them had shown any interest in them, but still they made him nervous. It seemed like only a matter of time before something attacked them.

He couldn't even see what they were. They moved so quickly. He didn't think they were undead.

Among other things, Nadia mentioned something called "fester vermin," whatever the hell that was. It didn't sound pleasant, that was for sure. He kept picturing giant cockroaches or something. And that was the sort of thing these small, fast-moving things reminded him of.

Nadia said nothing out here ever died, which was a fair description of the undead things that he'd seen in these woods. But she also said that there were other things out here. Including things that were neither alive nor dead. That, he still didn't quite understand. But he knew that there were things in the Wood that weren't zombies. There were those carrion eater things, for one thing. Freakish, flying creatures that Albert and Andrea had sat down with him and described for him to sketch out. The results were nothing short of terrifying. It looked like something out of a nuclear apocalypse, he thought. Freaky, bow-tie shaped wings. No heads. Mouths on their bellies. Like their descriptions of the Keeper, he had a terrible time imagining them as real.

Whatever they were, they weren't zombies. Albert deduced that they fed off the zombies. It was why he called them carrion eaters. And Nadia did mention that there were scavengers here, among all the other terrifying things she said were waiting for them.

"What's that?" asked Everett, hurrying forward again.

"Don't get ahead of us," worried Olivia.

But he wasn't listening, of course. He was shining his light out at what looked like a forest of tall, copper pipes sticking up out of the ground and stretching high up into the black sky. "What do you think this is?" he shouted back at them, making him cringe. Wayne didn't care what kinds of protections the sentinels crafted into this weird road, the loud little fool was going to attract *something* before it was over. He was sure of it.

Besides, how the hell was *he* supposed to know what all those pipes were for? They looked like copper, but he didn't think they could be. They looked brand new. As long as all this stuff was supposed to have been here, real copper should've turned green. This stuff hadn't even dulled for some reason. It was either some kind of alloy or something had been done to it to prevent it from developing the regular patina of typical copper.

As he drew closer, he saw that many of them had fallen over and broken. A few were even lying across the path, revealing that they weren't pipes at all. They weren't hollow. They were solid.

Was it some kind of lightning rod farm or something? A part of some kind of power facility? A giant circuit board? He couldn't even begin to guess. If this was truly something from an entirely different universe, it was impossible to know for certain. Whatever their purpose once was would likely always remain a mystery. It was a frustrating thought. Just like back in the temple, there were so many questions and so few answers.

They went on and on, more and more of them emerging from the darkness as they walked. A handful of night trees loomed among them, but not many. For the most part, it appeared to be nothing but these odd metal rods for as far as they could see. And there was something spectacularly eerie about the sight of it for some reason.

Finally, Everett had stopped walking. He was standing in the road ahead of them, his light cast out into the metal forest.

Wayne looked out where he was aiming it and he, too, stopped.

There was something standing out there. Something big.

Olivia let out an audible gasp and pressed herself closer to him.

It stood on four stout legs, its body at least the size of a full-grown bull, with a long, serpent-like tail and a huge, bulbous head that hung downward. There were strange, wriggling things hanging from its snout and slithering about the ground among the fallen rods.

He was becoming aware of an awful smell, too. A faint whiff of dead and rotting things.

A scavenger? Like the carrion eaters?

It didn't look like the shape of any creature Wayne had ever seen before. And the longer he stared at it, the less he wanted to see more of it.

Everett, however, took a step closer.

"Don't!" gasped Olivia.

"It's okay," he said, as if he knew anything about it, and took another step. He was right at the edge of the road, literally toing the line between safety and peril.

"Goddammit, don't be stupid!" growled Wayne.

Olivia didn't tell him to be nice this time. She was staring at the monster, her remaining fingernails digging into his arm.

Thankfully, Everett didn't take that next step. He stood there, on the precipice of danger, his light shining out into that forest of false copper, illuminating a mangy, wrinkled hide of mottled gray and black. There were more of those strange, wriggling things dangling from its belly, Wayne saw with mild disgust.

"We need to leave," squeaked Olivia.

He nodded. She didn't have to tell him twice. He was ready to be gone and well away from this place. For all they knew, there could be a thousand more of those things just beyond the reach of Everett's light.

He gave her a comforting squeeze and started walking again. "We're leaving," he whispered firmly.

Everett finally seemed satisfied. He took a step back. "That's wild…" he sighed. "It's like something from an alien planet. Right out of Star Wars or something."

"Fascinating," grumbled Wayne, clearly not caring about the scary new lifeform they'd discovered. "Move your ass before you get us eaten by something!"

"Okay, okay,"

But as he turned away from the edge of the road, Olivia let out a startled gasp. "Look out!"

Wayne and Everett both froze, their eyes wide. Look out for what?

But then there was a loud, metallic creak from the other side of the road.

Wayne looked up, startled, to see that one of those towering rods was bending toward them, picking up speed as it fell.

It was going to land right on them!

He grabbed Olivia and pulled her backward, out of the path as the metal snapped with a resounding, echoing twang.

Everett jumped the other way and fell on his butt, barely avoiding it. It struck the ground where he was just standing with a thunderous crash.

Out in the metal forest, the beast let out a strange, reverberating roar and flared. Long, fins of sharp spines fanned out along the length of the thing's hunched back and great, stubby tusks unfolded themselves from its bulbous face.

Wayne prayed that it was only startled by the noise of the falling rod. But as he watched it, his heart hammering in his chest, he realized that it was turning to face them.

Then he noticed something else.

Everett had landed off the stone.

He looked down at where he was sitting and then looked up at them, his eyes wide at the realization of what he'd done.

"Oh, fuck me," groaned Wayne as the thing in the forest charged toward them. "Run!"

Still careful to keep to the road, the three of them took off. He had time to hope that perhaps the monster would lose sight of them and charge right across the path, missing them completely, but one glance back revealed that it was angling toward them as it picked up speed, very clearly tracking them.

Nadia did say the stone road wouldn't protect them once they were noticed. Apparently whatever magic kept them invisible was broken the moment something actually spotted them.

This wasn't good. That thing was much faster than they were. They had no chance of outrunning it. And they sure as hell couldn't fight something like that off. It was huge. And it was agile, too. It weaved through those copper-colored rods with ease.

This was going to be a very short run if he didn't think of something fast.

He scanned their surroundings, desperate. A weapon. That was what he needed.

"Keep going!" he shouted. "Don't stop for anything!"

"What?" gasped Olivia.

"Just go!" He veered to the left, off the edge of the path and onto the dry, cracked earth. "This way, you son of a bitch!" he shouted.

Thankfully, the thing veered to follow him.

But Olivia cried out for him and the thing changed course again, following her instead.

"No you don't!" he shouted, stopping and waving his arms.

Could the thing even see him? Did anything living out in this black wasteland have eyes? Or was he just making a fool of himself?

But it worked. The thing changed direction again and charged him. He sprinted away, his eyes open, searching the bare, black earth in front of him.

There!

He stooped over and snatched up a long piece of one of those broken rods. Then he stopped and lifted it above his head. With all his strength, he jabbed it into the ground at as much of an angle as possible. Then he turned and faced the charging beast, aiming the jagged end straight at its...face?

He had a moment to take in all those awful features. It didn't seem to have a face at all. The front of its head was a bulging mass of wrinkled, mottled flesh with those great, tusk-like teeth protruding outward all the way around it. Those weren't visible when he first saw the beast. They were folded up, like the spiny fins. It had no visible eyes or ears. Whatever served as its mouth must have been under it, somewhere in that grotesque mass of wriggling feelers flopping around as it ran.

This better fucking work! he thought, closing his eyes and bracing himself against the impact. If it didn't, this was going to be the end of the journey for him.

An instant later, he felt the rod jerk hard in his hands. It pushed through the ground for several inches, kicking up dirt and driving itself deeper. Then something heavy and reeking slammed into his shoulder, sending an agonizing bolt of pain through his body, knocking him onto his back.

When he opened his eyes, the beast lay dead in front of him, the metal rod rammed deep into its grotesque, bulbous head.

Those bony tusks were looming over him, ready to impale him. And they very nearly had.

He looked down at his shoulder and found that one of them had pierced his skin. A bright blossom of fresh blood was slowly spreading across his shirt.

Before he could fully take it all in, Olivia was at his side, her pretty eyes full of terror.

"You're hurt!" she cried.

"I'm okay."

"No you're not! You're bleeding!"

"It's not bad."

"You don't know that!"

"I do," he insisted. Although she was right. He'd barely glanced at it. It could have gone all the way through him for all he knew. But he was almost positive that wasn't where he kept any of his vital organs. He scooted himself backward, away from those awful tusks, eager to be out from under the thing, but she pushed him back down.

"You don't know anything! I'm the nurse, not you!"

"Oh yeah. I forgot."

"What were you thinking?"

"That I had to protect my future wife, obviously."

"You're so hardheaded!"

"I love you too."

"*Augh!*"

He chuckled a little in spite of himself. He couldn't help it. She was so cute when she was in panic mode. She did the same thing when he cut himself while chopping onions once. It was adorable.

The monster suddenly let out great belch of air, startling a terrified scream from her. She threw herself against him, jarring him and sending a fresh bolt of pain through his shoulder. But that was all there was. The beast was dead. It was nothing more than its corpse giving up its last breath. Or maybe it was a fart. He didn't know how the damned thing worked. Either way, it smelled awful.

He rose to his feet with a painful grunt.

"Slow down! You're still hurt!"

"I'm okay," he insisted. "We have to get back onto the road before something else comes to see what that commotion was."

She wanted to keep arguing, but he'd made a valid point. She looked around as if suddenly realizing that they were standing out in the open, vulnerable to another of these nasty things. Or any number of other horrors.

She grabbed his arm and tried to take his weight, as if she were strong enough to make much difference, and the two of them made their way back to the path where Everett was staring back at them with eyes that finally appeared wide with appropriate terror rather than that silly wonder.

"It's dead," Olivia assured him. "Don't worry."

Everett never took his eyes off Wayne. "It's not *that thing* I'm worried about..."

Chapter 35

"Where's Keith?"

"What?" Nicole turned and shined her light into the ruins. He was with them when Gina told them to kill their lights. She thought he was right behind them. Did he lag behind? Did they leave him stranded out in the open? Did that *thing* get him? She felt her heart leap at the thought.

But Gina simply pointed her flashlight at the rubble of the collapsed building behind them. "He's right there."

And indeed, she immediately caught sight of his shoes and the legs of his jeans through gaps in the debris.

"Oh," said Andrea. "So he is…"

But…*why* was he down there? Was he trying to hide? Did he get lost when the lights went out? Had he dropped a contact lens? "What the hell are you doing?"

"I recognized the darkness," he replied.

Andrea crinkled up her face, confused. "What?"

"How do you recognize *darkness*?" wondered Nicole. That made no sense. Wasn't darkness just…*darkness*? Especially *total* darkness. How was one darkness different from another? There wouldn't be anything to remember if there was nothing to see…right?

"It's hard to explain," grunted Keith. He seemed to be squirming farther into the rubble.

"Be careful!" gasped Andrea. "This whole place could come down on top of you!"

"Oh no…" muttered Nicole in an emotionless tone. "That would suck so bad…"

Andrea looked over at her, a pierced eyebrow raised.

"Harsh," observed Gina.

"I'm *kidding*," she huffed. And she *was* kidding, of course. She wasn't the kind of person who would ever wish anyone to be crushed under a building. Unless they were someone like Hotdog. And Keith was certainly nothing like Hotdog. He was a nice guy. He never hurt her. He never yelled at her or put her down in any way. It wasn't like that. It was *complicated*. And she didn't appreciate the fact that he actually scared her a little when Andrea thought he'd disappeared.

"Not funny," said Andrea.

Nicole crossed her arms and turned her attention to the open forest outside the broken window. It was just a stupid joke. Why was everyone so uptight?

"It was mixed in with all those dreams I was having," explained Keith, ignoring her. "You know, the ones where I kept having to save Nikki's ungrateful ass from certain doom?"

"What do you want?" she growled at him. "A cookie?" She changed her mind. She wasn't kidding. Let the whole place come down on him. What did she care?

"One dream kept repeating itself. It was strange because I seemed to be blind and deaf. I couldn't see or hear anything. Everything was black and silent. And in that darkness, there was something glinting. Something mostly buried in the dirt. I reached out for it, but I couldn't reach it. There was something in the way, blocking me. I had to wriggle around it sideways and squeeze myself through the gap to reach it. But by the time I dug my fingers into the dirt and grabbed it, I always woke up. So I never found out what it was."

Andrea knelt down and tried to shine her light where he was reaching, but his body was blocking the opening. "You think *that's* where your dream was pointing you?"

"There's not exactly a shortage of dark places out here," Nicole pointed out.

"Yeah, but while the lights were out, I saw something glinting, just like in the dream."

But Nicole furrowed her eyebrows at his feet. "How does something 'glint' when there's no light for it to reflect?" Wasn't that the literal definition of the word "glint"? It wasn't giving off its own light or they'd probably have noticed it, too.

"It's a good question." He wormed his way in even deeper, huffing and puffing with the effort. "I'm wondering the same thing."

"If you get stuck under there, we're leaving you."

"No we're not!" insisted Andrea.

"Well don't expect *me* to help pull his dumb ass out."

"He's not wrong," said Gina, kneeling down and adding her light to Andrea's. "There's something there. I can sense it. I don't know what it is or why I didn't notice it before, but it's there. And it shouldn't be."

"What do you mean?" asked Andrea.

"It doesn't go with everything else here. It's different. Like someone put it there."

"What," pressed Nicole, "like, specifically for *him* to find?"

She turned those sleepy eyes on her. "Is that so hard to believe?"

She had no response to that. It was a good point. After all they'd been through, why *wouldn't* someone leave something hidden along the path that only Keith with his weird dream powers could find? Someone sent a magic spear-leaf-key thing to Andrea. Someone sent a mysterious box and its key to Albert and Brandy.

But wouldn't that mean that whoever left it had to know that they'd be forced to take shelter in this building? Someone knew that thing was going to pass through right at the same moment they were approaching *this exact spot*? Or did it mean that someone *sent* that thing here at exactly *that* moment to make sure he found it?

She remembered Ada telling them that nothing happened without the Keeper meaning for it to happen. She still wasn't sure how she felt about that. On one hand, it meant that he was keeping them safe all through that first temple, ensuring that they made it home in one piece. But she remembered Albert talking about how the Keeper was *using* them the whole time, that he only considered them *tools* and that there was nothing stopping him from throwing them away when he was done with them like he did with poor Beverly.

Who *was* the Keeper? *What* was he? And should they really be trusting him with their lives like this?

"Got it!" grunted Keith. He kicked his legs and started wriggling his way free again.

Andrea grabbed his ankle and tried to pull him out. Beside her, Gina did the same with his other foot.

Nicole, true to her word, only stood and watched.

"I'm good now," Keith reported once his shoulders were clear of the obstruction. He pushed himself up onto his hands and knees and backed out, clutching his mysterious prize.

"What is it?" wondered Andrea, her voice bursting with eagerness to see what was so important.

And Nicole didn't blame her. Her own imagination was running wild with the possibilities. Was it some kind of ancient treasure? Maybe a mythical weapon that would protect them in this harsh landscape? Or a map to guide them? Or even some kind of magical talisman?

Because why not? Andrea had a magic spear-leaf-key thing.

But when he turned around, he was holding only an empty glass bottle.

"Well, good thing you risked contracting alien tetanus for *that*," chided Nicole. It *was* a rather strange-looking bottle, she thought. Teardrop shaped, pointed on the bottom, with a short stub of a neck sticking up at the top. It wouldn't have stood on its own. It appeared to be designed to hang by the lip around the opening on some kind of stand. It looked like something you'd see suspended over a Bunsen burner in a science lab. But she could think of no good reason for anyone to have gone to that much trouble to retrieve it. "Waste of time."

"No…" said Gina, stepping closer to it. "It's not what it seems. It's important. I can tell."

"Important *how*? It's *junk*."

"But if he saw it in his dreams, it *must* be important," reasoned Andrea. "Right?"

Gina nodded. "That's probably true. But I can just tell. It's not an accident you found it."

Keith turned it over in his hand, examining it. "I'm with Nikki this time, though. It really does just look like junk. If you can tell it's important, maybe *you're* supposed to have it." But when he held it out to her, she shrank back, those sleepy eyes widening.

"No!" she gasped. "I don't think I can touch it."

Andrea frowned. "Why not?"

But she shook her head. She didn't know. "Just something I can feel," was her only answer.

"Okay," said Keith, bemused. "I'll carry it. Just…let me know if you figure out what it's for."

She nodded, but didn't dare take her eyes off it, as if she expected him to jab her with it as soon as she let her guard down.

"I still don't understand how it 'glinted' when the lights were off," said Nicole. "That's not how light works."

"Oh yeah," said Andrea. "That still doesn't make sense, does it?"

Gina switched off her flashlight. The rest of them realized what she was doing and did the same.

That suffocating, absolute darkness swallowed them whole again. But something there in the middle of them did, in fact, glint. A tiny flash of light, barely seen, but undeniable. Something deep inside that seemingly empty bottle…

"Cool," said Andrea.

Chapter 36

"Not hot here," observed Corey.

"I was thinking the same thing," said Violet.

"That *is* odd," agreed Albert. They were still speaking in hushed tones, still wary of anything that might be able to hear them, but the wreckage of the displaced ship was finally thinning out again, allowing them to see farther into their surroundings. And it had been a while since they heard the "tokka-tok-tokka" noise of those frightful monsters. She'd felt confident enough to give them an abridged version of the story of just how they first stumbled across those things. One thing she mentioned, however, was the temperature difference between the sweltering interior of the hive and the frigid Minnesota weather outside. "I guess they don't need it hot. They just can't tolerate freezing temperatures."

But Corey had a different theory: "Lotsa machinery in that ship," he observed. "Might still be stuff runnin' in there. Givin' off heat. Maybe even some kinda reactor."

"What, like it's *nuclear*?" scoffed Brandy.

"Why not?"

"That could explain it," reasoned Albert. "If anything is still functioning in all that mess, it could be producing heat, and that would probably make for an appealing place to build a nest."

Brandy shuddered. She didn't want to think about it. "Let's just hurry up and get back to the road before we get lost."

But as Albert glanced around, he wasn't entirely sure he knew which way was which.

Corey was contemplating the same thing. He pointed back at the bulk of the debris. "Boat's back there somewhere," he reasoned. He swung his arm about ninety degrees and pointed toward Albert's left. "Road should be somewhere that direction."

But Albert was staring across the wreckage, thoughtful. "No..." He looked one way, then the other. "It's not." He turned and pointed the other way instead. "It's that way."

Corey's pudgy face scrunched into a deep frown. "That don't make sense."

"It doesn't," he agreed, looking back in the other direction. He was quite sure they didn't make much progress trying to navigate that labyrinth of broken steel and concrete. But that didn't change the fact that the road was the other way.

"How do you know?" wondered Violet.

"Psychic stuff?" asked Brandy.

"Possibly." It made sense, given all they went through back at the hotel. Wasn't that what the pervert shaman was trying to teach them? "A little, maybe. But mostly it's the wind. It never changed direction when we were following the road. I remember thinking it was blowing toward our destination, practically *pushing* us toward it. But now it's blowing *that* way." He pointed out into the surrounding night trees.

"Maybe the wind changed," offered Corey. "It does that."

It was a reasonable line of thinking, but Albert shook his head. "Not here, it doesn't." He wasn't sure how he knew this, if it was just his own natural intuition or if it was the psychic part of his mind or if someone simply put the idea in his head, the way the Sentinel Queen nudged him along in his quest to unravel the meaning behind her mystery box. But he *did* know it. The wind in the Denselands always blew toward its center. It was the nature of it. That strange, heavy sensation, like gravity running wild, pulling harder at them. The thickness of the air, as if the very atmosphere were being condensed.

(*A place where the forgotten remains of countless dead worlds have piled up over the endless ages. A wasteland, where the very air is heavy with the weight of the inescapable atrophy that awaits all life.*)

He felt a slight shiver creep up his spine at the memory of Lucianna's unsettling description of it, but that was exactly how it was. These ruins…the worlds they belonged to…it was all compressed into one place, drawing all the air toward the center…toward their destination…toward whatever they were here to find…

Corey didn't argue. He turned and looked in that direction. "You're the boss," he decided.

But this made Albert frown. He didn't want to be the boss. He was just telling them what he knew.

"So how did we get so far off course?" wondered Violet, looking back the way they came.

"Everything's compressed here," he said, almost before he understood it, himself. "That's why everything feels so heavy. It probably distorts time and space in extreme and unpredictable ways." He looked off into the black forest again. "I'm betting that's what the roads were built for. The sentinels left them as a safe route. It probably acts like a bridge across the places where we'd otherwise get displaced."

"But someone dropped a boat on ours," said Corey, nodding.

Albert glanced over at him, his thoughts still churning. Now he found himself wondering. Did the ship end up here when the world it came from died? Or was it possible that someone displaced it like that on purpose in hopes of getting them lost? It was an unsettling thought. What manner of force would be capable of such a feat?

He didn't think he wanted to voice that particular worry. Not while they were still out here in the open, especially. They needed to find their way back to the shadow road. And fast.

"Okay," said Violet. "Lead the way." She glanced in the direction he said the road should be. "I'm not going to argue with moving *away* from the tokkatok nest."

The wind, alone, didn't tell him which side of the road they should be on. But the fact that it was blowing at the angle it was suggested that the wreckage of the ship didn't lay in a straight line. It was likely broken in half when it crashed here. Some of it was logic, but some of it was just that he seemed to *know* that they were now somewhere near the stern of the ship, meaning they'd gone *past* the road at some point.

He didn't think about it more than that. He was worried he might start doubting himself and talk himself out of it again. He simply lined himself up with where he thought it should be and started walking.

The others followed along, sticking close to him as he weaved around the sickly night trees and the thinning wreckage.

The ground here was covered in a seemingly endless carpet of litter that the constant wind had blown from the ruins of the stranded vessel. Rotting paper, tatters of cloth, little wads of foam that had a dull, glittery sort of sparkle when he shined his light at them. There were strands of cottony threads of bluish gray stuff and great, long, tangled streamers of something thin and wispy that fluttered in the wind, some of them stretching as far as he could see. And there were countless little clear balls that looked like glass marbles scattered everywhere. And of course there were untold thousands of things that were utterly unidentifiable.

But as he shined his light around, he caught a glimpse of something that he was quite sure was a fragment of dingy bone.

There was the Wood he remembered, the one swarming with long-mummified corpses. Now that one had caught his attention, he scanned the ground and found another one. And then two more.

Whether those were *human* remains, he certainly couldn't be sure. They were only fragments of larger pieces. And if entire worlds had been dumped here when they ended, he was sure the remaining local fauna came with them. And Wayne had described plenty of "zombies" he and Olivia glimpsed during his rescue mission into the forest around Gilbert House that weren't even remotely human.

Still, the sight of bones among the wreckage was a sobering reminder of where they were.

This was the Wood. Where the dead didn't move on. Where souls became trapped inside their mortal shells forever, rotting with them, fusing with them, until they became a terrible mockery of the very life that they lost.

It was an *awful* place to die.

Albert had been staring down at the ground, distracted, but now he looked up, his thoughts scattered.

Where was he?

A long, dark corridor was laid out before him, empty and cold and stark like the inside of a tomb, with rough stone walls. He turned and looked behind him, only to find more of the same.

"Brandy...?"

But Brandy wasn't here. She hadn't been here since... He frowned. Since *when*? What was happening? How did he get here? Wasn't he just in the Wood? He could almost hear the "tokka-tokka" sounds of that strange monster nest in the wreckage of a past universe...

But that was...

He winced at a pain in his head. That wasn't right. That wasn't just now. That was *before*.

He closed his eyes for a moment and took a deep breath. But only for a moment. He didn't have time to stand around feeling confused. He had to find Brandy. She had to be here somewhere.

He opened his eyes and continued on. He shined his flashlight down at the shaman's book he was holding open in his hand. The words scrawled on the page looked strange. He felt as if he'd never seen this particular page before. But he also felt as if he'd already read it. It was both scrawled in Shanzer's sloppy handwriting and at the same time in those strange, illegible symbols.

Why was he so confused? Was there something about this corridor? Something in the air here, making him feel delirious?

He turned the page and found the next page folded and creased. He stopped and stared at it. He remembered that…

His thoughts swirled like a hurricane inside his head. *Full circle…* he thought. Half of him seemed to know what those words meant. Half of him remained confused.

But he knew what he had to do.

He closed the book and looked up at the empty corridor ahead of him. "Stay away from the castle!" he shouted into the emptiness. "Ignore the cries!"

His heart was suddenly pounding. Was that how it went? Did he do it right?

He looked down at the book again, but he wasn't holding it. His hand was empty.

"Albert?" asked Brandy from ahead of him.

He looked up to find that he was standing out in the black, litter-strewn forest again. Brandy, Violet and Corey were all staring back at him.

"You okay?" asked Violet.

"What happened?" he asked. Was he just…somewhere else…?

"That's what *I* was going to ask," said Brandy.

"You just sort of checked out," said Violet.

"All frozen, like," added Corey.

"Sorry…" He looked down at his empty hand again, but he couldn't remember why he was looking at his hand. Did he think he was holding something?

He looked back the way he'd come, as if maybe he'd dropped it…but that didn't seem right either. Whatever he was just thinking about, it was gone. Forgotten.

Brandy took his hand and pulled him along. "Let's just stay together, okay?"

He nodded. "Right. Sorry."

The four of them moved on and Albert let the odd sensation of something forgotten drift away.

Chapter 37

Everett walked a few paces ahead of Olivia and Wayne, his eyes peeled for any more of the Wood's dangerous creatures or more falling metal rods.

Wayne hadn't said a word to him, but he knew he was pissed. And he could hardly blame him. If he'd kept to the middle of the path and away from the edge like he was told, that monstrous encounter wouldn't have happened. Probably. Although, he could have argued that the noise of all that metal crashing to the ground was enough to make the thing notice them in spite of any magical concealing effects the stone road possessed...if he were a much braver person.

More than anything, however, he simply felt awful. Wayne got hurt because of him. That wasn't right. The choices he made, the chances he took...his risks...his gambles... He never intended for that to affect anyone other than himself.

And poor Olivia was so afraid. What would have happened if that monster had killed her fiancé? The thought of it made him feel ill. She'd been so nice to him. What a terrible way to show his appreciation!

Even now, she was worried sick. "We've gone far enough," she decided. "We should stop."

"Not yet," insisted Wayne, still looking back over his shoulder, convinced something else would be along any second to punch more holes in him.

"You're still bleeding."

"It looks worse than it is," he assured her. And Everett certainly hoped so. He was walking with one hand pressed against a dreadful-looking stain that had spread halfway down his tee shirt, applying pressure to the wound underneath.

"Let me see it," fussed Olivia.

"I'm fine."

But she was already yanking up his shirt to see for herself. "Move your hand."

"It's nothing."

"*Show me.*"

Wayne relented and stopped walking.

Everett looked back, worried that he was hiding a serious injury under there. And when Olivia hissed at the sight of it, he felt his heart leap at the grim possibility that they could be in real trouble.

"Ouch..." she sighed.

"It's not deep," he assured her. "It just gave me a hard gouge. Luckily those tusks weren't very sharp."

She prodded at the wound with her fingers, careful not to touch it directly with her dirty hands. "Yeah... You're right... I don't think it's *too* serious."

"Told you. Didn't even go through the shirt."

Everett turned away with a sigh of relief and shined his light out into the surrounding darkness, making himself useful by keeping watch.

"I'd feel better if we could at least put a bandage on you," she pressed. "I don't like that it's still bleeding."

Everett stood up straighter at this. "Oh yeah!" He slapped at his shorts for a moment, trying to remember where everything was, then stuffed his hand into one of his pockets. He'd lost his first aid kit along with his pack when Maeve's fairy circle fell apart. The last he saw of it, it was still chained to an angry, undead bear. But he wasn't left completely unprepared. He withdrew a small, plastic container and hurried back to her. "Band Aids!" he announced.

"Oh, thank goodness!" gasped Olivia, taking the container from him and opening it.

Everett grinned up at Wayne, proud of himself, but promptly wiped the look away and turned his attention elsewhere when he only scowled back at him.

Yep. He was pissed.

Olivia selected a larger sized bandage and pressed it over the wound. "That's better," she decided. "But I'd still rather be able to properly disinfect it."

"It'll be fine." Wayne tugged his shirt back down and looked over his shoulder, still paranoid. "That whole thing back there was weird, wasn't it?" he asked, eager to change the subject.

"You mean the part where you decided to be all macho and go jousting with that thing?" asked Olivia, exasperated. "*Yeah.* It was *really* weird."

He chuckled a little at this. "No." He turned his attention forward and continued walking. "I mean what are the odds of that one metal rod standing all this time and then *just happening* to fall right where we were standing, at just that exact moment?"

Everett glanced out at that strange, metal forest, surprised. He had a point. While there were far more of those mysterious rods standing upright, there was no shortage of broken ones, so he didn't think much about one falling at the time. But if this stuff had really been here as long as Nadia said it had, then that was something that simply couldn't happen very often. And after hearing the racket that one made coming down, they'd know for sure if any of them fell while they were passing through. Didn't that make the odds against one of these things almost landing on top of them nearly astronomical?

Olivia was processing all of this, too. She was looking out into the coppery forest. "You think something made that happen?"

"Sandy did tell us there was someone or something out there trying to sabotage the cycle." He urged her forward, wanting to keep moving. "They even killed that Erin woman."

Everett continued forward, staying ahead of them. He didn't ask who Sandy was. He'd heard them use that name. It sounded like she was like Nadia. Someone they met before all that business in Gutler's Weep. Someone a lot like this mysterious "Keeper" everyone kept talking about. Clearly there was still a lot of their story that he hadn't heard.

Was there an unseen enemy lurking in this vast, black wilderness? Someone who knocked over that rod in a blatant attempt to kill them? It was an odd feeling to think that a killer's eyes could be on him right now. It was definitely a frightening concept. Somewhere inside, he could feel a part of him spiraling down into those terrible old emotions his mother instilled in him, back when he was afraid of everything and everyone. Because wasn't that exactly what she always told him would happen if he ventured out into the world without her? Wasn't that what she always wanted him to believe? That it was an absolute truth that someone out in that big, cruel world would victimize him?

He wasn't afraid of the world anymore. He knew there were bad people in it, just like she always said, people who preyed on others, the greedy, the selfish and the sick. But he'd found that they were the exception, rather than the rule. And *truly* evil people were exceedingly rare. But they *did* exist. He wasn't so blind that he couldn't see that. History books were filled with the deeds of evil people.

But were *people* even a part of the equation now? The things he'd witnessed these past few days were proof of exactly what he set out in search of in the first place. That there were plenty of *inhuman* things out there. He could still remember the angel he saw the night his mother tried to drag them both to hell. A heavenly vision of feminine beauty, though he couldn't remember what she looked like, exactly. Looking back it seemed strangely as if it were at the same time both too bright and too dark to truly see her, not in any way he could properly remember. But he remembered that she had a tremendous presence. He remembered that she was beautiful. And he remembered that she *sparkled*.

Angels were real. And if angels were real, then heaven was real, regardless of the lies his deranged mother told him. And if angels and heaven were real, then couldn't *anything* be real?

He set out determined to find the truth as soon as he was able. And *this* was the truth. Nothing in the world was as his mother said it was. In fact, nothing in the world was as *anyone* said it was. And yet he suddenly found himself spiraling back to where he started. Because if there was something in this forest that conspired to kill them, something smart enough and sneaky enough to topple that rod almost on top of them and simultaneously set that monster on them...

They'll kill you! he thought in his mother's vile voice, remembering all the times she shouted those sick lies at him. *The world is evil! They only want to see you suffer and die and go to hell!*

He cast his light off to the left and saw that those faux-copper rods were thinning out. They were reaching the end of it. The night trees were crowding in again. Those strange, coiling branches looked somehow much more ominous than they did before.

Within twenty or thirty minutes, they were behind them and out of sight. Only the night trees remained.

"It was the thing Maeve and Nadia mentioned, isn't it?" said Olivia. They'd been walking in silence for a while now, contemplating what Wayne had said. "The *chaotic* whatever-it-is."

"Probably," he replied. He looked out into the night trees, worried.

"How are we supposed to even handle something like that?"

"I don't know. But we can. Why else would we be here?"

Olivia didn't answer, but she clearly wasn't convinced.

Everett said nothing, but his curiosity was eating at him. Something *chaotic*... It sounded like something out of a sword and sorcery tale, the kind of thing that would have fire-breathing dragons and shadowy necromancers at its disposal. The ultimate evil to test the might of the undaunted heroes.

But that was the problem wasn't it? Wouldn't Wayne say that this was no silly story? That they weren't exactly an intrepid band of battle-hardened adventurers thirsting for glory? They were just three people who happened to have stumbled off the park map and into the "staff only" area.

He'd sat and listened to their story on the train ride here. He knew what they'd been through. He understood why they were frightened.

Except...*were* they? They both walked into that Gilbert House place with no clue whatsoever what they were getting into. It wasn't their fault they were there. The things that happened inside weren't their fault. But the fact that really stuck with him was that Wayne walked out of that building and could have gone home. But he didn't. He said he continued into those tunnels under the city willingly, with no idea that Olivia was even still alive.

He was quite sure that he didn't have the whole story, that there were things Wayne had left out for one reason or another, even if only to save time. But no matter how he looked at it, that simply wasn't the sort of thing someone who was afraid would do.

And then later, after he found her, after they endured that terrifying escape from the Wood, *both* of them walked out of that nightmare...and *again* they chose to keep going. They walked together right back into that dark, scary world to face their fears all over again.

He understood that they never asked to receive those envelopes, but they had chances to turn back and they didn't. That kind of courage was inspiring. And it was more than clear that Wayne still possessed an astonishing amount of courage. Not many people would have done what he did back there just now.

Wayne wasn't afraid of the things in this amazing and perilous forest. He was afraid of losing Olivia. And no one could blame him for that.

Everett glanced around, realizing that the forest floor was changing around him. The black, baren earth was giving way to rocks and sand. The night trees were thinning out again.

They were somewhere new, he realized.

A part of him was as excited as ever, of course. But another part of him was apprehensive. What if he messed up again? What if he was the reason something terrible happened to one of his new friends?

He needed to get his head on straight.

This wasn't a game.

Chapter 38

Keith stared down at the empty bottle as he walked, thinking about that tiny twinkle of impossible light he saw somewhere deep inside, trying to wrap his head around what was in there. It *looked* empty. It *felt* empty. And there was no cork or cap to contain anything, even if it wasn't.

What could be inside? And why did he see it in his dream?

Was it just another part of this weird journey they were on? According to Andrea, she was carrying an object that found its way into their possession just as mysteriously. A spear that was also a key...but also a leaf...or something...? He hadn't actually seen it, but it sounded very important. And the same thing happened six years ago to their friends, Brandy and Albert. Except it wasn't a spear...leaf...key...*thing*. And it wasn't an empty bottle that...wasn't. Instead, it was a box and a key. Which sounded a lot less weird, to be honest.

He hadn't been able to fully follow Andrea's story back on the boat. Something about those tunnels under the city that people liked to talk about and some kind of ancient temple hidden somewhere under it all. Monsters and puzzles and statues that had the power to induce fits of lust, rage and fear. And apparently they were all butt naked the whole time?

That was a thing? That actually happened? That Albert guy was just...walking around down there with all those attractive, naked girls?

Lucky bastard.

He pushed the thought from his mind. This was no place to be dwelling on such things. And he certainly didn't care to think about his ex-girlfriend naked. That reminded him too much of the past. And it was weird to think about Andrea like that, too. She seemed so much younger than the rest of them. Especially with her fondness for those girlish pigtails. Instead, he focused on the bottle.

There was something about it. It was only about two inches wide and about three inches high, solidly made and heavy. The glass was old and clouded and dingy, but still transparent, allowing him to see all the way through it, and it was clearly empty. Yet for some reason he kept thinking that the thing he saw glinting in the darkness of that broken building was something *within* it. Something he couldn't see. Something deep down inside…

That was the phrase that kept swimming through his thoughts. "Deep down." As if it weren't a tiny little bottle at all, but rather a vast *ocean.* As if something could sink into its cavernous belly for dark and murky *miles* before reaching its bottom.

All the way into… Somewhere *else…*

It was ridiculous, of course. What did that even mean? And yet the thought was strangely stubborn. He stared into the empty glass bottle and again caught a fleeting glance of something glinting in the darkness…

Something *deep down inside…*

Ahead of him, Andrea stopped walking. Distracted by his mysterious bottle, he nearly collided with her before noticing.

"What just happened?" she asked.

Nicole and Gina stopped and looked back at her, confused.

"What?" asked Keith. He glanced around, but nothing new had appeared. The path had been mostly clear since they left the questionable safety of that ruined building and returned to the road. There'd only been those sickly night trees lingering at the far reaches of their flashlights. He wasn't aware of anything out of the ordinary.

Andrea pointed up into the darkness to her left. "What happened to the thing?"

"What thing?" asked Nicole.

"There was…" But she frowned. "*Wasn't* there a thing? Just now?"

Nicole tipped her head to one side and raised an eyebrow. "Sweetie, you're talking crazy again."

Andrea looked back at Keith. She seemed to be trying hard to think straight.

"Are you okay?" he asked.

But she blinked back at him, confused. "What was I saying just now? Something about the…the thing…?"

Nicole stepped forward and grabbed her hand. "Okay, you're starting to freak me out a little now."

"Sorry…"

"It's this place," said Gina. "It's broken. Everything's crinkled up."

"Yeah, you said that before," recalled Nicole. "But we still don't understand what that means."

"It plays with your mind."

"Are you feeling all right?" Nicole asked, looking Andrea over. She nodded. "I think so. I just… I was confused for a second."

"Do we need to stop and rest?" she pressed.

"No. I'm better now. Really."

"We should keep moving," urged Gina. "There are things around us. The road seems to hide us, but I don't know what might happen if they wander too close."

"I'm definitely good to keep going," decided Andrea, looking around with those wide, worried eyes.

The four of them continued on.

Keith took the rear and looked back the way they came. He hadn't noticed anything moving, but then again, he'd let himself get distracted by his curiosity about the bottle. He could easily have missed something. As dangerous as this place was, he needed to focus. This was no place to let his mind wander.

But when he looked forward again, everyone was gone.

He stood there a moment, confused, staring into the darkness ahead of him. "Where'd you go?" he asked, seemingly throwing the inquiry into the very darkness that surrounded him.

"Where'd *who* go?" asked Nicole.

He turned around to find all three of them standing there, staring back at him. "What…?"

"What's wrong?" asked Andrea. "Did you see a thing, too?"

"What? No. I just… How'd you get behind me?"

She frowned, confused. "What do you mean?"

He glanced back again. "You were just…"

"Are you sure you didn't hit your head when you were crawling around in that junk?" asked Nicole.

"Distortions," said Gina. "Playing with our minds. We should keep moving. And stay close together."

Again, they pushed forward.

Keith looked down at the bottle he was holding for a moment, still trying to wrap his head around what just happened, then he slipped it into the pocket of his jeans and continued onward, hurrying to catch up.

It plays with our minds, he thought. That's what Gina kept saying. That was all there was to it. He just needed to ignore the things that didn't make sense and focus on where they were going.

But were they still going the right way? He tried to recall how many times he turned around. It seemed like he was facing the other direction, but everyone else seemed pretty confident they were going the right way. And wasn't Gina sort of a human compass? It seemed like she knew where they were going far better than he did.

And a few minutes later, he saw something appear from the gloom ahead of them that wasn't there before, confirming that they hadn't turned around.

It was another night tree, its trunk crowded right up to the edge of the stone walk so that its branches drooped across the entire path. He could see the way those strange, fleshy roots bristled up from the earth along the edge, some of them creeping right up over the stone, making him wonder just how deep the path was laid. Shouldn't a normal stone path have been pushed upward by such big roots? It happened to city sidewalks all the time. How deep was the stone they were walking on?

It goes deep, he thought. *All the way into…somewhere* else.

He shook his head. What the hell did *that* mean?

No. He didn't have time to let crazy thoughts distract him. Now wasn't the time to think about ancient stone pathway engineering or the behavior of alien, man-eating tree roots. The proximity of the tree meant that those deadly tendrils were impossible to avoid while remaining on the path. Andrea said the trees were sleeping, that they'd only wake up when they'd absorbed enough light…which sort of sounded fake, but he had no intention of testing it.

All three of the girls made a wide berth of the monstrous thing, stepping clear off the path to avoid passing within striking distance, all of them hooding their flashlights with their hands and hurrying past.

Not quite daring to tempt fate, he did the same.

Around them, other trees were crowding closer, too, he saw. They were moving deeper into the strange, black forest. Those snatching branches were closing in from every angle. It was getting harder and harder to avoid passing beneath one of them.

"The way they're drooping," pondered Andrea. "That's going to make it a lot harder, isn't it?"

"The ones on the mountain path up the temple didn't do that," agreed Nicole. "Until they really woke up, we could still walk under them."

"So…what exactly happens?" asked Keith, curious. "They'll grab us and drag us up into their branches?"

"Like something right out of a horror movie," confirmed Nicole.

"Then what?" he wondered, peering at those limp, coiled branches that looked like dangling snakes. "Is it like a Venus fly trap kind of situation?" He didn't see anything that resembled a mouth.

"They strangle and bite," said Andrea.

"*Bite?*"

"They have teeth," said Nicole. "I've still got marks to prove it."

"Yeah, last time we saw one of these things, they nearly killed her," explained Andrea. "And Brandy and Albert. They were trying to save her, but they only ended up caught in it, too."

He grimaced at the thought and made a mental note to not get too curious about the death plants. "How'd they escape?"

"She set it on fire," replied Nicole.

"Oh." He nodded. "That would do it."

"I don't think that'll work again, though," said Andrea, glancing up at those motionless branches.

"Fire was a lot easier to come by last time," agreed Nicole.

"Yeah, the whole mountain was kind of on fire."

Keith frowned. An entire mountain on fire? Andrea had talked about what happened to them five years ago, but she wasn't the most concise storyteller. She had a tendency to lose her way as she talked. He was pretty sure he was still missing a lot of the story.

"They won't be too much trouble asleep like they are now," Gina assured them. "They take longer to wake up than it does for us to pass. Especially here, where the weird atmosphere hinders them. But they're still dangerous to touch." She lifted her light and pointed it toward one of the trees farther out, its coiled branches still tangled around a knotted mass of dry bones.

"No touchy," croaked Keith. "Important safety tip. Got it."

The path ahead was getting more crowded, but even so there remained enough space between each tree that they didn't really overlap. Keith wondered if that was a result of their nature. Did they entangle each other if they grew too close, ultimately cannibalizing each other? It only made sense, he supposed. It was easy enough to imagine them ripping an unfortunate sapling right out of the ground if it happened to sprout within grasping distance.

He turned and shined his light out into the forest and onto a dark shape crawling across the forest floor.

The sight startled him, making him jump. His heart leapt in his chest.

Panic overwhelmed him.

Everything was chaos and pain.

He stumbled through the trees, exhausted, clutching at his injured arm. How long had he been running? And how much blood had he lost? He barely managed to get his arm up in time to shield his face. But the thing's teeth had done a number on him. He definitely needed stitches. He was starting to feel lightheaded. But he very much doubted he was going to be lucky enough to find an emergency room out here in this black wilderness.

And he certainly couldn't stop for a rest. The monster was still back there. He could hear it behind him, slow but tireless, a relentless killing machine that never stopped. Every time he thought he'd finally lost it, he'd hear that awful dragging sound again.

How did it keep finding him?

"It won't hurt us," said Gina.

Keith blinked at the strange, pitiful shape crawling across the black floor of the forest. Then he looked over at his companions. All three of them had stopped and were shining their lights at it. Nicole and Andrea had crowded close together, afraid of it.

What just happened? Why was his heart racing? He'd only glimpsed the thing, and yet for a second it was as if he were being chased down by it.

Or by something much worse…

But the memory of it was already fading. He couldn't seem to hold onto it.

"It doesn't see us," Gina assured them. "The road."

"If you say so," said Nicole.

They turned and pushed onward.

But Keith stood there a moment, confused. It felt like something had happened. He looked down at his arm, half-expecting it to be covered in blood for some reason.

Distortions, he recalled Gina saying. *Playing with our minds.*

He felt like he'd forgotten something frightening. Was it something important? Some crucial revelation about this frightful forest?

He stared out at the strange, misshapen thing crawling across the ground nearby, trying to remember what went through his head when he was first surprised by it.

But it was gone.

He carried on, confused.

Ahead of them, something new emerged from the darkness, distracting him.

It looked sort of like one of those huge farm silos tipped on its side, but bigger. A great, crumpled cylinder of dull gray metal lay across the path, blocking the way forward. There was no sign of either end of it. And it was too big to go over.

"We'll have to go around," reasoned Gina.

"You think?" grumbled Nicole.

"It was kind of obvious," she admitted, wilting a little at her tone. "I only said it because it means we'll have to leave the path. And that makes me uneasy."

"Uneasy…" she muttered.

Keith could almost read her mind. Anything that made Gina uneasy certainly made *him* uneasy. And he could certainly understand why leaving the path would make *anyone* uneasy. He glanced over his shoulder, back toward the thing crawling across the ground. It wasn't that far behind them. And he doubted it was the only thing out there.

"We should do it as quickly as possible," said Gina. "There are holes in the forest."

"Holes?" asked Andrea. "What, like just in the ground?"

Gina fixed that sleepy gaze on her. "No. In reality. If we're not careful we could fall out of the Denselands and end up somewhere a lot worse."

"Fucking *perfect*," growled Nicole. "This just gets better and better."

"Sorry."

"No, you're fine. Let's just…get this over with." She shined her light one way, then the other. "Which way's shorter?"

But Gina shook her head. "I can't tell."

Andrea squinted into the darkness. "How can't you tell? I thought you could sense everything in your surroundings."

"I can. But this thing goes on a lot farther than my mind can see."

Farther than her mind could see? Keith looked up at it. That couldn't be a silo, then, as he first thought. What kind of structure was that large? Was it some kind of massive pipeline or something?

Nicole cursed and shined her light over the surface. It was almost forty feet high, with nothing to use as footholds. There was no way they were going over it.

"So we just pick a direction and go?" asked Keith. He didn't care for the idea of having to take some epic hike through this nightmare forest just to go around one obstacle.

But again, she shook her head. She pointed to the left. "Not that way."

"What's that way?" squeaked Andrea.

"I don't know. But it has lots of teeth."

"*Okay!*" decided Keith. "Right it is." The briefest of memories surfaced in his mind, something with huge, jagged teeth…but then it was gone again. "Let's get this over with."

Chapter 39

Brandy stepped onto the familiar gray stone, a sense of relief filling her anxious mind. And not merely because it meant they weren't completely lost. There was something about this particular stone beneath her feet that felt safe. And yet she couldn't decide if that was a real feeling or simply because Violet told them that those creepy twins said so.

"Told you this was the right way," said Albert, shining his light back and forth, illuminating the shadow road.

"Nice," said Violet, impressed.

"Good job," agreed Corey.

Brandy turned and gave him a quick kiss. "Always my hero," she teased.

"I try," he said awkwardly, sounding adorably embarrassed. (She *loved* doing that to him.)

She turned her attention to the path ahead as they continued forward. That soft but steady wind was blowing at their backs again, just like he said, pointing the way to whatever was waiting for them at the end of this nightmare journey. (At least it seemed like she was getting used to that strange heavy feeling. She didn't notice it as much as she did when they first arrived.) "But it's not like it's much safer here. We're still out in the open."

"True," he agreed. "But it still feels different being on the road. I can't really explain it."

"I feel like that, too," said Violet. "It's weird."

"There's something about it." He looked down at his feet as he walked. "Something…"

"Significant?" finished Brandy.

He chuckled. "Yeah. Significant."

The terrain around them was still covered in litter, but it was slowly thinning out. They hadn't encountered any more ruined buildings. Or any more crashed ships. Or anything else for that matter.

There were more night trees than before, crowding closer together, making them more difficult to avoid. Some were growing right up next to the road, forcing them to step off the path to keep from ducking under those dangerous branches. But only briefly.

Albert was right, she realized. Every time they did that, it felt strangely *wrong*. Like they were more exposed, even though it shouldn't make any difference if they walked a few feet to the left or right instead of straight down the middle.

If one of those giant tokkatoks came charging out of those woods, there was literally nothing to stop it. And yet, it didn't feel like that could happen while their feet were on the path.

Could that really just be the power of suggestion at work? She was finding it harder and harder to believe that she could only imagine it.

Did it have something to do with the stone? Albert had referred to it as "temple stone" when he saw the giant face carved from it. It was the same stuff everything was made of down in the temple. And Lucianna said the sentinels built both that place and these roads. Did that make them essentially one and the same?

Engineering marvels of a long-lost civilization, she recalled. That was what one of the creepy twins said back on January Street, according to Violet. Were they talking about the *sentinels*?

What *were* the sentinels, anyway? Lucianna called them the "Faceless Ones." The Keeper's architects who apparently built all this stuff way back when everything was still brand-new or something. *No one knows much about them*, she remembered the kooky old bat telling them, *where they came from, where they went*. But one thing was certain. The Temple of the Blind wasn't just passageways of stone and mysterious statues carved with impossibly realistic detail. They'd somehow crafted *raw emotion* directly into some of those chambers, enough to drive a person *mad*. And she couldn't possibly forget that room where something the rest of them couldn't see frightened Beverly so badly she fell to her death on those murderous spikes. And what sorts of things were hidden away in that darkness that they never laid eyes on? Albert mentioned a few times that there had to be an entire sustainable ecosystem somewhere in the temple to support a species of creature like the hounds. And then there was the fact that the whole thing, from top to bottom, was a giant dimensional gateway of some sort.

If they could do something like *that*, then why wouldn't there be something special built into this unassuming stone pathway to help protect them from the horrors of the Wood?

Because Albert wasn't wrong to wonder. Where *were* all the zombies? The only monsters they'd encountered since arriving here were the tokkatoks, and that was when they'd wandered well off the path.

She understood completely why Albert was so fascinated with all of this. The unanswerable questions were maddening. She wanted to understand it all. But she wasn't quite as brave as he was. If she thought about it too much, she'd have nightmares.

But she supposed that was inevitable anyway... She'd had enough scares since walking into that ridiculous sex museum to fuel her nightmares for months.

Ahead of them, Corey was leading the way. He was using the LED lantern again, conserving his far more powerful flashlight's battery while there was nothing worth seeing.

Violet followed close behind him, studying those twisting branches as she passed each drooping night tree. "Jasburg," she recalled.

Corey nodded. "I was thinking of that, too."

"It's the only other one I know of."

"What?" asked Brandy, confused.

"Killer flowers," explained Violet. "That's as close as we've ever come to trees like these."

Albert kept glancing back over his shoulder, keeping an eye on the endless darkness at their backs, making sure something wasn't sneaking up behind them. "You guys have seen stuff like this before?"

"No," replied Violet. "Just stories."

"No proof," agreed Corey.

"We've collected *lots* of stories. But the *vast* majority of them are bullshit. Nothing even worth investigating."

"How do you decide which ones *are* worth it?" wondered Brandy.

"Depends. Sometimes it's worth a look if there's lots of evidence. Or decades of police reports. Or if a story is particularly compelling for some reason."

"Gut feeling," said Corey.

"Or if Corey has a gut feeling," she agreed. "Sometimes."

Albert raised an eyebrow, curious. "So you guys are psychic too?"

"Oh, I don't know about *that*," said Violet, wrinkling her nose at the idea. "More like ordinary intuition."

"I might be a little psychic," said Corey.

"I don't think so."

"'Cause of my gut feelings."

"You're not psychic."

"I always know when I'm going to have those weird dreams."

"So do I," she countered. "Every time you eat spicy Thai food right before bed. That's not psychic."

"It's not just Thai…"

"That's indigestion. Not psychic."

"Mexican does it, too. Sometimes."

"We don't have anything like that," said Violet, ignoring him. "Although every now and then his gut feelings are pretty spot-on."

"Psychic," he insisted.

"We never knew we were psychic until five years ago," said Albert. "Never even really believed in it, I don't think."

Brandy nodded. It never even crossed her mind before that. And she wasn't sure she ever believed a word of it even *after* the Sentinel Queen told her she had such a power. Not until the pervert shaman's weird magic lessons started tuning her directly into people's intimate inner workings…

Now it was getting harder and harder to doubt that she had some kind of mysterious power to see the truth within people.

"What's it feel like?" asked Violet, curious.

"It's kind of hard to describe," said Albert. Again, he turned and shined his light behind him.

Brandy looked back, too. Magic sentinel-built road or not, it made her nervous being out in the open like this. But still, they weren't being followed. At least, not close enough to be caught in his flashlight beam.

"For me, it's this feeling of *significance.* Like, something can look completely normal, but I'll just get this feeling like it's meaningful somehow. Significant, you know?"

"Right," said Violet, waggling a finger at them. "You guys used that word just a minute ago, didn't you? That's what you were talking about."

Albert nodded. "We did, yeah."

"That's pretty cool," she decided.

Brandy stopped walking.

Albert paused, concerned. "You okay?"

Ahead of them, Corey and Violet looked back to see what was happening.

She turned and looked out into that endless darkness behind them, a concerned frown on her pretty face.

"Brandy?"

"Yeah… I'm okay…" But still she stood there, staring out into the blackness for a moment. Was it only her imagination? Her tired mind playing tricks on her?

"Seriously," pressed Albert. "What's up?"

"Nothing." She started walking again, but for a moment she was still watching that pursuing darkness.

It was only for the briefest of instances, perhaps a fraction of a second, little more than a flash in her mind. But it had seemed for that tiniest of moments that there was someone else here with them. A fifth person. Someone who didn't belong.

But it was gone now. There was nothing back there. And why *would* there be? This was no place for *anyone* to be.

"Nothing," she said again, turning her attention forward at last. "Just jumpy. Sorry."

Albert nodded, but his gaze lingered back there as well, uncertain.

Ahead of them, Violet and Corey continued onward.

Chapter 40

Olivia watched as something new emerged from the darkness in Everett's flashlight beam ahead of them.

Twelve-foot-high walls were blocking the way forward, made of what looked like reddish-brown sandstone. For a second or two, she found herself wondering if maybe they'd reached their destination, but the road just ended there, as if these walls had fallen out of the sky and landed on top of it. The way forward was blocked.

They shined their lights back and forth. There were doorways and windows offering an eerie preview of the dark space within. There was no glass, no doors of any kind to keep them from going inside the structure, but none of those openings were located in line with the road.

The whole scene was a stark contrast to the strange field of towering copper rods, the bizarre, translucent green structure and the vehicle that looked like nothing that ever rolled off an assembly line in their own world. This looked like it had jumped right out of the stone age.

"What the fuck *now?*" grumbled Wayne.

It was a good question. She didn't care for the thought of him having to deal with anything unexpected so soon after being injured by that monster. And those walls looked like they might contain any number of deeply unpleasant surprises.

"I thought we were supposed to stay on the road?" said Everett, bewildered.

"Yeah," sighed Wayne. "Me too."

She nodded. Wasn't that the hard lesson they just learned a little while ago with that mutant whatever-the-heck-it-was? Stay on the path to stay out of sight? But the path ended here. How could they keep to the road if someone dropped *downtown Bedrock* on top of it?

Everett shined his light farther along the rough walls. She followed the beam with her own as it moved, adding her light to his. The structure stretched beyond their sight in both directions, making it painfully obvious that they weren't going to be able to simply hurry around it. Instead, he turned his attention to the nearest of those open doorways. "We might be able to sneak *through* it," he suggested. It was only about twenty feet from the path. And they'd be partially shielded by the wall.

"And right into a whole nest of monsters," countered Wayne. "We have no idea what might be living in something like that."

Olivia made a face at the awful thought, but she wasn't sure what other choice they had. She aimed her light at a window that was between the road and the door, only about *eight* feet off the path. They should be able to see if there was anything inside through there.

She didn't need to tell him. Everett took the hint and stepped off the path, already walking toward it.

"Hold on!" hissed Wayne.

He turned and looked back at him. "If you have a better idea, I'm listening."

Wayne stared back at him, unhappy, unconvinced, but without a reply. He *didn't* have a better idea. Because there weren't any other options. They had to get around this obstruction or they weren't going to be able to continue. Instead, he glanced at Olivia.

"I don't feel anything," she replied without him having to ask. And if her psychic senses weren't telling her this was a bad idea, then nothing would happen to him. Right? Wasn't that how it worked? She met Everett's eyes and nodded. "Lead the way."

He nodded back at her, then turned and continued creeping toward the window.

She couldn't help holding her breath as she watched him peer inside, cautiously at first, then more boldly, aiming his light through it.

"It's empty," he informed them.

She tugged on Wayne's arm and then hurried over to him. Peeking in over his shoulder, she spied a small, rectangular space. The floor was the same dry, packed sand that surrounded the structure. There were no furnishings of any kind to indicate anyone had ever lived here. No barrels or crates to indicate it was some kind of storage house. There was only a tall step along one side, creating a sort of empty shelf space.

It was odd. The angles of the stone were rough like sandstone, but also perfectly even. They didn't look like someone had carved it out by hand. It looked more like someone poured the stone into place in some kind of mold, more like concrete. The inner corners were perfectly straight. And yet it didn't look anything like concrete. It looked like *sandstone.*

A corridor led off the back of this room to another farther in. They could probably climb through it, but it would be faster if they just used the door.

She turned and shined her light out into the forest behind them. Nothing appeared to be out there. And she didn't feel anything unpleasant.

"We okay?" asked Wayne.

She nodded. "Seems clear. Let's try to find a way through."

Everett didn't need to be told twice. He took off, pushing onward, and she hurried after him.

A larger room waited behind the open doorway. There was something on the floor that looked like long-rotten cloth, but whether it was a rug or just a discarded blanket was going to remain a mystery. Otherwise, it was as empty as the first room. There was another door on the far side, leading to another empty room and, for the moment at least, there didn't seem to be a way leading back toward the road. They'd have to push onward from here and hope this place had a back door.

She shined her light out into the forest again. This time, she caught sight of something dark and low to the ground scurrying out of sight. It looked about the size of a cat, not nearly as intimidating as that last thing. And nothing about it triggered that dreadful psychic alarm feeling, so she ignored it and ducked through the doorway behind Everett.

Then she stopped, confused.

"You okay?" asked Wayne, concerned. "Did you feel something? Should we leave?"

"No…" She frowned. What *did* she feel. For a moment there, it felt like she was somewhere else. Another room, much bigger than this one, its floor littered with countless bones…

But that was a strange thing to think. She *wasn't* in some other room. She was right here, in *this* one. And there certainly weren't any bones lying around. At least, none that she'd seen so far.

"What's up?" pressed Wayne.

"Nothing. Just…spooked, I think."

"You say the word and we'll get out of here," Everett assured her.

"Yeah," agreed Wayne. "Definitely."

"I appreciate that." She turned and looked out through the open doorway again, still frowning. That didn't feel like her psychic warning alarm. Although it didn't feel like someplace she wanted to be, it didn't have that same sensation of imminent dread.

Was that one of Sandy's amber threads? A glimpse of the possible future? Something *beyond* a simple danger alarm?

What did it mean?

"Do you need to stop for a while?" worried Wayne.

She shook her head and grasped his arm again. "No. We should keep moving."

"Okay," he said, kissing her on the forehead. "Whatever you say."

She wished she understood how all this psychic stuff worked. She hated not understanding her own brain.

Chapter 41

Gina really didn't like it out here. These woods were unlike anything she'd ever felt before. They filled her with an almost *primal* sense of dread, as if some long-buried survival sense from deep within her genetic coding were *screaming* at her that she shouldn't be here.

It was almost the opposite of all the other places they'd found themselves in these past few days. Tristesse Lane. That awful hospital. Cedric's Cove. Those places were all strangely *small*. They *looked* like they went on forever, but they were crumpled up and twisted back on themselves. Or they bled off into some kind of void. But this place felt *enormous*. It actually *did* seem to go on forever. And there was something uniquely terrifying about that strange endlessness.

She'd always felt small in the world…insignificant…*weak*…but not like *this*. Here, in this dark and endless expanse, she felt more vulnerable than she'd ever felt in her life, like an insect caught in a busy crosswalk, about to be crushed underfoot at any second. And that feeling was only growing worse with every passing moment.

It was a mistake to leave that stone path. It was the safest route through this deadly forest. There was something about it, after all. It looked so simple, just a road cut and laid through this vast, black wilderness, nothing more than a line for them to follow to their destination, their own, less-colorful version of the yellow brick road. But it was much more than it appeared. Her psychic awareness revealed that it went far deeper than any ordinary road, stretching on and on, deep into the earth, well beyond the line of sight of her mysterious psychic eye. And it had, after all, allowed them to maneuver an ordinary trawler across an unimaginably vast lake in an extraordinarily short amount of time, even with the depth of an entire lake between them and it. It had also done something to shield them from the monstrous things that lurked out here in this hellish forest. She'd felt it working, keeping the things around them from turning their dead eyes on them as they passed, very much as if something about that deep, deep stone concealed their presence. Even that thing they took refuge from inside the broken building only passed as close as it did by chance. It never noticed them. If it had, she was quite certain they'd all be dead right now.

But of course, staying on the path hadn't been an option. There was no way over the obstruction. And after what felt like an hour of walking—although it was impossible to say exactly how much time had passed in this twisted environment—there was still no end in sight.

The good news was that even from this distance, she could still sense the path behind them. It was like a lighthouse in the fog, a beacon calling out to her. Finding it again wasn't going to be a problem. They needed only to find a way around this *thing* in their way.

Was it a building? It wasn't very wide. There were no doors or windows. She sensed that it was mostly empty. It was nothing more than a forty-foot-high cylinder lying on its side, wrapped in thin, smooth metal. It wasn't rusted or tarnished, only dusty and covered in splotchy, mottled stains. But it was crumpled in places, battered and torn here and there, occasionally revealing a black emptiness inside to match the forest around it.

There were no other structures nearby that she could sense with her mysterious inner eye, but there were a handful of strange, blocky things sticking up out of the earth farther out than their lights could reach. Those things might have been *remains* of other structures, but she couldn't tell for sure. All she really knew was that they weren't natural. Just like this endless cylinder, they came from somewhere else a very long time ago. Somewhere that was both far away and not. Somewhere that wasn't there anymore...

It was all so confusing. She wished she wasn't like this. She wished she could have just been born normal. It was so exhausting feeling things like this, things she couldn't possibly understand and no one could explain to her.

"Are we making any progress at all?" asked Andrea, looking back the way they came.

"This thing just never ends, does it?" agreed Nicole. "I mean, what the fuck *is* it, even?"

It was a good question. One Gina certainly couldn't answer. She didn't sense anything inside. If it was meant for storage, it had long ago been emptied out. And there was nothing to indicate that it was suitable for dwelling, no utilities that she could identify, no individual rooms, certainly nothing that resembled furniture.

Keith stepped closer to the structure and shined his light into one of the many small gaps torn in the crumpled metal as he passed. "It looks hollow. You think it's some kind of tunnel? A path for avoiding all the dangerous stuff you said was out here?"

"Who would've built something like that?" wondered Andrea. "Aren't we, like, super far from home right now?"

"This thing was built by *someone*," he reasoned. "It didn't just *grow* here."

She wrinkled her nose. "I know *that*. I'm just saying. *Who* was here before? How? And *why*?"

"There's a bigger hole up farther," Nicole saw as she pushed onward. "Maybe we can go *through* it instead of around."

Gina didn't bother aiming her light up ahead. She'd already seen the fissure she was talking about with her psychic eye. A tear in the metal, about ten feet high. It was only a few inches wide, however, far too narrow to fit through, so she'd barely thought anything of it. But on second thought, the metal looked quite thin, sort of like tin siding on a barn. If they could pry it back just a little, it might yield enough to let them squeeze in. And that *might* offer some protection from the things wandering around out here.

Keith wasted no time. He shined his light into the crack, ensuring that he wasn't about to reach into some angry creature's nest or something, then he pressed his back against one side and used his foot to push out on the other, opening a gap wide enough for them to fit through.

The noise was deafening in the silence of the Wood. Gina winced and covered her ears. Andrea let out a startled cry.

"What the fuck?" snapped Nicole. "Are you trying to attract every zombie for a hundred miles?"

"Do you want to try finding a way through or don't you?" he snapped back at her.

Gina cast that psychic eye out over the forest. That hadn't gone unnoticed. Things were starting to turn this way. And there seemed to be more of them than there were before, though she didn't understand how that was possible. Were they hidden from her somehow?

"Just hurry and duck inside," grunted Keith. "I can't hold it open forever."

"It might be the only way," agreed Gina, careful not to sound too eager to get out of sight. She didn't want to lie to anyone, but she also didn't want to scare them.

"There's definitely a space inside," observed Nicole as she shined her light past him. "I see a lot of pipes and wires. Some kind of machinery, maybe?" She glanced back at Andrea. "You think it's safe to go in?"

Andrea only shrugged. How was *she* supposed to know?

"Let me go first," said Gina, stepping closer. "I can usually tell."

Nicole didn't question her. She had no reason to. If Gina said she knew things, she took her word for it.

Gina, on the other hand, wasn't really sure of anything under this strange, empty sky. But it *was* true that she sometimes knew things. For example, at just a glance, she sometimes knew that a fence was electrified. Or a that pan sitting on the stovetop was still hot. And she'd often found herself wary of certain places for reasons that she simply knew had nothing to do with the strange and unnatural things she was able to sense. Things like high electrical fields emitted from a basement utility room. Or slightly higher than ideal radiation levels bleeding off an aging X-ray machine in a hospital. Or headache and nausea-inducing low-frequency humming noises caused by old machinery. Or even dangerous molds growing in the walls. But those things were part of the natural world she was familiar with. This was entirely different. She still didn't know how useful her psychic abilities were here. What if there were dangerous things out here that were invisible to her? She couldn't see any of that mysterious cemetery Andrea described back in All Trails Crossing, after all. And although there hadn't been anything dangerous lurking in that ghostly place, it didn't mean there weren't plenty of very deadly things she couldn't see coming.

But they had to do something. It was too dangerous to keep straying so far from the path. They were eventually going to attract unwanted attention one way or another. Or else slip through one of those crinkles and find themselves hopelessly lost.

She ducked under Keith's outstretched leg and over a bundle of thick, black cables, shining her light back and forth. There were great, three-foot-diameter pipes running along the interior of the structure, made of some kind of shiny, copper-colored metal that probably wasn't copper because it hadn't oxidized in the open air. There were fat bundles of dull, gray wires running along the walls. And strange little gold-tinted pyramids protruding from the walls at regular intervals in a spiraling pattern.

There wasn't a floor to speak of. Only the rounded curvature of the cylinder. She was walking directly on the exposed metal, stepping over the heavy iron framework holding it in place. These were two feet thick and spaced about every thirty feet, making it impractical as a passageway meant for foot traffic and all but impossible for anything motorized. Nor would it make any sense as a water pipe or anything else that she could imagine.

There were strange, funnel-shaped devices attached to the framework at regular intervals, the narrow ends all curved and pointed in the same direction. Each one was some kind of electrical device, because they were visibly wired into one of those thick bundles of cable. And wherever there wasn't one of those devices, there was a block of shiny, bright red glass with a thin, silver-colored rod sticking straight out from it.

She shined her light on several of these rods and saw that the ends were scorched black for some reason. It didn't look like anything she'd ever seen before, but something about those scorched rods made her imagine that great, burning bolts of electricity had once traveled through this tunnel, potentially incinerating any creature unfortunate enough to have wandered in.

But that was only her timid imagination trying to scare her. How would something like that even work? The whole structure was made of some kind of metal. Wouldn't it short out or something? Still, she could almost feel the hair on her arms standing up in anticipation of a sudden flash of lightning ending this strange journey in a gruesome, white-hot fraction of a second.

She shivered a little at the thought and shined her light around again.

No… Not electricity… That wasn't what this place was about. Very slowly, she found a familiar certainty creeping into her psychic brain. Shadows of ancient memories, perhaps? Glimpses of whatever long-lost past this structure belonged to?

She didn't understand how she knew these things, but she knew well enough that it wasn't just her own wild imaginings. When she knew something like this, she knew it absolutely. And right now, she knew that this place was built for something different. Something she couldn't quite grasp, because it was something…?

Something *what*? What was it?

Andrea ducked through the tear in the metal behind her. "This place isn't going to give us cancer or something, is it?" she wondered, her imagination clearly as morbid as her own. "Because it sort of looks like it would."

"I don't sense anything dangerous about it," said Gina, as if she were remotely confident that she knew anything about it. But it also wasn't a lie. She was fairly sure she'd know immediately if they were in any kind of danger being in here. Whatever used to flow through this strange structure couldn't harm them now.

Because it didn't exist anymore.

She shined her light at one of those metal rods again, distracted by the thought. Something that didn't exist anymore? No wonder she couldn't quite wrap her head around it. What could it have been? How was it used? And where did it go?

What a strange and bewildering concept...

Nicole slipped under Keith's outstretched leg and peered around. "This is a bad idea," she sighed. "I just know it."

"You can go back out if you want," suggested Keith.

"Or *you* can," she countered.

He pushed his weight against the metal, making room for himself. The sound was even louder and more painful from inside. Gina and Andrea both covered their ears and grimaced.

"Sorry," he grunted as he squeezed his body through and let the metal ease closed behind him with another deafening screech.

"If the zombies show up, *you* get eaten first," Nicole informed him.

"Why not?" he responded without hesitation. "Anything's better than being stuck out here with *you*."

"No one's getting eaten by zombies!" grumbled Andrea. "Both of you knock it off."

Gina closed her eyes and tried to cast out that psychic sense. There were definitely things out there that were moving closer, but they weren't moving fast. They seemed to be hobbling, as if wounded.

Was Nicole right? Were those things zombies? The idea sent a shiver through her body. She'd always been scared of those kinds of movies. She was scared of any kind of horror movie, really. Watching them only reinforced the fears she felt every day of her life. But zombies were particularly terrifying. Something about an unstoppable army of flesh-eating monsters descending on humanity, growing larger with every living person they killed. The thought of encountering *real* ones in this nightmare forest made her feel almost sick with dread.

"We should go back the way we came, right?" said Andrea, changing the subject. "See if there's a way out closer to the path?"

"Unless we overshoot it," reasoned Keith. "What if we find a way out but don't know which way to go."

"I'll be able to feel the path," Gina assured him. "I can see it, even from here."

"Oh. That's handy. Okay then."

"Perfect," said Nicole, impatient. "Let's get going then."

But before she could take a single step, something somewhere behind them struck the metal wall with a resounding bang. The sound echoed up and down the passage.

All four of them stared in that direction for a moment, each of them holding their breath in awful anticipation of something monstrous rushing out of the darkness at them.

But nothing appeared.

Not yet.

"Yeah, let's move," decided Andrea.

Chapter 42

Albert's gaze kept drifting out into those surrounding night trees. They looked wilted and sickly, but he knew they were still dangerous. If they lingered in one place for too long, the glow of their flashlights would begin to wake them. Especially that super bright one Corey occasionally swung around. Fortunately, however, they weren't quick to wake.

He recalled the one outside Gilbert House that Wayne told them about. When Olivia was snatched from that third-floor window, Wayne left her flashlight on the floor where she dropped it. At the time, they all assumed she was dead, after all. How could she be alive after something like that? The thing had almost certainly killed her. She was either devoured or torn to pieces or…well certainly nothing peaceful. Wayne said he couldn't bear to take it with him. And turning it off felt wrong somehow. Like leaving it to fade out on its own was a better way to honor her memory or something.

In reality, someone had put that idea in his head on purpose. Either the Sentinel Queen or Kneede or even the Keeper, himself. It served a purpose, after all. It was too much of a coincidence to have any other explanation, as far as he was concerned. Because that was the only reason they were allowed to survive that awful ordeal. The ground floor doors and windows were all bricked up. There was no way into the building from the Wood side. But in the hours that followed, that little glow was enough to make the nearest of those night trees begin to wake up and lean toward it. When he eventually found Olivia, alive and well out in that black forest, that night tree was their escape route back into Gilbert House and, from there, back home.

That tree didn't devour Wayne and Olivia when they climbed it. It wasn't fully awake. The glow of that flashlight, high up in that third-floor window, partially blocked by the wall and pointed the other way, wasn't bright enough to bring it entirely out of its slumber. Not like on the burning mountain, which was lit up like Times Square by those blistering flames, where that one very nearly made a meal out of three of them.

What that meant to Albert now was that there should be very little danger of these trees waking up in the short time it took them to pass.

But he remained wary, nonetheless. After all, he didn't know everything about night trees. For all he knew, the rules could change in a place like this. So far, however, he hadn't seen one so much as twitch. And several of them were so covered in those strange sores and blisters that he wasn't entirely even sure they were still alive.

He was far more concerned with the other things Wayne found in this forest. Those zombies being foremost on that list. But where were they? If this was really where so many worlds ended up when they died, shouldn't this place be swarming with them? Somehow, the absence of those corpses seemed far more unsettling than if he'd actually caught sight of one…

But he didn't have time to ponder it right now.

Something was emerging from the gloom ahead of them. Something big and dark, looming just to the right of the path. A great, towering wall of rough, black stone.

"What now?" wondered Brandy.

It was a good question. It did seem like one thing after another out here.

As they walked on, those towering black walls unraveled themselves from the darkness, going on and on, revealing an enormous structure that crowded almost to the edge of the road, considerably closer than Brandy was strictly comfortable with, given the nasty surprises they'd found in far less ominous places these past few days.

"Looks like a castle," observed Corey as he turned on his powerful light again and swept it across the charcoal-colored surface.

Albert stopped walking, surprised. A castle…? A thought flashed through his head—*stay away from the castle*—but was gone almost as quickly as it came.

He squeezed his eyes closed and rubbed at a dull pain in his head. What was that about? It felt important…but he couldn't quite grasp it.

Corey fixed his light on a high window. It was round and small, with what looked like two horizontal bars across it. "Castle *dungeon*," he amended.

"That's kind of unsettling," decided Violet.

The structure was much taller than even Corey's powerful light could reach. More of those tiny, barred windows could be seen as those black walls stretched upward into that empty, black sky. And there seemed to be no end to it. It went on and on as they walked past it, a hundred feet…two hundred…four hundred…

There were places where the walls were cracked and crumbling, but unlike everything else they'd encountered since they arrived in these woods, it was surprisingly intact, probably owing to the fact that it did, indeed, look like a castle. It was built like a *fortress*, with thick, solid walls.

It was intriguing. Lucianna told them that the Denselands was a place where dead universes were piled up, the very universes, he could only assume, that the Sentinel Queen told them their ancestors migrated from many generations ago in their final days. That strongly suggested that the things they found here were all ancient beyond imagination, from worlds that were long gone. And a structure like this might contain clues to what kind of world it belonged to. A part of him was curious about what might be inside. What if there were books in there? Artwork? *Photographs?* Long lost images of sunrises that no longer happened. Of flowers that no longer bloomed. Of animals that no one remembered. Inside those walls could be records of one of those past universes, just waiting to be found…

And yet the idea of going in there filled him with a strange and chilling dread that he couldn't quite comprehend. Had he seen something like this before? Did it remind him of something? A nightmare he once had?

(Stay away from the castle!)

He grimaced at something that flashed through the back of his mind for only an instant. Something that chilled him to the bone…something *important*…but something that was gone as quickly as it came…

Ahead of them, a large, looming doorway came into view. A great, gaping archway with huge, iron gates standing open, as if inviting them.

Violet stopped and tipped her head to one side, listening. "Do you hear that?"

"Hear what?" asked Brandy.

"Wind?" suggested Corey.

But Violet shook her head. "It's not the wind…" She kept walking, drawing nearer to that gaping doorway.

Corey held his hand up to his ear, shielding it from that steady wind, and listened. "Oh yeah… Something there…"

"Is that a voice?" asked Brandy.

Albert was starting to hear it, too. It wasn't words, though…

(Stay away from the castle!)

He felt a shiver race through him. He turned and looked behind him, half-expecting to see someone shouting a warning at him.

Corey shined his light at the doorway as he approached, revealing a long, black corridor leading deep inside.

"It sounds like someone crying…" Brandy realized.

Violet nodded. "Like a little kid or something."

The sound did, indeed, sound like the weeping of a frightened child, Albert realized as he drew closer.

"Why would a kid be out here?" wondered Brandy.

It was an excellent question.

"*We're* here," reasoned Violet. "You said eight others were heading here, too. What if one of them is a kid?"

Corey stepped off the road, probing the empty corridor deeper. "We should check it out. Make sure."

"We have to be certain," agreed Violet, already following him.

Brandy was moving that way, too. Albert stopped, distracted, and watched her go.

Something flashed through his mind again, rapid-fire images filled with gut-wrenching emotions, too fast to process, too much to understand and then gone without a trace, as if his own mind were working against him, forcing them down. But one thing did remain when the rest was forgotten. A deep and crippling dread like nothing he'd ever felt before.

Corey was already at the doorway. He was going inside. Violet was right behind him.

And Brandy too…

"Stay away from the castle…" he breathed. "Ignore the cries…" A fierce panic welled up inside him. He darted forward and grabbed Brandy's arm, holding her back. "No! Nobody go in there!"

Corey and Violet turned and stared at him.

"Why not?" pressed Violet.

"It's not what it sounds like," was all the answer Albert could give her. "You've just got to trust me."

Brandy looked back at those towering black walls, her pretty face pained. "How can we be sure?"

It was a good question. All they had was his word.

Those terrified wails continued from somewhere within. It was heart-wrenching. It was almost *painful.* And yet somehow he knew, deep in his heart, that whatever was waiting in that black castle was no child.

He pulled Brandy close to him. He grasped the side of her face in his hand and stared into her eyes. "You can feel it," he said. "Close your eyes and tell me there's a crying child lost in there."

She stared back at him for a moment, then she closed her eyes.

He kissed her. Slowly. Gently. Taking his time. Reminding her to take hers.

The feel of her lips against his was warm and familiar. It was the feeling of home. The feeling of *happiness*. She was his bliss. His heaven.

He took that feeling and cast it out into the forest around them. He could feel the Wood. The night trees that populated it. He could *see* the shadow road, like a shining ribbon cutting through the trees, leading them to whatever lay waiting at the center of this nightmare wasteland. And he could feel the things that prowled these awful trees, too. Shadowy, twisted things that were neither alive nor dead, victims of unforgiving time and hopelessness. Most of them weren't even moving. They were just slumped out there, watching the eons of nothingness pass them by. There was one not so far from here. If it had eyes, it would be able to see them. But its eyes were like the life it once knew, nothing more than a long-forgotten memory of a past so distant it might as well have never been.

He took in all of these things his psychic mind perceived and he focused them on what was right in front of him. On those tender, beautiful lips pressed against his.

Brandy gasped and opened her eyes.

"See?" he whispered.

She nodded. She did, indeed, see.

"What just happened?" asked Violet.

Brandy pressed herself against him, kissing him once more. She needed a moment, he could tell. Just a few seconds. It was all so overwhelming. But then she pulled away and took a shaking breath. "We stay on the road," she told them.

"No castle?" asked Corey, sounding disappointed.

She shook her head. Hard. Her blonde hair whipped back and forth. "There's no one alive in that place," she said in a timid, shaky voice. "We have to leave."

Violet nodded. "Okay. If you say so." She turned and pushed forward, casting only one more glance back at those black walls and that awful, pitiful voice pouring out of them.

Corey reached up with the butt of his flashlight and scratched at his head. "Was that magic?" he asked, curious.

Albert nodded. "Yeah. That was magic."

"Cool."

"Sometimes," he muttered. Although he wasn't entirely sure how cool that particular experience was. He felt shaken. His gaze drifted out into the forest, toward that gnarled and broken shape hunched among the trees nearby, blind and deaf to the world, so lost in its endless misery that it wouldn't have noticed them even without the road's protection.

He now understood where the zombies were. They were still everywhere. But time had taken its toll on them. In this place, very few, if any, still roamed after all these endless ages.

The worst part of it all was knowing how easily that could become any one of them. Or *all* of them.

As the four of them pushed onward, he pulled the shaman's spellbook out of his pocket and opened it to a page that was still covered in that strange, cryptic language. Another memory flashed through his head. The same page, but written in plain English in Shanzer's sloppy handwriting...

Something about it all sent a shiver down his spine.

What would've happened? he wondered. But he wasn't sure he wanted to know the answer.

He pushed the awful thought from his mind and turned the page. He folded the next over and pressed it flat. Then he closed the book and returned it to his pocket.

Those strange, unfamiliar memories began fading away again. This time, he didn't try to hold onto them. Somehow he understood that he didn't need them anymore.

"Full circle..." he muttered under his breath...though he couldn't quite remember why...

Chapter 43

Everett swept his light around the room, taking in every detail. That next doorway ahead of him should be where they wanted to go. That should take them toward the back of the structure and hopefully outside again. With any luck, they could get back onto the path without anything noticing them. But as he entered the next space, his attention was drawn to a number of oddly shaped, dusty blocks lined up against the right side of the room. They weren't made of the same material as the building. These things were smooth and grayish blue in color. With odd little ridges running around them. Were they crates of some sort? Water containers? He saw no lids or spouts or other openings. He stepped closer, his light trained on the nearest one, curious.

Wayne, however, didn't waste a single second on them. He walked straight to the next doorway, Olivia still clinging to his arm. "Keep moving," he warned.

Everett's curiosity was almost more than he could stand, but he dismissed the mysterious blocks and followed him. He didn't want to get on his bad side any more than he already had, after all. But it was so hard to understand his total lack of interest. Did he really not wonder about this place? What it once was? Who built it? Why?

The next room was longer than the others, almost a hallway of sorts, with several doors on either side. Wayne walked to the far end of it, shining his light into each room as he passed it, but never pausing.

Everett followed along behind them, but he couldn't help taking a second or two to peer into those spaces, determined to see anything worth seeing. Disappointingly, however, each one was empty.

But as he turned away from one of those rooms, his flashlight went black. He stopped, confused by the darkness. His light didn't fade. It vanished. In an instant it simply blinked out. And so did Wayne's and Olivia's. But at the same time? How did that happen? And why didn't he hear them react to this strange new situation?

Except, as he stood there, blind in the darkness, he realized that he wasn't holding a flashlight at all. And why *would* he have a flashlight? He hadn't had one since…

He frowned. What was going on?

Then someone grabbed his hand and almost yanked him off his feet. He let out a surprised yelp and stumbled along, trying not to trip.

"What's happening?" he whispered, though he couldn't remember *why* he was whispering, or who he was whispering to.

"Just keep up!" someone hissed back at him in a voice that was somehow simultaneously familiar and unfamiliar.

Then, as quickly as it had gone dark, the light was back. He was standing in the corridor again. Wayne and Olivia were passing through the doorway at the far end, seemingly unaware that anything strange had happened behind them.

He looked down at his flashlight. Just a second ago, that was a hand…

He turned and scanned the space around him, confused, but no one else was there. What a strange thing to happen. Why would he imagine something like that?

He decided not to try to explain it to Wayne and Olivia. Wayne would probably just snap at him anyway… He dismissed it for the time being and followed them into the next room, where something curious again caught his attention.

On one wall, there was a sort of table jutting out. And on the table was what appeared to be a cloudy glass jar. Except it wasn't sitting on the table so much as sticking out of it, as if built into it. And the top was wrapped in some kind of coarse, black cloth that looked like it had weathered many long years.

He hesitated a moment, staring at it, freshly distracted, as his companions continued on, their lights dwindling behind them.

What was he looking at?

He stepped closer to it, curious.

"I found the way out!" called Wayne from another room.

But this mysterious foggy jar was even more intriguing than the blocks in that other room. He couldn't help himself. What was this? Why was it coming out of the table like that? What was under that black cloth?

Was it his imagination, or was something inside that jar *churning*?

He reached out and brushed his hand across the glass, wiping away the dust, but it didn't reveal anything more. It was either the glass, itself, or the contents that were foggy.

But as he stood there with his fingertips resting on the glass, he found himself distracted by a very subtle feeling, like a long-forgotten memory slowly stirring deep down in his subconscious mind.

Did it have something to do with that weird hallucination he had a moment ago?

What was inside? He felt as if he could almost grasp it. Something about that strange *churning* he could almost make out deep within. Something important? He just needed to see better. He leaned closer, over the top of the table, squinting into the fog. It was just a little too far away...

He rose up onto his toes and reached out to grip the table. Just a little closer... Maybe if he could manage to get his nose right up to the glass...

Then Wayne was there. His strong hand clamped around his wrist like a machine and yanked him backward, sending a sharp bolt of pain through his arm. For a moment he was looming there, his angry, scowling face hovering right in front of him.

Had he finally pushed his luck too far? Had he finally infuriated the big grouchy guy who never asked him to tag along in the first place?

"Watch what you're doing!" Wayne growled. Then, with his other hand he pointed at the table where he was about to place his hand.

Something was growing there, he realized. A strange, black vine with blood-red creepers clinging to the stone.

"Killing vines..." gasped Olivia, horrified.

Everett stared at them. They were growing up out of the ground and up the wall under the table where he hadn't noticed them. If Wayne hadn't showed up at that moment, likely to see what was taking him so long, he would've placed his hand right down on top of it.

A single prick from one of those will instantly tear your soul from your body, he heard Nadia saying in his head. *You'd be dead before you hit the floor.*

"Oh..." he gulped as he stared at the sharp, black thorns sticking out from the vine in every direction, just waiting to pierce his flesh.

Wayne let go of his arm and turned away. "Seriously, stop clowning around and pay attention. This isn't a game."

He nodded. He felt strangely numb. It was an odd sensation, he thought, looking at the object of his very near demise. And yet even so, as he followed Wayne and Olivia out of the room, he couldn't help taking one last look back at that mysterious cloudy jar...

Maybe Wayne was right. Maybe there was something wrong with him.

Chapter 44

Keith stepped over a piece of the structure's frame, then reached back and offered his free hand to Gina.

"I'm okay," she assured him in her sleepy voice, but she accepted the help anyway. "Thanks."

"You're welcome." He reached back and did the same for Andrea.

"You're so sweet!" she gushed.

Nicole rolled her eyes. "Yeah, he's a fucking *saint*."

Keith said nothing. But she noticed that he didn't bother offering *her* a hand. He didn't even look at her. He turned and continued on as if she didn't exist. Which was exactly what he was supposed to do, of course. Let her live her own life like a perfectly capable adult. It wasn't even a particularly big beam. No one needed help stepping over it. He was just being overprotective again, acting like some kind of obnoxious Prince Charming. Taking control of every situation when no one asked him to. Nothing would please her more than for him to leave her the hell alone.

So then why did it piss her off to see him ignore her like that?

She clenched her jaw against an urge to shout something hurtful at him and stepped over the beam. What was it about Keith anyway? Why did he get under her skin so much?

Another of those bangs reverberated through the structure from somewhere behind them. Was it her imagination, or was that one closer than the first?

Andrea let out a terrified squeak of a cry at the sound of it and shined her light back the way they came.

"We've attracted too much attention," said Gina, her sleepy gaze sliding across the walls around them as if peering right through them, out into that god-awful forest beyond. (Which, of course, was exactly what she was doing.)

Nicole glanced over at those walls, at the small gaps in the torn metal that offered fleeting glimpses of the black world beyond and realized that their lights were probably shining through those holes.

Back in Gilbert House, Albert had theorized that it was their lights shining from the windows that had attracted all those zombie things, making them swarm the building like they did. Was the same thing happening now? Were they attracting an army of voracious undead like in the movies?

But then again, they were just out there, boldly shining them out into the forest, itself. Why would the little bit of light shining behind those holes attract them when four bobbing flashlights out in the open didn't?

The answer, of course, was that they *were* attracting attention. They simply managed to slip inside before anything dangerous arrived. Now they were right on the other side of that wall. Hundreds of them, for all she knew.

And all that noise Keith made peeling back the metal had only made the situation worse. (That idiot!)

Another sound filled the chamber, not a bang this time, but a long, drawn-out sort of grinding sound, like something dragging across the surface of the metal, digging into it, trying to get in.

"Are we safe in here?" she asked, not entirely sure if she wanted to hear the answer.

"For a little while," replied Gina. "But we need to get back to the road as soon as possible."

Nicole needed no further encouragement. She continued on, careful not to trip and fall over the metal beams lying across their path. The last thing she needed was to turn an ankle out here.

"They don't look like much," observed Keith. They still looked rather sickly and wilted, with their drooping branches.

"They looked a lot healthier last time," admitted Andrea.

"Everything about this place is broken," explained Gina. "The ground and the air. Gravity and pressure. Space and time. It's all crinkled up here. It's constantly fighting against anything living. Those trees are struggling just to exist. And the same thing will happen to us if we're here long enough."

Andrea let out a frightened groan. "Don't tell me stuff like that!"

Nicole turned her light on her, confused.

"Hey!" she exclaimed, shielding her eyes from the glare.

"What's happening?"

Keith and Gina turned and looked at her.

"What's wrong?" asked Keith.

She shined her light around at the metal walls of the structure.

"When did...?"

"Are you okay?" asked Gina.

Was she okay? What the fuck just happened? For a moment there, they weren't inside this metal tunnel. They were back out in that open forest, back on the path. Andrea was talking about the sick night trees. And Gina was talking about everything being crinkled up again.

"Nikki?" pressed Andrea. She was frightening her, she realized.

"I'm okay. Just..." But she shook her head. She was just *what?* What happened? "Déjà vu? I guess? I don't know. Everything was weird for a second."

"It plays with your mind," Gina reminded her.

"All crinkled up," she muttered. "Yeah. I remember."

A series of bangs echoed through the structure, reminding her that they were supposed to be moving, not pausing to analyze some stupid, poorly timed psychological episode.

The four of them continued forward, moving a little faster now.

Nicole looked back the way they came, uncertain. What if this was a mistake? What if there wasn't another way out of this tunnel? What if something terrible forced its way in and they were trapped in here? How long could they run before someone tripped over the stupid framework?

She couldn't bear the thought.

Another bang, softer this time, but closer, just behind them, it seemed, startled another squeak of a cry from Andrea. "God, I hate zombies!" she squealed.

"They're really zombies?" asked Keith. "Like, shuffling corpses in the streets zombies?"

Andrea tipped her head to one side, her pigtails swinging with the motion. "Not exactly, I guess. They're not, like, contagious, like in the movies. You can't turn into one. Olivia and Wayne both got bitten and they were fine. Albert says they're more like mummies than zombies. They're just dead things that eventually got back up again."

"Souls don't pass on to the afterlife in the Wood," recalled Nicole, relieved to have something to talk about besides that déjà vu weirdness. "They get trapped in the body and rot with it until eventually they, like, *fuse* or something." At least, that was the way the Keeper described it at the end of that strange journey five years ago. It was how Wayne was able to come back from the dead. All the Keeper had to do was patch his body and keep it functioning for him until he came back to it.

"Wayne said most of them weren't even human," recalled Andrea.

"I can feel them," said Gina. "Not alive but not dead, either. But also different."

She nodded. He described a lot of things that looked more like animals than people. And even the ones that looked like people were usually wrong somehow. She remembered him describing zombies with bizarre limbs and facial features that had nothing to do with being dead.

He said once that it was as if he'd found himself in a zombie apocalypse on *another planet*.

"There are other things out there, too, though," added Gina. "Things that were never alive."

Nicole stopped halfway across one of the beams, straddling it. "How was something never alive?"

But Gina kept moving. "They're just different," she replied, as if that explained anything.

She looked over at Andrea, but she only shrugged and kept moving.

Never alive to begin with? Ada said something about there being a world separate from those of the living and dead. Was that what this was? Some third state of existence that she couldn't quite comprehend?

She stepped over the beam and continued on, her thoughts dwelling on what, exactly, something *was* if it wasn't living or dead. And just how the hell were they supposed to defend themselves against something like that?

But all four of them stopped at the sound of something new. A strange, drawn-out rumble of a noise that slowly rose in volume, then turned into a series of deep clicks. It was such an alien noise that she couldn't quite wrap her head around it. It sounded like something from a science fiction movie.

And it was coming from the wall on their left.

All four of them turned their lights toward a softball-sized hole in the metal wall. It sounded like it was right out there somewhere…

But then everything fell quiet again.

Nicole looked over at Gina. "What is it?" she mouthed, not daring to even whisper.

But Gina looked back at her with wide, worried eyes. "I didn't feel anything," she mouthed back.

She stared at her, unsure what to make of this situation. Something Gina couldn't feel? She turned and looked at Andrea. "Can *you* feel anything?" she mouthed. Maybe it was something spiritual.

But Andrea shook her head. It wasn't anything *she* could sense. But…what else could it be?

There was another series of odd clicks. A very faint scraping sound. A barely audible sort of sigh? Or was that only her imagination?

The four of them stood silent, holding their breath, not daring to move, their gazes locked on that small hole.

Was something looking back at them from the darkness beyond? Something neither Gina nor Andrea could see?

Keith took a step closer, his light fixed on the hole.

"Careful!" whispered Andrea.

He leaned a little closer, stretching his arm out, trying to pierce that stubborn darkness.

There didn't seem to be anything there.

He looked back at her, eyebrows raised. "I don't hear it any—"

Something long and sharp and black plunged through the hole, narrowly missing him as he threw himself out of the way.

Andrea screamed and grabbed Gina's arm, practically shoving her forward.

Nicole hurried after them, out of the monster's reach as it tore at the metal.

What manner of creature was it? Was that a leg? Was it some kind of giant insect? But she had no intention of sticking around to investigate. It was clearly well past time to be picking up the pace!

Chapter 45

"How are *all* of them dead?" asked Violet.

"Don't know how. They just are."

Not just the battery in Corey's big flashlight, but all the spares, too? It didn't make sense. She'd never seen that happen before. Maybe one or two, but not *all* of them. She didn't understand it.

"Something's drained 'em," said Corey.

Albert frowned. "What, like on those ghost shows?"

Violet nodded. She was sitting cross-legged in the middle of the sentinels' shadow road, looking at the six useless batteries laid out on the ground in front of her that should have lasted days. Paranormal investigators on television often talked about spirits taking energy from electronic devices in order to manifest themselves in some way. But this was no haunted asylum. Would there even be ghosts this far out in the Wood? Hadn't these ruins been here longer than their entire world? It seemed to her that even the most restless of spirits should've given up and moved on ages ago.

"No other explanation," decided Corey.

"There're probably other explanations," she reasoned. But she sure couldn't think of any.

"Why didn't it affect the batteries in the small flashlights?" wondered Brandy, looking down at the one in her hand. It was working perfectly fine.

"It's curious, for sure," Violet agreed. "The lantern's still working, too. I don't understand it. It feels weirdly selective."

"Lot more energy to drain from these," observed Corey. "Maybe better fuel for ghosts to manifest."

"But nothing manifested," she reminded him.

"Nothing we *saw*," he countered.

"Are we seriously going with the whole 'a ghost did it' explanation?" asked Brandy.

"No," replied Violet.

"Yes," replied Corey.

Violet packed the useless batteries back into the bag. "Whatever the reason, there's nothing we can do about it now. We're not exactly going to stumble across a charging station out here."

"So will the same thing happen to *these* lights, too?" wondered Brandy.

The last thing Violet wanted was to be a pessimist in this frightful forest, but she also had no intention of lying to anyone. "We can't say. We don't know what caused it. Even if we go with the ghost theory, it's like I already said, nothing manifested. We didn't even have any disembodied footsteps to blame it on."

"Could be a possession," decided Corey.

"Nobody's possessed."

"Might be. You never know. Sometimes they're sneaky."

"*Nobody's possessed*," she said again.

He scrunched his pudgy features into a squint and fixed his gaze on her. "Exactly like someone possessed'd say."

She rolled her eyes and then stood up and continued walking.

Corey watched her for a moment, as if still trying to decide if she were being possessed by an evil spirit or not. But then he seemed to dismiss the idea and simply gathered up his bag and followed her.

"Have you guys run into a lot of paranormal stuff in your research?" wondered Albert.

"Occasionally," Violet replied. "Like I've said, that's not really our goal. We already know there's paranormal stuff out there. But one of our earliest theories about portals was that maybe some of those ghost stories floating around were actually connected to undiscovered rifts between our world and another."

"Were they?" wondered Brandy.

"Not really. Most of those places we explored, especially those first few years, never yielded any data. It wasn't until about five years ago that we finally started collecting physical evidence. But during that time we definitely ran across our share of freaky ghost stuff."

"Like Hedge Lake," said Corey, nodding. "Voices in the water. Lights in the sky. People in the woods."

"Wow," said Albert.

Violet felt a shiver as she recalled that quiet shoreline. "Yeah, that place gave me the creeps." *Especially* the people in the woods. It seemed like every time they looked around, they caught sight of someone just walking out of sight in that eerie forest, but no one was ever really there. Corey was convinced there must be a portal in that area somewhere. He could have happily investigated it year-round, but she was delighted when it was time to leave and was in no hurry to ever go back.

Corey stopped and lifted the lantern up over his head, casting the light out as far as it would reach. Something in the forest had caught his attention.

Violet aimed her light in the same direction and saw that something was moving over there. A dark, hunched shape shuffled along the baren, litter-strewn earth. The very sight of it sent her heart beating faster.

Everyone stopped and remained silent, their eyes all fixed on the thing as it disappeared back into the gloom beyond the lantern's halo.

"It's like they don't see us," observed Albert, his voice soft.

"Not going to complain about that," said Brandy.

"Something about this road."

Violet looked down the stone beneath their feet. Something about this simple stone path? She didn't understand what it could be doing to protect them.

Ahead of her, Corey lowered the lantern and kept walking, seemingly unfazed by the undead horror that just passed before their eyes. "Odenshippen," he said as if nothing had happened. "That place was wild."

"It was *awful* was what it was. Pervy ghosts groping at me the whole time we were there, whispering obscenities in my ear. Gross."

"Ew," said Brandy.

"I know, right?" The owner of the property warned them that women sometimes attracted that kind of attention, but it seemed like they took a particularly sleazy interest in *her* for some reason. It was another place she never had any intention of going back to.

"Fort Loddenmire," said Corey.

"Now *that* place was interesting," agreed Violet.

"I feel like I've heard of it," said Albert.

"You might have. It's not the most well-known, but it's one of those stories you sometimes hear about on creepy podcasts and stuff. It's one of those stories where everyone just mysteriously disappeared and no one knows why."

"Like Roanoke," said Corey.

"Sounds Creepy," said Brandy.

"If I had to pick a place we've been to that there might be a portal that we just haven't found yet, it would be Loddenmire. I mean, *something* happened there. I could feel it." There was an eerie sort of atmosphere in that town that was like nowhere else she'd ever been. Unlike the other places, she often thought about returning there to conduct more research. But she was also more than a little afraid of it. After all, something spirited away all the people there, never to be found again. It would be arrogant of her to think the same thing couldn't happen to them.

"Hodelmer," said Corey.

"Hodelmer," agreed Violet. She looked out at the black forest surrounding them. "That place was trippy, too."

"Where we found that hidden room with all the writing on the walls."

"It was so weird. It was just there and then it was gone. We never could find it again. I still can't explain it."

"Pocket dimension," grunted Corey.

"Pocket dimensions," repeated Albert, shaking his head. "That sounds like something out of *Star Trek*."

"It does," agreed Brandy, looking back at the straight path laid out behind them.

"It might have been a pocket," agreed Violet as she probed the surrounding forest with her light. "But it was just that one room, so if it was, it was the smallest one we ever found."

"Never found anyone who could decipher the writing in the pictures you took, either," he recalled.

"Never," she agreed.

"That *does* sound trippy," said Albert.

"Sounds *creepy*," decided Brandy.

Violet stopped walking, confused. Around her, everyone else did the same. "Did anyone else just have déjà vu?"

Brandy looked up, her blue eyes wide. "Yes! Totally! Just now. Like, did we have that same conversation once before?"

"It sort of feels like it..." She frowned, confused. "I can't remember, though..."

"Déjà vu ain't usually a group thing," puzzled Corey.

"It was this time," said Albert.

"This place is *so* weird..." sighed Violet. "What's even going on?"

Chapter 46

Olivia, Wayne and Everett emerged from the back of the stone structure only a few yards from the path and were back on it before anything could attack them. However, those not-quite-sandstone walls were barely fading back into the darkness behind them before more of the same appeared on either side, as if they'd stumbled into some ancient, stone-age metropolis.

Olivia turned her light on one empty window after another, paranoid that at any moment something awful would emerge from one of them and attack.

And yet, her psychic alarm bells hadn't gone off since right before that metal bar nearly fell on them.

So far, it hadn't steered her wrong. Not on this trip.

Although she still couldn't help wondering why it didn't warn her five years ago about the corpse monster outside the solarium windows. Or the troll thing that attacked them. For that matter, shouldn't it have warned her to stay out of Gilbert House altogether? Or even better, to never waste her time dating Andy Lanott.

(*You knew it was going to happen. You knew...and you never said anything...*)

She shivered at the memory of that awful talking corpse in the never-children's horrid little puppet show they subjected her to. Nick Shrewd with his head bashed in. Poor Trish with her body battered and broken. And Andy, whose remains she didn't stick around to see, but was quite certain was the worst of the three by far. All of them shouting awful accusations at her, *blaming* her for what happened back then...

(*You could've saved us...but you didn't...*)

She pushed the awful thought from her head with a grimace. That wasn't real. It never happened. She couldn't let those words poison her mind like that.

And yet, she couldn't stop wondering if there might be a grain of truth to it all...

If she could see those Amber Threads of Fate that Sandy spoke of, even subconsciously, why was it that it didn't help her those times? Was she too blind to understand those feelings back then? Or did something intentionally block that part of her mind? The Sentinel Queen admitted to using her own psychic abilities to toy with people's heads, giving Albert little nudges in order to bring him to her. Did she somehow shut off her early warning alarm?

Could all of those nightmare-inducing events have been avoided?

But then again, if she never went into Gilbert House that night, she never would have met Wayne...

This was all so confusing!

But that was then and this was now. She pushed all of it out of her mind and tried to focus on the path ahead of them. That was what was important. She needed to stay aware. She needed to protect everyone. Wayne had already given her a scare.

She glanced at him, still worried. She hated the sight of that bloody stain on his shirt. But she'd seen for herself that it was a relatively shallow gouge. And he wasn't clutching it any longer. He didn't look like it bothered him at all. But she knew him well enough to know that if it *did* hurt him, he wouldn't let her know. He hated to worry her, which was sweet, but it also only made her worry about him that much more.

The big, wonderful dummy...

Ahead of them, the landscape began tilting upward and the stone path became a stone stairway ascending it. The sight of it reminded her of the stairway leading down to Sandy's mysterious home from the feet of the stone angel.

God, but that felt like so long ago.

The steps didn't slow Everett down in the least. He shot up right up to the top of them, then stopped and looked around as they climbed after him.

Wayne grumbled something under his breath that she didn't quite catch, then called out to him to not get so far ahead.

"Do you think this hill is natural?" he called back. "Or do you think it's part of all these stone buildings?"

"How the hell should we know?"

Olivia shined her light out over the vast hillside stretched out on either side of them. She hadn't noticed before, but it *did* sort of look man-made. It wasn't a single slope, but three. They were staggered like steps, too evenly to be natural. Were there more of these stone structures buried under there? Was all of this only the very top floor of something much, much larger? But then, wouldn't that mean that this part of the road was laid *over* the structures? Which came first? Or did things not so much *land* here as *fuse* with the surroundings? How did any of that work?

She reached the top of the steps, embarrassed by her own heavy breathing. It wasn't that arduous of a climb. In her defense, they *had* been walking for some time, and everything here still felt a lot heavier than it did back home, but it still made her feel self-conscious, like she was the fat girl who couldn't handle a single flight of stairs... She looked around at the stone structures crowding in on either side of the path, hoping no one saw her flushed cheeks.

Everett was already ahead of them, sweeping his light back and forth, taking in every detail of these bizarre surroundings. He only stopped when his light fell on a very large night tree next to the road, its great boughs stretched across it and those coiling tendrils drooping all the way to the ground. It would've been impossible to avoid them completely without stepping off the path, but the thought of doing so didn't fill her with any imminent dread, so they dared to go around.

As they stepped back onto the path a moment later, she glanced at a nearby doorway in the stone walls and felt a jolt of something dreadful at the sight.

She picked up her speed and hurried forward, not daring to pause even a second to ponder the feeling. She didn't need any time to know what it meant. She knew instantly that there was something terrible lurking somewhere beyond that doorway, something she didn't want to go anywhere near.

So much for her inner alarm not going off. *Back to zero days since our last incident*, she thought wearily to herself.

But that dread feeling faded away as soon as she moved on. Although, she'd come to notice that there was always this constant sort of background level of dread from simply being here in the Wood again. It was difficult to know if that was because of the inherent danger of being in the Wood or the simple fact that she knew how dangerous this place was.

She looked back over her shoulder, half-expecting to see something chasing after them, but there were only those nightmare tree branches vanishing back into the gloom.

When she looked forward again, she saw that Everett was shining his light onto one of the stone walls, where more of those creepy black and red vines were growing.

"Better watch where we step," grumbled Wayne.

She nodded. If Nadia wasn't exaggerating about those things, it would only take the slightest prick of one of those thorns to kill any of them. She wasn't sure if they were sharp enough to pierce all the way through the soles of their shoes or not, but tripping over one would probably be the end of the line for sure.

She stared at them as she walked by. Night trees and killing vines… Even the plants were monstrous. Was *everything* in the Wood deadly? It seemed like overkill to her.

She scanned her surroundings with her light and found several more of those same black vines climbing up various walls. *Too many* of them, she quickly decided. What if they kept growing in number? What if they reached a point where they were growing on every surface? What would they do?

One thing at a time, she supposed…

"I guess none of these things need sunlight to grow," Everett observed. "That's kind of weird. How do you think they live?"

"I guess there used to be light here," said Wayne, eying those deadly branches with obvious distrust. "A really long time ago. The trees are supposedly in some sort of suspended animation. It's like they're in a really long winter, waiting for spring to come. The vines are probably like that, too. Someone once told me if the sun were to ever come up here, they'd all wake up again."

"Cool!"

"No, I really don't think it would be," he said, sounding exasperated.

Olivia couldn't exactly disagree. The idea of all those monstrous trees fully waking up—all at once, no less—was downright terrifying.

"You're not even a little bit interested in this stuff?" pressed Everett. "It's like discovering life on another planet!"

"Which is how a shit ton of *horror movies* start!"

She giggled at this. She couldn't help it.

"Well, *I* think it's fascinating," said Everett.

"Maybe we should introduce him to Albert," suggested Olivia. "They can talk about all this stuff for *hours*."

"Sounds good to me," grumbled Wayne. "*Anyone* else but me."

Albert would be fascinated to hear about all these things when they were back home. He liked talking about the night trees and the hounds and those freakish spider-squid things that lurked in the waterways down in the temple. And the Sentinel Queen and her blind children. Those two would probably get along great.

She felt a sudden and unpleasant chill creep through her. She turned and shined her light behind her just as something shadowy disappeared from view behind one of the stone walls.

She lingered a moment, frowning. What was that sensation that made her look back? Was that her psychic alarm? Her amber threads, as Sandy called them? Was it a warning of some kind? It didn't feel the same as that unnerving dread, but it also wasn't exactly a pleasant sensation.

And what was that thing she just glimpsed? Was it dangerous? Was it trying to sneak up behind her?

"You okay?" asked Wayne, shining his own light around.

"Saw something moving," she whispered.

He squeezed her hand and scanned the area, searching for anything out of place.

"Gone now," she assured him.

He didn't take her word for it. He searched the surrounding area and listened for any sound that shouldn't be there.

She tugged at his hand and continued onward. Everett was getting ahead of them. She didn't want to risk getting separated. The stone road still felt like the safest route. Focusing her attention on walking straight ahead, following it, gave her the calmest feeling. Thinking about setting off in any other direction, even back the way they came, filled her with an unsettling anxiousness that bordered on absolute dread.

Ahead of them, Everett's light revealed another of those stone walls blocking their path. This time, however, there was a door just a few steps off the edge of the road. They'd barely have to leave it to step inside this time.

He didn't wait for them. He didn't ask them what they thought was the best course of action. He simply walked right up to the door and shined his light inside. "Vines," he called back as they approached. "Be careful." Then he slipped inside and out of sight. Only the glow of his flashlight remained visible.

When Olivia peered through the doorway, she saw that he was cautiously making his way down a long, corridor with more open doorways on either side, shining his light around at the thorny vines that had spread across the walls and ceiling, looking eerily like black veins.

They were on the floor, too, she saw. They sprouted from the dry, cracked earth and reached for the nearest wall, some of them creating just the sort of tripping hazard she'd envisioned a few moments ago.

"Careful now," breathed Wayne, motioning for her to go first.

She nodded and stepped through the doorway, making her way into the narrow room while he lingered a moment to scan the area behind them for any other emerging dangers.

She kind of loved the way he was always going out of his way to look after her. Letting her go ahead of him so she'd be between him and Everett was just like him. He did that sort of thing all the time, not just here, and for all sorts of little things. He was always holding the umbrella for her in the rain. He was always there to grab the hot pans out of the oven when she cooked, just to be extra sure she didn't burn herself. And he even went out of his way to drop her off by the door when they went shopping and there were no close parking spots, even though he hated being behind the wheel any longer than was absolutely necessary. It was sweet. It made her think of Nicole again, and how different they were in that regard. Her last boyfriend was a sweetheart who treated her like that, too. But far from being charmed by it, Nicole became frustrated with him, and then downright infuriated. She supposed she understood not wanting to feel like an invalid, especially after what she went through in Gilbert House. If she could survive that, she certainly could get a casserole out of the oven by herself. But it wasn't really about that, was it? Being fussed over was just a sweet gesture. And she knew from experience that there were plenty of men out there who didn't do that sort of thing.

To each her own, she supposed.

But she didn't have time to think about things like that. She loved Nicole and she desperately hoped that, wherever she was right now, she was safe. But right now she needed to stay focused on the space around her. On those awful killing vines.

There was plenty of room to move around. But just knowing what they could do was enough to make the space feel ten times smaller. They were far too close for comfort.

But thankfully there were fewer of them as they moved farther into the stone structure.

She shined her light on the wall to their left. If the path continued straight, as it had roughly done since they left the station, then it should be just beyond that wall. And yet when she peered into those rooms, she saw no sign of that smooth, gray stone.

Was the path still there, under that sandy surface? Or had this structure displaced it somehow? She had no idea how this sort of thing worked.

But as she swept her light across the floor, it fell on a dingy, dust-covered shape in the corner. Something long dead lay there, seemingly a victim of the vines.

Bones, she thought with a strange shiver. Wasn't she thinking about bones for some reason a little while ago? She couldn't quite remember now, but for some reason the thought was unsettling. She didn't like it.

Everett was shining his light into open doorways as he went, checking one room after another. She tugged on Wayne's arm and hurried after him.

The rooms here were all small little spaces with no doors or windows, offering no way back out. Olivia still had no idea what these structures might have been used for. Was this some kind of city once? Were these the equivalent of bedrooms? Maybe this particular structure was some kind of inn. Or maybe it was like a military bunker kind of thing and this was the barracks. Or was it a warehouse of some sort, instead? A factory? There was no end to the possibilities. It was an entirely different universe, after all. Where there were once things that no longer are and where things that are now never were…

Yeah, this was getting way too confusing.

The important thing was that they hadn't found a way out yet. And they were running out of building. There were only a few doorways remaining and there was only a wall at the far end.

In the next room, she glimpsed more remains. Another unfortunate victim of the killing vines. But as with the first one, it was too dried-up and shriveled to tell what it might have once been. It looked like a gnarled lump of cracked leather and hair.

She turned and shined her light backward, making sure nothing was sneaking up behind them. But she was suddenly standing in the doorway, peering in at Everett as he shined his light around at the thorny vines creeping along the walls and ceiling.

What…just happened…?

"Careful now," breathed Wayne, motioning for her to go first.

She looked up at him, confused. "What?"

Wayne looked down at her, his eyebrows raised. "What?" he repeated.

"What did you…?" But when she looked back, she wasn't standing in the doorway. She was right where she was supposed to be. "You just said…?"

"I didn't say anything."

Everett shined his light back toward them. "You guys okay?"

"Are we?" worried Wayne.

She nodded. "Sorry, I just… I was confused for a second there."

"I guess there used to be light here," said Wayne. "A really long time ago."

She looked up at him again. "What?" Then she glanced around. When did they get back outside?

"The trees are supposedly in some sort of state of suspended animation. It's like they're in a really long winter, waiting for spring to come."

He said that earlier, didn't he? She turned and looked around. They were walking along the path again, those sandstone walls on either side of them, the killing vines creeping up some of them.

"Someone once told me if the sun were to ever come up here, they'd wake up again."

"Cool!"

"No, I really don't think it would be," he said, sounding exasperated.

"You're not even a little bit interested in this stuff?" asked Everett.

She looked up at Wayne again. "Why're you—?"

"Seriously," he pressed. "Are you okay?"

She blinked up at him, then looked around again. They were back inside. The walls were crawling with those deadly black and red vines. Wayne and Everett were both staring at her, looking concerned. "I think so?" she replied timidly.

"What's up?" asked Wayne.

"I don't…" She looked back toward the doorway they walked through. "I'm not sure. I felt like we were somewhere else for a second there." But already she was having trouble remembering where that somewhere was. Weren't they just talking about something?

Wayne slipped his arm around her and looked around, worried.

"I'm okay now," she assured him. "Really." And she was. She couldn't even remember what was thinking about a moment ago. It was as if it had just vanished from her mind. As if it never happened.

"Let's keep moving," said Wayne.

She nodded. She remembered looking back to make sure nothing scary had come through that doorway… But the way was still clear. Everything was fine.

Weird…

She pressed herself against Wayne's arm and pushed onward.

Ahead of them, Everett led the way, satisfied that nothing was amiss.

There were two doorways left. He shined his light down both of them and then reported, "More doors."

"Perfect," grunted Wayne. "Let's get out of here and away from these vines."

But as soon as Everett stepped through the doorway on the right, Olivia let out a startled gasp. "Not that way!" she cried.

He stopped and looked back at her, his eyes wide with surprise. "What's wrong with this way?" he wondered.

"I don't know." And she didn't. That wasn't how this thing worked. That strange, psychic eye didn't show her visions of what was in store for her. It only spoke to her in feelings. And the feeling it screamed into her head when she watched him step through that doorway was utter, icy terror. "But it's bad."

Everett nodded. "Okay, then," he agreed, stepping back through the door and giving the space beyond one last uncertain glance. Then he stepped toward the other doorway as he looked back at her, an eyebrow raised in a look that clearly said, "How about this way, then?"

She almost laughed. It felt absurd, freaking out about feelings in her head that she didn't even understand. And yet wasn't that why she was here? Wasn't that why she was there five years ago? To use her strange, psychic powers to navigate everyone safely through the Wood's countless dangers?

Everett nodded and very slowly crept forward, ready to jump back if she gasped like that again.

But no such feeling of terror enveloped her this time. Instead, she distinctly felt calmer watching him walk through that doorway.

She nodded. "Yeah. That way. For sure."

"That way," agreed Wayne, giving her one last squeeze before urging her to go ahead of him so he could watch that other doorway for danger.

Chapter 47

The monster's thrashing had died down by now and nothing had come charging after them, but still Andrea kept a wary eye on the darkness at her back, unwilling to let her guard down.

They were each walking with one hand over the lenses of their flashlights in hopes of not drawing any more attention, but in the process the darkness had closed around them, making this strange tunnel feel considerably more claustrophobic than it did before.

She really didn't like it in here. As much as she appreciated a metal wall standing between her and all the awful things in that forest, there was just something spectacularly spooky about this tunnel. Something about the way the shadows danced around them as they swung their lights back and forth. Something about the way their voices echoed whenever they spoke. And most of all, something about how she couldn't see what might be waiting for them in that darkness up ahead.

"Are we close to the path yet?" she asked, careful not to raise her voice above a whisper. It seemed to her that they should have found it by now. And yet there was no sign of another break in the metal large enough for them to squeeze through.

"It's still a ways ahead," Gina replied in her soft, sleepy tone. "It's farther going this way than it was going the other way."

Keith glanced back at her. "How does *that* make any sense?"

"I keep telling you, everything's crinkled up here. Time and space don't follow the same rules in all worlds. Nothing is constant everywhere."

"Crinkled," agreed Nicole. "Pay attention for fuck's sake."

"*You* don't understand it, either," he challenged.

"*I* don't understand it," said Andrea.

"I'm not really used to trying to describe this stuff to people," said Gina. "Sorry."

"You're fine," Andrea assured her. "There's nothing to apologize for. Nothing made sense five years ago when all this happened the first time, either."

"That's right," agreed Nicole.

"Okay…"

Andrea watched Gina for a moment as they continued forward. She'd noticed a while ago that the poor girl was constantly apologizing. The word "sorry" rolled off her tongue as easily as vulgarity rolled off Nicole's. It was starting to pain her to hear it.

Not for the first time, she wondered what this timid, soft-spoken woman had been through in her young life to make her so contrite. Had she been abused? She certainly hoped not. But it happened. It was a cruel world out there. Cold and harsh and filled with terrible people doing terrible things to each other.

A series of loud bangs echoed through the structure from somewhere behind them and they all twirled around, startled, their lights flooding the space behind them.

But there was nothing.

"Outside," Gina assured them. "Too far back to be a concern."

She sounded so calm and brave. That sleepy voice made her seem completely unfazed, even when her eyes were clearly filled with fear. It was something of a contradiction to all those unnecessary apologies.

"We should keep moving," Gina said, already turning and pushing onward. "There's something different up ahead. It may be a way out."

"Finally," grumbled Nicole, continuing after her.

But Andrea lingered a moment, her light fixed on that ominous darkness at their backs, her gaze washing over every shadowy crevice. This place was starting to get to her. An uneasy feeling had been creeping up on her, as if something bad were going to happen. But that was only natural. This was a bad place. Something bad was *bound* to happen. Bad things had *been* happening. And yet somehow this felt different. Was it only her fear getting to her, or was there something more instinctual about it?

Or did it have something to do with her supposed spiritual abilities?

Unconsciously, her hand drifted toward her pocket, where she could feel the weight of the leaf still resting. Something about it felt comforting, though she wasn't entirely sure why. Wasn't it the reason they were in this mess in the first place?

Finally, she turned and pushed forward.

But her thoughts continued to linger on that ominous darkness at her back…

She wondered where Ghost Girl was. She was right there with

them back in that crumbling building, assuring her against those intrusive thoughts. But that was the first and only time she'd spoken to her since her harrowing experience on that Cedric's Cove rooftop. Was she still nearby, keeping an eye on her? She was only a voice, after all. The closest she ever came to seeing her was when she attacked Hotdog. And even then she was little more than a glimmer and a mist.

Ahead of her, Gina stopped walking.

"What's wrong?" asked Nicole, her guard instantly up.

"Something ahead of us?" prodded Keith. He took a step forward, ready to defend them. Andrea couldn't help being reminded of Wayne and Albert back in the depths of the temple, always ready to defend them if needed.

But instead of answering, Gina only stared into the gloom ahead of them and said, "Strange…"

"*What's* strange?" pressed Nicole.

Another noise echoed from the emptiness behind them. This was less a bang, however, than a long, drawn-out creaking that Andrea, for one, found considerably more ominous. Again, she felt as if something weren't quite right. She turned and shined her light back that way and an odd, lightheaded sort of feeling washed over her for the briefest of moments, barely long enough to even register in her startled mind.

What was happening?

"Keep moving," urged Gina, already pushing forward. "There's a way out up ahead."

"Finally," sighed Andrea.

But Nicole wasn't done with the previous conversation. "Are you not going to tell us what's so strange?"

"Crinkles," she replied as she stepped over the metal frame and continued onward.

"Crinkles," grumbled Keith, mocking her back for her previous jab.

"Fuck you."

"Behave, children," sighed Andrea.

Ahead of them, the endless monotony of the structure finally changed, but not in any way that she considered an improvement. The right side was crushed inward, leaving only a narrow gap on the left for them to pass through.

"What happened *here*?" wondered Keith.

Gina didn't attempt to explain. She never even paused. She continued right up to it and sidled into the gap ahead of them.

"Wait up!" Nicole called after her, already easing herself in behind her. "We can't get separated!"

Keith stopped and urged Andrea to go ahead of him. "In case it gets tight," he said. "I'll be right behind you."

She paused long enough to take one more look back into that pursuing darkness. The uneasy feeling hadn't let up. If anything, it was only getting worse. Was it merely her imagination? Her nerves? It was only natural to feel anxious in a place like this. And yet something about this feeling wasn't sitting right with her.

Did it have something to do with Gina's sudden hurry?

It didn't matter. She said there was a way out up ahead. And Gina knew things like that. She turned and squeezed through the gap, careful not to catch herself on any sharp edges. She'd already lost sight of Nicole. All she could see was the backlight from her flashlight around a jagged sheet of twisted metal.

She stepped carefully over a twisted beam and ducked under several drooping cables, then found her path blocked by something that didn't belong here. It looked like a large column of shiny black stone.

Was this part of something that had collapsed onto the structure?

But she never saw anything like this when they were walking the other way. Shouldn't they have noticed if a part of it was crushed? Did this mean they'd gone too far?

But she didn't have time to ponder such things. Nicole's dwindling light revealed that she'd followed Gina under the obstruction, so she dropped down and did the same, crawling on her hands and knees, doing her best to avoid any jagged metal.

This felt like a really terrible idea. Someone was going to end up needing stitches.

The thought had barely crossed her mind when something snagged the sleeve of her tee shirt, tearing a hole in it and scratching her arm. A few seconds later, something scratched the side of her calf.

And from the sound of a very vulgar exclamation from somewhere in front of her, Nicole wasn't having much better luck, either.

She felt something under her bare hand and looked down to see that she was crawling over a carpet of frayed cables, reminding her what a good thing it was that there was no electricity running through this structure.

"It's opening up!" Nicole called back to her.

Finally, some good news. But as she cleared the obstruction and finally managed to get back on her feet, she was struck by a fierce chill that washed through her entire body. Her skin prickled with goosebumps. The hair on the back of her neck stood up. And a feeling of intense dread blossomed like an icy flower somewhere deep in her gut.

What was that?

She turned and looked behind her. Keith was still back there. His light was wriggling its way under the obsidian obstruction, following close behind her.

But there was something else there as well... Something that bubbled up like an unwanted memory, chillingly menacing and also weirdly familiar.

She'd felt something like this recently...

Back at the reception. Shortly after that first encounter with Hotdog. She felt this same sensation wash over her for an instant. Then it was gone. She remembered dismissing it as a trick of her mind. A product of the heat, perhaps. But that was exactly where all this insanity started...

"Andrea?" called Nicole from somewhere up ahead. "You okay back there?"

"I'm coming," she called back.

"I'm fine, too," said Keith. "Thanks for asking."

"Don't give a fuck," she informed him.

Andrea turned her attention back to the narrow path ahead. She was almost through. She could see lights just beyond a curled sheet of metal dangling down from above.

The feeling of dread was gone again, faded away just like last time. But unlike last time, she didn't simply shrug it off.

This time she was beginning to understand.

They weren't alone out here.

Chapter 48

Corey stopped walking.

He stood there a moment, blinking at the fleshy trunk of a night tree standing in his path, confused.

Where'd the road go? It was here a moment ago.

He turned and looked behind him, but there was no sign of that smooth, gray surface anywhere. It was only black forest for as far as his light could reach.

"Violet?" he called. But Violet was gone. Albert and Brandy, too. He was all alone out here. He didn't even have his bag. He'd lost it. He'd lost *everything*...

He frowned at himself. Why did he think Violet was still here? How could he have forgotten what happened, even for a moment? Why would he have any delusions of still being back on that road? Was he really that tired? Was the strange gravity of this black world getting to him? Or was there something in this heavy, stale air that was slowly poisoning him?

Cheerful thoughts, he knew...but that was the way his mind worked. Violet would understand. She always understood.

If she were here...

No. He couldn't let himself be dragged down. He couldn't let himself be distracted.

He wasn't afraid. Not really. This place was scary, sure, but he knew the risks when he came to places like this. He was prepared if he had to fight. And he was prepared to lose, too. Instead, it was a deep sadness that gripped his heart.

Violet...

How could he have let that happen? He promised he'd always look out for her. And he failed...

"Hey!" Violet snapped her fingers in front of his face, scattering his thoughts.

He blinked down at her, confused.

"Oh, *there* you are," she chided. "Houston, the roly-poly has landed. Welcome back to earth."

"What?" He looked around, dazed. Albert and Brandy were standing behind him, watching him. Brandy looked worried. They were standing on the same stone road stretching forward and backward into the same endless darkness. "What happened?"

"You tell us," she said. "You just stopped walking and stared off into space for a minute there. Did you have a nice trip to Wonderland or something?"

She was being especially snarky. That usually meant that he'd frightened her a little. He didn't mean to. He was just...

He frowned. What *was* he doing? He couldn't remember what he was just thinking about. He glanced over at a nearby night tree as some vague snippet of a memory came fluttering almost to the surface, but then it vanished again.

"Dunno," he said at last. "Can't remember."

"You can't remember what you were doing literally twenty seconds ago?"

"Guess not."

She rolled her eyes and looked back at their companions. "No worries. He's back to normal."

"That was weird," said Brandy. "Kinda scary."

"Sorry..." He didn't understand what happened. They were just walking along and then... He didn't know. It was like there was a gap in his memory. It felt a little like that group déjà vu thing they all had a little while ago, except it was apparently just him this time.

Weird.

"Something's off about this place," decided Albert. "Try not to get distracted."

He nodded. "Off," he repeated. "Yeah."

"Come on," urged Violet. "Let's keep going. We need to make up time in case you make it a habit to go out to lunch on us like that."

"Not trying to," he grumbled. "Just did."

But she was walking on ahead of him, not looking back.

Yep, he'd definitely spooked her. Now he felt bad. And he wasn't entirely sure why. What happened back there?

He looked down at the road beneath his feet. Again, some subtle little thought fluttered up from the depths of his mind, little more than a flicker in the darkness—*all alone out here*—and then it was just gone again.

But he felt a strange sadness creeping into his heart that he didn't quite understand.

Chapter 49

Wayne ducked through another doorway and found himself back under that empty black sky again. It was strange to feel relief at the sight of that starless darkness. Even the sight of a large night tree looming in front of them, its lower branches unraveled and drooping all the way to the ground was oddly welcome.

"Where's the path?" worried Olivia.

"Should be right over here," replied Everett, already following the stone wall to the right.

Wayne didn't like that these structures were laid over the top of the path that was supposed to keep them safe, forcing them to keep stepping off it. It defeated the purpose of having a safe path in the first place, didn't it?

On the other hand, however, these walls almost certainly offered a little bit of protection. He doubted the thing he killed back in that field of copper rods would even fit through these doors. But the downside, of course, was that they were probably an excellent place for other things to hide. Like whatever it was that Olivia sensed beyond that other doorway.

At least he wasn't seeing any of those deadly vines.

Everett pushed onward. "I mean, it *should* be right over here…"

But as Wayne watched, Everett's light revealed no path. Instead, another of those rough sandstone walls appeared, blocking his path. He stared at it for a moment, then looked back at him, puzzled.

"Did we lose it?"

"We can't *lose* the path," said Wayne. "We didn't go that far." But it certainly wasn't there. Did it curve somewhere under the building? Or had the stone structure led them off course? He turned and scanned the walls behind him with his light, stifling a grimace of pain in his shoulder.

He was determined to put on a brave face, but the injury that beast gave him was aching. It felt bruised all the way down to the bone.

Just lifting his arm sent a dull bolt of pain through it.

"You okay?" asked Olivia.

"I'm fine," he assured her.

"Let us know if you need to stop. Don't push yourself."

"I'm *fine*," he said again, knowing damned well that she knew better. She didn't need to be psychic to tell when he was lying. She was his fiancée. His best friend. She knew him better than anyone in the world. But while he might not be, strictly speaking, "fine," as he insisted, he wasn't lying to her. He was good to keep going. And that was all that mattered out here.

He needed to focus on the task in front of him, was all. He forced his attention away from the pain, then turned and shined his light after Everett, who was following the wall, revealing more and more of that rough, red-brown stone, but no doorways or windows.

It wasn't that hard, even, to take his mind off it. The loss of the road bothered him more than the injury.

He frowned down at the sandy earth under their feet, then looked up at those walls again. How did any of this even work? This structure didn't just fall out of the sky and land on the path. Regardless of whatever kind of alien material it might have been made from, he was fairly sure the whole thing would've broken to pieces and collapsed. The same with that field of copper-colored rods. He recalled the way the rocky sand just sort of melded into the forest soil as they walked. Exactly what happened to a world when it ended? If it was some violent, cataclysmic disaster, wouldn't it have torn all the buildings apart, too? But this made it look as if the worlds had become *fused* somehow.

Was it weird that this felt worse? He could almost imagine the people who once lived or worked here simply looking up one day to find that the sun, moon and stars had vanished from the sky and a deadly black forest crawling with monsters suddenly surrounded them.

The Sentinel Queen once said that tearing down Gilbert House could rip a hole in the barrier between their world and the Wood. She said the Wood, because it was much larger, could swallow theirs whole. And even worse, it had happened before. To other worlds.

He couldn't help wondering about the people who were living in the world these walls belonged to. What became of them when all of this came here? Did the trauma of such an event simply kill them? Or did they survive long enough to face the terrors of the Wood?

Everett's light illuminated another wall jutting off the one he was following. "Are we in some kind of courtyard?"

Wayne turned and walked the other way, casting his light in that

Brian Harmon

direction. Sure enough, there was another wall on this side, with still no sign of another opening.

They hadn't left the structure at all, really. They'd only entered a sort of interior garden area.

Everett continued around to the left, curious to see where it went, and Wayne circled around the night tree toward the right, intending to meet in the middle.

He reached back and took Olivia's hand. The motion sent another jolt of pain through his arm, but that didn't matter. It made him feel better having her at his side. It made him braver. Part of it was that strong desire to protect her. He'd felt that ever since he first laid eyes on her, when she stumbled out of that bathroom stall, threw her arms around him and asked if he'd come to save her. But that wasn't all of it. She filled an emptiness that used to be inside him. In every aspect of his life, she made him feel whole. She was the reason he was able to do everything he did. Whether it was here under this endless black sky or behind the wheel in heavy traffic feeling overwhelmed or sitting at another obnoxious family gathering listening to his grandfather's stupid lectures, she was the reason he could always keep going.

He felt an odd sort of tingle pass through him at the feel of her skin against his. His arms prickled with gooseflesh. The hair on the back of his neck stood up.

Sometimes it was like that. Sometimes the simplest touch could set his very nerves alight with energy.

"There's another door over here," reported Everett, revealing another dark opening.

"Be careful," Olivia begged him.

"I will."

Wayne looked back at her. She was several paces behind him, shining her light up at those rough walls.

Wait…

He looked down at his empty hand, confused. Wasn't he just…?

"There're more doors inside," Everett reported. "We should be able to keep going."

Olivia caught up and took his hand, urging him along.

It was the exact same thing he felt before, only without that prickly, goosebump-inducing feeling that she sometimes gave him. Instead, it was strangely surreal this time. Did he only imagine taking her hand the first time? Why would his mind do something like that? It didn't make sense.

Suddenly, it seemed as if that prickly, shivery feeling were something far less romantic, as if it might have been some kind of warning instead of his love-sick brain fawning over his lovely fiancée.

They reached the doorway where Everett was waiting and followed him into the empty room beyond. There was a raised platform in the far corner and a square sort of shelf notched out of the wall on the left. There were none of those black vines this time, which was good.

But Olivia squeezed his hand as she looked around. "I don't like it in here," she decided.

Wayne looked down at her, concerned. "Should we leave?" There was no other way out of that courtyard area, but there might be another path back in the maze of rooms they came through to get there.

She turned and looked back at the doorway behind them. For a moment, she contemplated it, staring out into that darkness. Then she turned and looked forward again. "No," she said finally. "I think we have to go this way. Going back feels worse."

Going back felt worse? He looked out toward the slumbering night tree.

"It feels like we should go this way," she decided. "But it also feels scary." She looked up at him, her eyes filled with worry. "I can't really say more than that."

He nodded and squeezed her hand. "You know best."

"Do I?"

"Yes," he said, the word bristling with confidence. He looked up at Everett, who was looking back at them, his eyebrows raised, waiting for their decision. "Keep going."

Chapter 50

Gina stepped through the strewn debris, her flashlight fixed on the ground at her feet. She didn't need it, after all. Her strange, unnatural brain could detect every contour of this alien environment. And right now she was using that part of her mind to scan much farther out than her light was able to reach.

This wasn't right. Everything had changed.

Nicole swept her own light across the littered forest floor around them. "It doesn't make sense," she said.

And of course she was right. It didn't. They only left the road to circle around the obstruction in their path. They kept close to it until they found a way in. Then they walked back the way they came, inside instead of outside, but it was fundamentally the same path.

"We obviously overshot the road," reasoned Keith.

"We didn't," insisted Gina. Although that would be the most logical explanation back in their own world, things were simply different here. "We've moved."

He frowned. "What do you mean 'moved'? Moved *where*?"

"Somewhere else."

"That's…not really an answer to the question."

"Crinkles," sighed Andrea.

"Fucking crinkles…" grumbled Nicole. She turned and shined her light at the other structure, the one that had collapsed onto the first. They could only see a little bit of it. It was too big for their lights to reveal in its entirety.

Gina, however, could see it *all*. And yet, there was really very little to see. It was nothing more than a great, mangled mass of shiny black…*something*… It wasn't stone exactly. It looked almost like glass, but it wasn't fragile. It was hard like marble and broke apart in large, heavy chunks. She was fairly sure it was a material they didn't have in their own world. Like whatever it was that used to course through that strange tunnel like lightning but wasn't electricity. It had toppled over like a stack of toy building blocks. Its pieces lay scattered across the land, almost as if some irritable fairytale giant had come along and kicked it apart.

There were things buried in the ruins, she could tell, but nothing she could identify. It was either too crushed and broken or too strange and unfamiliar for her to tell with any certainty whether they were part of the structure or furnishings or something that was once stored here. All she could be sure of was that it had all arrived in this place at the same time.

"So…the road's just gone?" asked Nicole, turning to face her.

"I lost it when we moved." Gina was slowly turning around, scanning the unseen horizon of this endless world. The entire landscape was different. The ground was uneven. There was a steep slope on one side, descending down into a rocky valley. And beyond that, a large hill. "It was there and then it just wasn't anymore." It was as if she blinked and everything was different. There were things here and there out in that darkness, like twinkling lights in the distance that only the psychic part of her mind could make out. But none of them were the path.

How far had they gone? Where had they ended up?

"This is *not* the place to get lost," groaned Nicole.

"It's not like we had a choice," Keith reminded her. "Someone dumped that building in our path, remember?"

"Well we obviously fucked up *somewhere*."

"It's not her fault," said Andrea. "She warned us there were crinkles."

"I know it's not her fault. But we have to figure something out. This is the fucking *Wood*, in case you've forgotten."

"No one's forgotten," insisted Keith.

"You stay out of this!" she snarled. "No one invited you!"

"Stop it!" pleaded Andrea.

"No one invited you, either," he reminded her.

Nicole turned and glared at him. "Excuse you! I'm here to make sure nothing bad happens to my friends!"

But Keith wasn't listening to her anymore. He was frowning down at the ground, a confused look on his face. "How did I know that?"

She blinked, surprised by the sudden shift in topic. "What?"

He looked up at Gina. "You said she wasn't involved. The goddess only sent you to Briar Hills for *Andrea*."

Gina stared back at him. "That's right…"

"But how'd I know that?" He glanced at Andrea. "*You* didn't tell me."

"I didn't." She glanced over at Nicole, distracted. "I'd kind of forgotten about that, actually…"

Gina could understand why. After all, what would they have done without her? That maniac would've killed Andrea up on that rooftop if not for Nicole. In fact, she wasn't sure they would've made it *that* far if they'd left her behind.

"Dreams…" Keith said under his breath, understanding dawning on him. "I saw it in my dreams. I saw a *lot* of things in my dreams. But it's so hard to remember it all… Things just…bubble up sometimes…"

Gina stared at him for a moment, distracted. Dreams… What was it about dreams? He told them when they first met up with him on the boat that he'd been having strange dreams for the past few weeks, dreams of Nicole in all the various troubles she'd gotten herself into. And somehow he was even able to help her from within those dreams, setting her free from the barely-there's trap, from Tristesse Lane and even from that maniac's nightmare hospital *twice*.

It wasn't so far-fetched. Psychic powers often manifested themselves in the form of dreams. She was fairly sure that was the only way the human mind knew how to process some of the things a psychic mind perceived. One of her roommates back in Cakwetak even kept a dream journal of artwork based on all the weird dreams she had.

But it was curious that he was able to appear to Nicole in those moments of peril. And even more curious that he was able to appear in a form capable of physically pushing her out of harm's way.

She could tell he had some kind of special abilities, but she couldn't read him like she could Andrea or that Hochog man. He was almost certainly more than he appeared to be, but not in a deceitful way. She didn't feel like he was lying to them. Whatever it was, he didn't fully understand it, either.

Nicole shook her head and turned around, scanning their surroundings. "Should we go back the way we came? See if it takes us back to the path?"

"No," said Andrea, her blue eyes widening at the mere suggestion. "That tunnel thing was giving me the creeps *bad*."

"It doesn't work that way," said Gina. "It's probably more likely we'd only end up even more lost."

She noticed the relief on Andrea's face to hear her say that and wondered what she sensed back there.

"Well we can't just wander around here blind," reasoned Nicole.

"We're not blind," said Gina. "I can see a long way. And we're not entirely lost, either." She turned and set off through the scattered ruins. "The wind was blowing at our backs while we were on the road. That felt significant."

"Significant..." sighed Nicole, distracted.

She wasn't entirely sure what it was about that word. It just sort of popped into her head. But she sensed that it held some kind of meaning to Nicole and Andrea. They seemed to take notice whenever she used it. Her weirdo brain did stuff like that sometimes. It was just another of her freaky supernatural powers that she'd always wished she could flush away forever.

She made her way across the baren landscape, weaving around those sickly, drooping trees, steering clear of the bigger obstructions, and of course keeping that third eye wide open for anything dangerous.

She kept her *human* eyes open, too. There were blind spots out here, after all. Like that thing that shoved its spindly arm through the hole in that metal wall. She didn't sense it until it was already attacking. If that happened again, she might not have time to warn anyone.

It didn't make sense. That thing wasn't spiritual, like the things Andrea could perceive that she couldn't. It seemed no different from the other creatures that wandered around out here. Ancient and long dead, yet somehow awake and aware. Twisted and broken, prowling this endless black forest in search of something it was no longer able to understand, yet yearned for with an unbearable aching.

It was an awful thing to comprehend. Terrifying and pitiful at the same time. She, of all people, understood wanting impossible things so badly it hurt. It could be maddening at times. But these poor creatures had endured such torture for a veritable eternity.

To them, this place might as well be hell. It wasn't so unlike Tristesse Lane. There was no escape. There was no relief. And there was no *hope*.

They'd end up like that, too, if they couldn't find what they were looking for before something awful found them. And now they didn't even have the protection of the road.

Was that the intention? Did something arrange for them to have to stray from the path? Had they been sabotaged?

"Where are all the zombies?" asked Andrea. "Not that I'm complaining, but isn't it supposed to be like a *Living Dead* movie out here?"

"Don't jinx us," groaned Nicole.

Gina pointed off to the right. "There's something crawling around over there, but it hasn't noticed us. I don't think they can see. Their eyes. Soft tissue."

"Okay, ew!" squealed Andrea.

"Sorry."

She pointed left this time, at one spot somewhere out in the darkness, then another, then a third. "I can feel them out there, but they're not moving. They can't. They're too broken. They've been there a very long time. We should be fine as long as we stay clear."

They pushed onward, the wind at their backs, deeper and deeper into the black wilderness.

Gina tried to look calm for everyone's sake, but deep inside she was terrified. It was true that she could sense where most of the dangers were, but she wasn't remotely confident that she could keep them alive out here. Her stomach was twisted into burning knots. Her heart was pounding. She could feel tears threatening to well up in her eyes and had to make a conscious effort to control herself. This was no time to be weak.

But why did it have to be her?

There was something rummaging around a scattering of barrel-like shapes off to the right, so she veered to the left, toward a white shape just emerging from the darkness.

It looked sort of like a large satellite dish, at least thirty feet in diameter, but it was flat, rather than concave, and there were no other visible components. It was jutting up from the ground on a rusty metal post as big as a large pine trunk, canted unnaturally to the right and covered in scratches and dents.

"Hey!" exclaimed Andrea, pointing up at it as they approached. "I've seen that thing before!" She scrunched up her pretty features, confused. "Somewhere?"

Gina glanced back. She remembered her saying something odd back before they left the road. (*What happened to the thing? Wasn't there a thing? Just now?*) Was this the "thing" she was talking about? A glimpse of their future?

This was a broken place. If they weren't careful, they could end up very lost here.

"So confusing," grumbled Andrea. "Makes me feel like I'm going crazy."

"We all feel like that," Keith assured her.

"You don't know what all of us are feeling," growled Nicole.

"I never said I did. I'm saying it's perfectly natural to feel like that."

"You don't get to speak for everyone,"

"He's not wrong," said Gina. "I feel that way."

"Doesn't matter if he's right or wrong. He doesn't get to just presume to know what's inside our heads."

Keith turned to face her, irritated. "What is it with you?"

"I don't have to explain myself to you."

"I was never anything but nice to you."

"*That was the fucking problem!*" she shouted.

"We really shouldn't be yelling out here," said Gina, cringing. A sensation washed over her, a vision of countless unseen things turning their rotting faces this way.

"So, *what?*" said Keith. "You wanted me to treat you like *shit?*"

"I didn't want you to 'treat me' like *anything!* I wanted you to let me be my own person!"

"I never said you *couldn't!* I just wanted to show you I *cared!* That I was there if you needed me!"

"I never *needed* you! Can't you get that through your fucking skull?"

From somewhere in the darkness came a strange and terrible shriek that seemed to shake the very ground beneath their feet.

"I told you we shouldn't be yelling," groaned Gina. Strange and grotesque things were stirring all around them, blossoming into her mind like the opening eyes of waking dragons. Far more than she could sense a moment ago. Each and every one of them filled her with dread, but the worst, by far, was the source of that awful shriek. That came from somewhere *beyond* her psychic line of sight. And it filled her with such an overwhelming terror that she thought she might vomit.

"Oh my god, you two…" whispered Andrea.

"Yeah…" breathed Keith, his face blanched with startled fear. "Our bad."

"Stop speaking for me!" hissed Nicole.

"*Seriously?*" snapped Andrea.

Chapter 51

Brandy shined her light back into that ever-present darkness crowding at their backs.

"Everything okay?" asked Albert, adding his light to hers.

"Just jumpy still," she replied. After all, there didn't seem to be anything back there. But every now and then she felt oddly paranoid about that darkness. Was it just the bizarre nature of the Wood? Some strange, lingering remnant of the life that used to thrive in this place? A fleeting glimpse of a ghost? Her psychic mind simply trying to wrap its head around one of the not-living-but-not-dead things roaming endlessly among those night trees?

But sometimes it didn't feel like the four of them were alone out here…

According to the pervert, she was sensitive to people. She could connect to their minds and see the truth in them. That, apparently, was how she could glimpse people's lives the way she did back at that sleazy party and in the hotel. But there weren't any people out here. She couldn't feel the things in this forest. They weren't human, after all. Not anymore, at least. And according to Wayne, a great many of them never were. It wasn't just humans who ended up like that. There were beastly things, too. Animals. Creatures.

Whatever it might have been that she thought she felt, it was gone again. For the moment, it was only the four of them. She turned and continued forward.

Everyone else did the same. But they all remained alert, their eyes peeled for danger.

"I still kind of want to know more about this magic stuff," said Violet.

"*Sexy* magic," said Corey, nodding.

"We don't need to hear about the sexy part," said Violet. "I'm just curious about the magic."

"*I'm* curious about the sexy part," he said.

"Don't be a creeper."

"Not a creeper. Just wanna know how it works."

"It's none of your business."

"Still wanna know."

Brandy giggled. "I don't know if we can really explain it. We only just found out that sex magic exists."

"But you've been using it," she reminded them.

"That doesn't mean we know what we're doing," countered Albert.

"About the magic," explained Brandy. "We're good at the sex thing."

He glanced over at her, surprised.

"What? We *are*. We're married. Sex is the part that's actually *normal*."

"That's true, isn't it?" laughed Violet.

Brandy flashed him that mischievous smile and giggled again as he shook his head, baffled. But it *was* the truth. She'd been thinking about it for a while now. Magic was one of those things that wasn't supposed to be real but was everywhere you looked. In books, on television, in movies. Meanwhile, sex was an absolute reality, but society had decided for some ridiculous reason that it shouldn't be acknowledged.

(Also, she kind of wanted an excuse to say out loud that they were married. That still made her feel kind of giddy. And that was an extra nice feeling in this dark and scary world.)

"So do you guys have, like *spells* or something?"

Brandy shook her head. "It's not like that."

"Well, we *do* have some of those," Albert reminded her, tapping at the pocket where Shanzer's spellbook was stashed. "But we haven't learned how to use any of them."

"Oh yeah... I forgot about those." Then she wrinkled her nose as she recalled the weird way those so-called spells were written out in there. "I'm not sure I want anything to do with anything that pervert wrote, though."

When she woke up from her rest in the back of the carriage on their way to this strange nightmare of a world, she found that he was already awake and was studying the pervert's book, reading through what had made itself legible to him. So if they needed something in there, maybe he'd remember it when the time came.

"The stuff we've done..." said Albert. "It's kind of hard to explain. But it's not what I would've thought sex magic would be, you know?"

Violet nodded. "You said it was emotional, not physical."

"Yeah. It's kind of like channeling those emotions into something productive," he went on. "You take those feelings, acknowledge them, embrace them, and just sort of convince yourself to direct them into finishing that job you have to do. It's like that."

Brandy nodded. That was a pretty good description of it, she thought.

"Sort of get that," said Corey, nodding.

The pervert did say something about *all* emotions possessing energy and magic being about *utilizing* those energies. Lucianna even mentioned something about sex being the quickest and easiest way for them to harness their latent psychic abilities. All of that strongly suggested that they could use *any* emotion to perform magic. They were just such a slutty couple that this was the most efficient way to teach it to them…

Should she be ashamed of that? Or proud of it? She wasn't entirely sure.

"You make it sound like anyone can do it," contemplated Violet.

"They can," recalled Brandy. "The pervert said so." She glanced at Albert. "The magic part, anyway. Not so much the psychic part, I don't think."

"Yeah, it sounded like that was just us," he agreed. "But I'm guessing anyone with any kind of latent psychic abilities might be able to amplify them the same way he taught us."

"Yeah…" She found herself thinking of Olivia. She was supposed to be psychic, too. She was able to tell which direction to go when the path up the burning mountain forked. Attempting to go one way often gave her an intense feeling of dread. She wondered what would happen if *she* attempted to use this kind of magic.

"Wonder if we could use something like that to help us search for portals," said Corey.

"You don't have a girlfriend," Violet kindly reminded him.

"Oh yeah… I'd have to use a different kind of emotion," he decided with a definitive nod, as if he'd cracked the code.

Ahead of them, something appeared out of the gloom to the left of the road. For a moment, Brandy thought it was the black castle again, that they'd somehow become turned around and were going the wrong way. But it wasn't the same black stone they encountered before. It looked more like dark stucco than any kind of masonry. And it didn't reach high up into the sky like the castle did. Whatever this thing was, it was much more squat, barely eight feet high, with a series of very small, oval-shaped windows filled with a black wire mesh instead of glass.

Looking up at one of those windows, she was again struck by that brief sensation of there being too many people here.

She turned and shined her light around, but there were still only four of them...

"You okay?" asked Albert.

Was she? What was happening? Why did she keep getting these awful feelings? Was something about this place making her psychic brain short circuit or something?

"Babe?" he pressed, concerned.

"I'm fine," she assured him. Although she wasn't exactly convinced.

The building was only about fifty feet long, with no visible doorway from this side. Something about the lack of a door and those screened windows bothered her. It looked very prison-like.

Were these buildings and that castle behind them related somehow? Did they originate from the same world? And what purpose did they serve?

"Another one over there," reported Corey, shining his light on a second structure off to the right, seemingly identical to the first. Except as they approached it, she realized she could make out a number of large cracks running up the side of the wall.

"Whoa!" gasped Violet, freezing in mid-step. Her light was fixed on a large, monstrous shape lumbering out from behind the first building, just a few yards from where they were passing.

"Zombie..." breathed Albert.

Chapter 52

Everett didn't hesitate. If Olivia said to go this way and Wayne said to keep going, then this was the way and he was going to keep going. He turned and pushed forward, through the next door and into the next room.

Wayne and Olivia followed close behind him, their eyes peeled for danger. He still found the kid's enthusiasm unnecessarily reckless, but at least it kept them moving forward.

Almost immediately, they were presented with three more doorways. This time, Everett didn't bother shining his light into any of them. He turned, instead, and looked directly at Olivia.

Already, her gaze was sliding from one to the next, studying the identical darkness behind each one.

"Left," she decided.

Again, he didn't hesitate. He turned and stepped through the doorway on the left.

There was a single killing vine creeping up one corner of the room, its blood-red feelers fanned out across the stone on either side. It looked to Wayne like a snake climbing up the wall.

A very *dangerous* snake.

He pushed the unhelpful thought from his mind and turned his attention forward.

There was only one way to go from here. Another door waited on the far side of the room. Everett walked through it without pausing and shined his light around.

He felt Olivia squeeze his arm tighter as she fixed her light on some small bones scattered along the base of one wall. He didn't blame her. It was a stark reminder of just how dangerous this world was. He pulled her a little closer and led her forward.

Now there were four doorways to choose from. Again, Olivia scanned them one by one. "Right."

Everett went right. There was a long, narrow corridor here, barely wide enough for Wayne and Olivia to walk together. Their shoulders brushed the rough stone as they walked.

Fortunately, there weren't any killing vines in here to have to worry about.

"Why do I feel like we're getting more and more lost?" grumbled Wayne.

Olivia didn't say anything, but he saw her gnawing worriedly at her lower lip and knew she could feel it, too. They had no choice, really, but to trust her psychic senses and make their way through this red-brown labyrinth, but even she had no idea where they might end up.

"Hey," said Everett, shining his light down at his feet. "Check this out!"

They looked down and saw that the packed dirt and sand beneath him was cracked and crumbled. Familiar gray stone was peeking out from under it.

"The road..." sighed Wayne.

"It's still here," marveled Olivia. "We're not so lost after all."

"I wouldn't celebrate yet." He swept his light across the floor ahead of them. It wasn't cracked anywhere else. It appeared that the road continued on under the walls. They'd have to keep going and make their way back to it.

"Well, I still think it's a win that we haven't wandered completely off course," decided Olivia. And she did have a point about that. They could just as easily have been going the wrong way this entire time.

He frowned as another of those strange, shivery sensations passed through him. A sort of chill, creeping up his back, raising gooseflesh on the backs of his arms and the hair on the back of his neck.

He turned and shined his light back the way they came.

There was nothing, of course. Just the same empty doorway they entered through. But for just a second or two, he found himself convinced that someone was standing there, looking back at them.

Everett continued onward ahead of them and Olivia followed.

Wayne didn't linger. There was no reason to. They didn't have time for him to be letting his imagination get the better of him. They followed Everett through the next doorway and found themselves in a much larger space.

This room was circular, with a domed ceiling and doorways spaced evenly all around them.

"*Lots* of doors..." breathed Everett, looking back at Olivia.

"This is getting harder," she groaned. She couldn't even *see* all the doorways in here. The entire far side of the room was still bathed in darkness.

"Just take your time," said Wayne.

"That's right," agreed Everett. He was already setting off across the room, illuminating more of the space for her.

"There's an odd feeling in here," she decided. "I don't think I like it."

Wayne swept his light across the floor, looking for more cracks revealing more of the road's gray stone. Instead, he caught sight of a dingy white bone lying near the wall.

It looked like part of a rib. Long and flat and curved. About the size of a human's.

Concerned, he quickly scanned the rest of the floor. Now that he was looking, he realized there were scraps of splintered bones scattered all around them. A much larger piece lay near one of the doorways, possibly part of a broken leg bone, though he could hardly be certain. His knowledge of human anatomy was limited to his art degree, after all.

He felt Olivia's grip tighten as she looked around at it, too. Did she only find the presence of the bones ominous, or did something about them subtly trigger her psychic alarm? He decided to remain vigilant, just in case.

He turned and shined his light through the nearest doorway. There was a smaller room in there with another doorway waiting beyond. There were more dingy white splinters lying in the dirt between it and him.

Olivia was slowly turning, aiming her light through each doorway. She shivered and let go of him to rub at the goosebumps on her bare arms. "Come on…" she breathed. "Which way?"

"You've got this," urged Wayne. He turned his light on the next doorway and stopped.

What was he looking at?

It looked like another small room, but there was something wrong with the space at the back. It was a lot darker there, as if his flashlight were coming up short.

He stepped a little closer, confused.

A strange, black shape seemed to be absorbing his light. It looked like a great blob of shadows all tangled up together.

Another of those eerie shivers raced through him as he began to process the danger he was in. *Nest* was the word that popped into his head as he began to back away. Then Nadia's voice spoke up in his memory: "Fester vermin…"

Behind him, he heard Olivia suck in a sudden gulp of air. He looked back and met her wide eyes.

"Find something?" asked Everett.

Then that great, wriggling mass of shadows woke up and poured into the room.

Chapter 53

Erin stood there a moment, struggling to make sense of this inky darkness.

Odd memories, like fragments of forgotten dreams, swam through her confused mind, struggling to collect together into any semblance of sense. Floating in a vast and churning ocean of nothingness... Riding a train that wasn't really a train... A forest of fleshy black trees with coiled and twisted branches... Walking on an ancient road built by men without faces... Holding hands with a stranger beneath a sky where no moon or stars ever shined...

The last thing she remembered clearly was sitting at the Elysium Fog with Horatio, talking about the job she still had to finish in spite of the fact that she was quite dead.

Although...she didn't *feel* dead... She felt perfectly alive. And yet everything was so *confusing*. Dead but not dead. Alive but not alive. Here but not here. She felt as if she were going crazy.

Was it wrong that she wished it were as simple as that? For all of this weirdness to be nothing more than a product of an unraveling mind?

But it *was* real. And she was right in the middle of it all.

There was a reason she was here, but in this physical form, it was difficult for her living brain to grasp all of what was going on. In this state, the absolute blindness was startling. As was the *weight* of this world. She felt herself being pushed downward, as if by some great, invisible hand. And it was hard to breathe. The air felt strangely thin and thick at the same time, so that she had to work harder just to fill her lungs. She wondered for a moment if this body was getting weaker the longer she was dead, if this extra time she was granted in the world of the living was only temporary, and the thought frightened her.

But she knew it wasn't her. It was this place. It wasn't known as the Denselands for nothing. Everything was compacted here. Shoved together. Piled up like rubbish in a junkyard.

She couldn't remember the times she spent in her spiritual form very clearly when she was in this body, but she'd spent far more time this past week like that than like this, meaning she wasn't as used to this body anymore. Feeling a little strange in her own skin was going to be the normal from now on, she was fairly sure. And she certainly hadn't adjusted to the weird physics of this place like the others who'd traveled here.

She gave herself a firm shake and stood up straighter. She couldn't let herself get distracted. She needed to focus. She had a job to do and it was only a matter of time before she forgot why she came here.

She couldn't see the wall in front of her, but she knew it was there. And she knew there was a sort of shelf set into it. A narrow little pocket of space, like a little cubbyhole in a children's classroom. She was looking right at it, though there was no light to see by, reluctant to turn her useless eyes away for fear of losing it in this utter blackness.

She was clutching an object in her hands. She couldn't remember what it was, but she knew it was the reason she was here. She was supposed to place it on this shelf. That was all. Just leave it here in this darkness and go back where everything would be clear again.

But for some reason she felt *bad* about what she was about to do.

I can't kill *anyone!* she heard herself saying in her head and cringed. She thought of the pretty bridesmaid she passed the thorn to and felt sick at the thought of what was happening.

But this was the job she was given. This was what had to be done. And she didn't have much time. They'd be here soon. They'd already disturbed the nest.

Except she didn't know what that meant. What nest? Nest of what? Somewhere in her broken memories she recalled a black and pulsating mass of something foul in the inky darkness of an empty room.

She could almost recall whispering that word to someone…

"Nest…"

She could hear frightened voices from elsewhere in this lightless labyrinth. Shouts of panic, quickly getting louder. They were coming. It was time to go. Things were about to get complicated for everyone here in the Denselands.

She placed the object on the shelf, then melted back into the ether from which she came.

Chapter 54

"This way!" gasped Gina, taking off into the darkness. "Stay close!"

That outburst had drawn *way* too much attention. There were things moving all around them. If not for the psychic intuition she'd cursed all her life, she wouldn't be able to see any of them. There'd be no way to avoid them.

But she wasn't about to take it back. That stupid stuff was also the reason she was out here in the first place, getting scared half to death by awful, not-dead things in this nightmare forest. This was like that terrifying tower the goddess sent her to in Cakwetak. This was all her awful psychic abilities were good for.

She veered to the right, away from something small and broken that was half-crawling and half-rolling across the lifeless dirt. There was something close by on this side, but it didn't seem able to move. Inside her head, she caught a frightful glimpse of a broken and rotting hand groping for the cold and empty sky above.

Somewhere behind them, something much larger was on the move. Something she couldn't quite comprehend. Was it the source of that awful shriek they heard? Or was it possible there was more than one of them?

She glanced back. Three flashlights following close behind her. Three companions still in tow. She already knew that, of course. She could feel them back there. But somehow it felt better seeing them with her human eyes. "Don't fall behind," she warned, struggling to keep her voice steady.

She veered to the left again, making a wide berth of something with too many arms that was scuttling the other direction. As soon as she was past it, she angled right again, avoiding something under the ground.

Another of those earth-shaking shrieks rolled across the landscape like thunder, chilling her to the bone and wrenching a barely stifled cry from Andrea behind her.

She could hear Nicole cursing under her breath.

But perhaps the noisy giant wasn't all bad news. The things around her were reacting to it as well. Some of them had turned to flee. Others hunkered down, as if to hide. Almost everything she felt out here turned its attention toward it. And away from *them*.

She pushed onward, weaving through the minefield of horrors, steering clear of everything she could sense.

It was working. The thing behind them wasn't following.

But there was trouble ahead of them. She could sense more than one of those not-dead things prowling around up there. These weren't slow like the others. They were quick. They were dangerous.

She reached back and grabbed Nicole's hand. "Stay together," she whispered. Then she turned left and began making her way around the worrisome things.

There was something over here, too. But it wasn't moving. It was just lying there. She could sense some kind of consciousness in it, but it felt weak and distant.

"Quiet," she whispered. "Don't draw any attention to yourselves."

Nicole nodded. Andrea had her other wrist. And Keith had Andrea's, forming a chain by which they could stay together and follow almost step-for-step the path she was mapping out for them.

It came out of the gloom, a frightful shape that wasn't remotely human. It was long and hairy and broken and dried, little more than a tangle of knotted leather and bone with clumps of filthy, matted hair clinging to it.

It didn't even stink.

The sight of it raised an audible gasp from Andrea, but she managed to keep it stifled enough that those livelier things didn't seem to notice them.

The thing on the ground, however, did. She could feel that distant consciousness stir a little. A flicker of alien emotion, sparks like fireflies in the twilight. A futile effort to make something in this long-ruined body move again. But then it faded back into the distance, surrendering to the hopeless eternity that had consumed it ages ago.

They moved on, the darkness at their backs once again swallowing the pitiful thing.

Elsewhere, those that could still move easily enough were still prowling. Most were continuing on the other way. One, however, was moving toward them.

Had it heard Andrea's surprised gasp? Was it zeroing in on them?

It was difficult to tell what these things were thinking. They weren't human, but they weren't mere animals, either. There was a hint of lingering reason somewhere in the chaos that was their consciousness. But it was garbled beyond recognition.

She kept moving, determined to keep putting distance between it and them, terrified that she'd feel it rushing toward them at any moment.

Somewhere ahead of them, another monstrous form appeared as if from nowhere and immediately turned its awful gaze toward her.

She froze. Behind her, the others did the same. None of them asked her what was wrong. They didn't dare make a sound.

She stared into that empty darkness, her gaze fixed on the place where she sensed it, and she felt it staring back at her. Where did it come from? Did these things move around the forest the way they did when they lost the path? Could they simply appear and disappear at random? Or worse, might they have developed the ability to do so *at will*? It was a terrifying thought. If she let it, it would paralyze her with fear. And she couldn't allow that. She needed to keep moving.

Nearby, the other one she'd been worried about shifted its attention toward her as well. Had it noticed her? Was this newly arrived one somehow drawing attention to her?

Her stomach gurgled in the unbearable silence. She felt sick. This was too much. How long could she keep this up? She closed her eyes and forced herself to breathe.

Something was different, she realized. She'd been focusing hard on those eerie, inhuman presences, but at some point the landscape had changed again. The shoreline of the lake loomed ahead of them. It was right there, just beyond the reach of their flashlights. She could see its black surface rippling in the ever-present wind.

It was still blowing against her back, as if they hadn't moved at all, but this wasn't anywhere near where they were. Had they somehow been sent back to where they started? She couldn't sense the trawler anywhere, but it felt as if they'd started over from the beginning again. Or somewhere even farther back, for all she knew.

Was this merely the twisted nature of the Denselands? Or was someone—or some*thing*—sabotaging them?

But she wasn't going to get the chance to ponder it. There were more of those not-dead things out there now. A *lot* more. And they were all moving *toward* them.

Her heart was racing again. Boiling fear spread through her belly. Had they been found?

Forward wasn't going to be an option. She turned and pulled at Nicole's hand, steering her back and to the right, where there were fewer monsters. But there were more appearing every second. Within ten paces, another awakened within the endless gloom ahead of her.

It was no good. There was no way out.

Nicole pressed herself closer and whispered, "What's going on?"

Should she tell her they were surrounded? Or would it be less cruel to pretend all was well right up until these things were close enough to tear out their throats? Because it was becoming harder and harder to tell herself that any of them were going to get out of this alive.

"They're coming, aren't they?" whimpered Andrea.

She couldn't speak if she wanted to. She could barely breathe. An icy terror had swallowed her whole. She couldn't make her feet move.

What did they do wrong? Were they careless? Did they make too much noise? Or was it only because they left the safety of the lake road?

Andrea let out a stifled squeal as her light fell on a horrible shape crawling toward them.

Keith turned to lead them away from it, but a tall, emaciated form was staggering from the gloom on that side.

Again, Nicole cursed.

No... This wasn't their fault. Somehow, somewhere deep down, Gina realized that something else was drawing the attention of these things.

"Tell us what to do," said Keith.

But she didn't know. Tears spilled down her cheeks as she watched a great, hairy thing emerge from the darkness, dragging half its mutilated corpse behind it, rotten teeth bristling from its dangling jaw.

It wasn't fair. The goddess said she'd find what she was looking for. She promised. This wasn't the ending she worked so hard for.

But then something changed again.

They didn't move. Not exactly. They were still standing in the same spot. And those not-dead things were still surrounding them. But in an instant, they all turned and retreated back into the darkness.

"What's happening?" squeaked Andrea.

"Not that I'm complaining," whispered Nicole, "but what the fuck was that?"

But Gina had no answers. She was as baffled as they were.

She was also concerned. Something about this felt wrong. What changed? What were they running from?

She turned and looked behind her, half expecting to find some horrible monstrosity bearing down on them. But they remained alone. Then she lifted her face and gazed upward. The sky was no longer empty. It churned with gloomy clouds. A drizzle of rain fell down around her.

She blinked and wiped it away.

This definitely wasn't right. She looked down, but the lighting had changed. The darkness was gone. It was suddenly twilight. Those deadly trees were bathed in hazy shadow. The ground was covered in a cool mist. And that cold, slow rain...

"Oh no..." she croaked. She squeezed Nicole's hand as a familiar feeling of weary dread washed over her.

But when she looked up, it wasn't Nicole standing there.

"Found you!" sneered the towering, shadowy shape clinging to her hand with mottled, corpse-gray fingers.

Chapter 55

"Zombie…" breathed Albert.

Or whatever you wanted to call those walking corpses, Brandy supposed. He'd said on a few occasions that they might more accurately be called mummies. They weren't contagious, like Hollywood zombies. And they weren't fresh by any means. Most of them weren't even remotely human. They were just dried up, ancient corpses whose souls never departed.

But that seemed pretty irrelevant, all things considered.

This particular monstrosity was either dressed in an ugly, rotting fur coat or, more likely, covered in long, shaggy fur, and was at least as big as a full-grown grizzly bear.

Wayne saw more of these things than anyone else five years ago. He described things of all sizes and shapes, from things with horns and bird-like beaks to things with ears that dangled to their chests to things that bounded through the forest like apes and wolves.

It wasn't moving toward them, thankfully. Nor did it seem to notice them at all. In fact, it was traveling at such an angle that it was already slowly disappearing back into the darkness.

"Can they really not see us?" whispered Violet.

"It seems like there's something about this path that hides us from them," Albert whispered back. "I don't really understand how that works, but it's the only explanation."

"Cool…" grunted Corey.

While everyone else was focused on the monstrous thing in the forest, Brandy felt another of those dreadful flashes of awareness.

This time, she turned and shined her light at the second building, directly at one of those little oval windows.

She couldn't see anything over there…and yet she felt the hair on the back of her neck stand up as she stared into that darkness.

Was someone staring back at her?

But again, the sensation was gone.

She turned and looked back the way they came, then out at the monstrous form everyone else was watching fade into the eternal darkness of the Wood.

Something wasn't right...

But no one else seemed to notice anything. As soon as the zombie—or whatever the hell that thing was—had disappeared from sight, they all pushed onward, picking up their pace, hoping to be gone before it could decide to stop and wander aimlessly for a while in *this* direction.

"I don't like the dead things," decided Violet, her voice still hushed. "They give me the creeps. Big time."

"Good," said Albert. "If those things didn't give you a major case of the creeps, I'm pretty sure I'd be more afraid of you than them."

Violet chuckled at this.

There were more of those squat, black buildings as they pushed forward. It looked like some kind of bizarre little city.

Some of them were turned at such an angle that they revealed their single doorway, but it didn't make the structure any less intimidating. It was little more than an archway filled with heavy black bars, similar to the ones they saw in the windows of that castle-like structure.

Was this all part of some kind of *prison*?

Another squat, black building appeared from the gloom, this one partially collapsed, its crumbling, stucco-like walls spilled like gravel across the litter-strewn forest floor.

Then something strikingly different emerged from the shadows. Something large and shiny was reflecting their flashlight beams in the darkness. It was a rounded structure, about two stories high and at least a hundred feet in diameter, made entirely of smooth, untarnished metal. There was a groove running around the middle of it and several large, rusty machines encircling it. To one side was a narrow tower of a structure built of some kind of white brick, with large gray pipes running up the side.

Brandy's first thought was that the rounded portion reminded her of the water treatment plant on the southern outskirts of Briar Hills. But what this thing might have been used for was beyond her.

"That doesn't look like it belongs with the rest of this stuff," observed Violet.

"It might not," reasoned Albert. "Lucianna said there were remains from *lots* of dead universes piled up here. These might be from entirely different points in time and space that just happened to land next to each other."

She shook her head. "So weird to think about..."

Brandy thought so, too. It hurt her head trying to keep up with it all. It was as bad as the time traveling thing.

This particular structure, whatever it may have once been, looked brand new in places, like that shiny silver tank that was dusty and grimy but otherwise appeared mostly untarnished, while other parts, like those machines surrounding it, were so badly rusted it was difficult to tell where the moving parts even used to be.

Some metals were naturally resistant to tarnish, she recalled. Like gold and platinum. It was possible that there were other metals in past universes that didn't exist in their own. It was also possible, she considered, that the distribution and availability of metals were different, changing the way they were used.

Which, of course, made her wonder...if she knew the difference, could it be possible to return home with her pockets loaded with precious metals? It *would* be nice to get something out of all this trouble...

But then again, weighing herself down with loads of gold and platinum probably wouldn't be the smartest idea when at any moment she may find herself running for her life from some undead monstrosity or another... That kind of greedy character rarely ever made it out of the movie alive, after all.

"I can almost feel it," observed Albert as he eyed the soft glow of the tower's white bricks. "Like these things never should've been in the same place. I can't really explain it."

"Psychic stuff," grunted Corey, as if that were all the explanation it needed.

"Can you get any kind of feeling about what it was used for?" wondered Violet.

But Albert shook his head. "Nothing like that. Only that it doesn't belong here."

As they pushed forward, more strange machinery came into view. Blocks of shiny silver the size of busses were lined up beyond the round structure, each one with large ventilation slits in the sides, revealing long-rusted guts within. Huge, gray pipes protruded from the sides and then plunged down into the earth. Stiff, black cables were strung from barrel-shaped things mounted on top of them that ran back toward the main bulk of the structure.

Beyond these were the remains of a sagging strip of black fencing that looked a lot like chain-link but wasn't, made up of a strange, hexagonal pattern in a single, molded sheet. Behind the fence was what appeared to be a sort of cracked and crumbling parking lot, but had a strange, orange tint to it. At the back of this lot, just visible in the shine of their flashlights, was another silvery shape, like a barn silo stretching up into the black sky.

The whole thing looked like some kind of futuristic science-fiction movie set.

And as soon as they were past the strange, orange parking lot, they found another of those squat black buildings with one of its walls having collapsed onto that strange, black fence.

They looked so utterly different from each other, looking very much as if someone had dropped one of these things almost right on top of the other.

More night trees had cropped up around this structure, their gnarled, coiling branches seemingly clawing at the mesh in those windows.

On the other side of the path, a much larger night tree had stretched its branches well over the shadow road, those drooping tendrils coiled on the cold stone like slumbering snakes, forcing them to step off the path and much closer to the gaping doorway of the black structure than Brandy felt particularly comfortable with.

Corey was still in the lead. He aimed his flashlight inside, revealing an empty interior devoid of any kind of furnishings. Even the floor was bare earth.

Something about the sight gave Brandy an uneasy feeling deep in the pit of her stomach. Again, she wondered if these were part of some kind of prison. And if so, just what kind of people were locked away here? Was this a place where bad people were sent? Or was this the sort of place where bad people with power sent *good* people?

She pushed the thought from her mind. Why did her mind go there? What did it matter? If half of what they'd been told about this place was true, then whatever went on here ended many, *many* centuries ago.

It was just the eeriness of this place, she supposed. It was unsettling just being here. And to be off the path like this, even for a moment, was unnerving.

She stepped forward and reached for Albert's hand. That was what she needed. His touch always gave her extra strength. But before her fingers could close around his, she was frozen in place by another of those strange and dreadful sensations.

Someone was here with them. Someone who didn't belong. She was sure of it this time.

Her gaze twitched from Albert to Violet to Corey and back again. Three of them. She made four. That was all there was supposed to be.

And yet there was another.

And it wasn't going away this time...

She turned around, scanning their surroundings, her heart beginning to pound with sick anticipation. But there was no one else here. She could see nothing.

She'd fallen behind. The others hadn't noticed she'd stopped. They were eager to get back onto the safety of the sentinels' shadow road, just as she should be doing. She turned to hurry after them, but that sensation hit her again, stronger than ever, an ice-cold feeling of stark terror that sucked the breath right from her lungs and made her entire body clench tight.

She tried to cry out to the others, but her throat wouldn't open.

What was this feeling? What was happening? Slowly, she managed to turn her head and look through that gaping doorway.

The figure standing there was something out of her worst nightmares. Huge, cavernous eyes. Moldy flesh. Wide, gaping mouth filled with greenish teeth far too big to fit inside. Long, black, filthy hair floating about its head like a drowned corpse.

Skeletal hands reached out and seized her.

By the time she managed to scream, she knew it was too late.

No one could hear her now.

Chapter 56

Fester vermin were freaky things.

They didn't look anything like the vermin in Everett's world, that was for sure. These things didn't look like *anything* from his world, or anything he'd ever imagined, even. They weren't bugs. They weren't rodents. They weren't reptiles. In fact, he could think of nothing even remotely like these things.

It was as if they were living globs of black ink. They were about the size of tennis balls, but flattened, as if melted. And they didn't scurry across the floor so much as sort of *swim* across it, trailing a black stain behind them that strangely faded away a few seconds after they were gone.

It was hard to tell if Olivia managed to use her psychic abilities in time to know which way to go or if she just panicked and ran into one at random, but so far they hadn't hit a dead-end, which was good because the passage behind them was swarming with living black goo that seemed to want to eat them.

It was all both totally terrifying and extraordinarily cool.

He just couldn't help himself. Even as he ran for what was almost certainly his life, he wasn't able to stop wondering just what these crazy things were. Did their freaky black color simply absorb all the light, masking the real shape of their bodies? Or did they even *have* bodies under there? Had they discovered some kind of real-life slime monsters? And just what would they do to him if they caught him? Did they have teeth? Or stingers? Or did they just dissolve their victims on contact?

He couldn't even get a proper look at them. They were too fast, keeping him running, not giving him a chance to look back.

Wayne was directly ahead of him, following Olivia as she led the way, weaving through a seemingly endless maze of open doorways. He'd already lost track of how to go back the way they came.

Then he glanced back at the strange swarm and found that they were suddenly gone.

He stopped running and looked back.

There were only two of them left. One retreated back down the black corridor almost as soon as his light hit it. The other was zooming back and forth in the doorway as if agitated.

"Guys!" he called, keeping his eye on that one remaining restless glob in case it reacted to his voice, but it only continued to dart back and forth for a moment. Then it, too, disappeared back into the darkness. "I guess they made their point," he panted, chuckling a little. Whatever those things were, they seemed to be territorial. They only wanted them away from their nest.

Ahead, Wayne and Olivia were peering back at him, their bodies still tense, ready to bolt again if necessary.

He still wanted to know what those things were. He couldn't help it. They were just so *unusual*. He had so many questions.

"That wasn't fun," gasped Wayne. There were beads of sweat on his forehead. He didn't look like he was used to a lot of vigorous exercise.

"I didn't do it," Everett reminded him.

"I know you didn't," he grumbled.

Olivia giggled in spite of her racing heart.

Wayne glanced around, confused. "Any idea where we are?"

"You're kidding, right?" replied Olivia. "I don't even know where it is we're *supposed* to be. I was lucky to be able to find a path that wouldn't trap us in a dead end."

He looked back at her, surprised. "Sorry..."

That made sense. Everett thought that she must have been using at least a little of her psychic ability to navigate. The odds of just randomly picking doorways that continued to lead somewhere other than a closed room wouldn't have been ideal.

And now that he was thinking of it, that would've been a terrible time to have come across a room filled with those killing vines, too. He found himself glancing around, half-convinced he was standing right next to one, fractions of an inch from certain death.

But there weren't any that he could see. Only more of those ominous, scattered bones.

It was strange how things just kept working out like that. Right from the beginning, even. The three of them ending up in Gutler's Weep together, with his ability to navigate the broken landscape and her ability to sense danger. Even Wayne, without any particular special ability, but physically strong enough to keep that scarecrow man's monsters distracted so he could focus on finding the story of that place. It was as if they all had a role to play there, without even knowing it. And even before he came along, they were like that. He found himself thinking of the stories they'd told him of mysterious abandoned dormitories and ancient, underground temples. The Keeper and his mysterious plans... People with just the right special thing to get them out of tough spots just like this one...

Just who *was* this secretive planner? Was he God? Like, the actual, capital-G God? Or some kind of angel doing His work? What would something like that mean for all of them?

Olivia turned and stepped through another doorway, her pretty eyes searching the space beyond. "I don't know which way to go. I feel like we're lost."

"We're not lost," Wayne assured her. "You'll figure out the way back. I know you will."

But she didn't look like she had nearly as much confidence in herself. Those fester vermin had frightened her, Everett knew. She was shaken. She needed a moment to calm down.

He turned and shined his light through one of the doorways, his eyes peeled for any more of those black slime things. (*And those killing vines*, he reminded himself. *Can't forget about those again.*) There was a ledge protruding from the wall on either side in here. They reminded him of kitchen countertops, or perhaps workbenches in garages. A place to do *something*.

What was this place? What did it used to be? What went on here? And who were the people who built it? It reminded him of similar ruins he'd seen on television in exotic places like Africa and Central America. Was it something like that? Was this already some kind of ancient city even in the final days of its own world? Was that why there were no artifacts left inside it?

It would be like their own world dying and someone, millions of years from now, happening across the Pyramids of Egypt in the middle of the Wood.

There was another doorway on the far side of the room. He stepped toward it, curious.

"Don't go getting lost," called Wayne.

"I'm right here," he called back. The next room was small. It seemed to be a dead end. There were no killing vines *or* fester vermin in here. But it wasn't empty. Something caught the light as he swept it across the walls and reflected it back at him. A twinkle in the gloom.

There was a small, square hole in the left wall, about the size of a shoebox. And something was resting inside it.

He crept closer, fascinated.

It was a disk, about the size of a dessert plate and about half an inch thick, made of a strange, greenish gold metal. It was etched with intersecting lines in an odd, flower-like pattern.

"Get back out here," Wayne called. "We need to keep moving before something else shows up."

"Okay," he called back. He reached out and picked the strange object up, curious. It was remarkably heavy. Was it made of lead or something?

Why was this the only thing left here? It didn't make sense.

He turned back toward the door as he studied the patterns on each side. There was something weird about it, but he couldn't put his finger on exactly what it was.

He'd ask Wayne and Olivia. Maybe they'd have an idea. After all, they'd seen a lot of strange things. Maybe they'd seen a pattern like this somewhere. Maybe in that crazy-sounding temple they went to.

But when he stepped through the doorway, everything changed.

In an instant, the oppressive darkness of the Wood was gone. He stood squinting out across an endless red desert beneath a blinding, boiling sky. The wind was howling. Sand stung his unprotected face. And it was suddenly very hot out, much hotter than it was back in that humid, Tennessee forest, even.

"What...?" He turned to look back through the doorway, but there *was* no doorway. He was alone in this blistering red wasteland, with nothing for as far as he could see.

Nothing made any sense. Where was he? What was this place? How did he get here?

Then he looked down at the mysterious object in his hand. Was this what brought him here? Should he not have touched it?

"Oops..."

Chapter 57

"Andrea?" gasped Nicole. "Gina?" She didn't understand what happened. One moment they were all standing in the Wood, watching those horrible zombie things vanish back into the darkness, the next she was all alone again.

She was standing far out on an old wooden pier in a cold, drizzling rain, dark water churning all around her for as far as she could see.

She didn't need to be psychic to figure out what happened. It was that emotion-eating freak, Glum. He found them somehow, figured out how to sneak past Gina's special senses and ambushed them.

"Andrea!" She turned and looked out over the dark lake. "Gina!" Just like in the barely-there's strange, twisted version of her apartment, everything seemed to be illuminated by some invisible, bluish light source. Although the sky was overcast and dark, she could see far off into the distance, as if Glum wanted her to witness just how alone she was in this place. "Keith!"

She tucked her flashlight into her pocket, saving its battery, and called out their names again.

Where could they have gone? They wouldn't be in the water, would they? The thought sent a thunderbolt of terror through her. The lake stretched well beyond the horizon. What if they were drowning out there right now and she couldn't see them?

They were all holding hands, like they were supposed to! It wasn't fair.

She couldn't go through this again... She couldn't deal with all those horrid emotions. She *wouldn't*.

She stepped up to the edge of the pier and looked down at the water below. Maybe it was just the gloomy light, but it looked unnaturally dark and inky.

A manifestation of his own physical form, she thought, remembering how Hotdog described Tristesse Lane. *A universe within his own body...* She thought about how he'd described that world as a sort of *stomach* and suddenly the sight of those black, churning waves made her sick to her own.

She backed away from the edge. Maybe it was only a metaphor, but she *really* didn't want to risk falling in.

She hurried back toward the shore. She felt so *stupid*. How could she let this happen?

Ada said Glum wouldn't kill them. She said he wanted to *use* them, not destroy them. If Gina's so-called goddess was telling the truth about that, then she had to believe that he wouldn't have dumped them out in those waves to drown. This was just like Glimmering Sunrise Place. He'd separated them. It was probably easier that way for him to suck away everything positive in their brains and poison them with his sick, crippling hopelessness.

She had to find them. If she was all alone here, then they were probably all alone, too. And she already knew what this place was capable of. The despair would come in like a tide, swallowing them, drowning them.

And she already knew she wasn't strong enough to resist it. Certainly not by herself.

She could already feel the tears welling up in her eyes.

"Please be all right," she cried. "*Please.*"

Chapter 58

Albert stopped walking, confused. Something seemed wrong. But...what?

He turned and looked back at Brandy.

She was standing right behind him, staring back at him, her eyebrows raised inquisitively. "You okay?" she asked him.

He glanced around, uncertain, but he nodded. "Yeah... I think so." But he reached back and took hold of her hand. He felt very much as if he didn't want to be separated from her. And something about her standing so close to the dark doorway of that creepy old structure made him uncomfortable. He pulled her toward him, urging her forward, and she pushed her body against his with one of those familiar little half-smiles he liked so much.

"What's up?" she asked him.

"Nothing..." He wasn't really sure how to describe it if he wanted to. It was just an odd rush of barely felt emotions that he couldn't quite sort out. All he really knew was that he suddenly didn't want to be apart from her. "Let's keep going."

Ahead of them, Violet and Corey had passed the intruding branches of the night tree they were circling around and were stepping back onto the shadow road.

He gave Brandy's hand a squeeze and they hurried after them.

What was it about this stone path that made it feel so much safer? It made no logical sense. There was nothing to stop the living-dead things in the forest from just shuffling right onto it after them. And yet nothing did. It was as if they were invisible to those things as long as they remained on the path.

Did it have something to do with the way the statues affected their heads back in the temple? Was the same force that made him and Brandy lose all control in the sex room making them invisible to the monsters of the Wood?

It was frustrating to understand so little of it all. He wished someone could explain these things to him.

He held onto Brandy's hand as he walked, still not wanting to let her go. She didn't try to pull away. In fact, she leaned against him as they walked, her cheek almost resting on his shoulder. It was nice. He could almost believe for a moment that they were on a nice stroll on a moonlit beach instead of some long-forgotten suburb of hell.

And yet, for some reason something in the far back of his mind was nagging at him, telling him that something somewhere had changed...

"Intergalactic communications tower," said Corey, pointing his light up at a strange, brown, spherical shape emerging from the darkness to their right, suspended on great, bluish-colored columns.

"Or a *water tower*," countered Violet, wrinkling her nose at him.

"Could be," he admitted. "Or water towers in that world looked a lot different than ours do."

"Or they looked a lot like ours because they were built for the *same purpose*."

"Maybe... Or maybe they looked like something else and that's what intergalactic communications towers looked like."

"You don't know anything about it."

"Neither do you. So you can't say I'm wrong."

Albert chuckled a little to himself. These two were fun. The big guy was funny. He couldn't tell if he was being serious or just teasing her, but he was leaning strongly toward the latter.

Brandy slipped her arm around him, resting her hand on his hip. He loved the way it felt whenever she touched him. It never mattered how brief or how unromantic the touch might be, whether she was straightening a misplaced lock of hair or wiping at a smudge on his cheek or prodding at a bug bite on his arm. There was just something deeply meaningful about her touch.

"Even if it *was* something other than a water tower," sighed Violet, "why would it be an intergalactic communications tower of all things?"

"Gotta have intergalactic communications towers. How else're you gonna communicate with people in other galaxies?"

"Why would there be people in other galaxies?"

"If all these universes are here 'cause they died out, then they were lots older than ours, right? They prob'ly had way more technology than we do. Bet they had lots of time to explore the galaxy."

Albert hadn't thought of it that way. Whether these other worlds had ventured out beyond their skies was a debate he wasn't prepared to get into, but he wasn't wrong. If he assumed that the life cycle of all the universes were approximately equal in length, and their world hadn't ended yet, then those other universes must have been older than theirs. If so, they easily could have possessed significantly higher levels of technology in almost every field.

But that, of course, led to another, far less cheerful thought: what happened to all that knowledge and technology? Was everything automatically reset to the stone age when everyone migrated into the new universe?

"Why are you so talkative all of a sudden?" grumbled Violet.

"Dunno," replied Corey. "Just excited to see an intergalactic communications tower, I guess."

"You're such a dork."

Albert felt Brandy's hand slide down the back of his shorts. Before he realized what was happening, she gave his butt a firm squeeze. He glanced over at her, an eyebrow raised, but she was pretending to look the other way. "What're you doing?" he whispered?

"Playing," she whispered back. Now she looked up at him and bit her lip in that mischievous way she had. "Wanna play with me?"

"Not exactly the best time, don't you think?"

"We'll sneak off for just a minute," she pressed. "They won't even miss us."

"What? Of course they'll miss us. What's gotten into you?"

Now her smile disappeared. "I'm just thinking we should recharge our psychic powers. It might tell us something about our surroundings. Like before, with that castle."

"I feel like we should just stay on the path and stay together for now. That just seems safer."

She pouted at him. "You're no fun."

He frowned at her, confused. "Where's this coming from suddenly?"

But she looked off the other way, refusing to respond.

This...seemed a little odd. What was up with her? And it didn't go unnoticed by him that she still hadn't let go of his butt.

"Don't have to be intergalactic," decided Corey. "Might just be for talkin' to other planets in the solar system."

"If you say so," sighed Violet.

Albert stared at Brandy for a moment. Something was definitely off. He was sure of it. But he couldn't quite wrap his head around what it was. "Seriously," he whispered. "Are you okay?"

She pressed one hand between her legs as she walked. She looked uncomfortable. Her face was flushed. She looked like... Well, she looked like she did back in the sex room, now that he was thinking about it. The thought sent a thunderbolt through his body. Was something happening to her right now? He glanced around, paranoid, half-expecting to see those pornographic statues appearing out of the gloom. But there was nothing more than another of those squat black buildings.

She turned and pouted up at him. "Wet..." she mumbled.

This caught him by surprise. "*What?*"

"*I'm gonna wet myself!*" she whispered, her face flushing bright red at having to say it aloud.

"Oh..." he said, those thoughts scattering in an instant. "Oh!" He turned and looked around, a different kind of panic springing up inside him. "I'm sorry!" It made sense, now that he was thinking about it. How long had it been since their last bathroom break? He couldn't even remember. It was almost weird that he didn't have to go, himself. But where were they supposed to go way out here? He doubted if any of these buildings had usable toilets.

"Can't hold it much longer..." she whimpered.

"Right. Sorry." He squeezed her hand and turned his attention to their companions ahead of them. "Hey, I need a quick rest stop."

They turned and looked back at him.

"I've seriously got to go," he told them.

"Sure," said Violet, looking perfectly unfazed. She glanced over at the nearest of those black buildings. "Try back there, maybe? Careful, though. Don't let your guard down."

"She'll keep watch for me," he said, tugging Brandy along.

"Yell if anything happens," she called after them.

They could probably see that it was her, not him, who was in distress at the moment, but he was doing his best to take the blame for her. It was the least he could do since he was too dense to take the hint before she had to spell it out for him.

Either way, though, they didn't seem to care. They turned back to the structure they'd been arguing about. It was right beside them now, looming almost overhead.

"You're right," decided Corey. "It's prob'ly a water tower."

"Uh huh."

Albert led Brandy around the corner of the building, just out of sight, then turned and shined his light around. "I'll keep watch," he promised. "Just relax and do what you need to do."

But instead of doing her business, she slipped her arms around his waist and slid her hands up under his shirt.

"Um...? Hi?"

She pressed her face against the back of his shirt and giggled.

"What're you doing?"

"Nobody can see us now," she informed him.

"Yeah..." Because she said she needed to pee... What was going on here? Why was she acting so strange? It wasn't like this was the cabana at the Lucianna Mysteria's pool. This was the Denselands, and all the horrors that came with it. They couldn't sneak off for a roll in the hay in a place like this. That was how horny teenagers ended up with machetes rammed through their chests in slasher movies.

Those wandering hands slid downward. With incredible speed, she unbuttoned his shorts and slid her hands inside.

He let out a startled gasp as she closed her fingers around that part of him.

"We never made it home," she reminded him. "So this is technically still our honeymoon, you know."

This wasn't right. This was *dangerous*. But when she touched him like that...when he felt her warm hands on his skin...the rest of the world always melted away. He couldn't help it.

She was as much his weakness as she was his strength, after all.

But *no*. He grabbed her wrists and pulled her hands away, then turned to face her. "What's happening here?" he demanded.

She smiled that gorgeous, flirty smile again. "I'm helping myself to your dick," she informed him. "Are you really this adorably oblivious or do you just like it when I take charge?"

He stared at her. That...kinda *sounded* like something she'd say to him...especially this past week...but *here*? *Now*?

She pulled her hands free and then grabbed hold of him again.

The world swam out of focus around him. Why did *he* have to be the voice of reason in this black wilderness?

"Just shut up and let me enjoy my honeymoon."

But this couldn't be their honeymoon. This was the Wood. This was an endless black forest full of dead things that wouldn't stay dead and man-eating trees and monstrous tokkatoks and carrion eaters and...

But she sank down to her knees in front of him and suddenly everything else was washed from his head.

This feeling...

He couldn't stand it. It overwhelmed him. He felt like he was melting.

Sure… Why not take just a little break from all this darkness?

An incredible pressure was building inside him…threatening to burst…

Except everything about this was entirely and dreadfully *wrong*.

His eyes snapped open, fresh fear exploding inside him.

When he looked down at his wife, she was gone. A horrible nightmare of a face was rushing up at him instead.

He tried to scream, but the darkness was faster.

Chapter 59

"Hey," Wayne called back. "Move your ass. We can't stay here all day." How far had he wandered off? He couldn't even see the kid's light anymore.

Olivia turned and looked back toward him, a frown on her pretty face. "Something feels off again."

Wayne glanced back at her. Then he turned and shined his light back and forth. "Shit..." he grumbled. What now? More fester vermin? Something worse? He stepped through the doorway. "We need to go," he urged. "*Now.*"

But the room was empty.

"Everett?"

"What's happening?" asked Olivia. There was a clear note of rising panic in her voice.

He stood there a moment, confused. Where did he go? He came this way. And there was no other way out. It didn't make sense.

Then Olivia was crowded beside him, peering into the empty room with him. "Where is he?"

"I don't know. He was right here." This was where his voice came from when he told him to hurry up. He stepped farther into the room and shined his light all around, looking for an opening. There was a small recess in the wall, about the size of a shoebox, but that was all. Was there a secret passage or something? "Everett?" he called, raising his voice. He reached out and pushed at the walls, trying to determine if any of them moved. It seemed kind of absurd, like something out of an Indiana Jones movie or an old Scooby Doo cartoon, but he didn't know what else to try. People didn't just disappear into thin air.

Except, he knew better than that. Of course they did. They all did it back in that broken fairy circle. Again and again.

Olivia turned and ran back out into the hallway, shining her light back and forth. "Everett?" she called.

Wayne backed out of the room. This wasn't good. This wasn't

just some West Virginia forest. This was the Wood. If Everett was lost somewhere in *this* wilderness, the odds of ever finding him were next to none. And if it happened to one of them...

He rushed back out to where Olivia was standing and grabbed her hand. "No letting go of each other," he insisted.

She looked up at him, tears shimmering in her pretty eyes. "Where did he go?"

"I don't know."

"Did something take him? Like those awful never-children did to me?" The thought filled her face with panic. A tear streaked down her cheek.

"I don't know," he said again. "But he's fine. Trust me."

"*How do you know that?*" she begged, her voice turning shrill with rising panic.

"Because that kid's *way* too stubborn to get himself killed. He's like a damn cartoon character or something. Just...trust me. Wherever he is, he'll be okay."

He could tell she didn't believe him, but she said no more about it. She gnawed at her lower lip and shined her light at the doorways around them.

"Besides," he added, "the Keeper sent him here with us. That means we need him. We'll probably meet back up with him by the time we get wherever it is we're supposed to be going. In fact, I'm betting *you* can find him."

"Me?"

"Yeah. Follow those amber threads or whatever they are."

"I still don't understand any of that!"

"I know. But you've been using them this whole time. You've kept us out of danger."

"Until now!"

"He's not dead. He's just lost. Like back in Gutler's Weep. He's wandered off. That's all. Just trust me. Trust *him*. And let your threads guide the way. Keep us out of danger, show us the way forward. I'll bet we cross paths again by the time we find our way out of this stone age maze."

She still didn't look convinced. She really didn't want to leave this spot without him. She was worried that they'd lose any chance at ever finding him again. And he didn't blame her one bit. He was afraid of that, too. He was *terrified*. What if he was wrong? What if Sandy's amber threads didn't lead back to him. Would they have simply abandoned him in this dark world? But the fact was that she *did* trust him. And she trusted Everett, too. She steeled herself, wiped away her tears and then turned and shined her flashlight at the doorways in front of them.

"Threads," she sighed.

Wayne nodded. "Yeah. Threads. Just like Sandy said. I'll bet you'll find the one that leads us back to him."

Still clinging to his hand, she started walking. "I guess…maybe this way?"

"Okay."

But she glanced back again, a mask of worry painted across her pretty features.

He didn't blame her. He felt it, too. There was a sick knot burning deep in his gut. He *really* hoped he was doing the right thing. But what else were they supposed to do? They couldn't just stay here forever. At some point they were going to have to move on. And what if staying in one place too long meant they missed him somewhere up ahead.

Damn that kid… Why'd he have to wander off like that? He knew how dangerous this place was. How many times had they warned him?

Olivia wiped at her eyes again and pushed forward. "I'm not even sure I'm doing this right."

"You're doing fine," he assured her, as if he knew anything about it.

If nothing else, she should be able to keep them out of trouble as much as possible.

She made her way through one doorway after another, weaving back and forth, following that strange sense. Every now and then she'd stop suddenly and change direction. He didn't quite dare ask what she felt when she did that. He didn't think he wanted to know. He had a sick feeling that if he could see what was in the rooms she was avoiding, it would haunt his nightmares for the rest of his life. He felt like a rat in a maze full of rattlesnakes, slipping past deadly dangers by nothing more than instinct and luck, one wrong turn from becoming prey for a monster.

How deep inside these stone walls had they ventured? He couldn't remember the last time he saw a window.

Olivia let out a gasp and stopped cold.

"What is it?" he whispered, still not sure he wanted to hear the answer.

"Something's here," she breathed, her gaze sliding back and forth between the two doorways in front of them. "We have to go back."

He didn't question her. He backed away, pulling her by her hand. When they reached the previous door, she slipped through it and hurried across the next room without looking back. But she stopped at the next doorway, too.

"No…" She stepped back. "Not there, either." She turned and tugged him back the other way, back through the door, retracing their steps to *another* doorway. Then she stopped. She stood there, looking around. "Something's not right."

Wayne didn't like this room. Those black vines had climbed up one of the walls, those deadly thorns bristling from it, just waiting for a chance to kill.

She stepped closer to him, as if frightened. "I don't understand what I'm feeling. It's not coming from any direction anymore. It's like it's all around us."

He shined his light around. There was nothing in the room with them. Nothing he could see, anyway.

She pulled at his hand again, leading him through another doorway and down another corridor, past more and more of those black vines. She hurried past three dark rooms, then quickly ducked into a fourth. Then she stopped.

Wayne turned around, scanning every surface with his light. There were killing vines on *all* the walls in here. "It's getting worse!" he gasped.

"I know!" Another tear streaked down her face. "I feel like something's going to happen! I can't find a way out!"

"It's okay," he assured her, squeezing her hand. "Just calm down. Take a breath. I'm right here."

She nodded and closed her eyes for a moment. Another tear slipped down her cheek. "My heart won't stop pounding. It feels like a bomb is about to go off or something. I don't know what to do about it."

"Stop and breathe," he said, pulling her closer. "It's okay. I'm not going to let anything happen."

But she was shaking her head. She knew as well as he did that he had no such power in a place like this.

Then she stiffened. Her teary eyes grew wide with mounting terror. "She's here…"

He stared at her. She? She who? What was she talking about? He turned and shined his light back at the doorway they came through.

Something was there. A sort of mist, he thought. It poured into the room and circled around them, occasionally taking shape, giving him a glimpse of a long leg, a slender arm, a trailing silver dress, a flash of yellow flowers.

It was like the way Maeve looked when she rose from the fountain, he recalled. More fog than person.

But this wasn't Maeve.

...so sorry... he heard a soft voice say somewhere in the back of his puzzled mind.

Then the shape rushed at him, turning solid in the process, and knocked him backward.

He heard Olivia scream his name, but he could do nothing to assure her that it would be okay this time. His back struck the wall. He felt a searing pain as those deadly black thorns passed through his shirt and sank into his flesh.

In a single, terrible instant, he was adrift in those endless, churning waves again.

Fresh terror overwhelmed him. No... Not this... He couldn't be here. Not now. He needed to get back to Olivia. She was all alone!

But he couldn't go back.

He couldn't move.

He couldn't even scream.

Chapter 60

Andrea stood in the darkness, her flashlight clenched in one hand, the spear in the other, staring down an ominously familiar stone tunnel. "Okay…" she whispered. She turned and looked the other way. There was no end in sight. "So I'm back *here* again…"

Journey of the Dead. The tunnel of light on which all the departed souls of the world made their final pilgrimage to whatever waited beyond. Although apparently if you weren't dead yet, there was no light. For the living, there was only endless darkness.

Five years ago, after that carrion eater thing knocked her over the ledge to what she really thought was her doom, she found herself here. Except, unlike now, it wasn't until she was reunited with her friends and their flashlights that she actually *saw* what it looked like. Until then, she'd followed it utterly blind. It was the passage she used to rescue her friends when the temple collapsed.

That was such a crazy ordeal. It was sometimes hard to convince herself that it wasn't just a wild dream. It was so *surreal*. She remembered somehow ripping the tunnel in half, bending it up and into the heart of the collapsing temple to catch her friends who were plummeting to their deaths after Brandy threw open that door. And then everything just snapped right back into place, good as new, with everyone safe and sound, if a bit scraped and bruised by the rough slide at the end of their fall.

It was like something out of a cartoon! And it didn't seem like it should've even worked. They fell from a fatal height and landed against the stone wall of the tunnel. Albert had theorized that it was only the slope of the tunnel, transitioning from vertical to horizontal, and the slickness caused by the water flowing along the tunnel floor that made a safe landing possible. It was either a tremendous stroke of luck or something out there was looking out for them, and she was leaning heavily toward the latter.

But how did she get back here? One second she was standing

there, looking out at the lake, the next she was enveloped in eerie darkness. She felt as if she'd simply blinked and missed something important.

She wasn't dead. She was, like, ninety-eight percent sure she wasn't, anyway. Because the dead in this place didn't have bodies. They felt like tiny little horizontal raindrops zooming by.

But she didn't feel any of those right now. The tunnel felt eerily empty.

And in her panicked state, she failed to notice another key detail as well. The water. She was standing on dry stone. The trickling stream that once flowed through here had dried up.

Was this the same tunnel?

"Hello?" she called. Her voice didn't echo. There was nothing at either end for it to bounce off of. For the living who managed to enter it, this tunnel went on forever. And she wasn't sure that the normal laws of physics worked in places like these anyway.

Last time she was here, a mysterious voice spoke out to her, assuring her that everything was okay, that she was precisely where she was meant to be, but no one answered her this time. She seemed to be utterly alone in this place.

"Nikki?" she tried. "Gina?" Then she looked the other way again, "Keith?" *Calm down*, she told herself. She needed to think. Last time, there was a reason she was brought here. She was everyone's way home. Without her, they would've been buried in the burning rubble of the Temple of the Blind as it came crashing down around them.

But there was no temple this time. They were supposed to be looking for someplace called the City Beyond Memory.

This was all so confusing…

Then she remembered the ghostly voice that had been following her since those hospital hallways. She might have been separated from Nicole and Gina, but the ghost girl, whoever she was, was *inside her head*.

Right?

She closed her eyes and bit her lip, hoping. "Are you still there?"

"Yes."

"Oh!" She opened her eyes and looked around. That wasn't inside her head. And it wasn't just a whisper like in the hospital. It sounded like she was standing right next to her. But she couldn't see anyone. "Oh, thank God…" For a moment, she thought she was alone again. "Um… Okay. This is good. Do you know where we are?"

"Spirit highway," replied the voice.

She turned around, listening. It was strange to hear someone talking so clearly and so close, and yet not be able to see anyone.

Spirit highway? She'd heard that phrase before. Gina called it that. Way back in Glimmering Sunrise Place.

"One of the dead ones," the voice added. It sounded like it was moving around her, but she couldn't quite follow it.

"Dead ones?" She frowned. "What does that mean?"

"When worlds die, their spirit highways are severed and the dead can no longer reach their destination."

"That sounds awful…"

"Doesn't it? But that's the cruel truth about the cycle. Not everyone gets a happy ending."

Was that why she didn't feel any souls whizzing by like last time? And why the water was gone? The tunnel floor was discolored where it used to flow, but it had long ago run dry. Now that she was looking, it occurred to her that there were cracks in these walls that weren't there the first time, as if the tunnel were slowly crumbling away. There was something sad and strangely disturbing about the idea.

"All the worlds that ever live are doomed to someday die and collapse into the ever-expanding vastness of the Wood, along with anyone, living or dead, unfortunate enough to still be in those worlds."

"Oh…" She wasn't sure what to say to that. It was a seriously depressing thought.

"Didn't you ever wonder why there were so many undead in the Wood? The vast majority of them are those unfortunate souls who were denied their final destination."

"Um… Wow." It was a lot more information than she was expecting. Ghost Girl wasn't just able to speak more clearly in this place, she was a lot chattier, too. Again, she turned and shined her light down one end of the tunnel, then the other. "So…any idea how we got here?"

"Yes. I brought you here."

She frowned. "Wait, *you*?"

"Yes."

"*Why*?"

"Why not?"

She blinked, confused. "What?"

"Let's see what happens when one of the Keeper's precious little puppets goes missing."

Andrea was still turning around, still shining her light at the tunnel walls, trying to glimpse even a peek of whoever was with her, but it was nothing more than a voice. And she was realizing now that it wasn't the voice of a friendly ghost.

What was it Ada said? Something clinging to her? Something stronger than a mere spirit? Something even she, with all her goddess powers couldn't quite see?

It seems to attract unwanted things.

"Who are you?"

"Wouldn't you like to know?"

She started forward, pushing the darkness back a few paces with her light, then quickly turned and looked the other way. Her heart was racing. This was seriously bad. "Um...*yeah.* That's kind of why I asked."

The voice laughed. There was something oddly familiar about that laugh.

"Where are Nikki and Gina?"

"I wouldn't waste time thinking about them. They'll be deep inside gross Gwilym's greasy guts by now."

"No!" She lurched forward, stabbing at that looming darkness, pushing the light farther into the endless tunnel. "Give them back!"

"They're not mine to give. Gwilym and I had a deal."

"What?"

"I helped him get past the freak girl's psychic senses and he let me have *you.*"

"*Why would you do that?*"

"Why not?" she asked again.

It delights in your misfortune, she recalled, her heart sinking. This was really happening. She was really trapped in here, with no way to help her friends. "You're as much a monster as he is..."

"Well, who isn't these days? I mean, really?"

No... There *had* to be a way out of this place.

"Have fun in here. I'll try to remember to check back in a few months and see how you're doing."

"What? No! Let me out of here! I have to help my friends!"

But the voice had fallen silent.

She was all alone. Again.

She groaned and leaned against the wall. This definitely sucked. Now what was she supposed to do?

Wasn't the Keeper supposed to have planned all of this? Everyone kept bringing him up. How could he let something like this happen? Or what about Gina's goddess? Where was *she?*

This was so stupid!

Could this day get any worse?

Then her flashlight flickered and died, and the inky blackness swallowed her completely.

"Oh come on!"

Chapter 61

"What's taking so long?" Violet called out. Albert and Brandy should've been back by now. It didn't take this long to piddle, not even if they were both going. "You two okay back there?"

But the forest was quiet. No one was answering.

"Don't like that," said Corey.

She didn't like it either. Not at all. Had something happened? She could still see the glow of their flashlights from around the corner of the black structure.

"I'm checking on them," she decided.

"Careful."

She stepped off the stone path and headed for the corner of the building. "What's going on?" she called as she approached. She didn't want to sneak up on anyone while they were trying to answer nature's call, after all. That wasn't a memory picture she wanted. "I'm coming to check on you," she warned.

But still no one answered. And when she turned the corner, she found both flashlights lying abandoned on the ground. There was no sign of Albert or Brandy anywhere.

She stared at the flashlights for a moment, her heart racing, then turned and looked back at Corey. He was standing there, staring back at her, his expression grim.

What happened back here? Where could they have gone? They wouldn't have just dropped their flashlights and walked off into the darkness. But she never heard any kind of commotion, no cries or scuffling, as if something had attacked them. And they weren't far enough away that they wouldn't have heard any odd noises.

Corey walked a few steps out into the forest, shining his lantern into the surrounding trees, looking for any sign of them.

"Careful," she called to him as she knelt down and studied the area. There was nothing to indicate that someone had been dragged away and she could see no sign of blood, which was good. But the earth here was dry and hard, revealing no footprints for her to follow. Did something get into their heads and lead them away? Were they snatched into the black sky?

She turned her light upward, her heart leaping at the memory of what everyone kept telling her about the trees out here, about those deadly, twisted branches that grabbed and strangled and devoured unwary prey. For a moment she was convinced she'd see their bloody corpses dangling overhead and those inescapable branches already reaching for her. But there were no branches over this spot and there was nothing to be seen in any of the surrounding trees.

She breathed a sigh of relief, but it was shallow. Albert and Brandy were just gone. It was as if they'd stepped back here to take care of business, just as they'd said, and then vanished into thin air.

"Not good," said Corey.

That was a hell of an understatement. They'd just lost half their party. Worse, Warner Harr made it sound as if they and their freaky-sounding, psychic sex magic thing were a critical part of this weird mission they were all on. What were they supposed to do now?

She picked up the abandoned flashlights and switched them off. It was best to conserve their batteries as much as possible. And yet a part of her wondered if it was a bad idea to take them. If Albert and Brandy came back...

Except what were the odds of that? She had no idea where they could be right now, but they had no light to see by. They weren't likely to find their way *anywhere* in this pitch-black wasteland. She tucked both flashlights into the pocket of her shorts and cursed under her breath. She didn't like this.

"Don't hear 'em anywhere," reported Corey.

The only sound was the constant droning of that steady wind.

"I *really* don't like this shit..." she groaned. This awful forest was scary enough as it was. Now it had snatched away both of their companions without a trace? Without so much as a shout? She backed away from where she found the flashlights and closer to Corey. The last thing she wanted right now was to be too far from him. They only had each other now, after all. "I mean, what do we do?" she wondered aloud.

"Get back to the path," replied Corey. "Albert said it was safe. The rest of these woods, not as much. Obviously."

She nodded. That was a good point. "Yeah, let's go."

But before they could head back, she caught sight of something dark moving among the trees in front of them.

She froze and watched it, praying that it was Albert and Brandy making their way back to them. But it was soon perfectly apparent that it wasn't them. It was something much stranger, something black and almost *fluid*. Something that *slithered* through those dangling branches. At the same time, it faded in and out of view, like something half-imagined.

It was bizarre…and yet it was strangely familiar at the same time. She felt like she'd seen something like that once before… A long time ago…

Black, undulating shadows danced across the baren earth, gradually combining together into a single form. A black shadow of a man seemed to step from it, moving purposefully toward them.

Then the shadows parted, revealing a man *not* of shadow, but of flesh and blood.

A man with a heart-wrenchingly familiar face.

"Jeremy…?" Violet whispered, her thoughts broken apart into a confounding kaleidoscope of emotions.

Impossibly, he smiled back at her. "It's been a while," he said.

More than eight years, to be exact.

They met Jeremy Gleer the day of the Tunipet Boom. He was their big secret. The true cause of the mysterious blast that they never told a soul about. Just an ordinary man with the unfortunate luck to not only be caught up in that bizarre phenomenon, but to be physically ejected from a second-floor window by it. He landed on the roof of a sport utility vehicle right in front of them. They thought the fall must have killed him, but he survived it.

At least, for a while…

Jeremy was a part of her life for such a brief amount of time. Mere hours. But he managed to change both their lives forever before he left them.

There are many worlds besides this one, he told them that strange night. *Some of them more significant than you can possibly imagine.*

The day Jeremy fell from that window was the day she and Corey found their purpose in life. He was what set them on this path to discover those other worlds, to find the truth.

"But you're dead," she said. She should know. He died in her arms.

But he only smiled back at her. "No. I didn't die. Not really." He spread his arms out, gesturing at the forest around him. "I just came home."

The place I'm from is the foundation for all worlds, even this one. It's a very dark place. A very hopeless place.

Could this horrible forest be the dark and hopeless place he spoke of all those years ago? Had they actually found his home dimension? And could he really have escaped death and simply returned here that night?

The idea filled her with such profound joy that she could barely stand it.

"I always knew you'd find your way to me eventually," said Jeremy. He was still walking toward them, his hand now stretched toward her. "Now I can show you *all* the worlds."

She reached out for him, eager to take his hand.

"That's not Jeremy," said Corey.

Violet barely heard him. She was still reaching out for the hand of her old friend.

But Corey's big hand closed on her shoulder, halting her. "Don't listen to it."

She frowned, confused. "What?" Somewhere in her head, alarm bells were going off. He was right. Something was dreadfully wrong here. And yet, even as she processed this, she realized she was still holding out her hand to the thing that claimed to be Jeremy.

Something cold and unnatural closed around her wrist. She was yanked forward. For just a moment, Jeremy's face became something different, something *horrible*, with great, empty sockets for eyes and huge, greenish teeth that barely filled its monstrous, gaping jaws.

She screamed…but it was already too late.

Chapter 62

Olivia knew her wailing sobs were carrying through these awful stone walls, but she couldn't help herself. Her chest ached with the force of it. The tears flowed like a river. She was doing everything she was taught to do in her training to bring him back, but Wayne was gone. CPR wasn't working. Mouth to mouth was useless. She was so tired. She couldn't go on much longer. How long had it been?

She kept hoping he'd come back. He'd done it before. Twice he'd been to the other side and returned. Why not once more?

She didn't even understand what happened. Something was in the room with them. Something misty and wispy and spooky, something she felt well before she saw it. A familiar, female presence. And a vision of sunflowers that blossomed clearly in her mind. It crossed the room so quickly, colliding with Wayne, pushing him back against the wall, into those deadly thorns...

Was it really Erin Laplede? But why would she do such a thing? Wasn't she one of the good guys? She gave her life protecting the thorn. She came back from the dead to save her in that awful fairy circle. Why would she want to kill Wayne? It didn't make sense!

She collapsed over her fiancé's lifeless body with an agonizing wail.

She couldn't do this alone. She couldn't do *anything* alone, much less *this*. She *needed* him. Didn't the Keeper understand that? If he knew so much, if he could plan every detail of his convoluted plans across the lifetimes of entire universes, why wouldn't he know that she couldn't do this without him?

It wasn't fair.

She didn't want to go on without him...

She couldn't...

She *wouldn't*...

Chapter 63

Gina lay curled up on the floor, tears streaming down her face, her hands clasped over her ears. But those voices reached her anyway. She couldn't block them out because they weren't coming from the other side of the wall, from the next room, like they did all those years ago. They were churning up from those awful places buried deep inside her.

"I saw your sister today."

"That freak is *not* my sister."

She could feel something squirming around inside her brain, dredging up all the garbage that had settled there over the years.

"What is *wrong* with her?"

She didn't want to hear these things again. She left that place behind a long time ago. It wasn't supposed to be able to hurt her anymore.

"Did you see the way she was acting?"

"She's a fucking psycho, I swear."

"Why won't Mom just send her away?"

She rolled onto her back, her hands pressed against her ears hard enough to send bolts of pain through her head. "*Leave me alone!*"

This was her old room, way back in Indiana…way back in that horrible house she swore she'd never set foot in again…

They never even tried to keep their voices down. They *wanted* her to hear all those awful things they said about her.

"Someone said she was talking to herself in the girls' bathroom."

"She's such a *freakshow.*"

And yet, this wasn't that house. It wasn't any kind of room at all. She could see it even through the tears and the gloom and that ever-present haze. The walls here weren't walls. They were soft and bulbous and slimy. The ceiling oozed and dripped. And there were slithering, wriggling things all around her, prodding her, groping her. She couldn't pull them off. There was nothing to grab onto. It was like they weren't there when she tried to touch them with her hands, but they were all over her body. And they were *inside* her. They were in her guts. They were in her chest. They were in her *brain*.

"Did you hear about the class trip to the museum? She totally started screaming at some random exhibit and then pissed her pants in front of everyone!"

She couldn't stop sobbing. She could barely even *breathe*. Why was this happening? What did she do to deserve this? Wasn't it enough that she'd gone through these horrible things once? Why couldn't she just leave those terrible things buried in the past?

"Her mom probably died of embarrassment."

"Someone needs to lock her up."

"She's probably going to end up murdering one of us in our sleep."

"Psychopath."

"Total freak."

"Why doesn't she just fucking kill herself?"

She screamed. But no one could hear her. Not in this place. She might as well be in hell, because no one was coming for her.

Not ever.

Chapter 64

Corey had his hands on Violet's shoulders. He told her the thing approaching them was lying. He warned her. He should have been able to stop it.

He should've just grabbed her and ran back to the path.

But he never expected the thing to move so fast. It yanked her from his grip and both of them shot off into the trees at an unnatural speed, disappearing in an instant.

He ran as hard as he could, following the sound of his best friend's screams, desperate to bring her back before something terrible happened.

The strange, twisted branches of those man-eating night trees slapped against his face and arms as he charged through one after another. He stumbled over rocks and roots. But he pressed onward with everything he had.

Her screams faded, but he could still see her flashlight. She wasn't gone yet. She was just up ahead. He was gaining on her, even. She was *right there!*

But when he reached the glow in the woods, he found only the flashlight.

Violet was gone.

And he was all alone in these terrible woods.

Chapter 65

Keith stood in the darkness of the Wood, beneath that endlessly empty sky, his pulse pounding in his ears.

What happened? Where did everyone go? They were right here just a moment ago. He looked down at his empty hand that Andrea was literally just clinging to. He had no recollection of her letting go. She was just gone, as if she'd never been there in the first place.

This wasn't good. He was all alone. He had no idea where the lake road went. His dream map ended back at the dock. He thought it was Gina who was supposed to lead the way from there. And then there was the not-so-insignificant fact that he was surrounded by *actual undead monsters*.

He couldn't even call out for anyone.

He'd never felt so lost in his entire life.

Chapter 66

Austin shined his light up at the towering wall waiting at the center of the Denselands. He couldn't see the tops of them, nor had he expected to. Legends said the walls reached upward forever, impenetrable, uncrossable, impassible. The City Beyond Memory was said to be unreachable, after all.

Not without the Whispers.

One of the three gates stood before him. Physically, it was nothing more than a depression in the surface of the stone wall, about ten feet high, with a round indentation at its center. The way wasn't open yet. Nor *would* it open. Not until all three of the ancient keys were used. And even then, the window would be very small. Anyone left behind would be stranded forever in this black hell. Wandering off, for even a moment, could be a fatal mistake. He wouldn't leave this spot until the gate was open.

But he had time. He'd arrived first, just as he'd known he would. The others would be along soon. They all had their trials to endure, after all. One by one they'd all have to prove their worth to the Faceless Ones' incomprehensible machines.

He'd just have to be patient. And he was good at being patient.

He turned and looked out at the surrounding black forest from which he'd just walked, undaunted by the things he saw creeping around out there. They were of no significance to him. In fact, he turned his back on the Wood entirely, sat himself down cross-legged in front of the locked gate and opened his book again.

Maybe the others would be kind enough to give him time to finish reading.

That would be nice.

About the author

Brian Harmon is an independent author of horror fiction, suspense and dark adventure. He grew up in rural Missouri and now lives in Southern Wisconsin with his wife, Guinevere, and their three children.

For more about Brian Harmon and his work, visit
www.BrianHarmonBooks.com